THE THREAT WIT[...]
THE ENEMY WITH[...]

FITZ, THE PATRIARCH—The War was over.
   Now was the time to rebuild Wyndward and
   to find the woman he couldn't forget.

MARK, BASTARD GRANDSON—He came
   back to claim his legacy—and stayed to meet
   his fate.

CLARISSA, THE "GUEST"—She came to
   Wyndward as "hostess"—and comfort to a
   man who loved another, but wouldn't let her
   go. . . .

ADALIA, THE YANKEE SCHOOLTEACHER
   —She was too smart, too beautiful, too close
   for comfort. Mark couldn't resist her. But
   would he ever belong in her class?

JONATHAN, THE SON—He was a dead man,
   returned from battle filled with hate. His war
   would never end—till the world that betrayed
   him burned in his wake.

Novels by Norman Daniels

Wyndward Fury
Wyndward Glory
Wyndward Passion
Wyndward Peril

Published by
WARNER BOOKS

Norman Daniels
Wyndward Glory

WARNER BOOKS

A Warner Communications Company

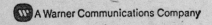 A Warner Communications Company

Printed in the United States of America

First Printing: December, 1981

10 9 8 7 6 5 4 3 2 1

Wyndward Glory

1

On the narrow veranda two men lounged in rocking chairs, drinking whiskey and spring water from tall glasses. Their shirt collars were open, their feet were propped up on the veranda railing.

The silver-haired man was Fitzjohn Turner, once owner of the largest horse-breeding, slave-breeding, to-bacco-growing plantation in Virginia. The other was his grandson Mark, the offspring of Fitz's son Jonathan and a recently dead New Orleans prostitute, a circumstance that didn't bother either man in the least.

Fitz drained his whiskey, lowered his legs, and stood up to stretch and yawn. "Reckon I'll take a ride," he said. "Sho' ain't nothin' to do 'round heah. You comin', Mark?"

"Ain't stirrin'," Mark said. "Too damn hot. Best you stay heah too. You're an old man now, an' ridin' 'round in the sun sho' goin' to kill you one o' these days."

"Who you callin' an old man? I could take you any time I wants, an' you bettah not forget it."

"Ha!" Mark scoffed. "You talkin' big, old man."

Fitz regarded him solemnly. "Thinks I gots to take you down a few pegs, son, but ain't got the time right now."

"You knows whut's good fo' you, bettah not find the time."

"Times I thinks mighty hard on kickin' your ass out o' this house."

Mark looked up, grinned, and waved a hand. "Too damn hot to fight now."

"Seems to me," Fitz replied, "there's 'nuff fightin' goin' on with this heah war turnin' brother 'gainst brother an' father 'gainst son." He paused for a moment, and his forehead wrinkled into the furrows brought on by his years. "'Members when this war starts. Heah in the South ain' no man thinks we kin be whupped, 'cept me, reckon. An' I sho' got myse'f in hot water by sayin' the North was stronger. Bein' I'm half Yankee an' seein' I was educated in the North, reckon I knowed mo' than most, but they call me a traitor anyways. 'Members the grand marchin', the pretty uniforms, the hothaids achin' to fight. Look at 'em now! We been licked fo' a yeah, an' ain't nobody admits it."

"My, my," Mark said indifferently, "ain't we talkin' like a real politican now, old man."

"Mayhap when I git back an' it ain't so damn hot, I'll show you how old I am. Goin' fo' my ride."

"Goin' down to the old plantation an' talkin' to the graves of your kin. You ain't foolin' me any, Gran'pa. You stand theah like an old fool an' talk to the tombstones like they kin heah you. You sho' old an' crazy. Talkin' to daid people."

Fitz shrugged. "Don't know why I keep you heah 'cept you're mo' company than Elegant. Figgered you went back to N'Orleans, you stayed theah. Wish you did."

"Went back to N'Orleans to sell Mama's whorehouse, an' I sold it fo' a mighty good price."

"Why'd you come back?"

"Thinkin' you a rich man once befo' the war an' mayhap you gots a little put away. Like the three million

8

in a Northern bank. You got nobody left. Your gran'sons got blowed to hell in the war. Your son, Jonathan, my pa, he likely daid. You got to leave your money to someone, an' might's well be me."

"Told you when you first comes heah I gots two, three million dollahs in a Northern bank. But I'll have 'em burn it 'fore you lay a hand on it. Now go to sleep. Best thing you kin do, an' be rested when I gets back 'cause I sho' aimin' to bust you up some."

"Gran'pa," Mark said, "likes you anyway."

Fitz sighed. "Trouble with me too. Cain't help likin' you, ornery as you kin be. Sees Elegant 'bout suppah."

He walked into the house, through the moderate-sized parlor to the small kitchen at the rear. It was a far cry from the kitchen at Wyndward, the plantation mansion now a pile of ashes surrounded by burned fields. Elegant, the cook, named by Fitz's father who named all female slaves after ships he'd once known, had had half a dozen scullery maids there to help and take her orders.

At least her old high stool had been salvaged from the ashes. To Elegant that was a godsend, for she was a three-hundred-pound, five-foot-two ball of ebony-black good humor and faithfulness, and the best cook in the South. No chairs could accommodate her bulk, so she relied on the high, backless stool for resting her gross body.

She sat there now, a bowl on her lap, while she shelled peas. She looked up with a big grin. "Fixin' fine suppah, massa. Hong Kong brought me a fat hawg so the eatin's good."

"That's fine. I'm goin' down to the plantation. Likely I'll see Hong Kong. Want anythin' I kin tote back?"

She wagged her head. "Reckon ah gots all ah needs, suh. Thanks you kin'ly, suh."

Fitz looked around the small kitchen. "Ain't like it used to be, Elegant, but one o' these days, when the damn war is over, I'm goin' to build Wyndward again, an' you gets the finest kitchen you evah saw. Promise you that."

"Sho' likes to think on it, massa."

"Time you stops callin' me massa, Elegant. The days

o' slaves are over an' will nevah come back. Ain't no call fo' any nigger to call any man massa no more.'

"You're my massa, suh, an' ain't no Northern kin tell me it ain't so. Way ah likes it. You sho' 'nuff thinks you kin build Wyndward agin, suh?"

"Know it. Soon's the fightin' stops I start buildin'."

"Can't wait fo' the day, massa. Whut 'bout that shiftless gran'son settin' on the porch like he's growin' from it?"

"He's all right, Elegant. Lazy, sho' 'nuff, but got him a bullet somewhar in his miserable body from bein' shot by a Yankee soldier. Mayhap that's slowin' him down some."

"Tells you one thing, suh, ain't nevah goin' to call him massa. Don' care a button fo' the likes o' him."

"He got good blood in him. Plenty bad too, but mayhap he'll turn into a real member o' the family. Be back 'fore suppah."

Fitz left by the rear door, walked down to the stable, and saddled his only horse. He rode slowly down a worn trail because often the road was not safe. It was a short ride to the place where his mansion had once stood and the fields where a thousand or more slaves had been kept at work.

It was often painful for him to return to what had once been the glory of Wyndward, to see again the stark, bare chimneys that were all that remained of the mansion. The small overseers' cottages were still there, but they were too small to suit Fitz, who had gone to live two miles away at a house he had taken over long ago. Well behind the burned-out mansion were the slave quarters, a series of small cabins where the multitude of slaves had once lived. The line of cabins seemed endless. The larger dormitory-like structures were also intact. The bachelor slaves had lived there. The old birthing house and hospital were intact also, along with the commissary, whose food had been looted. The reasonable Northern officer in charge of the raiding force had spared the cabins on Fitz's plea that the slaves had to have somewhere to live.

Only a dozen of the cabins were now occupied, most

of the slaves having fled long ago. Hong Kong and his wife Seawitch occupied the largest cabin. Hong Kong, named by Fitz's father, had been the plantation driver, in charge of the slaves. He was a thoroughly capable man, a huge man, strong enough and big enough to keep the slaves orderly and quiet.

Hong Kong and Seawitch came out of the cabin to meet Fitz as he rode up. Hong Kong promptly removed his wide straw hat as he had always done, and bowed his head politely. Fitz dismounted.

"You ain't come by in a long time, suh," Hong Kong said. "Think mayhap you ain't feelin' good these days."

"I'm real good, Hong Kong. You're gettin' kinda fat, ain't you?" He glanced at Seawitch. "Thinks you feed him mighty good, Seawitch."

"Ain't the feedin'," she said. "Ain't nuthin' fo' him to do, an' he gits fat doin' nuthin'. Mighty good to see you, suh."

"Elegant says thank you fo' sendin' the hawg. Thinks there's any left?"

"Reckon a few, suh. Mighty good thing we turns 'em all loose in the woods when the war comes. They's kinda wild, an' ain't so tender like we had 'em, but they's good eatin' anyways."

"How is everythin' else, Hong Kong?" Fitz asked.

"Jes' like always, suh. Nuthin' seem to change. Got nineteen families livin' in the quarters. They's mighty lazy, too, but they's also kinda old."

"You an' me an' Seawitch, we ain't gettin' younger, Hong Kong. We's jes' like them, you come to think of it."

"Whut you aimin' to do, suh, when the war ends?"

"Told you often 'nuff. Goin' to rebuild the mansion, goin' to plow the fields an' plant 'bacco. Goin' to get us all the old slaves we kin round up an' new workers to take the place o' them whut ran too far. Goin' to be like it used to be, even better."

"When you thinks this heah war goin' end, suh?" Seawitch asked. She spoke deferentially. The old habits remained.

"Endin' now," Fitz said, "only the hothaids don' know it yet. Won't be long they find out it's been over fo' months already. They'll stop fightin' pretty soon now."

"Cain't wait fo' that day, suh. You heahs anythin' 'bout your son Jonathan?"

Fitz shook his head. "Reckon he daid. My gran'son, Jonathan's boy, he tell me he fought alongside his papa an' sees Jonathan hit an' a Yankee soldier aimin' a bayonet at him. Sho' reckon he daid."

Hong Kong shook his head. "Ain't many o' us left, suh. Makes no mind. We does whut we kin when the fightin' ends."

"Pray God that comes soon," Seawitch said.

"Gots to, Seawitch. Ain't much left to fight with. Hong Kong, you heah anythin' 'bout raidin' parties 'round heah?"

"Heahs there's some, suh. Northern soldiers all over heah these days."

"They ain't soldiers, 'zactly. Some say they Quantrill's raiders, but they sho' ain't. He does his raidin' an' killin' in Missouri an' Kansas, not Virginia. Yo' heahs anythin', come an' tell me."

"Yassuh. Sho' tell you."

Fitz nodded and, leading his horse, walked away in the direction of the little iron-fence-enclosed graveyard. There, in an orderly row, lay those who had been so great a part of his life. His mother, a stalwart New England Yankee who had hated slavery and had died because a slave had refused to rescue her. Then there was Jonathan, his father, who had become rich as captain of a slave ship, operating in that awful trade to get enough money to build a plantation. Fitz had sailed with him and painfully recalled what a slave ship was like. His father had never been able to get rid of the stench of that ship. Years after he had established his very successful plantation, he had boarded and burned the ship, dying in the flames. Some had said it was by his own choice, but Fitz had never believed that. Benay, Fitz's beloved wife, lay there too. She had died so young, trying to help slaves afflicted with smallpox, which had threatened to wipe out the plantation. And, strangely, beside Benay lay Nina, a near-white

12

mulatto who had been Fitz's mistress and had born his son Dundee, now somewhere in the North. Finally, there was Daisy, Jonathan's lovely wife, who had been raped by a renegade slave and then had lost her mind because of the ordeal. She'd died as the war began, turning Jonathan into a Negro-hating rebel who had likely died fighting those who were to set free the blacks he had hated so intensely.

Fitz stood facing the graves. He spoke aloud, first in the perfect English of the North where he had been educated, for the benefit of his Yankee mother.

"It has come to pass, Mama. The slaves are free. The North is winning the war. It can't last much longer. I know you'll be pleased to have me tell you, your side won. But Mama, it was a war that should never have happened. There've been thousands on thousands killed. My grandsons were blown to pieces. They were not yet sixteen, and they died fighting for a lost cause. My son Jonathan has not been heard from, and I believe him to be dead. All that's left of this once-proud family is my daughter Melanie. She was like you, Mama. She hated slavery, and she left me to marry a Northerner. A congressman no less. I saw him about two or three years ago. She's the loveliest girl I ever laid eyes on. Independent as you were yet warm and loving, but not to me. I represent the South she hates."

Fitz moved a step to the left. "Papa, fo' your sake, I'm talkin' Southern again. You tell me, when I comes to the plantation, to talk like a Southerner so nobody would know I got some Yankee blood. Did it to please you an' been doin' it evah since. Comes to like it, suh. Well, I told you befo' that the mansion got burned to the ground. Burned it myse'f rather than let the Yankees do it. But got me plenty money up North an' goin' to build Wyndward again. Finer than evah. Ain't no mo' slaves. They's all free, an' they all run. Don' know whar to, but they sho' run. Feel sorry fo' 'em, poor ignorant bastahds ain't got no sense 'cause we nevah let 'em get any sense. Gots to say this, it was a mistake. Slavery had to go even if the South you knowed an' loved went with it."

Fitz knelt at a spot between the graves of his wife

Benay and the once beautiful Nina, his mistress, for these two had been the closest to him. The loves of his life.

"Benay, an' you, Nina, wish you were heah to help me when this's over an' we goes back to wuk. Misses you two so bad it hurts me inside so much I don't go whorin' 'round no mo'. 'Corse I gettin' old fo' that anyways. An' I hope Daisy lyin' theah 'side you is restin' easy. Reckon, I kin find Jonathan's body, I brings it heah, but cain't count on it 'cause so many died nobody knows whar they buried. Do my best. Wait only fo' the day I kin start rebuildin'."

He looked up. A rider was heading his way. Fitz stood. "Don't know whut in hell's goin' on, but this heah rider comin' like the devil ridin' behind him. Gots to go now. Tell you whut happened later."

He closed the iron gate of the cemetery fence and mounted his horse to ride toward the rapidly approaching horseman. He soon recognized him as Cass Sedley, a planter with a small farm ten miles to the north.

Cass sounded the warning as Fitz turned his horse to ride alongside. "They done burned an' looted the town, Fitz. Killin' the men but savin' the women. Say they're Quantrill's boys an' goin' to keep on raidin' an' killin'. Comin' this way, reckon."

"I thanks you, suh," Fitz said. "Keep on ridin' an' warnin' others. Ain't Quantrill's boys, but sho' ain't any bettah, way I heahs it. Best you warn as many as you kin."

"Take care, they's sho' in a killin' mood, Fitz. Got clear of 'em by the skin o' my ass."

Sedley kicked his horse into motion and rode off. Fitz began riding hard toward Hong Kong's cabin. The couple had already been alerted by the speed and shouts of the rider who had come with the warning. Hong Kong, with that instinct that made him so invaluable to Fitz, handed up a rifle and a box of ammunition.

"Raiders comin'," Fitz said. "Get all the others outen their cabins an' run fo' the woods. I thanks you fo' havin' a rifle ready."

He turned the horse and at top speed rode to warn Mark and Elegant. Before he reached the house a party of about a dozen men galloped up.

It was too late for Fitz to take refuge. The raiders had already seen him. He pumped a cartridge into the repeater rifle and kept riding. He hoped Sedley had been able to warn Mark.

They were not yet within range when Fitz heard the faint crack of a rifle, and one of the horsemen toppled from his saddle. Fitz saw the others slow down, not quite knowing what had happened. Fitz was by now almost within rifle range. A gun cracked again and another man fell. Fitz suddenly knew what it was about. He raised his rifle, aiming it, though he was still out of range. Though he didn't fire, a third raider fell, then a fourth. The others turned tail without firing a shot. They had no desire to go up against a man who could kill so efficiently at such a distance.

Fitz rode slowly now. He passed beneath a row of tall, heavily leafed oaks and looked up.

"You kin come down now, Mark. They's gone, an' reckon they won't be back."

Mark scrambled down from the tree, jumping from the lower branch. He got to his feet, picked up the rifle he'd dropped, and waited with a big grin until Fitz rode up and dismounted.

"You got some sense, anyways," Mark said. "They nevah saw me an' didn't know whar the bullets were comin' from. Thinks you doin' the shootin'. Way they looked, so damn skeered, almost gave myse'f away laughin'. How many did I get?"

"Four, I thinks. Bettah see if any still alive."

The first three were dead, shot through the chest. "You sho' mighty good with that gun," Fitz said.

"Learned how in the war. Look theah, Gran'pa, that one is wigglin' some."

They knelt beside the only survivor, who was surely not going to live much longer. Fitz turned him on his back and raised his head.

"Goin' to ask you one question," he said. "You tell me who ridin' as head o' these heah raiders or I put a bullet through your fool haid right now."

"Go to hell!" the man mumbled.

Mark pumped a cartridge into the chamber of his

rifle and brought the muzzle down to an inch from the dying man's face. The man opened his mouth in terror.

"Asking you once mo'," Fitz said. "We gets you to a docter, you tell the truth."

"Bibb," he said.

"Reckoned so," Fitz said. "You sho' ain't ridin' fo' Quantrill."

"Told us to say we Quantrill's boys," the dying man admitted, realizing he'd gone too far to hold back anything more.

"Who this heah Bibb?" Mark asked.

"Planter I been feudin' with fo' yeahs. Fetch my hoss, Mark. We'll take this man back to the house an' do whut we kin fo' him."

"Ain't goin' to last that long," Mark predicted.

"Damn it!" Fitz exploded in wrath. "Get the hoss like I says."

Mark nodded. "Gets him, old man. Reckon you shakin' so hard yo' cain't fetch him yourse'f."

They lifted the man and draped him over the saddle. By the time they reached the house, he was dead. They placed the body under a tree for burial later. They went back to the house and fixed tall, stiff drinks. They seated themselves on the veranda and drank slowly, not talking much at first.

"Reckon I owe you my life," Fitz said calmly. "Might have rode right into that bunch o' scum. How'd you know they was comin'?"

"By listenin'," Mark said. "That's all, jes' listenin'. I got good ears."

"Reckon we gots to do somethin' 'bout this heah Bibb. Sho' no account, but long as he runs 'round I got to keep lookin' over my shoulder. Been havin' run-ins with that bastahd fo' yeahs. Runs when I call him out, but sho' ain't mindin' shootin' me in the back he gets the chance."

Mark nodded and sipped more of his drink. "We'll ride some day an' find him an' kill him. Only thing left to do."

"Reckon. But he got friends, an' mayhap we get mo' trouble than if he lives."

"You skeered o' these heah friends, old man?"

Fitz balanced his glass on the porch railing. "Let's get it over with."

"Get whut over with?" Mark asked.

"You called me an old man once too often. Jes' step out an' see how old I am."

Mark arose, drained his drink, and ran down the veranda steps after Fitz. He faced the older man and began to maneuver for a quick rush to end the fight. Fitz stood with his arms down, seemingly uninterested in protecting himself. Mark lunged forward, keeping his eyes on Fitz's face, neglecting to look down. He tripped over Fitz's outthrust foot and went sprawling in the dust. Fitz made no move to take advantage of Mark's momentary disadvantage. Mark arose warily, this time watching all of the man he opposed. He chuckled in good humor and charged. He ran straight into a knee that stabbed into his stomach and a fist that grazed his chin. Mark turned, wiping a little blood off his lower lip. His eyes were narrowed and watchful. But Fitz merely waited for another attack.

Mark, a dozen feet away, began his rush. At the same instant Fitz hurled himself at Mark. Their bodies met in a crash that sent Mark back on his heels, the wind knocked out of him. Fitz was upon him, fists slashing, pounding, until Mark howled in pain and tried to move away. Fitz charged, wound his arms around the almost helpless man, and threw him heavily to the ground. He stood above Mark, one foot poised for a kick that would end the fight and probably break Mark's jaw.

Fitz lowered the foot. "You're too damn pretty to bust up some." He reached down for Mark's hand, hauled him to his feet. "One o' these days I'll teach you to fight Virginny style. N'Orleans style ain't very good."

" 'Preciates you teachin' me. If I kin get my jaw open, I'd like another drink. You fetch it 'cause you sho' ain't as old as I feel."

"Kinda winded," Fitz said. "Get your own drink."

On the veranda he settled himself in his rocker, whirled the chunks of ice remaining in his glass and took a long drink. Mark came out with two filled glasses and plenty of ice.

"Tell you one thing," he said, "that's the last time I evah tangle with you."

"Why I ask you out," Fitz declared complacently. "Now we kin settle down an' talk 'bout whut we aimin' to do with Wyndward."

"Jes' the two of us, suh?"

"Who else? You see anybody fixin' to help us?"

"No, but there were others . . . so I heahs."

"There was your papa. Think he daid. There was my daughter Melanie, but she mo' Northern than Southern an' hates my hide. Had two good slaves, Dundee an' Two Bits, but they up North an' ain't likely to come back 'til the war's over. Now who else you thinkin' 'bout?"

"Jes' the two of us," Mark conceded.

"There was one other," Fitz said dreamily. "Gal name o' Sally Beaufort. That's the name she lived under when she livin' at Wyndward. I was settin' to marry that gal. Reckon I loved her 'bout as much as I loved Benay, and that was plenty. But Sally turned out to be a Northern spy, tellin' me she was settlin' the estate of an old lady she wukked fo'. Took to goin' to Richmond ev'ry chance she got, lookin' 'round, countin' the wounded, the new soldiers goin' to the front, the cannon. Ev'rythin' that would help the North."

"Whut they do, hang her?" Mark asked.

"When the war started, she got away fast. I helped her in a way, I reckon. Don' know she alive or daid. Her real name was Elizabeth Rutledge, but in my mind reckon she'll always be Sally."

"She come back, you still aimin' to marry her?"

"She rides back heah I runs to meet her if she still a mile away. Nevah forget her. Hope she ain't forgotten me."

Mark touched his face tenderly. "You haul off an' bust her on the chin, reckon she wouldn't forget. Let's talk 'bout whut we aimin' to do about Wyndward. Whut we plant, whar we get niggers to help us. Whut we pay 'em an' how we raise the mansion 'thout Southerners gettin' het up we got money an' they ain't."

"That'll take a mighty lot o' talkin', son. Think we do it bettah with fresh drinks. You get 'em?"

"Yes, suh," Mark came to his feet. "Fetch 'em fast as I kin run, suh. Kinda dry myse'f."

2

Fitz had often ridden the train to Richmond, but there'd never been a journey such as this. It was during the first days of April. Part of the train was filled with wounded for whom little could be done. There were, as one medical officer admitted to Fitz, no drugs, no anaesthesia, not even opiates.

Among the civilian passengers were wary-eyed, downcast men not in uniform, though their ravaged faces were silent testimony that they had been soldiers for four agonizing years and were now deserting, returning home with the empty spirit of defeat.

Fitz didn't reach Richmond until midmorning on a Saturday. The city was a confusion of people moving about in search of food, drink, friends, and relatives. There seemed to be no organization. It was every man for himself. Faces were grim, tired.

Fitz had left Mark at home, for there was always a chance of marauders moving about to burn and loot.

Fitz walked the crowded streets, unnerved and for the first time filled with a sorrow at the defeatist attitudes of those he spoke to. They were all convinced the South had lost and the war ought to be brought to an end.

Fitz had business with his old bank, owned by his friend Paul Robin. The bank had once been a busy place in which Fitz was received as an honored client—and the owner of savings to the sum of more than a million dollars. Now it had grown dingy. The once-bright gilt sign above the door had faded to a point of being barely visible. Even the bars on the windows showed signs of rust, and over the entire building there hung an aura of neglect.

Only two elderly tellers were behind the grilled screens. They greeted Fitz without enthusiasm. No one in Richmond had much vitality left for anyone or anything. The door to Paul Robin's office was wide open, and Fitz walked in to find Robin tilted back in his chair behind the big desk, sound asleep. He was in need of a shave, his hair had grown too long, and his clothes were shabby.

Robin awoke and came to his feet to reach out for Fitz's hand. "Damnation," he exclaimed, "I'm sho' glad to see you still alive. Haven't heard from you in months."

"Ain't been no reason fo' me to come to Richmond, Paul. Reckon you know there's nothin' heah fo' me."

"That goes fo' every manjack in town. Fitz, we're beaten, whupped, licked. We're at the end of it, but Davis won't admit it."

"Well, there've been a few battles in our favor lately. Sherman was stopped for three days by Gen'ral Johnson and his Army of Tennessee."

"Oh, sho'ly that's the truth. An' Lee been havin' success north o' heah. But what did it all mean, Fitz? Not a damn thing! Listen to this. You got one gold dollah in your pants, I'll give you sixty Confederate dollahs fo' it. Shinplasters! Our money's no good any mo'. Chattanooga an' Atlanta lost, Sherman still on his way to the sea, burnin' everythin' in sight. But you know, I attended a meetin' last week. A political meetin'."

"Kin guess whut it was like," Fitz said with a sigh.

"There was nothin' but talk 'bout the north bein' drained o' blood an' treasure an' achin' to end the war now. They were sayin' we had a chance of compromise an' in our favor 'cause the North was sick o' the fightin'. As if we ain't."

"You minds if I talk frankly, Paul? Mayhap I sound like the traitor they once brought me into a military court fo'."

" 'Member it well. You sho' made fools o' them whut tried to get you hung. Go ahead. You cain't evah be a traitor to me."

"On the way heah I talked to soldiers desertin' 'cause they cain't see no use in fightin' any mo'. I saw cars filled with wounded an' dyin'. The whole goddamn thing is over, but politicians don' do the fightin' an' they the last to admit it. Reckon won't be long 'fore Richmond is taken."

"They kin have this bank," Paul declared with a wry laugh. "Ain't nothin' left in it anyways."

"Whut I come to see you fo'. Once you turned over a million an' a half o' my money to the cause."

Paul nodded. "An' they calls you a traitor."

"Jes' between us, Paul, I got near three million in a Northern bank. It wasn't like I hid it theah. I kept half my money in the North 'cause Papa an' me had lots o' dealings theah. When the war came, I couldn't get it out, so it still theah an' buildin' some with interest."

"Three million," Paul said with a shake of his head. "Cain't believe theah's that much gold anywhar on earth."

"Figgered when the war ends, I bring most of it down heah, to you."

Paul sat up in astonishment and happiness. "Mean that, Fitz? Three million?"

"Two. Leave the rest up theah. For now. Whut I want from you is access to this ready cash so I kin rebuild Wyndward soon's I kin get started. Wants to hire men back from the war, busted an' lookin' fo' wuk."

"That includes ev'rybody in Richmond. Hell, in the whole South. You want me to handle the money end? I'm proud to do that an' mighty grateful I kin begin doin' business like I used to do. With that amount o' capital on deposit I kin do 'bout anythin', 'thout a risk to your money, suh."

22

"Good. Soon as it's possible I'll send fo' a draft to your bank. It gets heah, we talk some mo' an' I starts lookin' fo' help."

"It won't be long now 'fore you kin begin, Fitz. Know whut these fool politicians talkin' 'bout now? Makin' soldiers outen the slaves."

"Givin' 'em guns an' all?" Fitz asked in disbelief.

"What they aimin' to do. The hothaids all fo' it, but I say it cain't be done, an' I got plenty on my side. You send a slave to fight, he's fightin' to still be a slave. That sho' ain't much in the way o' inspiration."

"They gives a uniform an' a gun to a slave, they emancipate him right there. He ain't nevah goin' to be a slave again."

"Whut I think, but talk of emancipation gettin' stronger in the South. Hear they sent an envoy to England with an offer to emancipate ev'ry slave if England will recognize the Confederacy an' give us some help."

"Whut they fightin' fo' they think that way?"

"Reckon it's the honor o' the South. That means the honor o' the politicians. England turned the offer down flat."

"Ev'rythin' sho' goin' to hell," Fitz agreed. "But sho' 'nuff plenty o' folks on the street."

"They got little to do 'cept roam around. Lookin' fo' food mostly. Sometimes I think hard on clearin' out, but where kin I go? All we kin do is wait fo' Lee to surrender. You think the North comes down to hang Jeff Davis an' Lee an ev'rybody else they been fightin'?"

"Talk o' that?" Fitz asked in wonder.

"Lots of it, Fitz. Some believin' it too. Keeps the fightin' goin' on account of that. Wonder if it kin be true."

Fitz shook his head. "You knows I was educated in the North. My mama was a New Englander. I got Yankee blood in me an' reckon I knows Yankees. There ain't goin' to be no killin' or lootin'. Sho' there be trouble. Mo' than we kin handle sometimes, but not any mo' than that. Whut Lincoln aimin' to do is bring us together."

"Cain't be done, not even by him," Paul said. "Too much hate on both sides. Too much killin'."

23

"It will pass," Fitz assured him. "It's got to or we ain't got a country no mo'. Takes time, but it'll all simmer down. Walkin' 'round the streets, I don' see nobody talkin' o' killin' Yankees, they comes down heah. Way I been thinkin', ain't no war evah was heah. Folks all laughin' an' carryin' on."

"They don't carry on, they go crazy," Paul said. "Reckon knowin' it's over gives them a right to laugh an' have fun even if they lost. An' been mo' weddings than 'fore the war. Folks talk o' settlin' down, raisin' families, an' wukkin' fo' a livin' 'stead o' killin' an' bein' killed."

"Good to heah that, Paul. Well, soon's it kin be done, the money come an' Wyndward begins to rise up out o' the ashes."

"Heahs from your son Jonathan?"

"On'y that likely he daid. Poor Jonathan."

"I'm sorry, Fitz. I liked Jonathan."

"Ain't many o' us left, Paul. Got me a daughter in Washington, but she tells the Yankee officer who asks her, to burn Wyndward. Knowed whut she'd say so I burn it myse'f. Not much satisfaction in that, but some, reckon. See you again soon's this damn fightin' finished with."

"You stayin' in town tonight, Fitz?"

"Aimin' to."

"If there was an extra speck o' food in my house I'd sho'ly be honored by your company, but. . . ."

"There'll be better times, an' I'll take you up on that then."

Paul offered his hand. "If there's good things to be done out o' all this, we'll do 'em, Fitz."

Fitz walked out of the bank, feeling much better. On the street he saw couples walking about, talking with animation. He saw some men on the verge of drunkenness, their only way out of pain. He entered the lobby of the best hotel in town and inquired at the desk for Clarissa Apperson. She was still living here.

He climbed the stairs to the third floor, and as he walked slowly down the corridor, he thought of Clarissa. She had once been obsessed with getting Fitz in bed. Likely she had ambitions of the same nature as those of many men. Her hatred of Fitz, because he consistently rejected her, had grown more and more intense. Yet, when Fitz had been in trouble she had defended him. Long ago she'd married the homosexual son of a planter named Apperson, who had become Fitz's archenemy over the years. Apperson had immediately rejected Clarissa when she had aided Fitz, so Fitz had arranged for her to live, cost free, at any hotel she chose. He paid the bills.

At one time, he'd have gone miles out of his way to avoid Clarissa, but those days were gone. She'd put on some weight, but she was still attractive enough and usually horny enough to accommodate any man.

Fitz knocked on the door. Presently it opened a crack, and Clarissa peered out. She threw the door wide and went into his arms with a cry of joy. He kicked the door shut without taking his arms from around her.

"Kind o' like holdin' you like this, Clarissa. You thinkin' whut I'm thinkin'?"

"Been thinkin' 'bout it fo' months. Whar in hell you been?"

"Skeered to leave Wyndward."

"You goin' to stay in Richmond fo' awhile? Like a month?"

"Cain't do it. Wish I could."

"We're wastin' time," she said and tightened her arms around him. Her body was pressed hard against him. He maneuvered her into the bedroom of the two-room suite. He half walked, half danced her to the side of the bed, and she slipped onto it without letting go of him.

"Take your clothes off," she said, releasing him to slip her dress over her head. "Don't keep me waitin', Fitz. Waited fo' you fo' yeahs."

He arose, bent to untie his shoelaces. As he straightened up and pulled down his suspenders, he hesitated a moment. "Think we kin still do it?"

"Why the hell not? We ain't a hundred yet."

"Last time we had a little trouble, I 'members rightly."

"Maybe we did, but I'm achin' fo' it an' lookin' at you, figures you ain't made o' ice either. Figure you plenty randy. Damn it, Fitz, take off your clothes!"

25

As she talked, she undressed, tossing her undergarments on the floor. She lay back in bed, her arms extended for him. He studied her ample, soft body, stripped himself, and got in beside her. The ache within him was strong. He needed her as she needed him, and they were professional at it. When he later rolled off her, their sighs were simultaneous.

"By damn," he said, "reckon I goin' to stay a month. Clarissa, fo' an old woman, you sho' still mighty good."

"In baid with you I don' feel old, Fitz. Feel like I did yeahs ago when I tried to get you away from Benay. Reckon I nevah been tossed out o' baid so often by any man. Now all I kin say, it was worth it."

"You in love with me?" he asked casually. He turned on his side and drew her closer.

"No suh, I ain't in love with you, Fitz. Know bettah than to be in love with you 'cause you nevah be in love with me. I take whut you offer an' makes me happy I get that much."

"Been thinkin' if Sally evah comes back, mayhap. . . ."

"You heah from her?"

"Not a word. How could I? She bein' up North an' bein' a Yankee spy 'fore the war starts so she cain't come down heah."

"War goin' to be over 'fore long. Whut if she comes back then?"

"I'll marry her, Clarissa. Cain't help it. I been in love with her all these war yeahs, nevah seein' her, nevah hearin' from her. Don' know she daid or alive, but nevah stop lovin' her."

Clarissa kissed him with an ardor that he quickly matched. "If you kin fo'get her fo' a little while, I sho' am ready fo' you, Fitz."

They remained in bed, alternately napping and making love while Fitz exulted in the fact that he was, after all, potent.

Early in the evening they went out to look for a restaurant with enough food to comprise a meal. Fitz used a gold coin in the best place they could find and got a bottle of whiskey, a steak of sorts, a small potato, a great deal of bread, and even a tiny pat of butter, which Clarissa exclaimed over as if it was expensive perfume.

"Whut you heahs 'bout your husband an' your papa-in-law?" Fitz asked.

"My husband got to be in N'Orleans. Sho' stayed out o' the war. He was no husband. You know that. He favored light-skinned boys, but he wasn't 'gainst takin' black ones either. Colonel Apperson, his papa, is still a colonel in the army but reckon he nevah heahs a shot fired, runnin' the army warehouse like he does. Heahs you hand him some Northern money, you get 'nuff to eat fo' a few days. He's a no-good sonabitch, Fitz, an' someday you got to kill him."

"Swear I would sometime back."

"Jes' be keerful. He'd rather shoot a man in the back than face up to him. Sneaky bastahd, but wearin' that uniform he sho' high an' mighty. Bet when the Yankees come, he the first one to surrender."

"Goin' to build Wyndward soon's I kin," Fitz told her. "You 'members the old Fisbee place?"

"Sho' do."

"That's whar I live now, 'til Wyndward rises up again. When it does, I fix the Fisbee place real nice an' give it to you. We both gettin' kinda old. . . ."

"After today you kin say that?" Clarissa asked, and her eyes gleamed with fresh desire and not a small amount of pride.

"Sho' was mighty good," he admitted. "But thinkin' far ahead, Clarissa, when you ain't so handsome a woman an' your hots gets cold. Bound to happen. Want you 'round me. If we cain't do anythin' 'bout it, we kin always talk 'bout old times. There's some satisfaction in that, reckon."

"You mighty good to me," Clarissa said. "Sort o' makes me think. Fitz, want to ask a favor o' you."

"Sho' aims to please you, Clarissa."

"Wants you to go to church tomorrow. It's Sunday an' Saint Paul's jes' 'round the corner."

27

"Who the hell you goin' to pray fo'?"

"Ain't aimin' to pray. Aimin' to say thank you. Fo' today."

"That bein' the reason, reckon I got to say my thanks too. Finish up your last drink an' we'll go back to bed. That gives us mo' to be thankful fo'.."

They were well fed, feeling the whiskey, and glowing with the kind of rare happiness that had been long gone since the war began to turn against the South. They were in no hurry, in spite of Fitz's plans for the rest of the night. They watched couples drinking, laughing, primed to make love, while the days of glory they had once known were crashing about them. Everyone knew it, knew they were unable to fight it, but until it happened, they were bent on getting all there was left out of the way of life they had once enjoyed. Fitz doubted that any of them bothered to think about hating the North. For them, there was only today.

Fitz and Clarissa took a brief walk along the street, but soon turned around, for the streets were too crowded with roisterers. They gratefully drank more from the bottle Fitz had carried out of the restaurant and then went to bed to sleep soundly, almost at once.

In the morning, Fitz awoke to hear Clarissa splashing in the tub. He went into the bathroom and managed to wedge himself into the tub facing her. They were like children. Fitz knew exactly how all those shouting, laughing people on the street the night before felt about their situation with the war closing in for its final gasp. They dressed, had a quick, Spartan breakfast brought forth by another gold piece. They walked arm in arm, to the still beautiful church where most of the politically important people of Richmond worshipped.

Fitz and Clarissa occupied a pew halfway down the aisle. A dozen rows ahead of them, Jeff Davis was worshipping. He was a man beset with all the troubles of the world. Discredited by some, admired by others, a man waiting for the final blow to fall.

Halfway through the service an officer made his quiet way down the aisle and bent to Jeff Davis' ear.

Davis immediately arose and followed him out of the church.

"Whut's that mean?" Clarissa whispered.

"Don' know yet. Lots o' officers heah, an' Davis' staff too. Keep your eye on 'em."

One after another of the important government people arose and left quietly, after being summoned by other officers.

Fitz said, "This heah service won't be over fo' an hour or mo'. Jes' get up real quiet, like mayhap you have to go to the necessary house. Walk out slow, with me. On my arm, like we got nuthin' on our minds."

They were able to leave the church, as the officers and the government officials had. On the street, they began walking faster at Fitz's urging.

"All hell goin' to bust loose," he said. "Know Lee losin' an' retreatin'. Means the Yankees are sho' comin' fast. Reckon the way Jeff Davis an' all the others left, Richmond goin' to be evacuated by the Confederate government. When all the Richmond folks heahs 'bout it, sho' goin' to bust loose fo' one final fling. Best we be somewhar else."

"You takin' me away, Fitz?"

"If we kin get away. Look about you. This is Sunday mawnin' on a nice day in April. You see any carriages? You see any riders? Know whut happened? Ev'rything that kin carry folks out o' the city been taken over. There's thousands o' government folks, an' they is leavin' quick as they kin."

Clarissa came to a stop in the middle of the sidewalk. "I don't want to go, Fitz. I want to stay heah. Folks goin' to need help, an' I'm stayin' to do whut I kin. Please don' ask me to go. So far I done nuthin' in this war. Time I did."

"It's goin' to be real rough," he warned.

"Know that, but don' matter none to me. Want to stay, Fitz. You stay with me, an' I sho' will be the happiest woman in Richmond. But know you cain't. So best you find some way o' gettin' to the railroad. If it still runs."

29

"Not 'til I'm sho' you be all right," he said. "Gots to go back, ain't no question 'bout that, but not 'til I know you be safe."

They didn't go back to the hotel, but remained on the street. Everything seemed quiet. They did notice a steady stream of all kinds of vehicles, piled with belongings and fleeing officials. It wouldn't be long before others would notice too and draw their own conclusions. After that, there would be pandemonium.

The dam seemed to burst in early afternoon. Suddenly, the Sunday-quiet streets were filled with anxious people, angry people. Someone shouted that Confederate soldiers were dumping kegs of whiskey into the gutters. There was a general avalanche in that direction. Filled kegs were wrested away to safety. People gathered at the big commissary buildings. The shouting began. Windows and doors were forced open or broken. In a matter of a few minutes the commissary was looted, and people were staggering away laden with sacks of flour, hams, port, and beef sides. The looting was very efficient—no animosity shown, no great amount of violence.

The now-churning, noisy streets were suddenly silenced by the sound of bursting shells. At first, it seemed the Yankees were shelling the city. Everyone began running for whatever shelter they could find.

Fitz and Clarissa had been close to Clarissa's hotel. They'd run four blocks, battled their way through several more, and now were exhausted. The two of them sat down in the lobby to regain their breaths.

"Reckon the Yankees goin' to blow Richmond to hell?" Clarissa asked.

"There wasn't any shellin'," Fitz assured her. "Soldiers were burnin' the ammunition dumps an' the armory. Whut we heard was shells explodin'. Ain't no mo' now, but reckon there be plenty mo' noise."

"But the Yankees are comin'," she insisted. "Think they come rapin' an' lootin'."

"By the time they get heah, won't be anythin' left to loot. We's doin' it 'fore they come. You gots to 'member that Lee got him an army blockin' the way. Sho'ly he got sense 'nuff to give up, but that'll keep the Yankees out o'

Richmond fo' a little while. You sho' you wants to stay?"

"Fitz, like I said, I ain't done nothin' in this war. Time now I got to do somethin'. I don' know whut, but I want to stay."

"All right. You need money or help, you go to my bank. Paul Robin's bank. Tell him I say you gets whutevah you want."

She leaned over and kissed him. "Wishes we could practice not being old some mo', but if you got to leave, bettah you go now, 'fore there ain't any way out. Hold me a little while an' then jes' get your ass off o' this sofa an' leave fast."

"Won't forget you, Clarissa. Thinks you crazy fo' stayin', but know whut you mean. Be careful now, an' come to me if there's no place you kin go."

"Promise," she said. Her arms tightened around his neck, her lips pressed hard against his mouth. In that kiss was more of the same longing which had obsessed both of them.

Fitz stood up and, without looking back, walked swiftly out of the hotel. He left his luggage behind, for there was no time to retrieve it. If there was still a train out of Richmond, it would likely be the last one, his final chance to get away.

3

The streets were almost solidly packed with people who didn't know where to go or what to do. They milled about uncertainly, wild-eyed with apprehension. More armory ammunition had begun to blow up, worsening the situation.

Confederate soldiers were beginning to burn houses in their desperate attempt to leave nothing for the invading Yankees. They were opposed by the householders who could see no point in burning their homes—the only things they had left. Fights grew in fury, and parts of the city were already darkened by a pall of black smoke.

Fitz fought and elbowed his way through the crowd, trying to reach the railroad station. Here and there he saw small bands of ex-slaves milling about in a greater state of confusion than their one-time masters. Most were cowering in whatever refuge they could find. They were terrified of all the commotion, knowing only too well that any of these frantic people blamed them for the war. Not knowing where to turn, they either tried hiding or formed groups large enough to offer some hope of protection.

If Clarissa had meant what she said about wanting to help, she was going to find many opportunities to do so, for everyone about required some sort of help, a calmer figure to rely on. It wouldn't take much, Fitz realized, to cause true pandemonium.

And there was great resentment over the sudden and unannounced departure of the government with little or no regard for the fate of Richmond's citizens. Dissatisfaction, suspicion, and fear were a mighty combination of forces to inspire rioting, though the situation had not yet gone quite that far.

Fitz finally reached the depot to find a train just pulling in. The station was crammed with soldiers and civilians who hoped to board it. But people now began drifting away instead. The train, carrying soldiers, was headed for a fighting area, and nobody wanted any part of that. The fighting was getting close enough as it was. The crowd lost interest and began to leave the area at a faster pace.

There were, however, two cars for civilian travel attached to the rear of the train. The rush on the platform was thinning out. Fitz moved quickly toward one of the half-empty cars, but a screech of terror made him turn about.

At the far end of the platform, a group of about a dozen men were slinging a noose over the head of a lanky, terrified Negro. The noose in place they pushed and dragged him along the platform while they sought a makeshift gallows.

Fitz ran toward them and boldly pushed his way to the side of the Negro. "Whut the hell's goin' on?" he asked.

One of the men, a short, stocky man, thrust his face close to Fitz's. "Ain't none o' your business. Stay outen this."

"You aimin' to hang him?" Fitz was not intimidated by the man's belligerence.

"We ain't aimin' to drag him 'round fo' the hell of it. Keep out!"

"Whut's he done?"

33

"None o' your goddamn business. I'm tellin' you, keep out."

"You're hangin' a free man, suh. This ain't a slave hangin'. Ain't no mo' slaves. Means trouble if this goes on, an' you damn well knows it."

The leader of the group, which had suspended the process of searching for a gallows, waved a fist in Fitz's face. Fitz restrained himself. He had never backed away from a fight, but in this case he'd be beaten to death by a dozen men. He had the wisdom to recognize that, but he had no intention of surrendering.

"Whut I'm tellin' you," he said, "is the Yankees are comin'. There's lots o' folks on this heah platform see you hang this poor nigger. The Yankees goin' to be lookin' fo' somethin' like this, an' they sho' run you down. All o' you. Then there's goin' to be a dozen hangings. This is the kind o' thing they wants to happen."

"You nuthin' but a crazy man," the leader shouted.

"Crazy 'nuff to know whut'll happen you strings him up. 'Lessen he killed somebody. That's why I wants to know whut he done."

"Runnin' like he outen his mind an' knocks a white woman to the ground. Falls right on top o' her on purpose, an' you know whut would happen we didn't pull him off her."

"That sho' ain't good," Fitz admitted with a shake of his head. "But the Yankees goin' to say it could o' been an accident, an' you sho' cain't prove it wasn't. Now you wants to hang this heah bastahd, you're welcome to do it, but it's your necks I'm thinkin' 'bout."

As he spoke, Fitz casually moved closer to the Negro. He suddenly lunged for him and shook him until his teeth rattled and his eyes rolled in fresh terror.

"Tells the truth," Fitz roared. "You aimin' to rape that poor woman?"

He pushed and pulled at the man in what looked like a frenzy of anger. But when his lips were close to the Negro's ear, he spoke in a whisper. "I give you a big shove so you bust loose o' these heah men. Then you runs like hell."

Whether or not the man understood, Fitz could no

longer get away with this and he knew it. He gave the Negro an extremely hard shove that sent him reeling back on his heels, the rope trailing after him. The man freed himself of the noose, turned, and began running. His long legs, his terrible fear, lent speed to his escape, and he quickly vanished along the platform.

"Now whut in hell you do that fo', mistah?" the stocky man shouted angrily. "Thinks you a nigger lover an' you did this on purpose."

"Damn you," Fitz shouted back. "Ain't you got a smidgen o' sense in your fat haid? I'm tellin' all o' you, hangin' that nigger gives the Yankees a chance to show us a nigger as good as we are. That means they'll say you murdered him, an' they'll sho' hang you fo' an example. Saved your worthless lives, that's whut I done."

"You're a liar, suh." The leader turned to his somewhat bewildered men and aroused them with a shout. "This heah nigger lover sets him free, an' we ain't standin' fo' that. Take him!"

Fitz backed up hurriedly. He had planned on this happening and was prepared for it. Fighting all these men would be hopeless. He thrust a hand into his pants pocket and closed his fist around a handful of gold coins. He tossed the coins into the air, over the heads of those aiming to destroy him.

The glint of gold coins performed the miracle Fitz had hoped for. The men promptly forgot their hatred to scramble for the coins, along with everyone else close enough to reach them. Two fights broke out. Men were on their hands and knees scrounging for the coins. Fitz headed for the train's two last cars at a run. The train was already pulling out.

Fitz had reached for the grips to haul himself aboard when he saw the Negro he had befriended, moving about uncertainly. Fitz sprinted toward him, seized the startled man by the neck and the seat of his britches, propelled him at full speed to the train, and threw him bodily onto the platform of the last car. Fitz now had to run to make the moving train, but he managed to get aboard. The Negro, still terrified and certainly mystified, cowered on the small platform while the train gained speed.

Fitz seized him again, pulled him erect, and pushed him into the car, which was filled with startled passengers and an irate conductor who made his way to Fitz.

"Ain't no niggers allowed in this heah car, suh. No exceptions."

Fitz said, "Thass fine with me, suh. But you throws him out, not me. I ain't lookin' to kill him."

The train was now moving very fast. The conductor looked about helplessly, seeking advice no one was inclined to give.

"Bought this heah nigger last week," Fitz said. "He runs, but I catches up with him, an' I'm takin' him back home. Anybody wants to argue that, welcome to try. But I paid good money fo' him, an' I'll pay fo' his passage."

"Niggers ain't allowed," the conductor insisted.

"Know that, suh. We put him on the back platform. You got any cattle cars on this heah train, we put him in one o' them soon's we gets to a station."

"We ain't stoppin' 'til we get to Lynchburg, suh. You put him on the back platform, he sho' 'nuff goin' to jump an' run again."

"Show you he sho' ain't." Fitz seized the helpless Negro again and shoved him down the aisle to the rear platform. The slave wore trousers held up by a rope. Fitz untied the rope and used it to secure the slave's wrists behind his back and then to the iron supports at the rear of the platform. The conductor observed this and nodded in approval. The black man wriggled about, trying to keep his trousers from falling down.

"You got a ticket, suh?" the conductor asked.

"Got one fo' me. Didn' expect to go back with a slave, so I pays fo' him in gold."

"Gold?" the conductor exclaimed. "You got gold money?"

Fitz produced a five-dollar gold piece and pressed it into the conductor's palm. "This heah gets ten times whut it's worth, suh. You take out this heah slave's passage an' keep the rest fo' understandin' how I feel 'bout this."

"Suh, I respect you fo' tyin' him up like you did. Reckon he goin' to get loose?"

"Not while I stay with him," Fitz said. "Thank you, suh, most kindly."

The conductor happily pocketed the coin and withdrew, closing the door. Fitz removed his hat, drew his handkerchief, and wiped perspiration from his brow. He glanced at the puzzled and amazed Negro.

"You sho'ly makin' plenty o' trouble fo' me. Whar you comes from?"

"Wuk fo' massa in Richmond."

"Doin' whut?'

"Body servant, suh. Waits on massa."

"Whut you done to that white woman, those bastahds tryin' to hang you for?"

"They beats me fo' pleasure, massa. I run an' 'fore I kin stop, I run smack into a woman an' she goes down. Me on top o' her, but don' mean nuthin'. Jes' tryin' to get away."

" 'Bout whut I was thinkin'."

"You saves my life, suh, reckon."

"You bet your ass I saved your life. Whut your mastah say 'bout how you waits on him?"

"Don' know whut you means, massa."

"He whup you fo' movin' too slow?"

The ex-slave hung his head. "Yas suh, reckon."

"Say you sloths?"

"Yassuh, I sloths." The man raised his head and looked Fitz full in the eye. "But sweah I nevah sloths agin, suh, you lets me wuk fo' you."

"Got no place to go?"

"No, suh, ain't got no place to go."

"I'm takin' you to my farm. Whut's your name?"

"Ephraim, suh."

"No it ain't."

The slave looked at him inquiringly, again puzzled.

"Your name's now Calcutta Two. Kin you 'member that?"

"Yassuh. I 'member whut you call me."

"Kin you read o' write?"

"No, suh. Cain't read or write. Cain't do nuthin' 'cept wuk hard."

"You kinda stupid," Fitz said appraisingly.

37

"Yassuh. Massa say ah most stupid bastahd evah see in his life, suh."

"Good. That's whut I'm lookin' fo'. A lazy, good-fo'-nuthin' nigger."

"Thass me, suh. Sho' 'nuff, thass me, suh."

"All right. Goin' back inside. Trusts you not to bust loose an' jump."

"Stay heah, suh. Goin' no place 'cept with you, massa."

"All right, then. Soon's the train stops, we gets you somethin' to eat."

Fitz opened the car door and went inside. He sat down next to a woman in black mourning clothes.

"You have my sympathies, ma'am."

"Fo' whut?" she asked.

"Fo' the loss o' your dear one. You're wearin' black so expect you lost a loved one."

"I lost the rottenest bastahd evah wear a Rebel uniform. Wear bright red 'stead o' black, but he got too many relatives fo' me to take the chance."

"Congratulations then," Fitz said cheerfully.

"That theah slave you roped ain't much good. Know him. Wuks fo' a man who runs a big store. Sells ev'rythin' from thimbles to buggies. This heah slave fetches drinks an' food, but gets to servin' 'bout the time we's finished eatin'. Jes' no good. Bettah you lets him jump off the train an' busts his damn neck."

"He wuks fo' me, an' he sloths like that, he don' have to jump off a train. I bust his neck fo' him."

Fitz drew his hat down over his eyes and stretched his legs as far as the limited space would allow. He felt as if he hadn't rested for days, and he blamed it on Clarissa's prowess. He smiled contentedly and promptly fell alseep.

At Lynchburg he left his new body servant outside a restaurant while he went in to eat. He ordered heavily and wrapped some of the food in a napkin. Outside again, he handed the food to the Negro as they walked along the street, Calcutta Two behind him. They reached the blacksmith shop where Fitz had left his horse and buggy. Reclaiming these and paying the fee, he ordered Calcutta

Two to hitch up while he went shopping for items needed at home. He returned after an hour and found Calcutta Two just finishing a task that should have taken about ten minutes. Fitz nodded in satisfaction. This was exactly what he wanted.

On the journey home, with the slave beside him, Fitz talked. He liked company, and even this illiterate man could listen, though he didn't comprehend everything Fitz said.

"You ain't no slave," Fitz told him. "Ain't no mo' slaves."

"Whut they calls me, massa, I ain't no slave?"

"Whut they calls you when you a slave?"

"No-good, slothin' bastahd, suh."

"Then that'll be whut I call you, but there's goin' to be a diff'rence. You wuk fo' me, you get paid. One silver dollah ev'ry week."

The black jaw dropped. "You pays me a silver dollah ev'ry week, massa?"

"Thass whut I said, an' you don' call me massa. You don' call anybody massa no mo', you understan' that?"

"Silver dollah ev'ry week?" He scratched his head and looked highly pleased. "Likes bein' free, suh. Sho' likes bein' free."

"Cain't whup you no mo', but I kin kick your ass if I feels like it."

"Massa, suh, you kin kick my ass any time you likes, suh. I your body servant now, suh." A massive smile spread across his coal-black face.

"You fetch drinks when I hollers fo' 'em or when my gran'son hollers fo' 'em. Yo' kin fix bourbon an' water?"

"Sho' kin." The Negro's eyes gleamed at the thought, Fitz noticed.

"Reckon you jes' the man I been lookin' fo'. Now you takes the reins an' let me do some mo' sleepin'. Sho' nice to be back in the country whar they ain't no shootin' an' no folks runnin' 'round like crazy. Sho' nice."

"Sho' is, suh," Calcutta Two agreed with a sigh of satisfaction.

Mark emerged from the house as the buggy pulled

up. Elegant came out to welcome Fitz back. Both of them stared at the newcomer who climbed down first and stood by respectfully, head down, hands clasped.

"Who the hell's that?" Mark asked. "Thinks ain't no mo' sellin' slaves, or did we win this damn war?"

"This heah Calcutta Two," Fitz told them.

"Calcutta Two?" Mark asked. "Who Calcutta One?"

"He's daid," Fitz said. "Missed him I did, he the laziest nigger I evah seen."

Elegant moved up closer to survey the new man. "Kinda looks like Calcutta, suh. Looks kinda like a string bean. Skinny one. He got long laigs an' big feet an' reckon he sloth real good."

"Tells him to bring in whut I bought," Fitz said. "Then shows him whar you keep the bourbon an' spring water. Calcutta Two, you brings us drinks an' you runs, heah?"

"Yassuh, run I does."

"An' you do whut Elegant say."

"Yassuh, I do whut she say."

"He don'," Elegant said with a toss of her head, "I busts him so he gits a inch o' two shorter than he is. Come on, you no 'count an' ah shows you whut to do."

Mark and Fitz assumed their customary chairs on the veranda. Mark was puzzled. "Cain't figger this heah Calcutta One and Two business, old man."

"You want 'nother lesson?" Fitz asked. "You calls me old man once mo' an' this time you don' wake up fo' two days. Tells you 'bout Calcutta One. He was born on papa's plantation, growed up with me. He so dumb he didn' know when it was night. All he good fo' was fetchin' drinks."

"Whut happened to him?"

"One time the poor bastahd ran 'cause he skeered. A goddamn colonel comes heah to forage an' tells Calcutta to stop runnin'. Calcutta mo' skeered than evah. So the colonel rides him down an' damn near cuts off his haid with his sword."

"Whut he do that for?"

"Like I said, 'cause Calcutta runs an' don' stop. An'

reckon 'cause this heah colonel don' like me none. So I finds this heah nigger in Richmond, runnin' jes' 'cause he skeered. Needs a boy to take care o' whut Calcutta One did."

"Gran'pa, you sho' a crazy old . . . don' mean to say that, suh. I begs your pahdon. But still thinks you're crazy fo' bringin' him heah."

"Calcutta One, he toted drinks, spilled half o' 'em on purpose, an' when nobody lookin', he drunk whut spilled off the tray. Time we has all we want to drink, he ain't totin' no mo'. He ain't movin'. He skunk drunk. Kinda like that. Missed it so I brings this one back."

Presently, after Fitz had told Mark about conditions in Richmond and the abandonment of the city by the Confederate government, Calcutta Two appeared with two glasses on a bone-dry tray.

Fitz took his glass, Mark his. Fitz stood up and set his glass on the veranda rail for a moment while he inspected the tray.

"You sho' ain't Calcutta One yet," he said. "Don' knows how to serve a drink, so I'll show you."

"Brings 'em. Runs, suh. Whut else kin I do?"

Fitz placed his glass on the tray, held it up with three fingers, and moved unsteadily along the veranda, letting liquid from the glass spill onto the tray.

"You sees that?" he asked.

"Massa, suh, I get whupped, I spills that way."

"Not heah, you don'. Now I take my glass. Lots o' drink on the tray. See it?"

"Sho' do, suh."

"Now you carry the tray inside. You drink ev'rythin' on the tray. You spills plenty, so makes sho' the glasses filled to the rim. You likes bourbon an' water?"

"Yassuh, sho' do, suh."

"All right then. Serve the drinks that way an' keep 'em comin'. Me an' Mark got us a pow'ful thirst an' lots to talk 'bout. Now you runs an' fetch mo'.'"

"Crazier an' crazier." Mark wagged his head.

"No," Fitz contradicted. "He totin' like that makes me feel like I'm home again. An' thass whut we has to talk about. Comin' home after Richmond."

"Heahs anythin'?" Mark asked. "The war endin'?"

"Way I see it, Lee ain't blockin' the way to Richmond no mo' or Jeff Davis wouldn' be runnin' like he did. So if Lee's bad off as that, an' I knows damn well he got to be, then there's nothin' left fo' him to do but surrender. Gen'ral Lee sho' ain't the kin' o' gen'ral lets his men die fo' nuthin'. He sho' put up a good fight, but nevah had a chance. Nobody in the South could've won this war. Nobody!"

"Nevah figgered we could lose," Mark said. "But reckon ain't no use fightin' no mo' we got no chance. Whut happens now?"

Calcutta Two returned with fresh drinks and a goodly portion slopped over on the tray. He rolled his eyes after he served the drinks and moved off the veranda to tilt the tray as Calcutta One used to do. Calcutta Two was quick to learn. By the fourth drink, he didn't have to jiggle the tray to spill the drinks.

"Whut's goin' to happen now?" Fitz repeated. "Don' rightly know. In Richmond they skeered Lincoln goin' to send soldiers killin' an' rapin', an' they hangs Jeff Davis an' Gen'ral Lee first thing. They's wrong. Mistah Lincoln says many times he wants no retribution."

"Whut's that word?" Mark asked.

"Means wants no revenge. Wants to bring the whole country back like it used to be."

"Think he kin do it?"

"Not goin' to be done day after tomorrow. I kin tell you. Plenty o' hate on both sides, but gots to happen like he say. Gots to, Mark, or we ain't got a country no mo'. Slaves are all gone now. They livin' heah like white folks. Goin' to be mighty hard on them. Some blame the war on the slaves, sayin' it happened 'cause o' them, not thinkin' slaves had nothin' to do with it. White folks brought this on. White folks like my papa an' his slave ship. That's whut done it, son."

"Whut these heah slaves goin' to do? Ain't nobody wants 'em. Cain't whup 'em no mo'. Cain't drive 'em."

"Don' know whut the slaves kin do. They don' know anythin'. We nevah lets 'em learn. An' now we gots to pay 'em when they wuk fo' us."

"Pay 'em with whut?" Mark asked. "Most folks ain't got 'nuff money to buy whut they needs to eat."

"Know that. Soon's the war is finished an' we sho' o' that, I send fo' some o' my money. I has it transferred to my bank in Richmond. Talked to Paul Robin theah already. He owns the bank. Then we draw on the money an' pay fo' whut we need."

"You aimin' to build that big house, ain't no niggers goin' do it, Gran'pa. Cain't do that kin' o' wuk."

"Hires white folks. Soldiers comin' back goin' to damn near starve. 'Til the South gets back on its feet, ain't goin' be much to do, an' hard cash will do it. But it's carpenters an' masons an' painters . . . that's who's comin' back. Reckon they needs money bad 'nuff to wuk fo' me even if they think I been hoardin' money."

"Whut 'bout the slaves?"

"Ones we had are long gone. But the countryside full o' them. Send Hong Kong out to round up a coffle o' two, bring 'em back, an' put 'em to wuk. Pays 'em. One silver dollah a week an' whut they want to eat an' a cabin to sleep."

"Dollah a week," Mark scoffed. "You go bust mighty fast."

"No, suh. Gets richer. You'll see. An' these heah niggers come to wuk, they kin leave if they wants. Lots o' them 'round to take their place. They has a cabin an' they wants a woman, they make up to one, jes' like we do, an' they marry 'em. They wants to raise pickaninnies, that's their business. They raise 'em, they feed 'em. Sho' not like it was when papa started this heah plantation."

"Whut he do?" Mark asked with considerable interest. They paused while Calcutta Two served drinks unsteadily but with great respect.

"Gots to train him some mo'," Fitz said. "Calcutta One, he moved so slow I had to kick his ass ev'ry day or so. Now, whut did my papa do when he put his slaves to wuk? He lined up all the gals on one side, all the bucks on the other. He made two lists. Like I told yo', all bucks were named fo' ports o' call an' all gals fo' ships. So my papa yells fo' Bombay takes fo' his woman gal named Glorious. Comes out so some big buck hung low as a bull gets a gal so puny he near kills her. An' some big gal, bustin' with lust, gets a old man who ain't got much left."

"Like you," Mark said with a grin.

"No, suh, not like me. I been seein' a big gal in Richmond, an' I got me drained to last a month. Mayhap mo'. An' she theah waitin' fo' me, I gets the need."

"Sho' 'nuff?"

"Tells you that's whut happened."

"We kin do whut we has to do," Mark said. "Want to see that big house built again, wants to make lots o' money. Got some myse'f. Sold mama's whorehouse fo' a mighty fine price. Wants to turn it over to you, suh. Wants to do my share. Mean it, an' you take the money, heah?"

"Heahs," Fitz said. "Don' need it, but whut's mine is yours now, reckon. Nobody else left. You got good blood in you. 'Nuff to overcome the bad blood your mama gave you. Know whut happens when your mama got knocked up? She raped Jonathan. He didn't know much 'bout a woman, an' she taught him. Right heah in this house whar we lives now. This is whar your mama's folks lived 'fore I sent 'em packin'. They all daid now."

"Then this heah house mine," Mark declared.

"If you kin take it from me."

"This heah house yours, suh. All yours."

Fitz stood up. "Whar in hell that slothin' sonabitch, Calcutta Two? Gettin' dry. We talks too much."

Elegant heard them talking. She waddled to the door, pushed the screen open. "Calcutta, he sleepin', suh. Sho' drunk. Jes' like Calcutta One. Yassuh, sho' jes' like it used to be. Whooee . . . reckon it like comin' home."

4

Fitz, with the help of Mark and Hong Kong, was busy in the fields laying out plans for planting again.

"Sho' goin' to be a great need fo' food, so we'll raise corn an' truck. Still, we got to think o' Wyndward gettin' back to whut it used to be, so we plants half in 'bacco."

"Gots the seedlings comin' real fine, suh,"˙ Hong Kong reported.

"Good. Heahs the war over an' Lee surrendered. 'Course ain't got no official word 'bout that, but reckon the shootin' stopped mostly. News travelin' slower than Calcutta Two these days."

"See plenty o' Reb soldiers in town last week," Mark said. "Doin' nothin', so reckon they sho' ain't under orders any mo'. Means the fightin' stopped. Asked some o' them. They didn't know fo' sho', but nobody's goin' back to the lines. They's all waitin' fo' word it's over."

"Praise God!" Hong Kong said fervently.

"I'll tell you one thing," Fitz said. "We now goin' to start hirin'. Soon's we gets the word fo' sho' the war is finished, wants you, Hong Kong, to take ten o' twelve o' the men wukkin' fo' us now. Go into town, all the way to Lynchburg. Want you to hire two hundred good men willin' to wuk. They lives heah fo' nothin'. Get meat, corn, an' whiskey ev'y Sunday. Wuk from six to five an' no wuk on Sundays. Raise their fam'lies heah. Be like old times 'cept no whuppin', kin ask me questions they likes, keep their hats on their haids they sees me, an' if they don' like wukkin' heah, they kin walk, not run, any time they likes."

"Goin' to think that mighty nice, suh," Hong Kong said.

"Mayhap, but feels most goin' to sloth fo' awhile. 'Til they gets hungry. Them whut comes to wuk heah now goin' to stay, reckon. Them whut comes heah hungry goin' to feed their bellies an' walk off."

"I gets the best I kin, suh," Hong Kong said. "You tells me when to look fo' 'em, suh, an' I goes fast as I kin."

Mark said, "Gran'pa . . . you turns 'round you sees a man in uniform ridin' this way an' got a second hoss trailin'."

Fitz turned about quickly. "Looks like he got business heah. Mayhap we gets word now 'bout the fightin' bein' all over. Hopes so. By heaven, nevah hopes fo' somethin' so much."

The rider, dusty, weary, in the uniform of a brigadier, pulled up and slowly dismounted. He favored Mark and Fitz with a formal salute.

"Reckon you don' 'member me, Mistah Turner, suh. Last time we meets was in a military courtroom."

"Gen'ral Miller," Fitz reached out with both hands to grasp those of the officer. "Reckon I sho' ain't fo'gettin' whut you did fo' me, suh."

"Whut you did fo' me an' the Cause," Miller amended. "Sends me all your fine thoroughbreds fo' my officers to ride. Brings two back, mayhap fo' breedin'. Best I could do, suh. Asks on'y you provides me with some means o' gettin' to Lynchburg."

"You keeps the hosses," Fitz said. "Not goin' to raise no mo' slaves an' no mo' hosses. Things changin'.

46

Sho' reckoned the Yankees took all good hosses like that."

"Yankees didn' take anythin', Mistah Turner. We gets to keep our guns an' them whut has hosses or mules keeps them too."

"It's all over then?" Fitz asked. "We ain't heared nothin' official."

"Sho' is over. Don't know whut to think now. Rides with Gen'ral Gordon when part o' the army surrenders. We feelin' mighty low, ridin' to whar the Yankee army is waitin'. We figgers we get cussed an' mayhap busted some, but when we rides into the Yankee camp, all the Yankee soldiers standin' in formation. Ain't no cheerin', no cussin', nevah even saw hate in Yankee eyes. An' when we marches befo' 'em, they shift arms from 'Ordah Arms' to 'Carry' an' they salutes that way. Nevah saw anythin' like it in my life. Don' know 'bout others, but makes me feel good. Bettah than I feel in yeahs. Gen'ral Gordon, suh, he wheels his hoss, drops the point of his sword to boot-toe, an' we all passes like we bein' reviewed. Damnest thing! Reckon now make no diff'rence whut side wins or whut side loses. When the goddamn war over, ev'ybody glad an' ain't no mo' hate."

"Gen'ral, suh," Fitz said, "we win this war, same thing would happen. Now we gots to bring this fine country back to whut it was 'fore all this heah fightin' starts."

"Yes, suh, you sho'ly right. Times goin' to be poorly fo' many, suh. I thanks you fo' the hosses. This heah your son?"

"Reckon I got two mo' hosses I gives 'em fo' that, Gen'ral. This heah my gran'son, an' he says I too damn old. Reckon you thinks he my son, make him think bettah o' my age."

"Reckon so." The general laughed a harsh, cracked sort of laugh, as if he'd forgotten how until now. He tossed a casual salute to Hong Kong. It was the best he could do. Hong Kong bowed his head, not in any servile manner but in respect. The general mounted and rode away slowly. Fitz glanced at Hong Kong.

47

"You heahs whut he said. Fightin' over. You ride out to find men to wuk heah. Got to get the plantation goin' first."

"Whut 'bout the house?" Mark asked. "Wants me to ride to town an' see 'bout linin' up some folks to come to build?"

"Best thing you kin do. Take some gold. Man say he willin' to wuk heah, give him a gold coin to bind the deal."

"Whut if he changes his mind? Some o' them Rebs goin' to say you mo' Yankee than Southern, suh."

"With the money to find out they ain't worth much anyways. You sees to lumber an' hahdware. Finds 'em hahd to get, goes North an' fetches 'em. Ain't goin' to be much sleep heah from now on. Wastin' time is wastin' money. You leaves in the mawnin'. Both o' you."

"I'se sho' ready," Hong Kong said. "Mistah Mark, suh, you wants to ride with me in the mawnin'?"

"Why the hell not, Hong Kong? Whut the hell, might as well get used to ridin' with a nigger. Reckon you kin ask Seawitch to fix us some o' that treacle pie she makes. Bettah'n whut Elegant makes, but don' you let Elegant know I says that."

They turned back to deciding what and where to plant. Later they inspected the cabins, and Hong Kong agreed to set the ex-slaves already on the premises to work cleaning them up. He would send a wagonload of them around the countryside rounding up likely ex-slaves to work the fields. Everything was moving now just as Fitz planned it would when the war was over.

In the morning, Fitz watched Hong Kong and Mark ride a buggy to town. Elegant, at his side, slapped her thighs with her big black hands.

"Suh, ah too fat to dance, but sho' wants to. Reckon things goin' to be like they was."

"Not 'zactly," Fitz said. "But close 'nuff, an' when we gets used to it, like it bettah, I thinks. You want to keep wukkin' fo' me?"

"Whut in hell makes you say that to me, suh? This heah mah home, suh."

"Pays you two silver dollahs a week, Elegant. You

worth it an' mo', but you eats so damn much ain't payin' you any mo'.'"

"Keep your goddamn two dollahs," Elegant said happily. "Got no use fo' money. Jes' don' you tells me to go, suh, 'cause ah ain't goin'.'"

"Goin' to start buildin' Wyndward soon's I kin get the lumber an' the help. Cain't wait."

"Reckon ah gets the same kitchen, suh?"

"Gots the plans fo' the house, Elegant. My papa gives 'em to me long ago. Ev'rythin' goin' to be 'zactly the same. Wants to walk in theah an' feels I comin' back home at last."

"Bless the Lawd, suh."

"Reckon," Fitz said. He wandered down to the barn and saddled his horse. He rode slowly to the stark chimneys of the old house and from his horse sat visualizing the new Wyndward rising out of the bare ground. He continued on to the graveyard, dismounted, stepped over the low white iron fence and faced those he had loved in life and still loved.

"War over," he said. "Killin's finished with. Got to get busy now makin' plans. Come back soon an' tells you whut goin' on."

Fitz broke into song on his way back. It had been a long time since he'd done that. Then he leaned over the saddle horn, dug his heels into the belly of the horse, lifted his head, and gave vent to a whoop of delight as the startled horse broke into a gallop.

Once home Fitz cooled the animal, watered and fed him, returned to the house, and went at once to his desk. There he contemplated how he'd write to Melanie, his daughter who detested him. Somehow he had to overcome that hatred because he wanted a favor of her.

He finally dipped his pen in the inkwell and began a letter he knew he was going to find difficult.

My dear Melanie,

I am very much aware of your feelings toward me, but now that the war is over, I think it's time we forgot our differences because they no longer exist. Wyndward was destroyed, as you asked for in answering the wireless sent you by the commander of a raiding party of Yankee soldiers. If this has been on your conscience, you may forget it because I burned the mansion, not the soldiers.

I am now about to begin rebuilding, and I shall restore it exactly as it was. I have no idea how much you suffered in this war, but the South is now destitute. Your brother Jonathan has not returned, and I have reason to believe he was killed in action. His twin sons were also killed at the outbreak of the war. So all the suffering is not on your side.

I write this letter for one specific reason. Shortly before the war began, I met and fell in love with a woman I knew as Sally Beaufort. When war broke out, she was compelled to flee, for she was, really, a Northern spy. However, we were in love. A true, genuine love. It broke my heart that she had to make a run for it, and I'm not even sure she reached the Northern lines. I pray that she did.

I have not heard from her since and it is on my conscience that she may feel she betrayed me and that I no longer love her. She gave me her real name. It is Elizabeth Rutledge. It's more than possible she was, or is, a well-known woman in Washington, or New York, or even Boston. I beg of you, try to find her for me and if you are fortunate, tell her that I am deeply in love with her and that I pray constantly for her return.

Do this for me, as my daughter. I hold no hatred for you, only the love of an adoring father for an exceptionally beautiful daughter. If there ever comes a time when you wish to return to Wyndward, I shall welcome you as I would welcome Elizabeth Rutledge—with all my heart and all my affection.

I am in good health and trust you are the same.

Respectfully and lovingly,
your father

50

Fitz read the letter over, sealed it, and left it on the desk to be mailed in Lynchburg, where he intended to be very soon. Then he leaned back in the big chair and thought how complete his life would be with Wyndward rebuilt and the girl he knew as Sally returning to him. It was a dream that would not go away, even if only half of it would be finally fulfilled.

He busied himself with the blueprints, making a few changes to conform with more modern ways. He would have a closed hallway from the main house to the kitchen, which previously had been separate. The springhouse would be larger, with room enough for the storage of ice cut from a pond on the plantation. The old corn crib would become a root cellar where vegetables could be stored for a long time. There would no longer be a commissary or dining hall. The farm hands would have their own cabins, well furnished, and they would support themselves entirely. The hospital would be restored, of course, but not the birthing house.

By late afternoon, Hong Kong had managed to bring back half a dozen men and four women. The ex-slaves who had been sent out to recruit more help had brought back three men.

Fitz addressed these people from the veranda of the small house while he thought back to the days when he had stood on the veranda of Wyndward and, at Christmas, handed out presents and coins to a thousand slaves.

"You brings your fam'lies," he said. "You kin pick any cabin you want an' see to it you gets all the furniture you needs. No sleepin' on the ground. Cabins ain't got wood floors, don' move in. 'Til you gets settled, we provides food an' gives you each two silver dollahs to buy more an' cook your own. You wuks from seven 'til five, an' you gets one hour off at noon. 'Spects a good day's wuk an' you gets paid ev'ry Saturday. One dollah to start. Mo' if you wuks hard an' the plantation makes money. Up to all o' you. Times kin be good or bad. You makes them whut they be. Thass all fo' now. Takes your orders from Hong Kong. You begins wuk tomorrow mawnin'."

He turned away as the blacks moved off, then did a

51

sudden about-face. "I thanks you fo' comin'," he said. And he wondered what his father was thinking down there in the little graveyard.

Mark returned the next day, thoroughly disgusted. "Cain't get anybody to come heah an' begin wuk on the house. They say they ain' goin' to wuk fo' nobody. Reckon all they thinks is slothin'. They sho' ain't much good after the war, Gran'pa. Whut we goin' to do?"

"Bide our time some," Fitz said. "They gets hungry. Their women an' childrun gets hungry, they sho' goin' to think some mo' 'bout wukkin'. Goin' to Richmond tomorrow 'bout my money. Sees whut I kin do there. You stay heah an' look after the men Hong Kong brought in. Treats 'em like they your brothers, heah? We needs 'em mo' than they needs us these days. Don' wants any o' 'em to walk."

"Ain't takin' much guff frum a nigger," Mark said. "They treats me fine, I treats 'em the same way, but sho' ain't takin' no guff."

"The war is over," Fitz said quietly. "Slavery over. Cain't figger whut's goin' to happen 'tween us an' the niggers, but the whole damn South goin' to need 'em like we needs 'em now. Things changin'. Been sayin' that fo' months an' it's nevah mo' true than now. Got to learn how to live with the change, Mark. This sho' ain't no time to get out o' step. We got to start from nuthin' an' turn the South back to whut it used to be. Think on that, son. Think hard."

Mark shrugged, obviously unimpressed with the lecture. Fitz went to his room to pack for the journey to Richmond in the morning.

A timid knock at the door brought him to open it and stare at a young, near-white ex-slave who smiled hesitantly at him.

"Fo' God's sake, it's Calla," Fitz cried out. "You comes back. Whar in hell you been?"

"Runs, massa suh, 'cause I skeered."

"Nothin' to be skeered 'bout no mo', Calla. You wants to come back, you sho' is welcome."

"Wants to come back, massa suh. Wants it bad, I does."

"Come in," he said and opened the door wider. "Sit down. Tell me whut you've been doin'."

She sat down very hesitantly. No slave ever sat in the presence of the master. Fitz bent and placed his hands against her cheeks and then bent lower to kiss her on the lips.

"Calla, you nevah be skeered again. You ain't a slave no mo'. You don' call me massa no mo'. We buildin' the big house, an' when it done, you takes charge o' all house slaves." He made a wry gesture. "Kinda hard gettin' used to it. You takes charge o' all the folks wukkin' in the house."

"I gets to be in baid with you, suh?"

"Well, cain't say as to that right now. Means fo' when the big house is built. But tonight . . . welcomes you. Sho' needs it, an' you pretty good at it."

"Wants to please you, suh."

" 'Preciate that, Calla. You evah heah from Domingo? She used to be my son's wench."

"She hidin', suh. In the woods. Skeered to come back."

"Now, Calla, you goes right now an' brings her back. She's welcome as much as you. Goin' to be like old times. Cain't say I kin take care o' both o' you gals, but got me a gran'son thinks could take care o' twenty like you. Go fetch Domingo."

"Yassuh," she exclaimed happily. "Brings her quick. Thanks yo', suh. Cain't call you massa no mo'?"

"Ain't no mo' massas, Calla. Ain't no mo' slaves."

When she returned with Domingo, Fitz was downstairs to greet them. Mark was at the plantation, so Fitz handled the situation himself. He brought both girls into the small parlor and urged them to sit down. They were so unused to such a request that finally Fitz grasped Domingo by the shoulders and pushed her into a chair. Calla had seated herself on the edge of her chair.

"Both o' you needs fat'nin'." He looked them over carefully. "Ain't lost none o' your looks. Elegant feeds you much as you wants an' pretty soon you gets kinda soft an' bettah in baid than a gal who is all bones. Damnation, you is skinny. Whar you been?"

"Jes' walkin', suh," Domingo said. "Gets hungry. Cain't find no wuk. We asks an' they drives us off. . . . Your son ain't come back from the war?"

"I'm 'fraid he's daid."

Domingo covered her face, holding back tears because no slave was supposed to cry before a master. Fitz went to her side and gently pulled her hands away from her face. She looked up at him with tears in her big, brown eyes. She was surely a good-looking girl, he thought. It would be hard to choose between Calla and Domingo. Perhaps he wouldn't have to choose. With better times, his prowess might improve.

"You sho' welcome to come back. You get paid if you wuks fo' me now. Kin talk 'bout that later."

"Massa suh . . . ," Domingo began.

"Tells you, don' call me massa."

"Mistah Bibb, he say I don' call him massa, he whups me."

"Bibb?" Fitz cried out. "Whar in hell yo' see that sonabitch?"

"Wuks fo' him, suh. 'Til he tries to rape me. I runs. . . ."

Fitz shook his head. "That man sho' gets in my way. Did he whup you?"

"No, suh. Say he was goin' to."

"Next time I meet him. . . ."

"Suh, he comin' heah."

"Bibb comin' to see me?"

"Comes 'long five, six others, suh. They aimin' to burn an' kill."

"When they comin'?"

"Tonight, suh. Thass why me an' Calla, we comes heah."

"Each of you gets five silver dollahs. Case Bibb got somebody watchin', bettah you run fo' the woods. Keep runnin' to the plantation. Seawitch theah an' gives you a cabin. Stay inside."

The girls hurried out of the house and took the trail through a wooded area. Fitz went into the room he called his office. From a closet there, he took out four rifles and a pair of pistols. He also had plenty of ammunition, dumping it out of the boxes onto the desk. He was humming, feeling very good. He welcomed the arrival of Bibb on a mission of arson and murder. For some years now he'd sought to rid himself of this dangerous enemy, and his chance was coming soon.

Mark returned, sweaty and tired. Fitz waited until Elegant served supper and then, at the table, told Mark how Calla and Domingo had come back.

"Calla's my wench. Domingo your papa's. Reckon she kinda in the heat, an' no mo' than right she gets into baid with you."

"Sho' ain't denyin' it sounds mighty good, Gran'pa. But it ain't like it used to be, we jes' takes 'em to baid an' they gots nothin' to say. Reckon we kin do this?"

"Hell, Mark, times ain't changed that much. They wants to get pestered, reckon ain't no law says we cain't pester 'em. But don't forget. They ain't whores like you growed up with in your mama's whorehouse. They servants now. Damn, whut make you think times change that much?"

Mark smiled happily. "When I gets to meet this heah wench?"

"Soon's we takes on Mistah Bibb. He comin' heah with five o' six men to burn us out an' kill us if he kin. Your wench heared 'em talkin' 'bout it an' comes to tell me."

"Ain't goin' to take all night to send this heah Bibb packin'. You tells Domingo to come back tonight?"

"Reckon after the fight is over, they both comes back."

"How you aimin' to stand up to six o' seven, Gran'pa?"

"Thinks o' a way. They won't come 'til near dark or after. Bibb ain't much good at fightin' in the daytime."

"We could bushwhack 'em. We get lucky we might take care o' the lot."

"Too risky. Sho' ain't got no wish to get killed now. Too much to do. Gots to raise Wyndward again. You stays heah an' keeps an eye out. You got a rifle an' a

55

sidearm in your room. Fetch 'em. See 'em comin', fire a shot an' come runnin' down to the slave quarters. They don' come, you sit tight 'til I gets back."

Fitz began to gather up the guns and ammunition. Mark watched him until he was on his way to the door.

"You fixin' to turn yo'se'f into a one-man army, Gran'pa?"

"Reckon, mayhap. Keep your eyes open now. You sees dust on the road, get off that shot quick as you kin."

"You're the gen'ral," Mark said amiably.

Fitz saddled his horse, and with the guns across the saddle, he rode down to the quarters and brought Hong Kong out of his cabin. He turned over all rifles, except one he kept for himself, and most of the ammunition along with orders. Hong Kong listened and nodded eagerly. He was never a man to back away from a fight. Fitz was back at the house long before he and Mark heard the faint sound of riders coming through the haze of near darkness.

"You get yourse'f into the bushes near the road so you be kinda behind them when they ride up. Wait fo' me to act 'fore you starts shootin', but once you start, kill as many o' the bastahds as you kin."

Mark stuffed ammunition in his pockets, strapped on the holstered pistol, and hurried away into the advancing gloom. Fitz sat down on the veranda with the rifle across his knees.

There were five men besides the burly, bearded Bibb. Fitz wondered how Bibb had ever rounded up that many, for his reputation in the county was quite well known. They paused halfway down the road and lit firebrands, holding them high as if to intimidate Fitz. Then they began riding again.

Fitz stood up, the rifle level, finger hard on the trigger. "Far 'nuff!" he called out. "Pull up or I starts shootin'."

Bibb held up his hand as if he were a cavalry officer giving orders to a squad of men. The riders came to a halt. Bibb rode ahead slowly, watching Fitz intently.

56

"You stops right theah," Fitz said.

Bibb pulled up his horse a bit late. A bullet sang its lethal song close to his ear.

"Raises that gun an' you sho' a daid man," Fitz warned. "You sick o' livin', try it."

"Askin' you to come down heah an' fight me man to man," Bibb shouted.

"When you gots five men ridin' to back you up?" Fitz asked derisively. "Come heah alone, you yella bastahd, an' you won' have to ask me out."

"All right, then," Bibb shouted. "We'll take you now, Fitz. You get one o' two o' us, ain't goin' to do you any good. You is a daid man!"

"Now I'd say you an' the rest o' you scum are much closer to bein' daid than I am. Jes' look about you, Bibb. Whut you an' your boys sees ain't whut you might call healthy."

"Bibb," someone called out. "There's niggers sidin' him. Niggers with guns!"

Bibb wheeled his horse. His five men were between two rows of ex-slaves, led by Hong Kong. All appeared to have rifles ready. Hong Kong fired off two fast shots, not aiming at anyone, purely to intimidate.

Fitz called out. "One o' you scalawags so much as raises your rifles an' the lot o' you is comin' outen your saddles daid 'fore you hits the groun'. As fo' you, Bibb, any time you wants to come back alone, you is welcome, but bring a wagon to take back your worthless carcass. Now ride! Ev'ry last one o' you bastahds, ride off. In two minutes the shootin' starts."

Bibb hesitated, but gave up when Mark emerged from the brush, rifle aimed straight at a range from which he could not miss. Bibb cursed bitterly. His men doused their firebrands by dropping them into the dust and rode off before Bibb finally made up his mind as to the utter hopelessness of the situation and joined the retreat.

When they had vanished into the dusk, Hong Kong came up to the veranda, holding all the rifles Fitz had given him, along with the ammunition. He placed the guns on the steps.

"Reckon yo' gave me no orders to shoot, suh, but I was wonderin' if those rednecks thought an ex-slave wouldn' shoot."

"You did right. You did fine, Hong Kong. So did the boys you brought heah. Sees they get a good reward. Whiskey an' all they kin eat. . . ."

"Thanks you, suh. Ain't lookin' to no rewahd, suh."

"Knows that. You gets it anyways."

"You wants me fo' anythin' else, suh? Seawitch she kinda worried some."

"That'll be all, an' I thanks you again."

Mark moved up beside Hong Kong. "You has my respect, Hong Kong. You sho' one smart . . ." he drew a long breath, "man."

Fitz chortled, "War's sho' over."

"Reckon so." Hong Kong laughed with Fitz.

"One thing mo'," Mark said.

"Yassuh, Mastah Mark."

"Sees you get word to Calla an' Domingo to come back heah fast as they kin. All this heah excitement got me kinda horny, an' fo' my papa's sake an' fo' his mem'ry, gots to take care o' his wench."

5

Fitz luxuriated in the deep bathtub while Calla energetically applied a brush and a sponge. She was stark naked, wholly unashamed of it, and worked industriously at getting him clean.

He finally got out of the tub and accepted the towel she handed him. She raised a foot to step into the water, but he laid a hand on her bare shoulder.

"You ain't takin' a bath in water me or anybody else left. Elegant got hot water on the stove all the time. Now you puts on somethin', go down an' fetch your water. Clean the tub first."

"Don' mind usin' you watah, suh. Always did."

"Damn it, do as I say. Start learnin' not to think an' act like a slave. An' be quick 'bout it. I get too damn tired, I ain's much good."

"I runs," she said.

Half an hour later, perfumed with toilet water Fitz had bought in Richmond long ago in anticipation of something like this, Calla slipped into bed, her warmth reaching him. He was in no hurry now, warm from her.

body and from the tub, tired but pleasantly so. He turned on his side and looked at her. She'd not yet blown out the bedlamp, and he saw in this girl a beauty he'd not noticed before.

"By damn," he said, "you sho' is a mighty fine-lookin' gal. You white, with a face an' a body like that, they standin' in line jes' to talk to you. 'Course you is as dumb as a rock, but that don' make much diff'rence. Not with whut you got to offer a man. You knows whut in hell I'm talkin' 'bout, Calla?"

"Says I ain't smart. You sho'ly right, suh."

"I said you are very attractive. No—that word is too much fo' you. Let's say it this way. You're a goddamn good-lookin' gal. You kin get yourse'f pestered by any white man you wiggles your little ass at."

She laughed, a silvery, soft laugh that intrigued him.

"Reckon I sees mo' in you since you not a slave. Knows whut you wants out o' life, Calla? You wants a man to treat you kindly, sees you get 'nuff to eat an' a little perfume now an' then. Mayhap you wants babies. That sho' ain't bad. An' no mo' takin' 'em from you an' sold. Someday you finds a man like that. Bound to happen."

"Yassuh," she replied softly. "You knows whut I wants better'n me, suh."

"Goin' to see you gets all that. Domingo too. You fine gals an' mighty good in baid. Yes, suh, goin' to happen like I say. A good man comes 'long, or we finds him fo' you. But right now, thinks I kin rape you. So—come closer an' let's see if I'm still good."

She snuggled next to him, moving sinously. He said, "An' ain't no need you gets outen this heah baid when I goes to sleep. No mo' sleepin' on the floor at the foot o' the baid. Them days is gone, Calla, an' I say good riddance."

Fitz woke late in the morning feeling fine. The other side of the bed was empty and he sat up to make certain Calla hadn't disobeyed him and slept on the floor. She was not there.

He was halfway through shaving when Calla came in

with a breakfast tray. She set it down carefully and stood waiting for him to finish. She held a chair for him. He sat down, leaned back, reached up, and drew her down for a kiss.

"Reckon I kin say I sho' am lucky you comes back to me, Calla."

"Wants to be heah all my life, suh. Wants to pleasure you ev'y day you wants me to."

"Calla, I'm gettin' on. You a young gal. Takes more'n me to keep you pestered. You talk to Domingo this mo'nin'?"

"She says you gran'son jes' like you, suh. Jes' like your son too. She say she nevah been raped so good."

Fitz nodded and reached for one of Elegant's hot biscuits. "Reckon so. I kin whup him in a fight, but I sho' cain't do my rapin' good as he kin."

Mark came by and joined Fitz at the small table. Calla discreetly withdrew. Mark seized the last biscuit as Fitz reached for it, and helped himself to the egg on Fitz's plate, snatching up Fitz's fork when he laid it down.

"You fixin' to starve me to death?" Fitz asked patiently.

"Mighty hungry, Gran'pa. Domingo sho' a fine wench. Nevah knowed a brown gal could pleasure a man so. Been to baid with lots o' 'em, all shades, but not one like this heah gal. Wonder why I 'preciates her mo'."

"Thass easy, son. Now you has to ask her she wants to be raped. 'Fore you didn' ask, you jes' took."

Mark looked up. "Sho' 'nuff?"

"She wants to pleasure you, like any gal, no matter whut her color, then it be bettah by a hundred times. Fo' you an' fo' the gal."

"Reckon I ain't too proud to ask again," Mark said with a laugh. "She tells me 'bout papa. Nevah heahs these things befo'."

"Like whut?" Fitz surrendered his cup of coffee.

"Says papa reál nice. Treats her like a lady. But after Daisy died he sorta changed an' jes' threw her down. Like she nuthin'. Breaks her heart, but says she know why. I sho' don'."

61

"Nevah figgered Domingo had that many brains to know. Your papa married to a mighty pretty gal name o' Daisy. They happy as two people could be. Then a slave, runnin' from some other plantation, comes heah an' rapes her. Nobody at the big house when it happens. Don' know 'zactly whut he done to her, but she goes outen her haid an' nevah comes back. Don' even know me or Jonathan when we goes to see her. Then she dies an' that makes Jonathan mad. Thinks 'cause this no-good nigger done the rapin', all niggers are like him. Comes to hate 'em. Even Hong Kong, an' all his life your papa think Hong Kong a fine man. Then the war comes an' Peter an' Paul, twin boys borned to Daisy an' Jonathan, enlists. We sends 'em to a military school 'fore that, an' they gets educated in how to kill people. The war comes, they swears they eighteen an' enlists right off. They were ridin' an ammunition wagon when it blew up. Wasn' nothin' left. They fifteen yeahs old."

Mark shook his head. "Whut Domingo says makes me kinda 'shamed o' myse'f. Mama tells me Jonathan rapes her an' I borned, an' she say it no mo' than right I kills Jonathan. Makes me hate him an' swears I shoots him some day."

"Yo' came damn near it more'n once."

"Mama say I waits 'til he worries fo' yeahs. Then shoot him down. Comes to Wyndward to do it, but he in the war. Finds out whar he is, enlists myse'f, an' looks fo' him. Thinks I kin kill him nice an' easy on the battlefield, an' nobody thinks I done it. Finds him an' waits. He didn' know who I was. Kept away from him. Then I gets my chance an' by damn, I couldn' do it. Tries twice. Had him in the sights o' my gun, an' I couldn' pull the trigger. Pleased now I didn'. Reckon he was a fine man."

"They's always a chance he ain' daid."

"Thinks we kin try to look fo' him?"

"Not yet. War's over sho', but ain' been time to get things sorted out yet. Mayhap he in a prison, or in a hospital. Nevah gave up hopin'."

"I sho' am hopin' too, Gran'pa. Reckon he treats me good he comes back?"

"Cain't say. He went into the war so full o' hate sometimes I didn' know he was my son. Mayhap the war changed him. Hopes so."

"Whut we goin' to do 'bout this heah Bibb?"

"Nuthin' right now. 'Lessen he gets too close. Then I kills him an' damn the rest o' it."

"Watch yourse'f. Kin see now he a yellow sonabitch an' most likely to shoot you in the back."

"Knows that. Reckon he'd shoot you too so I'd cry over you."

"Gran'pa, would you cry I get shot?"

"Reckon, but cain't say now they'd be tears o' sadness or joy. Leavin' you in charge now. Hong Kong got 'nuff men to start plowin' an' you go down to the plantation an' see things done right."

"You fixin' to jes' set an' let me do all the wuk?"

"No suh, wouldn' trus' you that much. I'm goin' to Richmond to tend some bankin'. Means you in charge. See that you stays out o' trouble."

"Got Domingo." Mark wiped his mouth with Fitz's napkin. "Ain't lookin' fo' anythin' else. Keeps ev'rythin' runnin' good, Gran'pa. Don' worry none."

"Worries some," Fitz told him. "Knowin' you as I do. You gots some growin' up to do, son. Reckon you gets steady on your feet an' dry behind the ears, you goin' to be tolerable. Jes' tolerable."

He arose and clapped a hand against Mark's shoulder. He could reach Lynchburg with time to search for artisans to hire—maybe he'd be luckier than Mark had been. In the morning he'd take a train to Richmond. He was eager to get going, to see that Wyndward rose from its ashes into what would be its greatest glory. Little else mattered to Fitz these days.

He reached Lynchburg early in the afternoon, put up his horse at the livery stable, and walked slowly along the main street toward the bank. There were men, still in uniform, mostly lounging about, looking tired and discouraged. Two of them were seated on a platform at the grain and feed shop. Fitz walked up to them.

"Reckon you boys lookin' fo' wuk?"

63

"Whut in hell makes you think that?" one of them demanded angrily. "Ain't we done 'nuff, riskin' our lives an' givin' up mo' than four yeahs o' our lives?"

"An' fo' whut?" the other man said in a toneless voice of despair.

"Sooner or later you goin' to need money." Fitz attempted reason. "You starts earnin' it right off, bettah fo' you."

"Ain't wukkin' fo' no man. You wants help, suh, you gets yourse'f some o' these niggers walkin' 'round free."

Fitz didn't reply. He walked away from them, disturbed by this first encounter with the lassitude he now sensed he was going to find wherever he went.

He reached the bank, not sure what sort of a reception he was going to find. Henry Tallen, who owned the Lynchburg bank, had testified against him when he was being tried in military court on a charge of treason. Henry had been clearly wrong, through ignorance of the situation, and Fitz had managed to make him look like an idiot.

Fitz walked into the bank. Employees were at work behind the grilled windows. They watched him indifferently as he crossed the lobby. A young man at a desk near Tallen's office arose to intercept Fitz, but sat down again, after a look at Fitz's face.

Fitz opened the door and walked in. Behind the desk, Henry Tallen came to his feet quickly, and a look of fear grew on his face. He seemed to be much older, and Fitz actually felt sorry for the man.

"Sit down, Henry," Fitz said. He dragged a chair from the wall to the front of the desk and seated himself. Tallen slowly resumed his chair.

"Whut you wants, Fitz?" Tallen asked.

"See heah," Fitz said, "the war over. Or ain't it?"

"Don' knows whut yo' talkin' 'bout, Fitz."

"I'm tellin' you, we had troubles 'tween us. You swears I was sendin' my money to the North to help them fight us. Whut you said wasn't a lie 'cause you didn't know 'zactly whut I did with that money. You didn't know I gave it all, the whole million an' mo', to the

Confederate States. Wants you to admit you was wrong."

"Admits it," Tallen said. "That all you wants?"

"Fo' a man under an obligation to me, you actin' like I fixin' to wring your neck. Like I said, the war over. Once you gets used to it, you sleeps bettah, Henry. Kin I cash a draft fo' ten thousand?"

"You talkin' 'bout dollahs, Fitz? This heah bank cain't cash a check fo' a thousan'. Lessen you lookin' fo' shinplasters. I gives you a million dollahs in them, jes' to take 'em away."

"Thought you damn neah busted. Now I wants a favor o' you."

"Cain't do anybody any kind o' favor these days, Fitz."

"This one you could. Want to rebuild Wyndward. Make it jes' like befo'. Aimin' to get the plantation goin' again."

"Fitz, ain't that much money in the whole South."

"I had some money in a Northern bank, Henry. When the war came, I couldn' get it out. It's a respectable sum now, plenty to do all I want to do. I need men to come an' help me. Carpenters, masons, brick makers, any kind o' help, an' I pays well."

"Umm," Tallen said as he leaned back in his chair, at ease now that he knew Fitz was not here to make trouble. "Mighty nice o' you to do this, Fitz. Could bring money into the town, an' we sho' needs it. Reckon I does whut I kin. Don' promise nuthin', but tries. Most men comin' back don' want to do anythin' 'cept sloth. But not all. Reckon I kin be of help."

"Good." Fitz arose and extended his hand across the desk. "Needs a good banker heah in Lynchburg. Sees Paul Robin tomorrow in Richmond, an' I has him send you a draft fo' a million dollahs. Draws on it fo' the house an' whut evah else I needs, but should be a balance to keep your bank solvent."

Tallen nodded. "We been mighty wrong 'bout you, suh. Mighty wrong. I begs your pardon, an' I 'preciates whut you doin' fo' the bank an' fo' Lynchburg. I am your servant, suh."

Fitz was pleased with the results of his meeting with

Tallen. He had had a real need for a banker closer to home than Richmond. He stopped at a hotel bar where he was once accused of being a Yankee sympathizer. The managers had long since learned how wrong they were, but Fitz was still welcomed quite coldly. He had his drinks and then wandered down to the railroad station to learn he was in luck. A night train for Richmond was due in less than an hour.

He passed the time with a Richmond newspaper that seemed streaked with doom. He learned from it that Jeff Davis had gone into hiding, but there seemed to be no concentrated effort to find him.

Fitz threw the newspaper aside. What the South needed most was some word of encouragement. It had suffered defeat and it was destitute, but until there was some sort of cooperation with the North, recovery from the war would be almighty slow. Fitz, with all that New England blood in him, felt certain that the hate would die, at least sufficiently to bring in Northern money, skills, and machinery. The South could not withdraw from the world because they had been defeated.

He endured the overnight ride to Richmond in a drafty, sooty, hard-seat coach. Southern railroads were in a terrible state of disrepair. At least this train was not filled with wounded soldiers. It was a slow ride, but it got him there by midmorning. He felt the need for more sleep and went to the hotel where Clarissa lived. Since he felt no need for her inducements, he checked into a room and went to catch up on some sleep. It had been an exciting five days since Lee surrendered.

When Fitz wakened, it was midafternoon. He had lost more time than he wished but still had enough in which to transact his business. He got a shave in the barbershop and went out to search for workers. He began at the old slave auction area with its cleared space for buyers and sellers, its platform on which the auctioneer had exhibited his stock and taken bids on men, women, and children. To one side was a small scaffold-like structure on which hung the auctioneer's bell, which had somehow escaped being melted down for bullets. Fitz grasped the rope and sent a clamor resounding through the neighborhood. It drew men and women, all puzzled by the ringing. Fitz also noticed two men in Yankee blue hovering at the edge of the group.

"Come closer, folks." Fitz imitated the cry of the old slave merchants. "Cain't see whut I gots to offer, you hangs back that way. Get in heah an' see whut I gots to sell."

"Whatever you gots to sell," a woman's voice called out, "ain't nobody heah gots 'nuff money to buy it."

"Thass whut I means. I got gold to sell." He tossed a gold coin into the air and caught it deftly. "Got mo' o' these an' gives 'em away to anybody who kin help build a big house. Owns Wyndward, an' it get burned down. Wants to rebuild an' needs good men with skills to help. Pays well, in gold. Do I get any takers?"

No one replied. The men looked at one another. There were whispers between husbands and wives, but the small crowd finally drifted away. Fitz sighed and stepped down from the platform, discouraged and mightily disgusted.

Before Fitz could move out of the slave trading area, a familiar figure strode up to face him. Fitz wagged his head in disbelief.

"Colonel Apperson! Whut in hell you doin' stayin' alive? Ain't many colonels livin' these days."

Colonel Apperson had aged considerably, but his disposition had not changed. "You cain't insult me with you cheap words," he said. "Wants to know whar Clarissa is."

"Now whut makes you think I knows whar she is?"

" 'Cause she got to be livin' someplace, an' ain't nobody but you who give her 'nuff money fo' that."

"Colonel," Fitz said, "I goin' to break your neck one day. You comes to my plantation wearin' your big new uniform, an' you kills one o' my slaves jes' fo' the hell of it. Ain't nevah goin' to fo'get that even if I fo'gets all the otheh things you done to me an' mine. So go to hell, Colonel, suh. An' get out o' my way fo' I kills you now."

"Clarissa's my daughter-in-law. Says she got to come an' live with me."

"She sooner live with a skunk."

"Reckon she tells you that. Means you know whar she is. I'll have the law on you, Fitz, you don' send her back to me."

"The law!" Fitz said with derision. "Last time you an' me was concerned with the law, me an' Clarissa made a big fool o' you. Ain't no law says she gots to go back to you. Or your son, s'posed to be Clarissa's husband an' who baids down with boys 'stead o' Clarissa. Now you get out o' my way or I dumps you in the gutter."

Apperson moved aside. His face was aglow with anger, but he knew better than to engage in a physical fight with Fitz.

Fitz, still boiling, walked rapidly down the street. He had to see Clarissa now, to warn her that her father-in-law was searching for her.

The aroma emanating from a cafe enticed him inside, and he spent fifteen or twenty minutes there. When he emerged, he saw a scrawny-looking Negro boy lounging against the wall. As Fitz walked away, the boy began to follow him. At least, so Fitz thought. To make certain, he turned a corner and ducked into a doorway. The boy came into sight, pausing in consternation that he'd lost his quarry. Fitz stepped out behind him and clamped a hard fist on his collar. He turned him around.

"Whut you followin' me fo', boy?"

"Ain't," the frightened boy said. "Ain't followin' you, massa. Jes' walkin'. . . ."

"You're lyin'. Don' you evah lie to a grownup, heah? You gets you ears boxed ev'ry time. Now answer me."

The boy hung his head. "I'se hungry. Ain't got no place to go. No place to sleep."

"Whar your folks?"

"Git none. My mama an' papa sold befo' the war ends, suh. Kin you give me ten cents, suh? Needs somethin' to eat real bad."

Fitz hesitated. "Whut's your name?"

"Chickory, massa suh."

"That sho' one crazy name. Whut plantation you come from?"

"Alson, suh. Long way from heah, suh."

"Never heared o' it. How you gets heah in Richmond?"

"Get on a train, suh. Don' know whar it goin'. Don' know whar I am."

"I see. I'll give you a silver dollah fo' buyin' food. But if you've been lyin' to me an' I finds you, I sho' take that dollah out o' your black hide."

The boy caught the coin Fitz spun into the air so deftly that Fitz thought this wasn't the first time he'd begged. He was an intriguing boy though, evidently quick-witted and resourceful.

Nearing the hotel, he came to an abrupt stop, turning quickly. He wasn't certain, but he thought he saw a small dark figure duck around a corner. Fitz shrugged and went on in. He didn't stop at the desk but walked up the two flights of stairs and knocked on Clarissa's door.

"Who is it?" she asked from behind the closed door.

"Fitz. Open up, Clarissa."

She opened the door and threw herself into his arms, kissing him wildly, pulling him into the room.

"Nevah been so glad to see anybody in my life," she said. "Whar in hell you been, Fitz? You know I cain't go too long 'thout gettin' in baid with yo'."

"Mayhap that come later, Clarissa. Stopped by to tell you I meet your papa-in-law an' the sonabitch wants to know whar you hidin'. He wants you back."

She shrank away from him in sudden fear. "He skeers the hell out o' me, Fitz. Please don't let him find me."

"Do my best, Clarissa. Gots to go now."

"You ain't stayin'?" she asked in renewed fright.

"Comin' back. Mayhap an hour. Gots to see my banker. Won't be long."

"Yo' aimin' to stay?"

"All night. Mayhap two o' three nights. Lookin' fo' people to help me build Wyndward, but cain't find anybody willin' to earn an honest dollah."

"They's waitin' to see whut the Northern soldiers

goin' to do. Waitin' to heah whut orders Mistah Lincoln gives. Ev'rybody jes' waitin' an' kind o' skeered, reckon."

"So that's it!" Fitz said. "Reckon you right, but got to hire men anyways. Ain't inclined to wait to see Wyndward all built again. Comes back soon."

She followed him to the door, closed it, and he heard her lock it after he left. He made his way to the lobby, looked about but saw no one he recognized. He walked the dozen blocks to the bank owned by Paul Robin.

Fitz spent about half an hour with him. He arranged for the transfer of a million dollars to Tallen's bank in Lynchburg.

"Know you an' Henry didn't get 'long too well," Robin said. "But reckon he's an honest man an' a good banker."

"Tallen made a mistake. Kin fo'give that. Tryin' to find workmen to help me rebuild, but nobody wants to wuk. You heahs o' good men, would be a mighty big favor to me if you sends 'em to Wyndward. Pay all their expenses an' give a bonus they want to wuk fo' me an' live on the plantation fo' a few weeks."

"I'll do my best. I think ev'rybody is tired, exhausted. The idea o' wuk, 'specially to mustered-out soldiers, is bad. They're sort o' catchin' up on things."

"Reckon cain't blame 'em fo' that. See Yankee soldiers heah. Sho' didn' take 'em long."

"Whole regiment moved in yesterday. Ain't sho' whut they wants heah, but so far seems all they doin' is police wuk. Been polite an' makin' no trouble so far. Heahs lots mo' of 'em comin'."

"Thass whut you get when you lose a war," Fitz said.

"Mistah Lincoln made a speech few days ago. Says he wants to bind up the wounds. Ain't lookin' to make trouble fo' us. Even say he hopes Jeff Davis got away to some other country."

"Davis lookin' to turn his soldiers into bands o' outlaws like Quantrill," Fitz commented.

"Crazy idea. Ain't nobody wants any mo' fightin'. Wouldn' do no good anyways. On'y make things bad fo' the rest o' us. I got plenty o' faith things goin' be all right pretty soon."

"Gots the same feelin'. Well, gots to go. Oh yes, sees Colonel Apperson a little while ago. Looks kind o'seedy."

"He's flat busted. Comes heah fo' credit, he sho' goin' to get turned down. Durin' the war he in charge o' a big warehouse heah an' struts 'round in his uniform like he mo' important than Gen'ral Lee. Ain't got no use fo' that stinker."

"Reckon I goin' to kill him someday. Well, I'll look in again fo' I goes back."

"Any time, Fitz. You sho' is welcome. You an' your money," Robin added with a wide smile.

Fitz walked the street for a short time, noticing more Yankee soldiers, armed and moving about, keeping an eye on things. Richmond had enjoyed no real police force in years. These soldiers were actually an asset to the community. Especially now that the war was over and there were many desperate men floating about.

Fitz returned to the hotel, intending to take Clarissa to supper. When he reached her door, his hand paused in midair before knocking—he heard a sharp cry from inside. He tried the door, found it unlocked, and pushed it open.

Clarissa was cowering in one of the chairs. Colonel Apperson stood over her, swinging his cane and beating her about the shoulders.

"You no good whore," he was saying harshly. "All you good fo' is sellin' yourse'f. Fo'gets you part o' my fam'ly. You runs away when I'm doin' my duty in the war. You comin' back now, heah? You comin' back an' do whut I says."

"You go to hell," she cried out, noticing Fitz's presence for the first time.

Apperson raised the sturdy-looking cane, but Fitz moved up behind him, wrenched the cane from his grasp, held it at both ends, and broke it over Apperson's head. He threw the two pieces aside, seized Apperson by the throat, and pushed him against the wall.

"You's the most miserable bastahd evah born," he

said. "Warns you to let Clarissa alone befo'. Warns you again, an' so you understan's whut in hell I'm talkin' 'bout, this might make you 'member."

He struck Apperson full in the face with his fist, drawing a geyser of blood from his nose. Then he held him by the collar and the seat of his pants and threw him bodily into the corridor. Then Fitz slammed the door and walked over to Clarissa. Blood was oozing from her temple, and she bared her shoulders to show the slowly blackening marks from the cane.

"He's crazy," she said.

"Sonabitch must o' followed me," Fitz said. "He come again, you call fo' help an' have this crazy man locked up."

"Ain't no police. . . ."

"Sho' is. Yankee soldiers patrollin' the streets, an' they sho' goin' to help a mighty handsome woman like you. Jes' don' go back with him no matter whut. Now gets yourse'f dressed an' we goes down to suppah."

In the bedroom she faced a mirror and cleaned the scratch on her temple, deciding a dusting of powder would hide it. She flexed her shoulders to offset some of the pain still lingering there. Then, while Fitz waited and read the Richmond newspaper, she dressed in the only good gown she had left.

Looking at her, Fitz decided she made a passable if somewhat hefty appearance. Her face was still pretty and remarkably unwrinkled. Her hair was the same soft shade of brown it had always been. She'd been about as immoral as she could be, she'd done her best to make trouble for Fitz and for his family, but now they were friends as well as lovers. It pleased him to notice that she managed to attract male eyes as he escorted her into the dining room of the hotel.

They ordered Fitz's preference, also Clarissa's: thick slices of rare roast beef, vegetables, a bottle of wine, and a slice of chocolate cake for dessert. A lavish feast. Food was being released by the army and meat was coming from farms nearby, now that all beef wasn't confiscated. That is, it was available to those with money or articles to offer as payment.

Clarissa finished her wine and turned to her coffee, also filling Fitz's cup from a silver service, which had mysteriously reappeared since the end of the war.

"Sho' like old times." Clarissa's breathing was shallow, for her corset was tight and her stomach full. "Reckon it comin' back, Fitz? The balls an' the picnics an' the banquets like we used to have."

"Goin' to take time, Clarissa. Lots o' time, but no reason those kind o' days cain't come back. Mayhap not quite like befo', but good 'nuff."

"Benay, she used to give the most wonderful parties. All the beautiful dresses an' fine food an' drink. Lots o' men tryin' to get next to the single gals. Slaves to bring anythin' you wanted." She smiled reflectively. "You know, Fitz, I had to learn how to brush my hair. Nevah knowed how, 'cause a slave did it fo' me."

"Whut you goin' to do now you broke off with the Appersons?"

"Don' know, Fitz. I ain't good fo' much. Cain't sew or cook, cain't even read much, an' writin' comes mighty hard fo' me. On'y thin' I'm any good at is in baid."

"That sho' ain't no overstatement." He patted her hand. "One thing 'bout you, Clarissa, no matter you jumps into baid kinda often with a man, nevah seen you lookin' like a whore. You always looks like a lady, neat an' tidy. You want to come live at Wyndward when it ready? Won' be no goin' to baid. Not with me, but you kin stay theah the rest o' your life. Jes' makin' sho' the house looks nice. Gives you all the servants you need."

She leaned forward. "You means that? 'Course you do. Nevah say anythin' you don' mean. Fitz, I sho' be the happiest woman in the South . . . in the world."

"Good. I also don' think it kinda safe you stay heah, that sonabitch wantin' you fo' his servant. Best thing you kin do is come back with me. Got room 'nuff. On'y Mark is theah. You 'members he Jonathan's son by Belle Fisbee."

" 'Members. He kinda crazy I 'members rightly."

"Not any mo'. Goin' to be a fine man he gets a little mo' sense. You willin' to come back now . . . tomorrow?"

"You says so, I walks all the way," she said.

"We leaves on an afternoon train. Gets us in Lynchburg awful late, but got my hoss an' buggy theah fo' the ride back to Wyndward."

"But tonight. . . ?" she asked, and her eyes appealed to him.

"Feelin' rested," he said. "Reckon we spends the night in your baid."

"Even if it the last time," she said earnestly. "I'm mighty happy."

"Pack your things in the mawnin'. Got to leave you now. Need to see if I kin find someone to come to wuk fo' me. Comes up later."

"I sho'ly goin' be ready," she said. "Lookin' to it, Fitz. Reckon we ain't too old."

"You ain't, I 'members last time I was heah. Reckon I get kinda weak, you knows how to makes me strong. You been drinkin' kinda much. Think you need help?"

"Got two big feet, two nice laigs, an' one fat ass that'll balance me, Fitz. Don' worry none an' come soon's you kin."

She was only slightly unsteady. Fitz left the dining room after she had gone and headed for the bar. There he ordered a bourbon and water, sipped the drink, and looked about for any likely candidates to work at Wyndward.

He was about to strike up a conversation with a group of young men, fresh from the battlefield. At least, he thought, he might get some kind of an approximate time when they'd be glad to go to work.

A Yankee lieutenant and two corporals marched into the bar. Instantly, all the lively conversation ceased. The lieutenant stepped up to the bar.

"Be good enough to point out a man named Fitzjohn Turner."

The bartender was about to swear he never heard the name before, but Fitz moved up to the lieutenant. "I'm Fitzjohn Turner, suh."

"I have a complaint against you, Mister Turner. You'll have to come with me."

6

Marched between the two corporals and followed by a very reticent lieutenant, Fitz was brought to Richmond's main police station. There he discovered that Yankee law had taken complete control.

Fitz said, "Lieutenant, wish you'd tell me whut in hell I'm s'posed to have done."

"Mister Turner, I don't know. I was given orders to pick you up at the hotel. I went directly to the bar, and there you were. Major Brand will tell you what the charge is."

Fitz was ushered into a back room just off the cells, which seemed about half full. Major Brand was young, efficient, and not hostile.

"Sit down, Mister Turner. I have to ask you a few questions, and it is possible you may be placed under formal arrest and locked up. Do you know a man named Apperson?"

Fitz sat down with a wry laugh. "Knowed him fo' fifty yeahs. Been goin' to knock his block off mayhap fifty, sixty diff'rent times, an' someday I'm goin' to do it."

"He was, until recently, a Rebel colonel."

"Runnin' a warehouse," Fitz said. "Closest he evah got to a gun is shippin' 'em in an' out."

"Nevertheless, he is an important person. He has made a charge of battery against you. Claims you provoked him and struck him."

"Sho' hit him, Major. When I meets him again, I'll hit him again, fo' havin' me arrested."

"Then you admit you struck him. I must place you under arrest. We cannot permit any sort of violence to crop up. As I am part of the Army of Occupation, it is my duty to lock you up, sir. For trial in the morning."

"You do whut you got to do," Fitz said. "I gets fined fo' hittin' that skunk, it be wuth ev'ry dollah."

"Your full name is Fitzjohn Turner. Your address, please."

"Wyndward plantation, suh. Kin I make bail?"

"There are no provisions for that yet." Brand frowned. "You said Wyndward?"

"Thass whut I said. A few miles out o' Lynchburg."

"Excuse me a moment, Mister Turner."

"Won't run," Fitz assured him.

Brand was gone but a few moments. When he returned, there was a brigadier with him.

"General Foster, Mister Turner," the major said.

Fitz braced himself for trouble. If it was trouble inspired by Colonel Apperson, it was apt to be serious.

"I wish to make certain of your identity, Mister Turner. Your wife is dead, is she not?"

"Been daid a long, long time," Fitz said, more puzzled than ever.

"You have a son?"

"Is that what this is 'bout?" Fitz asked. "Yo' heah from him?"

"Hear from him?" The general seemed equally mystified.

"He was a cap'n last I know, mayhap a colonel 'fore the war over. Heered he was killed. . . ."

"I know nothing about that, Mister Turner. You have my sympathies. I wish to know what his name was."

76

"Jonathan. Whut in hell's this 'bout, Gen'ral? I comes heah under arrest 'cause I whomped a sonabitch needs whompin'."

"The accuser is in the anteroom, sir," the major said.

"Let him stay there, Major. Or throw him out. I don't care which. Mister Turner, you are free to go, and you have the apology of the United States Army, sir."

"I'm free? Thass all there is to it? Gen'ral, I don' understan'."

"You are free to go, sir."

"Well," Fitz was not inclined to push his luck, "I thanks you, suh."

"What about Colonel Apperson?" the major asked.

"If he gets uppity, throw him in jail for awhile," the general replied.

The office door opened suddenly, and a man, his face somewhat white, came in with a wireless message. The general read it, then jumped to his feet and emitted a loud curse. His face grew dark with a combination of rage and sorrow.

"President Lincoln was shot last night," he said. "He is dead. Damn the South! And all you Southerners!"

Fitz, seated close to the major's desk, leaned forward and let his head fall upon the edge of the desk. He sobbed.

They left him there. The police station was alive with excitement. There were shouts and curses. Fitz arose slowly, using his handkerchief to dry his tear-stained face.

The general returned alone. Fitz half braced himself for a fight.

"I beg your pardon, Mister Turner," he said. "I was under the belief that the President was assassinated by some Rebel. He was not. A half-crazed actor shot him."

"Makes no difference who killed him," Fitz said. "I followed his career for years with complete admiration. His like will not come again for many a century. And my sorrow is deep, for him and for the South. Who knows what will happen now?"

"Who knows." The general regarded him critically. "For a moment there you sounded like a Yankee."

"I'm half Yankee, sir. I was born in New England. My Southern speech is an accommodation to the deep South where I have lived for many years and to which I owe an obligation. I'm sorry I made a fuss."

"You're rather a remarkable man, Mr. Turner. I'm proud to have met you. If there is any way the army can serve you, you need only ask. Good-bye, sir. I must leave now. The situation here has changed tremendously."

"Thank you, General," Fitz said, who was still mystified, but too preoccupied over the death of Lincoln. Everything else seemed purely inconsequential.

Outside the office, he found Apperson seated on a chair against the wall. Fitz was in no mood to argue with him. He began passing by.

Apperson said, "They have to lock you up. You can't jes' walk out."

Fitz said, "Apperson, I ain't feelin' very pert right now, or I'd bust you one. I advise you, however, to let me alone."

"They let you go!" he shouted. "I was goin' to tell them 'bout the spy you harbored."

"You gettin' close to losin' your haid," Fitz warned.

"She's daid! They caught her, an' they hung her."

Fitz stopped in his tracks. He nodded slowly. "An' you knew this all the time. Yo' are a bastahd of the highest grade, suh. When I gets 'round to it, I'm goin' to kill you."

A soldier working at a desk, called out. "Stop this fighting. It's no time for an argument. Pay some respect to President Lincoln."

"He heah?" Apperson gaped at the idea.

"He was murdered," the soldier said.

"Now ain't that jes' too. . . ."

Fitz's fist almost shattered Apperson's jaw. The colonel fell back into the chair from which he'd half risen. Blood spurted from loosened teeth and a lacerated lip. He was only half-conscious as Fitz started to walk out.

Fitz paused and looked at the soldier behind the desk. "You wants to make somethin' o' this?"

"Me? Mister, I saw that man fall on his face. I think

he's drunk. I'll have him placed under arrest and locked up for his own safety."

"You's," Fitz said, "goin' be a gen'ral some day."

He walked out, shoulders drooping. Sally was dead, then. If only she'd left earlier. . . .He walked down the street in the direction of the hotel, rubbing his right hand, which was bleeding slightly from contact with Apperson's jaw.

Before he went upstairs, Fitz learned that the assassin had fired a fatal shot into the President's head and then leaped from the theater box from which the President and his party had been watching a play. It had already been made clear that this was not part of an assassination plot by some hotheads in the South.

When she heard the news, Clarissa was not even in the mood for bed. Fitz was somewhat surprised at her deep sorrow over Lincoln's death.

"A shameful thing," she said. "Nevah, in all these heah yeahs did I heah him called names. Mayhap he was, but I nevah heared it. Reckon this goin' to mean a heap o' trouble, Fitz?"

"A heap," he said. "Don' know a damn thing 'bout the Vice President. Don' even know whut his name is, or whut he fixin' to do to the South. Way I see it, this is the worst thing could o' happened. But have to wait an' see."

"An' hope," Clarissa said. "Fitz, I'm sorry 'bout Sally. But mayhap my stinker of a papa-in-law say this to make you feel bad. He a mighty good liar."

"No, not this time, Clarissa. She waited too long. The Reb forces had sealed off the border. I nevah did think she'd make it. Prob'ly the Confederate military knew 'bout her somehow, an' jes' spread a net she was bound to fall into."

"Ain't nuthin' in you life but grief, seems like, Fitz."

"Oh, no. You're wrong, Clarissa. Daid wrong. I had those yeahs with Benay. I had my papa an' learned from him. I had my son an' my daughter. I had gran'sons. I've had Wyndward too, an' all it still means to me. No, Clarissa, I been lucky. A little anyways. Goin' to baid now."

79

"Wants to sit up a little longer," Clarissa said. "Gots some thinkin' to do. We leave in the mawnin'?"

"Afternoon," he corrected her. "Good night."

Clarissa got into bed beside Fitz much later. He stirred and murmured something in his sleep. Clarissa drew an arm around his shoulders, pushed her face against his back, and wept. She wasn't even sure why, except that this had been a day for weeping.

In the morning Fitz went down to breakfast and had a tray sent up for Clarissa, who was hard at work packing her scant wardrobe and few possessions for shipment to Wyndward. Fitz found the dining room very somber. After breakfast, he went out to see if he could find someone to work for him. The city seemed hushed. There was little traffic, few pedestrians. Reinforcements seemed to have arrived, for there were more soldiers about than ever. They paid Fitz no attention.

He had hoped to find groups of young men gathered whom he might address, but there were no gatherings this morning. It was no use. He'd have to rely on whatever workers he could pick up in Lynchburg.

As he turned back to the hotel, a small, black figure emerged from a doorway. Fitz stopped and looked sternly at the boy.

"You followed me yesterday, didn' you?"

"Massa suh, I gets my ass kicked I don' follow you, massa suh."

"I know who made you do it. Did he pay you?"

"Says he pay me a dollah, suh. Didn' pay me nuthin', suh." The boy extended his hand and placed a silver dollar in Fitz's palm. "You gives me this, massa suh, but I got no right to keep it, suh."

"Your name . . . ?"

"Chickory, massa suh."

"Oh yes. You're 'bout thirteen, eh?"

"Yassuh, massa suh, I'se thirteen. I thinks."

"You're a pretty bright boy fo' thirteen. Kinda sly too. Bet you kin lie 'til you're blue."

"Sho' kin, massa suh. Lies like hell I does."

"You lyin' when you say you got no kin?"

"Massa suh, got no kin. Sweahs it."

"Whut're you goin' to do? Nowhar to go?"

"Nowhar, massa suh. I finds somethin', suh."

"Wouldn' s'prise me if you did. Now you take back this heah dollah. Knows a place you kin buy somethin' to eat?"

"Yassuh. Sho' am hungry."

"You was hungry last night. Why didn't you buy somethin' with this heah dollah, boy?"

"Ain' mine, massa suh. You gives it to me 'cause you sorry fo' me, but I sho' did you bad, suh. Cain't spend you money that way."

"All right. You spend the dollah fo' food an' be at the depot at half past twelve. Kin you tell time?"

"No suh, cain't tell nuthin', suh. Cain't read. Cain't write. Cain't do nuthin', but lie like hell, suh."

"You a little bit crazy in the haid, boy. Ask somebody to tell you the time, but be at the depot like I say."

"Whut you aimin' to do with me, suh?"

"I ought to kick your ass, but kind o' likes you. Takin' you home an' puttin' you to wuk. Don' want you walkin' 'bout gettin' yourse'f in trouble. You be theah."

The boy raced off. Fitz wondered if he'd ever see him again. He returned to the hotel, packed his own bag, and saw to it that Clarissa's possessions would be sent on. He also paid the bill. It was only eleven. There'd be no food on the train, so he escorted Clarissa into the dining room for dinner.

"You gets anybody to wuk fo' yo'?" Clarissa asked.

"Ain' nobody out theah. Reckon they skeered the Yankee soldiers be mad 'cause Lincoln dead. Got somethin' on my mind. Want to know whut you thinks o' it."

"Tell me, Fitz," she encouraged him.

"Last night 'fore that gen'ral let me go, he made mighty sho' who I am, an' then he tell me I'm free. Nevah even asks whut I done. Jes' lets me go—like he got orders to do that. Seems like he told to let me go. Now who'd do a thing like that, an' why?"

"Thass easy," Clarissa said serenely. "I kin tell you."

"I'm sho' listenin'," he said.

"Cain't be but one person. Your daughter Melanie."

Fitz made a whooshing sound of surprise. "Nevah gives Melanie a thought."

"She the wife o' a mighty important man in Washington. Reckon he tell the army you ain' to be bothered. Real nice o' her. Thought she hated your guts."

'So did I. I'm pleased, Clarissa. I've wanted her affections back so much. She a pretty woman, like her mama. Loves her an' feels bad she hates me. Now mayhap she don', this war over an' all. Sho' goin' to Washington soon's I kin to thank her. Mayhap even bring her home fo' a visit. That's somethin' I sho' wanted fo' yeahs. Finish your coffee. Ain' got too much time fo' the train pulls out."

And wonder of wonders, Fitz even found a carriage for hire, something quite rare in Richmond during the war years. Clarissa sat up very straight, opened her parasol, and nodded her head with its big hat, to attract attention. Fitz couldn't blame her. He knew it had been a long time since she'd ridden in a carriage.

On the depot platform, the boy waited for them. He ran up to Fitz and wrapped his thin arms around his leg as if he was afraid Fitz would change his mind.

"Whut in hell this boy doin'?" Clarissa asked.

"Nuthin'," Fitz decided not to tell her the circumstances under which he'd met the boy. "Got nowhar to go, no kin. Too puny to get wuk, so I take him back. Mayhap we kin make him useful."

"Don' look like much." Clarissa studied the boy. "Skinniest runt I seen in a long time."

"You eats like I told you?" Fitz asked.

The boy dug into the pocket of his ragged pants and handed Fitz some coins. "Eats all I kin, massa suh, an' I gets back this heah money. Reckon it belongs to you, suh."

"He givin' back the change?" Clarissa asked. "Reckon you bettah take him on, Fitz. Be mighty nice to have somebody honest 'round the place."

"You keeps the change," Fitz told the boy. "You gets on the train. The last car. It full, you stands. You heah?"

"Yassuh, massa suh, I stands."

"I pays your fare so don' let anybody kick you off the train."

"Tells 'em you my massa, suh."

"I ain' your massa. Ain't no mo' massas. Now git."

The boy scrambled aboard the train. Fitz and Clarissa took their seats. They were mostly silent during the ride. Clarissa slept with her head on his shoulder part of the time.

"You sho' you got room fo' me in that Fisbee place whar yo' livin' now?" she finally asked.

"Got plenty. They's on'y Mark an' Elegant an', . . . ," he laughed softly. "There's Calla an' Domingo."

"Wenches?"

"Sho' 'nuff. One's mine, the other sleeps with Mark."

"You kick the ass o' yours. I sleep with you."

"How it goin' to be, reckon. Calla kind o' lookin' fo' one o' her color. Got some new boys in the slave quarters. Mayhap she find one, but Mark sho' ain't lettin' Domingo go. Mark's kind o' randy."

"Well now," Clarissa said enthusiastically, "if you cain't take care o' me. . . ."

"You stays outen his baid, heah me? Got 'nuff trouble with him. He thinkin' I'm gettin' too old to takin' care o' any woman."

"Yo' kin use me fo' a reference if you likes," Clarissa said good-naturedly. "Fitz, we talkin' like this sho' gettin' to be like old times. Ain't laughed so much since the goddamn war stahts."

"Time we began laughin' again," Fitz agreed. "Time to begin fo'gettin' the last four or five yeahs best we kin."

Upon reaching Lynchburg, Fitz and Clarissa looked about for Chickory. Finally Fitz boarded the last car to find the boy curled up under the last seat, sound asleep. Fitz dragged him out and set him on his feet while he blinked and rubbed his eyes.

"We's heah," Fitz said. "You sleepin' like you daid."

"Yessuh, massa suh, I'se pow'ful tired I is."

"All right. You kin sleep on the way back to the farm. Now get off this train."

Fitz led the boy and Clarissa to the livery where he

awakened the owner and set Chickory to harnessing the horse. The boy did a credible job of it, showing he'd been trained in handling horses at least. He then lit the lantern, suspended it under the buggy, curled up in the small space behind the seat, and promptly fell asleep.

"Reckon he been runnin' fo' days an' don' even know whar he goin'," Fitz observed. "Happenin' to lots like him. Wonders whut these slaves goin' to do. Ain't even 'nuff wuk fo' the soldiers."

"Way I sees it, Fitz, the slaves goin' right back to whut they used to be. 'Cept they kin leave if they likes, an' they gets paid somethin'. Won' be much. But they get no mo' clothes, no food they cain't pay fo', an' they get to pay fo' a place to live 'sides all that. Some goin' to think they bettah off befo' the war."

"Wonder how they goin' to be treated. Lots o' folks don't think they's mo' than an animal whut kin talk. Thass whut they used to say. Won't even call in a regular docter they sick, but sends fo' a vet, like they was animals. I nevah did that. Reckon my papa wasn't above it."

Clarissa snuggled closer to him, held his arm tightly. "Whut we gots to do is stop thinkin' an' we starts livin'. Back at Wyndward . . . o' at least near it. Nevah thinks I get back heah long as I lives. Mighty beholden to you, Fitz. Reckon me an' that boy sleepin' in back ain't much diff'rent. We gots no place to lay our haids."

" 'Til now," Fitz said. "Glad to have you, Clarissa. Goin' to see you get your own suite o' rooms when Wyndward built. Like you say, time to start livin' again."

The buggy rolled on through the night, the lantern beneath the vehicle bobbing along like a giant yellow firefly's light. Fitz was droopy-eyed himself by the time they reached the old Fisbee place.

There were lights in the windows, though it was almost midnight. Fitz worried that there had been trouble, but when Mark emerged, followed by Elegant, Domingo, and Calla, he knew they'd simply expected him and had waited up.

Fitz helped Clarissa down, and Mark, holding a lantern, raised it higher to illuminate her face.

"You brings one back fo' me too?" he asked Fitz.

Clarissa's face grew grim and angry. "Now you listen to me, you no-good bastahd. Knowed you mama an' her mama an' papa an' all the no-good aunts an' uncles hangin' 'round this heah house befo' you born. You mama nothin' but a whore. Her papa, he bad as she was. You comes of a rotten fam'ly, an' on'y good thing in you is Turner blood. Seems like it kind o' thin in you goddamn body."

Mark backed off hastily. "Ma'am, I begs you pardon. I'm sorry. Powerful sorry, ma'am."

"You lucky you ain't got a busted jaw," Fitz said. "This heah is Clarissa. She was Benay's cousin. Knowed her all my life. You treats her like a lady, heah? That goes fo' you too, Elegant."

"Ah ain't said nuthin'," Elegant exclaimed indignantly.

"Nothin' you know 'bout Clarissa goin' to be mentioned. Whut happen long ago is over. Clarissa stayin' heah 'til Wyndward is built, an' then she stays theah an' takes charge o' the house. She lives with us long as she wants, an' hopes it fo' the rest o' my life."

Mark saw Chickory emerge from the back of the buggy into the gloom. "Who in hell is this?" he asked. "Look like he been drowned an' comes back to life."

The boy moved closer uneasily, frightened and ready to run. Fitz could guess how badly he'd been treated through most of the war years.

"This heah is Chickory," he said. "He thirteen, but no kin an' no place to go. He goin' to make hisse'f useful. Elegant, he's in your charge. If you wallops him, do it gentle, 'cause he skinny 'nuff to blow away."

"Fattens him, an' then we sees whut's whut," Elegant said. "Come 'long, boy. You name sounds like somethin' you puts in coffee. When there is any coffee," she added with a sigh.

"Likes coffee, I does," the boy said.

"An' anythin' else you kin lay your hands on. Take my hand. Shows you the kitchen. You kin sleep back o' the stove."

Fitz, Mark, and Clarissa made their way into the house. They sat down in the parlor. Calla and Domingo had very quietly slipped away into the night.

Mark arose. "You got a letter from Melanie, Gran'pa. I'll fetch it."

He came back with a rather thick envelope. Fitz opened it eagerly. The letter he'd written to her fell out, still sealed. There was a torn bit of paper pinned to it. He read the message aloud.

I did not open your letter. I wish never to see you or hear of you again as long as I live. My husband was killed in that awful war you and yours began. I sent word that Wyndward should be burned to the ground, and I pray that it was. Do not waste your time writing me again, for I shall not read your letters. I have but one message to give you. The two ex-slaves you placed in my hands to be educated have turned into very bright young men. They will be going into the South to do what they can for the slaves. Perhaps they will seek you out. I did not tell them to.

Melanie

Clarissa said, "Fitz, I'm sorry."

"What kind o' woman kin she be?" Mark asked. "Writin' that to her papa."

"Knows whut I think?" Fitz said thoughtfully. "I think she ain't the one who got word to the Yankee gen'ral that I was to go free. Reckon it jes' a coincidence brought on by the death o' Lincoln an' lots o' other things I don't know 'bout."

"Whut you goin' to do 'bout Melanie?" Mark asked.

"Ain't goin' to do anythin'. You knows whut she said. Don't want anythin' to do with me. Kin see why she so full o' hate. She had a fine husband with a mighty big future, an' now she got nothin'. Reckon there's money 'nuff fo' her husband was the kind o' man makes sho' o' that. Aim to let her alone. Cain't fo'get her, but do whut she say."

He tore up the letter he'd written to her. His request was not important anymore. Sally was dead. Melanie would have refused to attempt to find her anyway. Fitz thought it probably best this way. He would concentrate on Wyndward and push everything else far back in his mind. Even though he knew full well how impossible that would be.

7

Fitz, Mark, Hong Kong, and several blacks taken from the tobacco fields worked on the first stages of the restoration of the mansion. They dug out the debris in the cellar. They cleaned the chimneys, which were intact and certainly could be used in the rebuilding. The immediate area was cleared of brush and tall grass, which had grown all around.

Then they were forced to stop. None of them was sufficiently skilled to do the masonry work required for the foundation. It was exasperating because there was gold to pay for workmen, but none came. A week after they'd about given up and Fitz was going to go into the cities in an attempt to recruit help once again, a lanky rider appeared.

"Heahs you needs a mason," he said, before he even dismounted.

"You might say that," Fitz observed dryly.

"Got mustered out last week. Got me a wife an' three kids. I don't get wuk, all o' us goin' to starve. Been 'nuff o' that already. You put me to wuk I sho' 'preciates it, suh. My name's Paul Stewart."

"Kin you begin now? Pays a full day. Want this to get started."

The man dismounted, reached for the sack of tools tied to the saddle, and walked toward the now-cleared basement. Mark, at work scrubbing debris from one of the chimneys, emerged to greet the newcomer.

"Name o' Paul Stewart," Fitz said. "Wants to help with the foundation."

The supply of new bricks, mortar, and mixing tools was already at hand, along with covered stacks of lumber, purchased and delivered days ago.

Within half an hour, the mason was at work. Mark worked alongside the man, carrying brick and stones, helping with the mixing. Though they worked only five hours, it was a start and, to Fitz, a most satisfying day. He paid the man in gold.

"I thanks you, suh," Stewart said gratefully. "Means I kin stop on the way home an' buy some corn meal an' flour an' a bit o' bacon, if I kin find any."

"Chickory," Fitz shouted, and the boy came running. "You run all the way back to the Fisbee place an' tell Elegant to get a ham an' side ribs ready fo' Mistah Stewart. He rides by in a little while. Put in a sack o' vegetables too. Now you runs."

Chickory was off. Fitz had already realized what an asset the boy was. He was quick, intelligent, and striving hard to please. Even Elegant admitted he was tireless.

When Stewart returned the following day, there were two men with him. One was a carpenter, and now the work really began. Still, there was a vital need for more, but no one came.

"Mistah Stewart," Fitz said, "you brings two men but no mo'. We need ten mo'. Ain't nobody doin' anythin' but slothin'. Knows there's not much wuk in the cities yet an' some must be mighty hard up."

"I tries, suh," Stewart said. "Hates to tell you this, but reckon I has to. There's word goin' 'round that you mo' Yankee than Rebel. That you pays in gold you

89

buried while the war on. They says you was tried fo' treason when the war broke out. Boys who fought the Yankees ain't in no mood to go wuk fo' one."

"Why did you an' the other two come then?"

" 'Cause we got mo' sense. You were found innocent o' treason an' even complimented fo' what you did fo' the Cause. Don' know whar you got this heah gold, but that ain't none o' our business. We needs wuk an' we eatin' now. Goin' to miss this wuk when it ends."

"By that time," Fitz said, "things will have improved. Believe me, there's more wuk fo' masons an' carpenters than they can handle. Want a favor o' you."

"Sho' willin' to help if I kin."

"Goin' to Lynchburg. Yo' an' the others quit early. I'll pay you fo' a full day. You know whar Gillian's saloon is. Go theah an' treats to free drinks sayin' you mighty glad to be wukkin'. I comes in an' mayhap some o' the boys heahs whut you sayin' an' I kin hire mo'."

"Be mighty glad to 'blige, Mistah Turner, suh. Means we kin keep wukkin' heah. We don' gets no mo' help, won't be nuthin' fo' us to do."

"Good. You kin leave now you likes." He produced gold pieces from his pocket and counted out several into Stewart's hand. "Pay the other boys their share. See you in the saloon."

An hour after the men departed, Fitz and Mark rode to Lynchburg with Chickory, who was to take care of the carriage while Fitz and Mark went about their business.

They entered the saloon late in the afternoon. Stewart and his two companions were at the bar with a large group of men gathered about gawking at the gold pieces being rolled across the bar in payment for drinks.

Stewart saw Fitz and Mark and with a whoop of joy greeted them and led them to the group. "This heah Mistah Turner an' his gran'son Mark. Been tellin' you 'bout them. They sho' a pleasure to wuk fo'."

"You pays ev'rybody in gold?" one man asked.

"Want carpenters, plasterers, laborers, an' a good plumber. Pays a five-dollah gold piece fo' each day's wuk. You want, you kin live in the overseers' cottages or in the old slave quarters, which are cabins with wood floors an' stoves fo' cookin'. No charge fo' that. They's wuk fo' mayhap fo', five months. On'y wants men who willin' to give me a good day's wuk fo' my money."

In an hour six men of varied skills had been recruited. It had required a good deal of drinking and toasting though, and by the time they were ready to go back, both Fitz and Mark were in a gay mood.

"Sho' gets mo' than 'spected," Fitz said. "Seem like they're good men too."

"We kin get whut we needs, nails, hardware, an' all, we kin have Wyndward all done by winter, Gran'pa."

"Reckon we kin. Goin' to give a big ball when we get it finished. Don' know how many will come, but it's one way o' findin' out jes' where we stand. Apperson an' Bibb doin' all they kin to make us look bad."

"They passin' 'round word you're mo' Yankee?"

"Ain't nobody else do a thing like that. They keep it up, an' I sho' goin' to have a nice talk with both o' them."

"Wants to be theah, Gran'pa."

"Why? You think I can't take care o' myse'f?"

"Showed me you could, but cain't tell they got somebody to back 'em up. I might come in handy."

"Then you sho' has my permission to come along. Gettin' to sort o' like you, son. Reckon you got 'nuff Turner blood in you to offset the blood of the Fisbee fam'ly. Now theah was a whole fam'ly o' dumb sonabitches I evah see."

"Yo' talkin' 'bout my mama's fam'ly," Mark warned in a serious voice.

"Sho' am, an' ain't takin' back one word o' whut I said. They pure trash."

"Nevah knowed 'em 'cept fo' my mama, an' ain't faultin' her any. She sho' made lots o' money runnin' that whorehouse. Kinda proud o' her I am. Reckon she not as dumb as the rest o' them. . . . Who that with Chickory?"

They slowed down their approach to the carriage at the curb. Chickory was waiting for them with a very large, very black man at his side.

"Massa suh, wants you to let this heah nigger talk to you?"

91

Fitz surveyed the man. He was neatly though poorly dressed, but there was intelligence in his face and not a trace of servility about him.

"Talk to us 'bout whut?"

The Negro spoke in a quiet voice. "Been doin' wuk in the saloon whar you drinks an' talks 'bout hirin' men to wuk. Heahs you say you needs a man to do plumbin'. Fo' an' durin' the wah, suh, wuks fo' Mistah Morgan, suh. Fo' the wah he run a greenhouse whar he grow flowers. They needs waterin', an' I puts in pipe fo' him. Learns all there is to know 'bout plumbin', suh. Wuks in Mistah Morgan's house takin' keer o' that kin' o' wuk."

"Whut's your name?" Fitz asked.

"Toby, suh."

"Toby whut?" Fitz asked. "You ain't a slave no mo'. You got to have a full name."

"Toby Morgan, suh."

"Take your massa's name?"

"Yassuh. Ain't got no otheh, suh."

"Got a fam'ly?"

"Sho' have. Wife an' son."

"You kin send word to 'em quick? I want you to come with us now, an' tomorrow you kin drive the carriage back fo' your fam'ly after wuk. Got a nice cabin fo' all o' you, an' charges nothin' you a good plumber an' you don't sloth."

"You kin give me five minutes, suh."

"Give you half a hour. Chickory, you stay heah with the carriage."

"Yassuh, I stays."

Fitz turned to Mark. "We close by the old slave market. You evah sees it when you a boy?"

"No, suh. Mama took me to N'Orleans, Gran'pa."

"Wants you to see this. Kinda dark, but they's 'nuff light fo' whut I wants to show you. Come 'long. Ain't mo' than two blocks from heah."

They walked rapidly along the street. Most of the effects of the alcohol they'd imbibed had worn off. Fitz turned into a spacious, cleared area predominated by the large cement block set in the center of the yard.

"They put up slaves theah to be bid on. Men, wenches, an' children. Man who buys a buck, don' wants his woman an' their baby, busts up the fam'ly. Mayhap even the woman an' the baby got busted up. Good-lookin' wenches got felt all over by bastahds in the heat an' wantin' to finger 'em. Nevah got 'nuff money to buy, but ain't no way stoppin' 'em from that. Bucks got to shuck down 'til they naked, so women with they husbands kin see if they hung good. Nevah could stomach that, even though my papa saw nothin' wrong with it. You thinks it was right?"

"Had to have slaves, suh, to do the wuk."

"No slaves now an' won't be agin. They goin' to wuk anyways. Got to or they starves to death. An' if they don't, then we do the wuk. We white folks, 'cause the wuk got to be done."

They stared at the slave block silently, both thinking of Wyndward, then returned to the carriage to find Chickory and the new black waiting. On the way back, Fitz learned that Toby's master had been killed in the war, and his widow had turned Toby loose. He'd managed to get through the war and even raise a family, but it had been difficult. Fitz quickly ascertained that Toby was no ordinary ex-slave. He was ambitious and, no doubt, skilled. Fitz felt lucky to have him. Toby had brought along his meager supply of tools and was prepared to begin work in the morning.

Fitz went to bed as soon as they returned. He was too tired to sit up with Clarissa and far too exhausted to bring Calla to his bed.

In the morning, while Elegant served breakfast, he received the first portent of things to come. Hong Kong brought the news as Mark joined Fitz at the table.

"Toby, the man you hire last night, suh, he up early an' ready to begin long 'fore the others comes. But when they gets heah, they sits down an' sloths."

"The white men? Whut in hell's the matter with 'em?"

"Declares, suh, they ain't goin' to wuk 'longside no nigger."

93

Fitz sat back. "I be damned!"

"Gran'pa," Mark said in a voice tinged with worry, "we sho' cain't 'ford to let 'em go."

"No, I kin see that. Hong Kong, you pull Toby off the job, an' you bring him heah. Tell the white men to get to wuk. They don' have to wuk with a nigger, they don' want to. I thinks they kind o' crazy, but don' tell 'em that."

Toby, heartsick and worried, came in after half running from the mansion to the Fisbee place.

"Sit down," Fitz said. "You wants a cup o' coffee?"

"No, suh," Toby said. There was belligerence in his voice.

"You don' have to get yourse'f on no high hoss, Toby."

"Eats with Hong Kong an' Seawitch, suh. They feed me good."

"I'm glad to heah that. Now you know your wukkin' heah ain't goin' to be easy."

"Goes back to Lynchburg, suh."

"You do that, Toby, an' you brings your fam'ly back today. Brings all your things yo' kin get into the carriage." Fitz raised his voice to a shout. "Calcutta Two, get in heah quick."

The ex-slave took a full five minutes to get there, which pleased Fitz.

"Calcutta Two, you the slowest man in this heah world. Get your ass kicked good, you sloths like that. Now you go down to the stable an' hitch up the carriage. You drives it heah an' turn it over to Mistah Toby Morgan."

"Whut Toby Mo'gan?" Calcutta looked around the room.

"This Mistah Toby Morgan," Fitz pointed at Toby. "He goin' to Lynchburg to fetch his fam'ly. Toby, you needs any help with your things?"

"Kin handle 'em, suh. But whut you gettin' me to bring my fam'ly heah fo' when I ain't 'lowed to wuk?"

"You goes to wuk soon's these heah high an' mighty boys quits. You wuks when they don', so they cain't say they gots to wuk with a nigger. Even if you got to wuk by lantern light. You willin' to do that, Toby?"

A broad smile crossed Toby's face. "Sho' am, suh. Yassuh, sho' am."

"Good. An' when this heah mansion all built, you stay on. Goin' to need a man got the kind o' skills you say you got. Means you live heah long as you likes; an' pays you whut a skilled man is worth."

" 'Bliged, suh. Mighty 'bliged. Wuks hahd, suh."

"You damn well better," Fitz said lightly. "Don't know whut in hell the boys wukkin' now think when they sees the plumbin' wuk done, but don' give a damn."

Later Fitz rode down to the site of the mansion. Mark had preceded him and emerged from the hammering and the activity to join him for a few minutes.

"They says they cain't wuk 'longside an ex-slave," he reported, " 'cause makes 'em feel they now slaves. Cain't figger that kind o' damn fool talk, but thass whut they say. Tell 'em we cain't get a plumber to come an' wuk, an' if the plumbin' ain't gettin' done, ain't no wuk fo' 'em by the end of this heah week. They talks 'bout it, but still say they won't wuk with no nigger. They agree if he wuks when they ain't heah, they sho' got no objection to that."

"Goin' to wuk out then. Worried 'bout that."

"Cain't use none o' the help we got wukkin' in the fields."

"Know that. Anyways, they gots all they kin do 'thout comin' heah to help. You stays heah an' see things get done. I'm ridin' into the fields an' see how the 'bacco crop comin'."

Hong Kong met Fitz at the edge of the fields. They rode together along the rows of tobacco plants. Fitz dismounted to examine the sprouts.

"Stalks gettin' fat," he said, "an' leaves sproutin'. Mighty good weather. Gots to start weedin' now, an' next got to begin toppin'. We needs mo' help, Hong Kong. You 'members we had a thousand slaves wukkin' heah. Wukkin' mo' hours than the men we gots now."

"Knows that, suh. Got on'y half o' the acres planted

this yeah. But got corn comin' good an' truck growin' mighty fast. Got a good crop o' sweet-scented 'bacco down near the woods, all the rest in oronoco. Best oronoco in this heah state, suh."

"It's like beginnin' all over again," Fitz said. "Kin make you think it ain't worthwhile sometimes, but got to grow food an' got to grow 'bacco so we does whut we kin. Goin' to try an' find mo' men to wuk the fields. Whut land ain't plowed this yeah, stays fallow. Don' hurt the ground to be idle. Mayhap we get mo' help next yeah, then we does mo'. Sho' ain't like it used to be."

"Sho' ain't," Hong Kong said. "Boys we gots wukkin' now doin' mighty good, suh. Cain't use a whup no mo', but kind o' whuppin' 'em 'nother way. Tells 'em they sloths, they gets fired, an' no mo' money. An' they got to leave the plantation. That sho' perks 'em up some."

"You're doin' fine," Fitz said. "It'll take time, but we goin' to be back near whut we were."

"You send Toby back to Lynchburg, suh?"

"He comin' back with his fam'ly today, an' he wukkin' at night. Sho' won't get as much done, but even if I could hire a good white man to do the plumbin', wouldn' do it now. Toby stays no matter whut."

"Sho' bad times, suh."

"Bad as the war, an' goin' to get worst."

"Heahs no niggers kin ride the train lessen they be extra seats, an' then they gots to ride in one car an' cain't complain 'bout it 'thout bein' put off. That bein' whut they calls free?"

"Goin' to take time. Mo' time me an' you got, Hong Kong. Goin' to be trouble."

"Reckon. Suh, gots to tell you that old Mitch died las' night."

"Sorry to heah that. He was a good man. Lived heah all his life, or most of it. My papa brought him heah on his ship when I was a small boy."

"He near ninety, mayhap mo'. Whut we goin' to do 'bout buryin' him, suh? Used to be we buries him, an' on Sunday we had a dance in honor o' his death."

"They won't be any mo' o' that. You buries him in the old slave cemetery, but we has a dance fo' him, we goin' to get in trouble. Got to wait an' see how things go. Reckon you sho' payin' fo' bein' free, but ain't no other way. Reckon I'm payin' too, this heah plantation goin' to bring in not even half o' whut it used to."

"How many field hands kin you use, suh?"

" 'Bout three hundred. Pay 'em good. On'y way you kin get good wuk. Mayhap next yeah we hires 'nother hundred."

"Does whut I kin to find mo', suh. Sho' glad the big house risin' up again. Misses it."

"Think how I miss it," Fitz said. "We'll try to make ev'rythin' as much like befo' as we kin. See yo' later, Hong Kong, an' says hello to Seawitch."

"Thanks you, suh." Hong Kong mounted and began riding along the rows of tobacco plants. Fitz led his horse down to the fence-enclosed family graveyard. There he reported briefly, addressing no one in particular.

"Times gettin' real bad. But war over at last an' that sho' is good. The big house risin' again an' goin' to be jes' like befo', 'cept you ain't goin' to be theah, so won't be the same. Feelin' kind o' low today, so won't say no mo'."

He rode back to the site of the mansion, watched the men working happily and doing a good job. Mark, stripped to the waist, was working as hard as any of them.

Fitz rode back to the Fisbee place. He greeted Calla with a friendly slap on the buttocks, bringing a squeal of delight from her. He found Clarissa in the parlor, reading an old Richmond newspaper. She flung it aside in anger.

"Northern money comin' in now, an' prices goin' crazy. A loaf o' bread is up to eleven cents. Ev'rythin' else jes' the same. Goin' up all the time. Whut's goin' to happen, Fitz?"

"We don' get back to wuk, North comin' down heah an' earnin' the money we ain't even tryin' to wuk fo'. Know the war ain't been over long 'nuff fo' even all the soldiers to be sent home. Folks goin' back to wuk fo' sho', but they losin' too much time."

At supper Mark reported that as soon as the carpenters and masons left, Toby had moved in with his pipes and tools and gone straight to work.

"We sho' lucky we got him, Gran'pa. Watches him fo' a little while, an' he knows whut he's doin'."

"Good. Been down to the fields an' things comin' 'long theah too. Won't be long 'fore we shippin' 'bacco agin."

"An' livin' in the big house," Mark added. "Nevah lived theah myse'f, an' cain't wait to move in."

Presently, Fitz yawned. Clarissa had already fallen asleep in her parlor chair. Fitz found Calla waiting in his room.

"Ain't goin' to pester you tonight," he said. "You finds yourse'f 'nother baid."

"Kin me an' Domingo go down to visit with Seawitch, suh?"

"Kin fo' all I cares."

"Thanks you, suh."

Calla closed the bedroom door softly. Fitz was in bed ten minutes later. Someone shook him by the shoulder. He had no idea what time it was, but he sat up, instantly awake. Elegant had entered with a lamp turned low. She turned up the wick.

"Whut in hell . . . ?" Fitz began angrily. Then he saw tears staining Elegant's fat face. "Whut's the matter, Elegant?"

"Calla daid, suh. Domingo downstairs, suh. She hurtin' awful bad."

"Calla daid! Hand me my pants. Some bastahd kills her, or she has an accident?"

"Some bastahd, suh . . . Domingo kin tell you whut happen."

"Wake up Mark. I'll go down an' see Domingo."

Fitz put on his shoes, didn't take time to don a shirt. He hurried down to the kitchen where Domingo was seated in a chair, bent over as if she was ill. Fitz gently raised her head and cursed savagely. Both her eyes were swollen, there was dried blood around her mouth, and dark marks around her throat indicated she had almost been strangled to death.

Fitz heard someone behind him and turned to see Chickory with a worried expression on his face.

"Go gets the bottle o' whiskey in the dinin' room," Fitz said. "An' brings a glass. Hop!"

Fitz poured whiskey into the glass, held Domingo's head steady, and made her drink. The whiskey revived her somewhat, but did little to relieve the terror that still shone in her eyes.

"Whut happened?" he asked. "You tells me, Domingo."

"Calla get raped." Domingo's voice was hoarse from the beating she'd undergone. "Tries to stop it, an' I get knocked out, suh. Jes' knocks poor Calla down an' rips her clothes off an' rapes her."

"Who?" Fitz asked. "You sees the man. You knows him? He a nigger, o' a white man?"

"Me an' Calla, we wuks fo' Mistah Bibb. Tell you that, suh."

"If this was Bibb. . . ."

"No, suh, was a man wuks fo' Bibb, name o' Perth. Tries to rape us when we wuks theah."

"Calla daid?"

"Thinks so, suh. Thinks he cuts her throat."

Mark was beside Fitz now.

"Whar this happen?" Fitz asked.

"Comin' back from Seawitch, suh."

Mark said, "I'll ride down, Gran'pa. Get out the guns. Chickory, you come to the stable with me, an' you saddle Mistah Fitz's hoss an' brings it in front o' the house. Be right back, Gran'pa."

Fitz helped Elegant clean the blood from Domingo's face and then ordered her put in his bed until she recovered. Fitz half carried the girl up the stairs, and while Elegant got her to bed, he finished dressing. He paused beside the bed.

"You sho' it was Perth?"

"Knows him, suh. I clawed him so he got mo' blood on him than I got. Clawed him good, suh, over his face."

"Good. I wish you'd killed him, but since you didn', I'll take care o' that chore. Stay with her, Elegant, 'case she mo' hurt than we thinks. I'll wake Clarissa now."

Fitz entered Clarissa's bedroom and shook her awake. She'd slept soundly through all the excitement. He told her what had happened.

"Goin' after the sonabitch who done this. Don' knows mayhap he come heah lookin' fo' Domingo 'cause she know him. Leavin' a gun fo' you downstairs. He comes, shoot him!"

"An' don' you think I won't," she said angrily. "Poor Calla! She nevah hurt nobody."

Fitz grunted something, picked up a coat on his way downstairs. He waited a few moments until Chickory arrived, riding the horse. Fitz mounted, held his rifle across his lap. He rode slowly toward the Bibb farm, taking his time so Mark could join him. Mark came up, with a terse report.

"Calla daid, Gran'pa. Been raped an' her throat cut. I ask the pleasure o' killin' the man who done that."

"Wuks fo' Bibb. Cain't sweah to it, but wouldn' be s'prised Bibb sent him. Now, when we gets near the Bibb house, you puts your hoss in the brush an' moves up slow on foot. That sonabitch in Bibb's house, I smokes him out, he fixin' to run. You take him, son. There's trouble later, we face up to it."

"Sweahs he won't get by me, he runs. You needs help, get off a shot."

Fitz nodded, spurred his horse lightly, and rode straight up to the farmhouse, which was in total darkness. Fitz had been there before. Once he was brutally slugged here with a rifle butt when he had tried to keep Bibb from hanging a man caught traveling the Underground Railroad.

Fitz dismounted, walked up to the door, and banged on it with his rifle butt until the door opened and a seemingly sleepy Bibb demanded to know what was going on.

"Inside," Fitz said tersely. "Get back in theah!"

Bibb retreated with the barrel of Fitz's rifle painfully

buried against his stomach. At Fitz's command he lit a lamp. Fitz wasted no time.

"You got a man named Perth heah?"

"Ain't seen Perth in a week o' mo'. Whut the hell you gettin' a man outen his baid this time o' night fo'?"

"You sleeps with your clothes on?"

"Kin' o' tired," Bibb explained weakly. "Jes' fell into baid."

Fitz left the room, walked down a short hall, and into Bibb's bedroom. He passed his hands under the rumpled bedsheets, found them cold. He returned to the parlor in time to see Bibb removing a pistol from a cabinet drawer. Fitz struck him on the back of the head with his rifle barrel and sent him reeling. Bibb fell onto a small sofa where he touched the back of his head tenderly and glared at Fitz.

"You a goddamn liar," Fitz said. "You ain't been in baid. You knows whut happened. Perth would o' come to you right off he gets through rapin' an' killin' my wench."

"You crazy, Fitz. I ain't seen Perth. . . ."

"Then you an' me waits 'til he comes, but if you lyin', I kills you right heah."

"Tells you, nobody heah. Jes' me. My wife left me. Runs out."

"Don' know how she stood the likes o' you long as she did. Asks you again, whar is Perth?"

"Tell you. Ain't seen him."

Fitz said, "Goin' to search the house. He heah, he dies an' so do you."

"He ain't heah," Bibb reiterated.

Fitz went down the hallway again, opening all four doors. There was an indentation in the covers of one bed, as if someone had occupied it. Fitz walked into the bathroom. From the light of the lamp he had taken with him, he saw the towels on the floor. Two of them were stained with fresh blood. He picked them up and returned to the parlor.

"Seems to me like somebody wiped blood off his face, Bibb. Now don' tell me you cut yourse'f shavin'. Whar this heah blood comes from?"

"Don' know. Got folks wukkin' fo' me, an' they comes in to use the bathroom. Mayhap one o' them cuts hisse'f."

"In the middle o' the night? This heah blood ain't turned dark yet. Perth comes heah. Knows it. Runs while you keep me busy."

Bibb's eyes grew cold and baleful. "Cain't prove nothin', Fitz, but next time it goin' be you an' not your damn wench."

Fitz smashed the rifle butt against Bibb's face. Blood spurted, and Bibb howled in pain. Fitz raised the rifle butt again, and Bibb went down to stay.

Fitz used his foot to turn him over. "Sort o' pays you back fo' the time you did this to me. Ought to finish you off now, but goin' to save that pleasure fo' later."

Fitz walked out. He mounted and rode slowly away. Half a mile from Bibb's place a low whistle brought him to a stop. Mark walked slowly out of the brush, leading his horse. There was a body lying across the saddle.

"Po' sonabitch comes runnin' straight toward me. Got a pistol an' starts raisin' it 'fore I shot him. Reckon this heah Perth?"

Fitz grasped the dead man by the hair and twisted his head around. "Light a match," he told Mark. In the light of the tiny flame they saw Perth's face, deeply gouged in a dozen places by sharp fingernails.

"Sho' is Perth," Fitz said. "Domingo did all that scratchin'."

"River's no mo'n a mile," Mark said. "Runnin' kinda strong these days. Mayhap we jes' dumps him in, an' he nevah found."

"Reckon thass whut we does. Cain't have a daid bastahd hangin' 'round Wyndward now, kin we?"

They found the river running strong, as Mark had said. They tossed the body as far into the stream as they could and saw it begin bobbing wildly as the current took possession of it.

Then they rode back to the Fisbee place, almost in silence. Mark's exhaustion from the previous day's work and being rousted out of bed, made him drowsy as he clung to the saddle. Fitz was too angry to be sleepy.

Nearing the Fisbee place, Fitz nudged Mark awake. "Busted Bibb like he busted me yeahs ago. He wakes up, he ain't goin' to know we finds Perth o' not. You an' me, we nevah did see him. Ain't that right?"

"Saw nuthin' but a big old log floatin' down the river, Gran'pa."

Clarissa was seated on the veranda, the pistol in her lap. Elegant and Chickory came out to meet them. Chickory took charge of the horses and led them away.

Fitz said, "Domingo all right?"

"Cryin' her poor heart out," Clarissa said. "Sends her down to Seawitch. She goin' to hurt fo' a week she busted so bad."

"Not as bad as the sonabitch whut killed Calla," Fitz said.

"He ain't evah goin' to get over it," Mark added.

"Mayhap Bibb goin' to make a fuss 'bout this," Fitz said. "When Perth don' come back, Bibb goin' to guess whut happen, an' mayhap he tells we killed him. Cain't prove nuthin' but tries anyways. So both o' yo' kin sweah you don' know nothin' 'cept me an' Mark we comes back an' says Perth got away."

"Man like him bound to run," Clarissa said.

"Whut we goin' to do 'bout poor Calla?" Elegant asked.

"I'll tell Hong Kong to see she gets buried," Mark said. "He can make a coffin fo' her in the mawnin'."

"Let's go back to baid," Fitz said. "Been a bad night."

8

It was a rule with Bibb never to allow a chance to cause trouble for Fitz to pass. Midmorning the next day he arrived at the Fisbee place with a sheriff and a Yankee captain.

Mark had already gone to the building site so Fitz and Clarissa came out to the veranda to greet the party as it rode up.

The captain introduced himself. "Captain Elias Morton, sir, of the Pennsylvania Army of the United States. The gentleman with me is County Sheriff Bill Townsend, representing civil law. The . . . ah . . . other man you likely know."

"Wishes I didn'," Fitz said.

"He has made a formal complaint that he believes you're responsible for the murder of one of the men who work on his farm. By the name of Perth. Mr. Bibb also swears you—well—altered his face somewhat."

Clarissa asked slyly, "You sho' that ain't the way he always look?"

Bibb, peering with difficulty through black eyes almost closed, bellowed through swollen lips, "She nuthin' but a common slut . . . leave her husband an' come heah to sleep with Fitz. Nuthin' but a whore."

Clarissa turned abruptly and went inside. Fitz sat down on one of the rockers.

"Clarissa happens to be the cousin o' my late wife, an' she sho' welcome in my home whenever she wishes to visit. Mistah Bibb got a mind that wuks jes' like a sewer. Tells first how all this began. Last night one o' Bibb's farm hands comes heah, rapes one o' my housemaids, an' then slits her throat."

"Cain't prove it," Bibb roared.

"Got a dead gal fo' evidence," Fitz said. "She down at Wyndward, my plantation. Goin' to be buried theah. Got me 'nother housemaid who was with the one who got murdered. She knows this sonabitch Perth 'cause she wukked at Bibb's place when Perth wukked theah. Says he near killed her too. Goes down to see if Perth hidin' at Bibb's place. Bibb swears Perth nevah did anythin', an' he wasn't theah anyways. Thinks mayhap Perth run out the back door when I rides up. Mistah Bibb riles me some, an' I busts him a little. Thass all theah was to it, Captain."

"You got any objection we searches fo' Perth o' his body?" Sheriff Townsend asked.

"Search all you likes."

"He gots a big graveyard down at Wyndward," Bibb said. "Thass whar he'd bury poor Perth."

"Wants to ride down, I goes with you," Fitz said.

"We'd better settle this thing one way or another, Mister Turner," the captain decided.

Fitz shouted for Chickory and ordered him to saddle a horse and bring it to the front of the house. Clarissa, carrying a large glass of what seemed to be whiskey, walked down the veranda steps and straight up to Bibb.

"You looks like you need a drink, Mistah Bibb. You also looks like you been run over by a train. Mayhap this heah make you feel bettah."

Bibb reached for the tall glass with an eager hand.

Clarissa flung the contents into his face. Bibb fell back against his startled horse and then shouted as he wiped the liquid from his face.

"Vinegah!" he cried out. "This heah whore got vinegah. . . ."

"An' molasses," Clarissa said meekly. "Hears tell vinegah an' molasses good fo' a busted-up face."

Captain Morton restrained a laugh with some difficulty, but the sheriff slapped his thigh and howled.

"Clarissa, you gots mo' sympathy fo' this sonabitch than I got," Fitz said.

"It my nature to be kind to animals," Clarissa said. "Even skunks."

Chickory appeared with a saddled horse. Fitz mounted and rode with the captain, behind Bibb and the sheriff. Clarissa went back to the veranda and collapsed onto one of the rockers, doubled up in laughter. Elegant waddled through the door, her wide face aglow with happiness.

"Wasn't that somethin'," she chortled. "Goin' take him all day get that stuff off his face."

Clarissa looked up. "Elegant, you mixes a mighty fine drink fo' a bastahd like Bibb." They roared again at the memory of Bibb's face when the mixture hit him.

Fitz, riding alongside the captain, explained his side of the story. "Knows you gots to do this, suh, but Bibb, he a no-good coward. Hates niggers, hates Yankees, hates me, an' reckon he looks in the mirror, he hates hisse'f. Ain't buried that poor gal who got raped an' killed last night. Bibb lookin' fo' Perth, ain't goin' to find him. But Bibb goin' to look at the gal's body, an' even you ain't goin' to stop me from makin' him look."

"Mister Turner, sir," the captain said, "I am in charge of law enforcement at Lynchburg and the surrounding area. Bibb complained to the sheriff, and he came to me. I had to ride out here with them. But I assure you that even if this man Perth is found at your plantation, you will not be held accountable for what happened to him."

"Even if I killed the sonabitch?"

"If you killed him, I would judge that it was no

106

more than justifiable. And quite likely I'd find evidence to suit myself, if not Bibb and the sheriff, that you were compelled to take some kind of action against this man."

"I thanks you, suh," Fitz said.

"And if you require any kind of help in the future, please come to me, or any Yankee officer."

"Reckon it won't come to that. I kin take good care o' my troubles, suh. But I thank you again fo' what you jes' said."

When they reached Wyndward, even the captain was impressed with the way the mansion was going up.

"It's a shame," he said, "that such places had to be destroyed, but in war nothing is sacred. And yet, I see no reason why they had to destroy this house. It certainly was of no military value, it's far out in the countryside. And yet," he looked around again, "they spared your slave cabins and the overseers' houses."

"Your army didn' burn my house, Captain. I did. Mayhap they would o' done so, but I spared 'em the trouble, an' reckon they spared me the cabins an' the two small cottages. Ain't complainin'."

"I see you still have Negroes working your fields."

"They gots to live, suh. I pay 'em a good day's wages, an' they doin' fine. But cain't get mo'. Could use two or three hundred mo', but they don' wants to wuk."

"I know. We're having trouble all over with them. I had no idea how much like children they are."

"Ain't their fault. We nevah let 'em get any schoolin'. Fo' a time theah, any slave whut got caught tryin' to read or write, got hung or, anyways, whupped 'til he near daid. Been that way fo' many yeahs. Now they free, the slaves don' knows whut to do, or how to live 'thout a massa or mistress carin' fo' 'em. Thinks they believe Yankee soldiers goin' to take the place o' their old massas an' will give 'em food, clothes, an' lodgin's."

"I've also come to that conclusion, Mister Turner. I confess I don't know how to handle them."

"They got to be made to learn they got to wuk, they wants to eat. Wuk fo' pay. If they sloths, ain't no mo' whuppin' sheds, but 'stead o' that, they gets fired an' no mo' money. Not goin' to be easy to teach 'em that, suh.

An' by damn, I feels mighty sorry fo' 'em 'cause how else kin they think?"

"You're a compassionate man, Mister Turner."

"Ain't half as compassionate as sensible. Kin see there's goin' to be nuthin' but trouble."

"It's already happening. I'm sorry to say that some white folks continue to treat the Negroes as slaves. They're fully aware that slavery has ended, but they still demand the ex-slaves be as subservient as when they were in bondage, and it's not going to work."

"Don't get into town often, Captain. Whut you mean by that?"

"Well, even if they had money enough, no Negro is allowed in a restaurant. They're expected to give way on a crowded sidewalk. Lots of other things. Doesn't amount to too much now, but someday it will. The time is bound to come when Negroes will realize they have the same rights as white folks."

Fitz nodded. "Reckon so, suh. Now will you look at that sonabitch an' the sheriff askin' questions o' the men wukkin' on the house?"

Fitz and Captain Morton watched the carpenters and helpers shake their heads as they were asked if they had seen any signs of violence. Bibb and the sheriff gave up and walked back to Fitz and the captain.

Fitz said, "Jes' so yo' ain't 'bout to sweah wasn't anybody killed last night, wants you to see this."

He led the party to one of the slave cabins. Seawitch had signaled Fitz and now stood beside it. She opened the cabin door and stepped aside. They filed into the small structure and stood before an open, newly made coffin in which Calla's body lay. She had been washed and dressed, but the severed throat was in clear evidence and so were the marks of the cruel beating she had undergone.

The captain turned away and closed his eyes. The sheriff gulped and backed out of the cabin. Bibb looked impassively at the dead girl. Fitz seized his arm and propelled him violently out of the cabin and sent him reeling.

"Now there's one mo' thing," Fitz said. He called out, "Seawitch, whar you got Domingo?"

Seawitch silently led the party to another cabin. In it Domingo lay in bed, her face still swollen.

Fitz said, "This heah gal was with the daid gal an' seen it all. Perth beat her up too, near kills her."

"You gots to prove it was Perth," Bibb said angrily. "Ain't takin' the word o' no slut."

Domingo was clearly frightened by all these white men staring down at her.

Captain Morton shook his head. "Mister Bibb, I hope you are not going to intimate that this girl did that to her face. This man Perth is going to pay the full penalty for what he did. When we find him, we'll certainly hang him."

"You hangs Mistah Turner, thass who you hangs," Bibb said. "Reckon he sho' killed Perth."

"Well," Captain Morton asked, "where would you suggest we look for the body, Mr. Bibb?"

"Fitz got him a slave cemetery jes' down past the cabins. Place to hide a body is in the ground, an' we looks theah first."

Before the group left for the cemetery, Mark walked over from the building site. He looked grimly at the captain and with disdain at Bibb and the sheriff.

"Whut's goin' on?" he demanded. "Askin' the men wukkin' on the house if they sees any fightin' goin' on."

"Mistah Bibb," Fitz explained, "say we kill Perth, an' he thinks we buries him in the slave cemetery. You buries anybody lately, son?"

"Knows who I'd like to bury." Mark eyed Bibb with contempt.

"Mister Turner," the captain addressed Mark, "did you know that your grandfather visited Bibb last evening?"

"Sho' did. Went theah lookin' to get Perth an' turn him over to the law."

"Do you know what happened there?"

"Knows Gran'pa busted Bibb an' lookin' at him right now he did a fine job. Been me, I'd o' killed him.

Gran'pa comes back from Bibb's place an' says he think Bibb was hidin' Perth, an' Perth runs when they sees Gran'pa ridin' up."

"Nevah saw Perth since day befo' yesterday," Bibb insisted. "But sho' goin' to see him, you digs him up. There's a new grave theah. Sees it from heah."

"We'll go down to the cemetery now," the captain said. "I want to see this new grave. I didn't notice it before."

Moments later they had dismounted and were standing beside the fresh mound of earth.

Bibb spoke triumphantly. "You sees it! You asks Mistah Turner who he got buried theah."

"Well?" The captain looked at Fitz.

"Don' know who buried theah," Fitz admitted. "You knows, Mark?"

"Sho' don' know, Gran'pa."

"Then we digs him up," Bibb insisted. "Sheriff, I'm askin' you to order Mistah Turner to dig up that grave."

Fitz shrugged. "I ain't diggin' up no grave."

"You see?" Bibb cried out. "He's skeered to open that grave."

"Ain't skeered at all," Fitz said tolerantly. "But thass hard wuk."

"You got slaves. . . ." Bibb began. "Least, yo' got niggers wukkin' fo' you."

"Gots to pay 'em, they digs up the grave," Fitz said.

"They ain't slaves no mo'," Mark added. "We ain't goin' to order 'em to do anythin'. An' we sho' ain't payin' 'em to do this even if they wants to."

Captain Morton glanced at Fitz with a glint of humor in his blue eyes. "Mr. Bibb," he said, "it appears that if you want this grave opened, you'll have to do the digging yourself. As Mr. Turner says, we can't order anyone to do that kind of labor."

"Willin' to supply a shovel," Fitz said mildly. "Best I kin do."

"Get me a shovel," Bibb said angrily. "I'll show you I'm right. Perth is buried in this heah grave."

Mark walked over to the building site and returned

with a shovel. He tossed it at Bibb, who went to work immediately. It was a new grave, but the earth had been well packed and the shoveling wasn't easy. Presently Bibb removed his coat and then his shirt as he shoveled out the grave. He sweated profusely, but when his shovel finally unearthed a corpse, he shouted in triumph.

"Now we got you, Fitz! This heah's Perth, I charges you with murder."

"You might see who it is 'fore you talks too much," Fitz said quietly.

Bibb eagerly uncovered most of the body and then, with a show of theatrics, he removed part of the blanket in which the body was wrapped to uncover the serene, deeply wrinkled, black face of an old man.

"Sho' don' look much like Perth to me," Fitz said.

"Not lessen he changed some," Mark added.

Captain Morton said, "Mr. Bibb, you will fill in that grave at once and the next time you make an accusation like this, I'll see to it you are locked up. Sheriff, as a civil officer, do you agree with me?"

"Gots to," the sheriff said. "Nevah did think Bibb knowed whut he talkin' 'bout. Mistah Turner, suh, fo' my part in this, I begs your pardon." He gave Bibb a hard shove toward the open grave. "Fill it in, you lyin' bastahd, an' you fills it in real respectful fo' this poor old man whose grave you violated."

Bibb, with a great sigh and a muttered oath, went to work. They made him tamp down each layer of earth and no one lent him a hand, just criticism about the way he filled in the grave.

Riding back with the captain, Fitz was chuckling aloud. Captain Morton riding alongside, glanced at him.

"Who was that in the grave?" he asked.

"An old slave, livin' heah on Wyndward most o' his life. Was told he daid an' I gives orders to bury him, but fo'got all 'bout it an' I sho' got some set back when I sees this heah grave."

"May I ask what you think happened to this man Perth?"

"Reckon he daid," Fitz said. "Jes' got me an idea he daid."

"Then we won't bother to look for him, sir. I'm sorry we put you to this trouble, but we have to investigate any complaint. There'd be the devil to pay if we didn't, and we've worries enough without that."

"One thing mo'," Fitz said. "How kin you say I didn't kill Perth? Jes' 'cause his body wasn't in that grave don' means I couldn' o' killed him."

"Mister Turner, sir, we judge a man by his record for honesty, and there is no reason why we should dispute your claim of innocence in this matter. I assure you, sir, that we hold you in highest regard. And that is a fact worth remembering."

"Sho' won't fo'get," Fitz said. "I thanks you, suh."

"Besides, if Perth is dead, we're saved the chore of hanging him."

Fitz turned his horse over to Chickory and seated himself on the veranda beside Clarissa. They both watched the captain ride away. After a few minutes, the sheriff and Bibb rode by, neither one looking toward the house.

"Reckon you convinced the captain you ain't seen Perth?" Clarissa said.

"Reckon," Fitz said. "Gots me wonderin'. Jes' comes to me whut the captain means when he says it didn't make no diff'rence they finds Perth daid. An' I get any mo' troubles to come to him, or any Yankee officer an' I gets help."

"Mighty nice o' him."

"Sho' is, but sounded to me like he got orders I get taken care o' no matter whut."

"Reckon," Clarissa mused, "you 'maginin' it, Fitz. Mayhap you're plain lucky."

Fitz nodded. He shouted for Calcutta Two and gave orders for bourbon and water. He and Clarissa sat in their rockers sipping drinks and talking about old times. The talk finally turned to planning for a big dinner and ball as soon as the mansion was finished, something Clarissa could delight in. Fitz liked her ideas. It would, they decided, be the biggest and best affair in the county since before the war.

"Whut the hell we talkin' 'bout?" Fitz said with a

laugh. "We invites one person an' feeds him sowbelly an' grits, an' it be the biggest soiree since the war. Ain't been no soirees o' any kind."

"We changes that, Fitz," Clarissa said contentedly. "Gives you my promise I won't go to baid with anyone who comes."

"Now Clarissa," Fitz admonished her, "we wants to make this heah soiree jes' like it used to be, an' you beds down most ev'ry time Benay an 'me gives a ball. Wants it jes' like it used to be. You get horny, ain't goin' to start lookin' in the bedrooms."

Clarissa shook her head sadly. "Mayhap I tries, but some things got to change, Fitz."

Fitz patted her knee comfortingly. "I'm mighty happy we good friends again. Wouldn' say it 'fore, but when we both young an' randy, you sho' looked mighty good to me."

"Gives you ev'ry chance." She sighed as the memories returned. "An' ev'ry time you makes a fool o' me, Fitz."

"You wrong 'bout that. Makes a fool o' myse'f. An' now, when we sees one 'nother all the time, we ain't got the juice to do much 'bout it."

She closed her eyes. "Reckon I could."

"Right now?"

"Right now, Fitz."

"Whut the hell you waitin' fo'?"

Her eyes flew open. "The invitation you jes' gives me."

"Gets Calcutta Two to bring us a bottle. Sometimes helps, 'specially you get kind o' weak."

Elegant watched them go upstairs, Fitz with the bottle of bourbon swinging from his hand. She compressed her lips tightly and shook her head.

Fitz didn't even take the cork out of the bottle. It was a strange yet satisfying romance. With all the passion they both enjoyed, there was no real love, only a mutual admiration for one another.

Clarissa opened her eyes and sighed in sheer bliss. "Mark couldn't o' been any bettah, Fitz."

"Takes that as a real compliment, Clarissa."

113

"Thinks now mayhap I kin do my part to see that the ball gets to be mo' like they used to be. Sho' goin' to try, 'specially a nice-lookin' man comes 'long. Dances with him, gets him randy, an' whoopee, goin' to be like old times sho' 'nuff."

9

Over the next few weeks the mansion took on size and dimension, and some of the finishing touches were begun. The dependency house, the corn crib, and the spring house were already built. Some of the ex-slaves, working in their spare time, had erected an icehouse close by the spring house. Fitz looked forward to having all the ice he needed for his drinks.

Elegant was already supervising the arrangement of her kitchen, which, though separated from the main house, was attached to it by a very short corridor to the dining room. Fitz had ordered a large range and water heater from a Northern manufacturer along with an over-size icebox and pantry equipment. Elegant moved about the small Fisbee place with her eyes shining, concerned only with how the new kitchen should look and how she intended to operate in it.

Clarissa was deeply engaged now in planning the decor, selecting the paint and the wallpaper. She made several trips to Richmond and Lynchburg to examine and often buy furniture, which she was determined must be as much like the old furnishings as she could make them. She was completely engrossed in her new responsibility and absorbed all she could from the furniture dealers and artisans, thoroughly enjoying her new role and deeply aware of the importance she played in the revival of Wyndward. She worked diligently to earn the respect in Fitz's eyes as he listened to her plans. She knew his surprise at her skill was no less than hers, but she was determined that he would never regret the trust he'd placed in her.

There was an air of serenity about Wyndward now. Fitz knew how false it could be, but he enjoyed it while it lasted. Bibb had quieted down, there'd been no further search for Perth. Domingo had recovered and gratefully occupied Mark's bed when he called for her.

In the fields the help worked far more diligently than Fitz had hoped for. Hong Kong had managed to bring in fifty men over the months up to late autumn. One of the first structures built was the enormous curing shed. Long before, the tobacco plants had been topped to check too much upward growth so a broader leaf could be produced. Once they were ripe, they were allowed to wither a bit before being cut and hung up in the curing shed to dry.

When the weather was suitable for the operation, not too dry or too humid, the stalks were taken down and stemmed. The leaves were then placed in a press, and their bulk reduced to a point where they could be squeezed into hogsheads. In the old days these hogsheads weighed half a ton, but Fitz was growing a finer tobacco now and he limited the weight to six hundred pounds or less. That made selling them easier. He could not only ask a better price for choice leaf, but the buyer could better afford to purchase it in smaller lots. Money was scarce in the South these days. Some of the tobacco went North, but more than half was sent to England where it had been in great demand since the end of the war.

At last the hard work was done, the curing houses empty, the fields ready to be replowed for next season. The corn crib was full, the smokehouse crammed with pork and smoked beef. Standing at the edge of the cleared space behind the mansion, Mark and Fitz surveyed the plantation, or what they could see of it.

"Know whut?" Fitz asked lazily.

"How kin I know whut, you ain't tellin' me anythin', Gran'pa."

"Feels now like the goddamn war over an' we back to the way it used to be. Or almost. Nevah be the same, o' course, but this goin' to be even bettah, folks get used to it."

"Sho' shipped off plenty of 'bacco," Mark agreed.

"A third mo' from the same 'mount o' land. Know whut that means, boy? We kin get rich mighty fast. Payin' help 'stead o' whuppin' 'em gets mo' wuk done an' bettah wuk."

"Ain't been one nigger walks off," Mark observed. "Used to have to hang some o' 'em to keep others from runnin', but now nobody wants to go off. Reckon you're right. We goin' to get rich."

Fitz nodded. "An' fo' whut! Ain't nobody to leave my share to, 'cept you an' be too much fo' one man. Even a man raised in a whorehouse whar money flows mighty free."

"You got to keep remindin' me o' that?"

"Used to be you were mighty proud o' whar you was raised."

"We ain't had a fight in a long time, Gran'pa, but you keep talkin' like that an' we sho' goin' to have."

"Kin take you now jes' like I takes you befo'."

Mark said, "Kin believe it. Mayhap yo' gets married again. Reckon you kin make suckers you wants to."

Fitz laughed aloud. "I don' think so, Mark. That'll be up to you. So why in hell you ain't lookin' 'round fo' a good-lookin' gal? Domingo mighty nice in baid, but you gots to think o' your future. Wants great-gran'childrun runnin' 'round heah fo' I dies. Wyndward didn' die durin' the war an' ain't nevah goin' to die. Whut happens to me ain't important. Whut happens to Wyndward mighty important. You 'members that, son."

"Reckon. An' whut in hell you means by sayin' I

should be lookin' 'round fo' a pretty gal? I ain't had no time fo' anythin' but helpin' build the mansion. An' you sees any pretty gals 'round heah, you tells me."

"Well, next week the furniture come, an' Clarissa get it all set up. Soon's that done, we sendin' invitations to ev'ry fam'ly round heah to come to the dinner an' ball. Mayhap there's a pretty gal or two then."

"Sho' looks like it be the finest house I evah sees," Mark said. "Reckon ain't any bettah than Wyndward."

"Tryin' hard to make it the best," Fitz agreed. "Was goin' to say we bettah get back fo' suppah or Elegant gets mad, but ain't that the plumber—ain't that Toby comin' this way?"

"Sho' is, like he wants to see us. Wavin' now. Reckon we waits."

Toby greeted them in his own independent way. "Suh, goin' to put pipe in the outhouse," he said. "Got Hong Kong to give me some he'p an' I gets a nice tank made o' bricks buried in the ground. Reads 'bout it, an' thinks I kin make it wuk, suh. Knows it will."

"Gettin' kin' o' modern, ain't we?" Fitz said. "Likes whut you done. It wuks, goin' to give you a nice bonus."

"I thanks you, suh. But that ain't whut I comes fo'. Wants to know you sendin' anybody to look 'round the mansion? Means at night when I'm wukkin' theah."

"Whut you sees or hears?" Fitz asked quickly.

"Ain't much, but thinks I sees two, mayhap three men watchin' the mansion from the woods, suh. Sees 'em flittin' 'bout like they don' know whut in hell they doin'. Sho' they ain't hunters. Jes' lookin' an' studyin'."

"Bibb!" Fitz said harshly "Fo' that you gets ten dollahs extra in yo' pay. Now you keeps watchin', Toby. You sees 'em again, you comes runnin'. That'll be all fo' now. Mark an' me, we goin' back to the Fisbee place fo' suppah, an' then one o' us comin' back heah ev'ry night."

"Mighty glad I tells you, suh."

"Mighty happy you did. Come on, Mark. We'll decide which of us is goin' to come back an' stay all night."

On the way back, riding side by side, Mark seemed

dubious. "You thinks Bibb got the guts to fire the mansion?"

"Bibb got guts fo' nuthin', but it don' take guts to set fire to a house when there's nobody 'round. He comes, I sho' 'nuff goin' to make him wish he hadn't."

"Reckon 'bout time to do some mo' killin'," Mark said. "That mansion burns down now, I gets mad 'nuff to kill ten men."

Back at the Fisbee place, they sat down to supper with Clarissa. Fitz revealed the new problem and what they must do about it.

"From now on, until we moves in, somebody got to be theah. Cain't let Toby o' any other black man take responsibility fo' it. Not even Hong Kong. One who goes theah stays awake all night an' sits with two o' three guns 'side o' him. Who goes tonight, Mark?"

"Reckon I kin do it."

"Good. Tomorrow night I goes."

"Ain't goin' alone," Mark said.

"Who you bringin'?"

"Domingo lots bettah now an' wants her."

"God damnit," Fitz exploded, "you goin' to guard the house. How you goin' do that you busy pesterin' Domingo?"

"Kin do it. Don' take ears to pester."

"I might's well save my breath," Fitz grumbled. "Takes Domingo. Mayhap she stays 'wake bettah than you anyways. But Bibb o' anybody else burns down Wyndward while you on guard, you bettah get on a hoss an' don' stop 'til you reach California."

"Gran'pa, you bettah keep you own ears open while you theah. Else it be you on a hoss headin' fo' Maine."

"Likes the way you two gets 'long," Clarissa said, smiling tolerantly. "Gots somethin' to say myse'f. Wukkin' mighty hard gettin' the house ready an' kin kill any sonabitch wants to burn it down. Goes with you, Fitz. You got any objections to that, Mark?"

" 'Course not. Mayhap me an' Domingo, we kin' o' fo'gets whut we theah fo', but that sho' won' happen with you two old folks."

"Goin' to strangle him some day," Fitz said.

"Let's do it now," Clarissa suggested.

"Don' wants to stay at the mansion ev'ry night o' mayhap I would. Take 'long plenty o' guns. Goin' to keep a hoss saddled an' tied up in front o' the house. I hears shootin', I rides, shirttail an' all."

"Gets Domingo an' go right after suppah," Mark said. "Toby's wukkin' some ways off at the curin' sheds tonight. Cain't leave the mansion 'lone fo' a minute after dark."

"One mo' thing," Fitz said seriously. "I ain't foolin' 'bout this. Way things are now, the Yankee soldiers in charge an' mayhap it ain' healthy to kill Bibb he comes. Needs killin', but ain't like it used to be."

"You kin do whut you wants, Gran'pa. The Yankee officer said so, didn' he?"

"He didn' come right out. Reckon he means I kin get away with much, but I thinks killin' too far. Bettah not kill him 'lessen you has to."

"Whut'll we do, kiss his ass?" Clarissa asked flatly.

"We kin find ways o' makin' him wish he wasn't borned," Fitz said. "Theah sho' are ways. But he comes shootin', that diff'rent. Fill his stinkin' carcass full o' lead. We got a right to defend ourse'ves."

"Goes down jes' 'fore it get dark," Mark said.

That night Fitz slept fitfully, and each time he awoke, he could visualize Mark and Domingo occupied in bed while Bibb and some of his men slithered through the grass, each holding a firebrand ready to be lit and hurled into the newly built mansion.

By morning Fitz was covered with sweat from these recurring nightmares. Immediately after dawn he dressed and hurried downstairs to mount the horse that Chickory had saddled and left for him in front of the house. He scanned the gray dawn for any sign of smoke, saw none, but still was not relieved of his anxiety. He kicked the horse into a gallop.

Coming within sight of the mansion, it seemed intact. Nothing around the countryside moved. It was just a late summer morning and a quiet one. A time to appreciate what Wyndward was going to be like in only a matter of a few days now.

As he rode up, he grew worried again. By now Mark should have heard him coming and be investigating, but there was no sign of him. He had almost reached the spacious veranda which ran around two sides of the mansion when Mark suddenly appeared directly in front of the horse, rifle aimed. Fitz wasn't even sure where he had sprung from.

"See you comin' a mile off," Mark said.

"Jes' the same, 'nuff of 'em rides up fast, you cain't take care o' all standin' heah in the open."

"Turn 'round, Gran'pa."

Fitz twisted around in the saddle. Domingo, a rifle at her shoulder, had him covered. Mark had set up a simple, but most effective trap.

"That gal kin use a gun good as you, Gran'pa. We been waitin' all night fo' Mistah Bibb to come."

"All right," Fitz said, "you sho' could o' s'prised a small party. Carpenters comin' in a little while. You kin go get some sleep."

Fitz dismounted and tied his horse. Mark and Domingo disappeared for a few moments and then came riding by, Domingo astride the saddle, her tan face alight in excitement. Mark rode behind her, one hand about her slim waist.

Fitz nodded in satisfaction. They were a good couple. It was too bad color would eventually keep them apart. Fitz went into the mansion. It was the first time he'd been there alone. Previously, someone had always been with him or the carpenters had been at work. Now, in the silence and the smell of fresh paint, paste, and newly cut wood, he felt the homeyness of the place surround him like a warm, comforting mantle.

As nearly as it could be, Wyndward was the same as the original mansion. His footsetps resounded in the hollow emptiness, and yet the past was there as if it had arisen from the foundation, the basement, and permeated the newness. This was where he'd grown from youth to manhood, where slaves had moved about, some happy, some arrogant. This was where Benay held him, laughed with him, and loved him. And here was where Daisy, so light-hearted and lovely, had spent some of her youth

121

with Jonathan—and where she had been savagely ravaged.

The emptiness seemed filled with memories that almost took visual shape before his eyes. There'd been the lavish balls attended by everyone in the county who could possibly make it. Outside, there'd been banquet tables during the warm days and, at night, Chinese lanterns strung from trees.

He recalled how his mother's New England sternness had finally melted under the influence of this wonderful life, and he could hear his father's bass voice booming orders to Calcutta to hurry or he'd get his ass kicked. He supposed, if he listened harder, he might hear the screams of slaves being whipped in the shed down near the stables. That had been part of it too.

Fitz walked upstairs and stood by a window at the rear of the mansion looking out over the fertile fields, making up his mind then and there that Wyndward would be bigger than ever. There were new strains of tobacco plants he wanted to try out. He planned a road stretching from one end of the plantation to the other, over which the work carts could move faster and more easily. Speed meant money, especially these days when the hands had to be paid in cash, not handouts.

He entered the empty bedroom, a duplicate of the one that had been Sally Beaufort's when she had lived there. He couldn't think of her as anyone but Sally. Her name was Elizabeth, she had written, but she was still Sally to him. He recalled her beauty, warmth, and the quiet love she'd shown for him. That she had schemed against the entire Confederacy had never bothered him, least of all now, when the war was over. He closed his eyes for a moment, trying hard to bring her back. He wanted to hear her voice, to see the softness in her eyes when she looked at him. Then a man's voice and the loud bang of a hammer broke the reverie. He went downstairs and surprised the workers.

He talked to them for a while, mostly about the progress of their work and a few minor changes he wished in what would be his office. Bookcases built against the walls were one thing, and his desk had to have its back to a large window.

He returned to his horse and led the animal as he walked slowly in the direction of the fields. Hong Kong was apparently busy elsewhere. The blacks, working steadily if not furiously, stood erect as he passed by, but they didn't bow their heads and clasp their hands before them. They looked him in the eye, and their greetings were genuine, in no way servile. Fitz stopped to talk to one of them.

"Likes it heah?" he asked.

"Sho' does, suh. Likes it mighty good. My woman like it too, an' my chilldrun gets to run whar they likes."

"Reminds me," Fitz said, "an' you kin pass the word, that soon's the mansion is finished, goin' to build a school, hire a teacher so your chilldrun learn how to read an' write soon's they kin understand."

"Was hopin' fo' that, suh. Sho' ain't no school gettin' ready fo' niggers in Lynchburg."

"This," Fitz said, "ain't Lynchburg. You get 'nuff to eat?"

"Nevah had it so good, suh. Wishes all folks who was once slaves gets it good as this."

"Not fo' a long time," Fitz prophesied. "It comin', but not yet."

" 'Cept heah on Wyndward," the black said with a broad grin.

"Get to wuk, you lazy nigger," Fitz chuckled. "Ain't payin' you to stand heah an' jaw with the man who pays your wages."

"Gits right to wuk, suh." The black began to turn away, paused, and looked back. "We thanks you, suh. We sho' goin' to give you a day's wuk wuth the money you pays us. Theah be any who don', we sends 'em runnin'."

"Good," Fitz said. "You gots anythin' you want to talk 'bout, you comes to the big house—when it ready."

Fitz rode back to the Fisbee place, hoping it would be for one of the last times. He was anxious to move into the mansion. Being there would mean less time riding

123

back and forth. But mostly he looked forward to it because when he left the Fisbee place, it would be like going home.

Fitz spent the day tending his bookkeeping, which had grown in proportion to the added workers he had hired. Everything had worked out better than he had anticipated. Word of mouth, between his early employees and blacks eager for work, had brought him the best of the ex-slaves. Not one shirked, and most even gave more than expected and Fitz cautiously raised their wages, being as quiet about it as possible, for other planters were hiring too. They paid as little as they could get away with, taking advantage of the near starvation which so many ex-slaves suffered.

Before too long, more and more would be expected by these workers and more and more the planters were going to resent it and try to bring back the old ways however they could. There was going to be trouble. Fitz knew it and planned so none of it would affect him, except to increase his profits by bigger sales to a hungry market.

Clarissa rode back from Lynchburg, excited over the news that much of the furniture had arrived by rail and was waiting at the depot. Fitz arranged for wagons to be sent next day. That evening they had an early supper. Elegant had packed a basket and, armed with this, a bottle of whiskey, four rifles, and a side arm, they rode down to the mansion, put the horses in the new stables, and sat in one of the front rooms on planks placed over sawhorses. Not a very comfortable spot, but a fine place from which to observe the entire front of the estate and much of its sides. Any attempt to burn the house was not expected to be made from the rear because of the activity around the workers' cabins.

"Wishes some o' that furniture was heah," Clarissa said. " 'Specially a baid. Jes' sittin' heah like this sort o' wastin' time."

"Cain't do whut you're thinkin' an' keep an eye out fo' Bibb," Fitz said. "An' don' start lookin' at the floor. We's heah on business not makin' love."

"I still say it wastin' time, an' when I looks in the

124

mirror I think ain't got much left. An' you wants to jes' sit heah on this goddam plank an' wait fo' somethin' you ain't even sho' goin' to happen."

"Goin' to happen," Fitz told her. "Bound to. Bibb swear he gettin' back at me, an' reckon he mean it. Worst thing he could do to me is burn this place jes' befo' we get to move in. An' Bibb, he always does whut he thinks is worst. He's comin'."

"You says you ain't goin' kill him?" Clarissa asked impatiently. "Why not? He pesters you all your life. Kill the sonabitch."

"Befo', it easy. Now I ain't so sho'. This whole country kinda growin' up. Best to think o' other ways o' makin' Bibb unhappy. But, he give me good reason, I sho' kills him. An' with some pleasure. The same goes fo' your papa-in-law."

"Wants to be theah when yo' does. He's like Bibb. Whatever he does is when your back is turned."

"Hears you say that 'fore. Now you stops that jawin'. How kin I listen fo' someone comin' toward us in the dark with you talkin' all the time?"

"Hand me the bottle," Clarissa said. "Cain't talk, I kin drink. Lessen you thinks they kin heah me when I swallows."

10

Time crept by. Seated in the darkness of the empty room, Clarissa dozed and Fitz had trouble keeping his eyes open. Once he startled Clarissa by reaching for one of the rifles, but he had just seen a couple of hands taking a late walk. Fitz relaxed, and Clarissa, after cursing him for disturbing her, went back to sleep.

The men came well after midnight. Fitz couldn't see them, but he could hear the crackle of dry branches being stepped on. Yet the sound came from places where there were no trees, only brush that didn't have branches large enough to crackle that way.

Fitz nudged Clarissa and clamped a hand across her mouth before she could start arguing about his interruption of her sleep.

"Takes a rifle," he whispered. "Go to the office where the window looks out on the back. You sees anythin' move, fire off a round. Don't go stickin' your fool haid out o' the window. Might get it blowed off."

"Ain't that short o' brains," she retorted, whispering

back. "Tells you, I sees Bibb I goin' kill him an' take my chances with the Yankees."

She crept to the back of the house, rifle clutched in her hand. She was a dead shot, Fitz knew, and she would do a good job of backing him up. He knelt at the large window to peer out into the night. If these men were sure the place was unprotected, they'd not be too quiet. Likely they'd simply run up, throw the firebrands, and run back. But to make use of the torches, they'd have to light them, and that was what Fitz was waiting for.

Moments later he saw a flicker of light followed by the far greater flaming of the first torch. Fitz took aim at a spot just below the light, but then held his fire. There would be others, and knowing how many would be extremely useful.

The firebrand suddenly seemed to wave in the darkness and then vanish. Fitz was puzzled. Another torch was lit and then a second. They were held high and then began to move in the direction of the house. Fitz aimed slightly to the left of one torch and pulled the trigger. The torch fell to the ground, and someone gave a loud yell of surprise and fear. The other torch was promptly extinguished.

Silence followed. The men were still there, waiting, Fitz knew. He also knew there were at least three of them. Any exit on his part would be highly dangerous. He hurried to the room where Clarissa was on guard.

"See anythin'?" he asked.

"Not a damn thing. You get one o' them?"

"Didn' aim to hit," Fitz said. "They's three so far, I think. They's out in the tall grass waitin'. Soon's they think it's the right time, they'll be comin' an' fast. Mayhap cain't get all three, an' it'll take jes' one torch to do whut they after."

"Whut are we goin' to do? Sit an wait?"

"Want 'em to come to the front o' the house. I'm goin' out after 'em an' you backs me up. You see a torch, shoot at it. Cain't worry none 'bout whether or not we kills 'em. Not any mo'."

"Don' like you goin' out theah alone, Fitz. But

knows whut you means, an' it's got to be done. I'll watch. I got 'nuff guns I needs 'em."

Fitz nodded and then made his way to the front door. He opened it very quickly, hoping he would not be seen. He tiptoed to the end of the veranda, vaulted the rail noiselessly, and, bent double, began to move out, making a wide circle of the spot where he believed the arsonists might be.

He was skirting the area where he'd seen the first torch briefly lit and mysteriously extinguished. He moved forward in a crouch. Suddenly he thrust the rifle forward and almost pulled the trigger. But the form lying on the ground was not waiting to trap him. Fitz knelt and turned the man over. He was dead. From the way his head flopped around, his neck had been broken. The extinguished torch lay at his side.

Fitz wondered if Mark could have come to reinforce him. He doubted it, for Mark usually obeyed orders, and Fitz had told him firmly to stay at the Fisbee place. That too had to be guarded.

Fitz rose, taxing his brain to solve this new mystery. But he forgot that when he saw a torch lit, then a second and, to his surprise, a third. There had been four men bent on arson. The torches were moving now, faster and faster. Then one of them went flying harmlessly into the air, and there was the sound of a scuffle.

There was more movement, and Fitz began to run. Someone, someone trying to aid him, was in danger. He heard a shout and a gunshot. Fitz ran closer. The two remaining torches gave enough light so that he could see the grim scene before him. The two men with torches were faced by a black man, unarmed and helpless. Bibb was moving forward.

"Who the hell are you?" he demanded.

The black made no reply, but stood there, his arms away from his sides, fists clenched and muscles tense either to take the bullet or to charge. One of those two things was going to happen within seconds.

Bibb said, "Well now, you cain't talk, mayhap you won't yell when I puts a bullet in you goddamn black belly."

Fitz brought his rifle to his shoulder. He aimed at the torch held by the second man, drawing a bead on the hand and arm holding the torch. He fired. The torch fell to the ground, and the man who'd held it emitted a screech of pain. Fitz transferred his aim to Bibb's back.

"You a daid man in two seconds, Bibb, you don' let go o' that gun."

"Gots me a nigger to kill first," Bibb called back.

"I'm pressin' the trigger hand 'bout now."

Bibb let go of the rifle. The black man sprang forward and picked it up. Then he moved to one side and picked up the second rifle. There was a wild yell, and someone crashed through the brush just beyond the tall grass and disappeared. Fitz moved forward, gun level. Bibb raised his hands high and kept his back turned to Fitz. The black was waiting.

"Two of 'em got away, suh."

Fitz peered at the man. "Knows you now. Ain't sayin' your name."

The black, a tall man, stood erect. From the house came a shot. The bullet whistled through the air. The black dropped to his knees. So did Fitz and Bibb in order to avoid being seen above the grass.

Fitz called out as loudly as he could. "Clarissa, stop that goddam shootin'. You near got me."

"You all right, Fitz?" she yelled back.

"Stay whar you are," Fitz ordered. "War is over. Got me a skunk name o' Bibb an' goin' to string him up."

Bibb fell to his knees. "Fitz, you cain't lynch me! They'll hang you fo' it sho'. You cain't do that."

"Kin, an' don' give a damn I gets hung so long as you daid. Had all I kin take o' you, Bibb. All an' mo'. This ends it, tryin' to burn my home. After I hangs you, I goes fo' the others. Ain't had a hangin' 'round heah since befo' the war. Kinda missed 'em." He glanced at the Negro. "Goes back to the stable an' brings a rope fo' hangin'. Run both ways. Wants this heah no-'count daid 'fore mawnin'."

"Fitz, sweahs I nevah pesters you again. Sweahs I goes 'way, mayhap to California. Goes anywhar you says. Please don't hang me."

"You comes heah to kill me. Ain't no reason why I shouldn' string you up."

"The Yankees 'gainst it," Bibb said. "They says no fightin', no killin'."

"You sees any Yankees 'round heah, Bibb? When you daid, I'll cut you down an' throw your body in the river. Ain't nobody goin' to look fo' you."

"Fitz, you kin have my farm. All o' it. Hosses, stock, ev'ry damn thing. Jes' let me go! Please, Fitz! Knows I done wrong an' pays you back fo' ev'rythin'."

"When I sees you squirmin' at the end o' the rope, then knows you sho' payin' me back. 'Course, yo' ain't in the mood fo' bein' hung, I kin shoot you, but far as I kin see, hangin's bettah. Cain't go shootin' off too many guns. Might be heard. Don' wants no witnesses to your hangin', Bibb. Goin' be real quick an' quiet."

Bibb was beginning to weep, muttering to himself since addressing Fitz got him nowhere. The black man came back promptly with the rope. Fitz said, "Go find a good, stout tree branch, throws the rope over it, an' we hoists him up."

Fitz prodded Bibb with the barrel of the gun, forcing him to walk to the fringe of forest. Fitz had picked up one of the firebrands. Once at the tree, he handed the torch to the black man and told him to light it. Then he expertly tripped Bibb. The man was too weak from terror to resist. Fitz bound his hands behind his back, tied his ankles securely. What Bibb didn't see was that the end of the rope was not in the shape of a noose and it was tied to Bibb's ankles.

Fitz seized the end of the rope that had been flung over the branch. He heaved at it. Bibb's body jerked up, feet first. The black man came to Fitz's side and grasped the rope as well. They hoisted Bibb well into the air. He dangled there, five feet above the ground, head down. Mewing noises came from his lips.

Fitz tied the rope to the trunk of the tree. "Comes by in the mawnin', Bibb, an' cuts you down. Hangin' by the neck too damn quick fo' the likes o' you. By sunup you'll be daid 'nuff to get thrown in the river. Ain't no way outen this, Bibb, but if you does get loose, next time

I don' waste this much time. I jes' puts a bullet through your haid. Good night an' good-bye."

Fitz extinguished the torch, and he and the black man left the scene. As they moved off in the darkness, Fitz spoke softly.

"I thanks you, Toby, fo' whut you done."

"Got a daid man in the brush," Toby said. "Breaks his neck when he tries to throw the torch in my face."

"Jes' twisted his fool neck," Fitz marveled. "He sho' daid. I found him."

"Plumbin' gives me big muscles, suh. Wasn't nothin' to bust he neck. Knows they comin'. Spreads dry branches 'round so they steps on 'em."

"We'd better pick him up an' bury him soon's we kin. Knows the place. Bibb dug up an old man's grave thinkin' there'd be the body of someone else. We jes' opens the grave again an' puts this poor jackass in theah. Nobody sho' ain't goin' to open that grave again."

"Suh, gots to bury Mistah Bibb too, don' we?"

"Toby, knows you killed this man 'cause yo' had to. But hangin' Bibb by the neck is lynchin', an' the Yankees ain't goin' to stand fo' that."

"He dies hangin' by he feet," Toby warned.

"Two o' his men runs off, but reckon they don' run far. Hears 'em in the brush. They comin' back to cut him down fo' he gets too much blood in his fool haid. Liked to have let him die with the rope 'round his neck but cain't do that now. Got troubles 'nuff."

"Reckon he ain't comin' back to do no mo' burnin'," Toby said.

"Nevah hears your name. He don' know you an' don' think he evah got a good look at you, even in the torchlight. He say you helped me with this, I'll deny it, an' my word a hell o' a lot bettah'n his. Don' worry none."

They found the dead man. Toby slung him over his shoulder as if he were a large rag doll, and they made their way past the mansion. Fitz called out to Clarissa that she must stay inside and keep an eye out.

Toby and Fitz made quick work of burying the dead man. The earth was still soft and the grave deep enough to accept another body. They filled it in, rounded it off. Fitz wiped perspiration from his forehead and leaned on the shovel for a moment's rest.

"Toby, in your pay next week, you finds a hundred dollahs mo'. An' you reports to Hong Kong an' tells him you wuks right under him now. You pay gets raised twice."

"Thanks you, suh. Nevah did help you 'cause I wants money, suh."

"Knows that. But it sho' comes in handy these days, Toby. You goes to your cabin now, an' you ain't been outen it all night. You nevah sees me, an' you don' know Mistah Bibb."

"Yassuh. Nevah knowed him."

"I'll see you tomorrow, Toby. I thanks you again."

Fitz carried the shovel to the stable where he cleaned off the fresh dirt and put it away. Then he returned to the house. Clarissa was seated on the steps of the veranda with one rifle across her knees and another at her side. She didn't get up, merely raised her head.

"You sho' ain't no gen'mun leavin' a lady sittin' heah by herse'f. Whut the hell goin' on? You comes from the stables. Heahs somebody out theah in the brush. Heahs talkin'."

"Less you knows, the bettah, Clarissa."

"I ain't movin' 'til you tells me whut happened."

"You sho' a pain in the ass, Clarissa, but I'll tell you. Out theah, 'thout me knowin' 'bout it, Toby hides an' waits. Mayhap you didn' see one o' Bibb's men light a torch an' gettin' ready to run an' throw it through a window. Toby gets him fo' he kin do anythin'. Then Toby goes fo' the rest o' them. He got no gun, but he sho' got plenty o' guts. But Bibb gets his rifle on him, an' I gets theah jes' in time to send Bibb's men runnin' off. I gets Bibb in the sights o' my rifle, an' he gives up."

"Fitz, you didn' put a bullet through his neck, you the biggest fool evah."

"Hung him," Fitz said.

"That's bettah. Lots bettah."

"By the heels," Fitz went on.

"Whut you means by the heels?"

"Ties his ankles an' hoists him up head down an' leaves him danglin' theah."

"Fitz, gots to hand it to you. Mighty good way o' gettin' rid o' bastahds like Bibb."

"Didn' get rid o' him. Knows two o' his men hidin' close by. Knows they comes an' cuts him down."

"I take it back, sayin' you did right. Damn it, Fitz, Bibb on'y goin' try again."

"Knows that, an' mayhap next time I kin kill him an' get away with it. But not tonight. Cain't give the Yankees a chance to lock me up fo' murder."

"You says you're special an' they don' arrest you."

"Not fo' most things, but killin' a man diff'rent."

"You get one killed tonight. Ain't that whut you said? This heah Toby. . . ."

"Kills him, an' we buries him in the old slave's grave. The one opened up by Bibb lookin' fo' 'nother o' his boys he sweahs I killed. You don' jaw 'bout this to anybody. Not Elegant or Domingo, not anybody. Reckon Bibb ain't makin' no complaint 'bout this heah daid man 'cause he'd have to 'splain whut he was doin' heah. 'Sides, Bibb so damn skeered right now he ain't goin' to get back any o' his nerve fo' weeks, reckon."

"Keeps my mouth shut," Clarissa promised. "Was heah too, wasn't I? Heahs the Yankees hangs ladies 'long with men they has to. But I wishes you hung that sonabitch by the neck. Would o' dug his grave with pleasure."

When they returned to the Fisbee place, it was almost dawn. They left the horses to graze and entered the smaller house. Fitz took a bottle of whiskey from a cabinet, poured drinks, and they toasted one another.

"Wonder why Mark nevah showed up," Fitz said. "There was shootin', an' he must o' heared it."

"Reckon Mark gots other things on his mind."

"Mark don' make promises he don' keep, Clarissa. Somethin' else must o' happened."

"Bets you five dollahs, or a night in baid with me, Mark upstairs right now, sleepin' off his pleasurin' o' Domingo. That boy mighty randy. Reckon he mighty good too. Mayhap like you used to be."

133

"Damn it, I still am," Fitz insisted. "Takes you up. Told him befo' he cain't pester Domingo when there's trouble all 'round us."

They went upstairs quietly and opened the door to Mark's bedroom. He lay with Domingo enclosed in his arms. Both were fast asleep.

Clarissa shut the door softly. "You pays me five dollahs or you gets in baid with me now, Fitz. That's whut you bets."

"Gives you five dollahs," Fitz said. "Too damn tired."

"You ain't like you used to be. No, suh, you're losin' your juice, Fitz. Hands me the five dollahs tomorrow. I'm tired too."

"Good night," Fitz said. He walked down the short corridor to his room. Clarissa watched him go and heaved a great sigh.

"He takes me to baid right now an' reckon I jes' faints or goes to sleep. Sho' am tired."

Mark was at the breakfast table when Fitz came down next morning. A brief glance at Fitz's stern expression made him realize he was in trouble.

"Whut you mad at this mawnin'?" Mark asked casually.

"Mad at you."

Mark drank coffee, set the cup down. "Now whut I done?"

"Nuthin'! Thass whut you done. Nothin' at all. Not a damn thing, but me an' Clarissa near got burned out 'long with the mansion." Fitz told him briefly what had happened, then said, "Tell you to come runnin' if there's shootin'. They was shootin'. Whar you been?"

"Sweahs I didn' hear no shootin'. Was listenin'. . . ."

"Was pleasurin' yourse'f, thass whut you was doin'. Man layin' on top o' a wench don' hear nothin'. Not even cannon fire. So Toby was whar you was s'posed to be. You pays him that reward outen your own pocket. Wants no argument 'bout that. He doin' your wuk an' you pays him."

"Ain't goin' to pleasure Domingo no mo'."

"Hah! Hears that befo'."

"Means it. Last night was the last time. Domingo tells me she ain't comin' to my baid no mo' 'lessen I makes her."

"What's come over that gal? She lookin' fo' you to pleasure her fo' a long time."

"She gettin' married."

"Domingo gettin' married?"

"Meets a young buck. One o' the new men we hires last week. Domingo sho' 'nuff in love."

"Whut you goin' to do now?"

"Don' know, Gran'pa. Been thinkin' lately, all these heah wenches now free. Cain't bring 'em to baid no mo'. Gots to stop. They ain't wenches no mo'. They ladies now. Thass whut Domingo tells me."

"But she came to your baid, didn' she?"

"She say she a lady beginnin' this mawnin'.'"

"We gives her a good weddin' present, Mark. She been a mighty good gal. Jes' like poor Calla. Thinks o' her last night an' mayhap I would o' hung Bibb by the neck an' not the feet."

"He hangin' all night, he sho' daid," Mark said.

"Don' think so. Knows we drives two o' his men off, but they didn' go too far. Reckon they came back to see whut happened. Or they heard Bibb yellin' he haid off."

"He sho' goin' to try again. You makes a bad mistake."

"Bibb so goddamn skeered last night, wets his pants when I hangs him upside down. Ain't goin' to get over whut happened fo' a long time an' won't be long we lives in Wyndward. He comes then, he gets shot, an' reckon he knows it."

"Goin' to be ready that soon?" Mark asked.

"Mayhap a few mo' days."

Mark heard the rumble of wagons and arose to look out the window. "Wagons comin' down the road toward the plantation. They's loaded with all kinds o' furniture."

"Told you we moves in soon. Bettah wake up Clarissa so she kin tell 'em whar to put things." Fitz raised his voice. "Elegant, come heah."

She appeared in the doorway. "Wants me, suh? Makin' biscuits so don' asks me to do nuthin'.'"

"You kin go upstairs an' wake up Clarissa. Furniture passin' by right now."

"Clarissa been at the big house fo' two or three hours by now, suh. Wakes up real early an' goes off."

"Gettin' so nobody waits fo' orders from me," Fitz complained mildly.

"Gettin' so nobody kin afford to wait fo' you any mo', Gran'pa. You slowin' down," Mark observed.

"Wants me to prove I ain't? Like I did befo'?"

"Had 'nuff o' that. Takes it back."

"Glad o' that. Loves you too much to push your face in agin. Goin' down to the mansion. Comin'?"

"Sees hosses grazin' out front. Be ready in a minute."

They rode down. The mansion seemed to be gleaming in the sunlight, inviting them to come. Even Mark was affected by the sight of it.

"Real pretty, Gran'pa. Don' 'members too much 'bout it, but sho' ain't many houses any bigger o' nicer. Wants to make sho' my room like I wants it to be."

"Like Clarissa wants it to be. You argues with her 'bout that an' you goin' to jaw fo' a week an' she don' change her mind. Mighty glad to have her doin' this. Was up to me, I wouldn' know whar to put anythin'."

"House needs a woman. Not Clarissa. She fine, but needs a woman to share it with. Like it ought to be shared."

"Then do somethin' 'bout it, son."

"Kind o' aimin' to. But kind o' skeered too. On'y gals I know were whores. Don' know how to find me a good gal. One I want to marry."

"When you sees her, you knows, an' you won't be bashful any mo'."

"Sho' 'nuff?"

"Lays eyes on Benay an' knows I loves her. She runs from me an' I gets mad. But I follows her 'til she knows I loves her. Same way with Sally. Sees her an' one minute later knows I loves her."

"Keep you eyes open, Gran'pa. Mayhap you falls in love again."

"No. Thass all over fo' me. When Sally runs off,

knows there's nobody kin compare with her. Nevah looks again. Up to you now. You the one gots the juice."

They reached the mansion, dismounted, and made their way to the front door, which was wide open for the men carrying furniture inside. Clarissa came rushing out.

"You stays away, heah me? This ain't your house 'til I get it all ready. Tries to come in now, you gots to walk over me first."

"When we comes back?" Fitz asked.

"Mayhap two mo' days. Not befo'."

"Comes at night an' stays outside like befo'," Fitz said. "Cain't take no chances Bibb comes back."

"You knows he daid or alive?" Clarissa asked.

"Come to think of it, don' know. Mark, we rides to whar I left the sonabitch upside down."

They found only the rope, still hanging over the branch.

11

Fitz and Mark rode from the now almost empty Fisbee place to Wyndward, driving the carriage over the dirt road instead of riding across rough country. Clarissa insisted they approach from the formal route so they might see Wyndward, risen from the ashes, in all its newfound glory.

They got out of the carriage and stood mute, regarding the edifice with solemn wonder. They'd seen it many times, at close and distant range, but somehow this time a majestic beauty was added to its grandeur. The mansion lay somewhat less than half a mile from the dirt road and had been reached by a fieldstone-paved road, which had all but vanished under the lush growth of weeds and grass. The latter had been cleared and the paved road swept clean and scrubbed until it glistened with cleanliness.

The mansion itself looked as though it had never vanished in fire and smoke. The architect had obeyed orders and duplicated this new structure from the blueprints of the old. The building was square, lacking ornamentation yet noble in appearance. There were eight chimneys, five of which had been part of the original house. The columned veranda ran across the entire front, then curved around each end. Even the cushioned wicker chairs decorating the veranda were identical to the ones that Fitz's father and mother had used in the evenings while Jonathan Turner sipped his bourbon and water.

There were twelve hundred acres, almost half of which was in production or being made ready. The other half was woods and permanent pasture, which would no longer be needed. Nor would the old fenced-in race track, where thoroughbreds had been trained and timed. Fitz had no intention of breeding horses any more than he had of breeding slaves.

Standing on the veranda steps was Clarissa, wearing her only good evening gown, a rather brilliant red and trimmed with a great deal of lace. To Fitz and Mark, she looked beautiful.

Elegant was beside her, in her black uniform and white apron. Domingo was also there, along with Calcutta Two, grinning broadly, and Chickory. Clarissa had dressed them up for the occasion, and they were fidgeting excitedly. Below the veranda, Hong Kong and Seawitch stood proudly by. Fitz sighed in recognition of their advanced age. Toby Morgan had also elected to come. But the main reception was that of the approximately seventy blacks lined up in formation.

"Now ain't that somethin'," Mark said softly. "Yes, suh, really somethin'."

"Kinda like the way it used to be." Fitz had relaxed the reins and his horse was barely moving. "If I close my eyes, I kin almost see papa an' mama, Jonathan, Daisy, Benay . . . all of them gone. . . ."

"Time to keep your eyes open," Mark said with understanding kindness. "This heah is whar we start again."

"You're right 'bout that. I am proud o' this planta-tion, Mark. Couldn' be prouder."

Fitz brought the carriage to a stop. From his seat, he spoke in a loud voice. "We thanks you, my gran'son an' me, fo' comin' an' welcomin' us like this. Sho' am proud this day. No mo' wuk today, an' you get a day's pay anyway. Sees to it plenty o' food an' a keg o' whiskey sent down so everbody celebrates. 'Nother thing. Later all o' you men an' your women an' childrun, all kin come an' see the inside o' the house, as my guests."

There were cheers, whether for the invitation or the promise of whiskey, Fitz couldn't be sure, but he liked the gesture anyway.

Mark said, "Wait'll folks hereabouts hears you takin' niggers in to see the house. They ain't goin' to like that nohow."

"Hell with 'em," Fitz said joyfully. "I'm so goddamn happy today, nuthin' kin make me worry."

Fitz shook hands with Hong Kong, kissed Seawitch on the cheek, and gripped Toby's hand warmly. He grinned at Calcutta Two and patted him on the shoulder. He scooped up Chickory, tossed him in the air, and set him down while the boy squealed in delight. He enveloped Elegant, as best he could encompass her bulk, and danced her about for a few steps. Then he embraced Clarissa and placed a warm, affectionate kiss squarely on her lips.

"You done fine," he said. "Looks like Wyndward was always heah. It jes' like befo'. Nobody could o' done this 'cept you."

Clarissa blushed under all the compliments. When Mark embraced her, she gave him a sample of what she had to offer in a way that left Mark somewhat breathless and Fitz laughing aloud.

"Now," Clarissa said, "you make sho' your feet are clean. Brand new carpet, brand new everythin'. Don't wants no smudgin' o' furniture, an' you walks light."

Fitz entered the reception hall and stared in amazement, for not one thing seemed to have been disturbed from the old mansion. Even the wallpaper along the curved staircase to the second floor was exactly the same. Clarissa must have gone to great lengths to find it, for the original mansion had been built and the paper applied many years before.

Fitz and Mark went from room to room, admiring everything and exclaiming over it. There were large chandeliers in the reception hall, more, along with sconces, on the walls of the spacious ballroom. The fireplace was as huge as ever, the large mantel of ebony was in stark contrast with the other lighter-hued furnishings. In the dining room, the very long table could seat thirty in a pinch. The chairs, table, and sideboards were all of dark mahogany. Heavy draperies framed the downstairs windows. The walls of the library, used as an office, were lined with bookcases, most of them filled. The desk and tall-backed chair had been transported from the Fisbee place.

Elegant insisted they inspect the kitchen which was larger than the old one and equipped with a gigantic range and boiler, its black surfaces shining as brilliantly as Elegant's black skin.

Upstairs, the bedrooms were tastefully furnished. Mark's two rooms had oak furniture, Fitz's walnut. Clarissa had chosen fragile period pieces for herself. She wasn't quite certain what period it was though, for the salesman had spoken some French words which she had him write down. But she had wanted that furniture, even if she couldn't pronounce the names of some of the pieces.

She opened the door to a parlor and bedroom suite done completely in pale pink taffeta. It was beautiful. Both Fitz and Mark, neither of whom were as appreciative of the furnishings as a woman might be, exclaimed over it, further delighting Clarissa.

"This heah a guest room," Clarissa explained. "Got mo' guest rooms but this kind o' special. Fo' Sally, she evah comes back. She nevah does, then fo' the gal Mark goin' to find someday. Now, whut you got to say 'bout this, Fitz?"

"One thing," he said. "Makes sho' you knows whut's my bedroom an' whut's Mark's."

Then he hugged her and led her downstairs where Calcutta Two waited with a tray, rather well floating in whiskey, with three glasses not quite filled. Chickory took a glass from the tray and wiped the wetness from it before handing it to Fitz. The same was done to the two remaining glasses.

Fitz raised his glass. "To Wyndward. Jes' like it used to be, soon's I kicks Calcutta Two's ass he sloths bringin' mo' drinks."

They settled down at the supper table later and were served one of Elegant's best meals of chicken, ham, and beef along with a collection of vegetables, biscuits, and breads.

"Gots everythin' fancy fo' the ball," Clarissa said. "Elegant gots ten young wenches from the fam'lies in the cabins, an' they goin' to wait on folks. Got music—five pieces from Richmond, but they cain't come in evenin' dress 'cause they ain't got any. All invites sent out an' think o' this, Fitz, not one returned. Ev'rybody's comin'."

"No wonder," Mark said. "This the first social event since the war."

"Been some mighty nice balls heah in the old days," Clarissa said. "Come to most, an' thinks I got my ass kicked out on'y once."

" 'Members that last ball we had hear befo' the war," Fitz recalled. "Had one 'fore that, an' ev'rybody came along with some gals waitin' to baid down with anybody. Includin' Clarissa, an' she sho' had her pick. All the women folks gets mad at all the wenchin' an' drinkin' an' hell-raisin'. Thinks I got to apologize fo' that so I has another ball an' invites them all back. Funny thing—not one woman comes, but not one o' the men failed to come."

"I sho' had my pick that night," Clarissa mused. "Some o' the men brought good-lookin' whores. Reckon this heah old house nevah saw anythin' like that befo'. Whut went on that night got talked 'bout fo' weeks."

"It was jes' befo' the war," Fitz said with an air of apology. "Ev'rybody kinda excited an' randy."

Shortly before dark, Calcutta Two and Chickory lit the candles in the chandeliers and the sconces. At dusk the mansion gleamed with light, and the field hands arrived to inspect the house. They were carefully dressed, the women in calico with bonnets, their faces scrubbed. The children, polished like apples, were on their very best behavior. Domingo had the task of escorting them through every room, a chore she was plainly proud of.

Clarissa said, "You tells me, Fitz, I kin spend all the money I wants, an' you says you wants ev'rybody on this heah plantation to be happy an' satisfied. So I bought presents fo' all the folks heah tonight. Gots lacy scarves fo' the women to wear on they haids. Got jack-in-the-boxes fo' the childrun, an' a little bottle o' whiskey fo' the men."

"Whar yo' finds all this?" Mark asked. "Last I knows ain't much fo' sale in Lynchburg o' even Richmond."

"Some o' the storekeepers hid lots o' things away. Brings 'em out now fo' anybody with plenty o' money. Fitz got plenty o' money, so I buys whut I wants."

"Goin' to be hell to pay, folks hears 'bout this," Mark said. "Way you treats the niggers."

"Don't give a damn whut they thinks. Got me a big plantation heah an' runs it like I wants. Way I sees it, we got good men an' they fam'lies heah. They get treated like reg'lar folks. That makes 'em happy, an' they wants to stay. Means they nevah run, they wuk hard so they kin stay, an' we turnin' out mo' an' bettah 'bacco than evah. It ain't I'm bein' go goddamn kind to the niggers. I'm lookin' out fo' a business, an' by damn I know how to run it."

"Hears most plantations got their slaves back," Clarissa said. "Some runs, but most stays an' nuthin' changed. They wuks 'em jes' like befo'. Pays 'em board, an' a cabin ain't worth a damn, but no money. Reckon the planters cain't get over the end o' the war an' neither kin the slaves."

"They wakes up one o' these days," Fitz said. "Ones we got wukkin' hahd, they's woke up already. Now if you all stops jawin', an' hands me some o' that puddin', I kin finish my suppah."

That night Fitz slept better than he had in months. He rejected the temporary feeling of loneliness because it could not help him in any way, and besides, he told himself, he was not lonely. By afternoon, neighbors, city folk, everyone on the invitation list would begin to arrive. It was going to be a good day. No man could go through such a day and feel lonely. Still, when he awakened very early, he dressed quietly, drew on a sweater, went downstairs, and let himself out of the house. It was one of those late summer mornings when everything seemed aglow with life. It was very quiet. The blacks had not yet risen from their beds. In the old days, they'd have been in the fields by now, for dawn had already broken. Fitz walked slowly along, knowing his destination was the cemetery.

He stood facing the graves, well back, as if he wanted to be sure he was heard by everyone. He raised his arms, spread them wide.

"We's back," he said. "Me an' Mark, an' Clarissa. Seawitch, Hong Kong, Elegant, some new folks. Early crop came in fine, we's goin' to make some money this yeah an' ten times as much next. Raises the mansion so it looks jes' like befo', an' Clarissa fixes it up so you cain't tell the diff'rence from when you-all lived in it. That's the way I wants it, so I kin 'member all o' you best. Wishes you were really heah, but that cain't be. Tells you later how things goin' 'long. Jes' thinks I'd come by."

He wandered over to the race track. The fence had been removed, but the oval was still plainly visible. Fitz had loved raising thoroughbreds, but such a luxury was not for the day and age he lived in now. Cash crops, food as well as tobacco, were what the South needed most. Fitz had never dreamed of not doing his part to improve and finally bring back the days when life had been easier. He knew those days would never return as they'd once been. But if some of the old life could come back, it would be an advantage.

The plantation was beginning to stir now. A young black, who was in charge of the stables, was already caring for the animals. He greeted Fitz with a broad smile and made not the slightest attempt to remove his cap or bow his head. The young ones were learning faster than their elders. Fitz talked to him for a few minutes and took a little more time to inspect the stables. He found them neater than he had ever seen them. It seemed this was the answer to treating his help like human beings: they were more than eager to repay him.

Back at the mansion, things were already well on the

move. Under Elegant's direction, the cooking had started. Clarissa, in a voluminous apron borrowed from Elegant, was directing girls to decorate the walls, arrange the flowers just delivered, set the table in the dining room, and generally prepare for the influx of visitors bound to begin in the middle of the afternoon.

Fitz circled the house, entered the kitchen by the back door, and found Mark there, eating off the kitchen counter.

"Sho' don' wants to get mixed up in all that fuss goin' on," he said.

"Thinks the same way. How you this mawnin', son?"

"Feelin' mighty good. An' goin' to feel mighty proud when the folks comes an' looks at whut we done to the plantation."

"Takes an early walk." Fitz poured coffee and buttered one of Elegant's freshly baked biscuits.

"You tells 'em we's back?"

"Tells who?" Fitz was still embarrassed by his visits to the graveyard.

"All o' them buried down theah. They sho'ly got to know."

Fitz nodded. "Tells 'em. Makes me feel good."

"Reckon," Mark said.

"You makin' fun o' me fo' talkin' to 'em?"

"Not this time, Gran'pa. No, suh, not this time."

"You keeps your haid on your shoulders then. Got no reason to knock it off. Kind o' skeered 'bout this aftahnoon an' tonight. I nevah was whut you could call popular with all the folks. Lots came 'cause Benay asks 'em. They says they comes, but mayhap they don'."

"Ev'ry last one o' them will be heah," Mark vowed. "Likes you or not, they comes."

"Hopes you're right, Mark."

By noon Clarissa was at the height of whut Fitz called fussing, but she managed to issue orders that he and Mark must get dressed to receive the first of the visitors.

Neither had much in the way of clothing, but then nobody would. They wore well-polished boots, ordinary trousers, and shirts with string ties, and black coats. They met in the corridor outside their suites.

"Sho' looks pretty, Gran'pa," Mark said. "Back in N'Orleans, in the old days 'fore the war, you could stand on the corner, hold out you hands, an' gets a few picayunes fo' eatin' money."

"You looks the same. Sho' ain't much fo' the lawd o' this heah manor, an' his randy gran'son."

The guests began arriving far too early. The first were Cass Sedley and his wife, probably because they lived the shortest distance from Wyndward. Their arrival sent Clarissa rushing to her room to dress.

"I be damned," Cass said as he stood in the ballroom and looked around. "Nevah thinks this could be done, Fitz. Ain't nothin' changed."

" 'Cept it all new," his wife added. "Cass, when you goin' to give me a house like this?"

"Knows I shouldn' o' come," Cass said in a dismal voice. "Gets sass from now on 'cause we gots nuthin' like this."

"Whut you gots pretty damn good," Fitz said.

"Suits us tolerable, Fitz," Mrs. Sedley said. "We didn' get burned out bad as you. Looks 'round heah an' thinks I sees Benay comin' to meet me, all dressed up real fine. An' Daisy, laughin' all the time. Reckon the house ain't changed much 'cept fo' that."

"You talks too much," her husband said. "Whar's the drinks? So I kin get started 'fore all the rest o' them comes."

The musicians arrived and quickly set up their instruments. Then the real influx began. Folks came in carriages, phaetons, landaus, in buggies, and some even in old country wagons. They came on horseback. Whatever means of transportation made no difference so long as it got them there.

Clarissa was on hand now, in complete command as mistress. She greeted the guests with a polish she had learned as a child on her father's plantation and thought she'd forgotten. Fitz and Mark discreetly left her side from time to time to visit with the men now actively engaged in consuming quantities of bourbon and spring water, served by Calcutta Two, who had never moved so fast. He'd not even had time to drink the spilled liquor, which was probably for the best. Chickory helped wherever his services were needed and surpassed Fitz's hopes for a good houseboy. Elegant, sweating profusely, shouted instructions to the girls helping her, and when inquisitive guests impeded the duties of the help, she ordered the curious from her kitchen.

It began to seem more and more like old times. Fitz gloried in it. Mark mixed well with the men and became popular with the women when the dancing began.

Toby, assigned to help ladies out of the carriages, gave the first alarm. Though Toby was a newcomer, he already knew that a Rebel colonel was among the folks Fitz held in contempt. Toby ran into the house, found Fitz, and spoke quietly to him.

"Reb colonel comes in uniform," he reported. "Reckon he the sonabitch you don' like, suh."

Fitz sighed and went to the door to greet Colonel Apperson. He was glad that Clarissa was with the ladies. Apperson was quite resplendent in his gray uniform with the yellow sash, sword at his side. The same sword that had maliciously cut down Calcutta One just to show authority and his hatred of Fitz. Fitz had never forgotten that. Nor would he.

"Fitz!" Apperson extended his hand. "Sho' am glad to see you."

"Whut in hell you doin' heah? Made sho' you didn' get no invitation."

"Figgered you fo'got, suh. Come o' my own accord. Represents the Confederate States of America, suh. Wears its uniform proudly."

"You kin take it off. War is over, or didn' you know that?"

"Nevah over fo' me, Fitz."

"You bettah go see Jeff Davis an' Gen'ral Lee 'bout that. Fo' now, cain't forbid you to my house 'cause it a happy day fo' me. You kin come in."

"I thanks you, suh."

147

Apperson strode into the ballroom, cleared his throat loudly, and began saluting the men, bowing to the ladies, and making his presence known.

"Who left the door open?" Mark asked.

"Cain't do nothin' but asks him in. He say one thing to Clarissa, an' I sweahs I kicks him out. Uniform o' not."

"Sho' makin' folks see the uniform," Mark said with a laugh. "Struttin' like he a gen'ral an' the war still on."

"Says it ain't over," Fitz remarked. "Kind o' means it too. Don't like that, Mark. Too many goin' to say the same thing, an' don't needs a sonabitch like Apperson to lead the way."

"Say the word an' I throws him out politely, Gran'pa."

"Let's see whut he does an' listen to whut he say. Kind o' likes to know how some folks thinkin' this long after the war. Jes' keep an eye on him."

Fitz hurried to the dining room where Clarissa was helping put the table in perfect order. Meals were going to be served at three seatings, thirty at a time.

"Gets outen my way," she told Fitz. "Ain't got no time. . . ."

"You favorite papa-in-law heah."

Clarissa almost dropped the platter she was setting down. "He crazy. Fitz, get rid o' him."

"Cain't 'thout makin' a big fuss, an' this ain't no place fo' it. But if he finds you an' he says one word you don' like, you kin bust him one an' whut you leaves o' him, Mark an' me will finish."

"Long as you puts it that way. But keep him 'way if you kin. Fitz, I hates him so much I'm shakin' inside jes' 'cause he in the same house with me."

"Don't show it, Clarissa. You lookin' real beautiful tonight."

"In this heah ol' rag?" she flounced the skirt in disgust. "Been wukkin' mighty hard fo' this heah party. Asks you when the new clothes comes from Paris, you lets me buy a new gown."

"When the clothes comes," Fitz said, "you gettin'

148

anythin' an' ev'rythin' your heart craves. Means it. Not one dress, ten, an' ev'ry damn thing goes with 'em."

Fitz returned to the drawing room. He went directly to Betty Lou Eldon, who was from a plantation a mile to the north. She was young and pretty and she danced well. But halfway through the number, Fitz was tapped and Mark moved smoothly into Betty Lou's arms, shouldering Fitz aside.

Fitz scowled and then chuckled. Betty Lou was more Mark's age, and it was high time the boy got acclimated to women of this class and forget the assortment of whores he had grown up with.

Colonel Apperson had corraled half a dozen men to whom he was explaining the military situation that still existed. "Long as we Rebs kin breathe—we real Rebs— we don' surrender to the goddamn Yankees. Way I sees it, the North still bloody from whut we done to 'em an' gettin' weaker all the time. Reckon our slaves runs theah now an' gives them mo' trouble'n they kin handle. An' when the right time comes, we starts the war again. . . ."

"Colonel," one man said, "you sho'ly outen you mind. We's licked fair an' square, an' if we wasn't, makes no diff'rence. Nobody wants any war to start again."

"You a real colonel?" another man queried.

"You sees my uniform, suh."

"You fightin' in the war, suh?"

"We all fights, suh, an' we ain't done yet."

"Cuh'nel, best I kin say is you a mighty lucky man the cannonball that hit your haid didn' take it off."

Apperson's small audience dispersed leaving him red-faced and seething with anger.

Fitz walked up to him casually. "Reckon it's 'bout time fo' you to go, suh. No colonel in uniform kin stay up late. Bad 'zample fo' his men."

"Ain't leavin' till I damn well feels like it. Ain't nobody kin throw a colonel of the Confederate States of America outen a soiree like this. Whar's Clarissa?"

"She say to you she daid."

"Goin' to speak to a lawyuh 'bout this. Clarissa my kin an' wants her back. Ain't right she livin' heah an' pleasurin' herse'f with you, who ain't no kin."

"Happens I am. Happens I don' like whut you says. Now you takes hold o' that sword yo' wears—the sword you kills a good man with—or I pulls it outen that fancy scabbard an' makes you swallow it. In two minutes don' wants to see you again."

Fitz turned and walked away swiftly before his temper exploded. Apperson raised a hand as if to stop him but let it drop. He looked around, wondering how many had heard Fitz's thunder. He considered the situation for a moment and came to the conclusion that he would hardly enjoy his sword rammed down his throat.

Then he drew himself up, adopted his military bearing, and walked across the room, nodding affably to people who didn't even look his way. He reached the door, turned and looked back to find Clarissa, saw no trace of her, and began crossing the veranda. He came to a dead stop.

A buggy had pulled up. There were two people in it. A man in uniform and a woman. The man got down from the buggy. Colonel Apperson gasped in astonishment. He went back into the house, to the entrance of the ballroom and began to shout. "Look heah whut's comin' to visit. Look heah, all you fine people, an' see whut I means."

Fitz, hearing the commotion, came forward. By this time Captain Elias Morton, in full Yankee uniform, was coming into the ballroom. The music stopped, the dancing ceased, there was a low murmur that rose and spread all through the house. People at the table in the dining room arose promptly and entered the drawing room. Fitz steeled himself. He walked straight up to Captain Morton.

"Welcome, suh. I'm glad to see you again, suh. Welcome to my home an' to my soiree."

"Heahs whut he says?" Apperson shouted. "Heahs whut he says to this heah . . . this heah . . . this Yankee. We Southerners, an' we don' has to take this from anybody. 'Members this heah sonabitch givin' this soiree tried fo' treason when the war starts? Looks like they sho' made a mistake they lets him go."

Captain Morton looked about in astonishment. The

150

guests were already leaving. Fitz stood by the captain's side, watching them go. Apperson, with a smile of triumph, seemed to be directing the entire exodus.

"Captain, suh," Fitz said. "You wins the war, but you don' wins these bull-headed Southerners. Look at 'em, runnin' off like you brings a big disease heah. Now you knows whut you up against, suh."

"Mister Turner, I didn't know you were having this soiree. I had no intention of interfering. I am here because I heard your house was open and I wished to show my companion, a young lady who waits in the buggy, unharmed I hope, what a real Southern mansion looks like. I'm very sorry. I'll leave now. . . ."

"This heah party goin' on, suh, an' you stays you wants to Got 'nuff food fo' a hundred an' 'nuff whuskey to keep drinkin' fo' a month. Which is likely whut I'll do."

The musicians were packing. Fitz said, " 'Scuse me, Captain. Be right back."

He crossed the drawing room with long strides and faced the five musicians, addressing the leader who played fiddle.

"Whut in hell you think you doin'? Pays you fo' a full night playin'."

"Cain't play fo' you, Mistah Turner, suh. Cain't play fo' no Yankee lover. . . ."

Fitz reached out, snatched the violin from the man's grasp, and drew it back. "Always wonders whut in hell inside this heah squeak boxes. . . ."

'Mistah Turner, suh. No, please! Don' bust it. Please, Mistah Turner, suh. We plays. We plays long as you wants. Please, Mistah Turner, suh."

Fitz tossed the fiddle and the musician caught it with a great sigh of relief. Before Fitz returned to the captain's side, music was playing.

"I'm sorry, Captain," Fitz said. "You tell me you got a lady waitin' in your buggy? Want her to see my house, suh. Be my real pleasure, suh." He turned to Mark who had come striding back from outside. "This heah my gran'son Mark Turner, Captain. Mark, this heah a friend o' mine name of Elias Morton. He a Yankee, case you thinks he wears his uniform like Apperson, to show off."

Mark hesitated only a second before he thrust out his hand. "Cap'n Morton, suh, my pleasure."

"Thank you," Morton said.

"Mark, they's a lady waitin' in the cap'n's buggy. You fetches her. Wants to see the house."

"My pleasure," Mark said again.

"You may address her as Adalia Morton," the captain said.

Mark nodded and hurried out of the house. Clarissa stood alone at the dining room door, not sure if she wanted to laugh or cry. She finally came forward slowly to be introduced—to the one remaining guest.

Outside, Mark approached the buggy. Most of the guests had driven off by now, though a few vehicles were still turning into the driveway.

Mark raised a hand to help the passenger down. And as she accepted his hand and stepped down, Mark looked into a pair of merry blue eyes belonging to the most beautiful girl his eyes had ever beheld.

12

"Clarissa," Fitz summoned her to join them, "wants you to meet Cap'n Elias Morton."

"Whut the hell happened?" she asked, looking around the almost empty room.

"Your big, important papa-in-law say he don' stand fo' no Yankee soldier in the same room, an' looks like all the others kinda agreed with him. Cap'n, this heah is Clarissa Apperson, sort o' a cousin o' mine."

Clarissa curtsied and accepted the captain's hand automatically, her puzzlement changing to open indignation.

"You means they all runs 'cause a Yankee soldier comes heah? Whut in hell the matter with 'em? Whut's one Yankee soldier goin' to do? Shoot 'em all?"

"Missus Apperson, Mister Turner," the captain's tone was apologetic. "I'm highly embarrassed by this. I should have driven away when I saw this party in progress. But it never occurred to me that my appearance or the uniform I'm wearing would create such hostility."

"Cap'n, you is welcome heah," Clarissa said. "On'y

thing, gots 'nuff food fo' a hundred, got this heah big dance floor. gots the music playin'. Fitz, how come they stays to play fo' us?"

"Kind o' persuaded 'em," Fitz said. "Tell you whut, Clarissa. We has the soiree anyways, in honor o' our guest from the North. Mayhap he a soldier an' mayhap he whips the bejesus outen us, but tonight he our guest, an' we treats him an' his lady.. . . . Oh my. You evah seen a gal pretty as that, Clarissa?"

Mark, with the girl on his arm, seemed slightly dazed.

"Sho' is pretty," Clarissa agreed. "Whut's the matter with Mark? Look like he drunk."

Mark led the girl up to them. 'Wants to present my gran-pa an' Clarissa Apperson, a cousin o' my gran'pa's dead wife. Gran'pa, Clarissa, this heah Missus Adalia Morton."

The girl emitted a silvery laugh. "Miss Adalia Morton, Mister Turner. Elias is my brother."

Mark said nothing. He seemed incapable of speech.

Fitz bowed over Adalia's hand. "Goin' to say it right now, Miss Adalia. Been a long time I sees a gal pretty as you."

She was fairly tall for a girl, almost Mark's height. She wore white with a blue sash around her tiny waist. She stood straight. her head tilted at a proud angle. Her blue eyes were clear, inquisitive, and lively. Her hair, visible beneath her tiny bonnet, had the sheen of spun gold. Possibly a shade darker than Mark's. Standing together. they made a striking couple.

Clarissa said, "Dinner gettin' cold, you wants to eat. Kind o' hungry myse'f."

"Tell you, Cap'n," Fitz said, "we gots the best cook in Virginny. an' somebody don' eat her food she goin' to feel mighty bad an' mayhap bust up the kitchen."

Captain Morton smiled gratefully. "Why, I'd not want that to happen, Mister Turner. And I am hungry."

"Whut about you, Mark?" Clarissa asked. She waited a moment. "Mark, whut's the mattah with you? Asks a question."

Mark wasn't even aware Clarissa had spoken. His eyes hadn't shifted from Adalia's face. He was completely mesmerized.

"Mark," Clarissa raised her voice. "Please escort this heah young lady into the dinin' room. We's goin' to eat."

"Oh! Oh yes, o' course," Mark said hastily, extending his arm. "Miss Morton, ma'am, may I have the honor?"

She rested her slim hand on his arm and gave him a warm smile. Color flamed his face, and he felt a wave of dizziness come over him, but he managed to lead her into the dining room. The table was fully set. The prismed chandelier glistened with candlelight as did the sconces on the mirrored walls and the candlestick holders on the table. The room seemed bright.

The table, covered with a fine linen cloth and set with crystal, china, and gleaming sterling, was an invitation in itself. But the savory smells from the covered dishes on the sideboard were even more enticing.

"Wants you to eat hearty," Fitz said. " 'Cause we got food fo' a hundred."

"You told them that," Mark said, now more in command of himself.

"How'd you know? You wasn't listenin' to anythin'. Mark, you got no manners at all? Seat the lady."

Mark pulled out the chair so hastily, he almost fell backward. Adalia pretended not to notice and gave him a grateful smile as she sat down. The scent of her perfume reached him, and he felt his senses soar again. He'd never known such a sensation before except when he'd drunk too much bourbon.

"Thank you, Mark," she said as he seated himself beside her. "Your home is beautiful, so bright and cheerful ... and so big! In New England our houses are smaller mostly. Also, we favor dark furniture. I don't mean I do." She amended her statement quickly. "I'm impressed with the colorful touches you have here."

"Thank you, ma'am," Mark said, loving the sound of her voice and her precise way of speaking, yet not very aware of what she was saying. It didn't matter. Nothing mattered except that she was close to him, sitting beside him, smiling at him as she spoke.

Clarissa said, "Calls you Adalia. Later shows you upstairs. Got one suite o' rooms I mighty proud of. Pink. All pink."

"It sounds beautiful, Clarissa."

"You ain't mad 'cause ev'rybody walks out on account o' you bein' a Yankee?" Clarissa asked in her typically blunt way.

"No. I can understand their pain and the loss they endured. They've not been able to accept it yet."

"Adalia, kind o' likes you fo' a Yankee."

"Thank you, Clarissa. I'm glad someone does."

"Who don't like you?" Mark suddenly came to life. "Any sona.... You tells me anybody insults you an' I sho' goin' to...."

"Mark, shut up an' eat," Fitz implored. "You actin' like a fool. Miss Adalia think you're an idiot."

Clarissa gave the order for the serving to begin, and eight uniformed maids began serving five people. Presently, Elegant waddled into the room. She surveyed the long table with only five occupants. The grim line of her mouth and her eyes conveyed her disapproval. Her glance shifted to Fitz.

"Heahs all them Sorthern ladies an' gen'mun bastahds leaves. Cain't believe it. Whut we goin' to do with all this heah food?"

"You eat it," Fitz said. "Ain't much mo' than an appetizer fo' you, Elegant. Wants you to meet our guests. Cap'n Morton an' his sister Adalia. They our hundred guests."

"Glad somebody heah to eat all this. Ah is Elegant, Cap'n. Been a slave on this heah plantation mos' o' my life. Nevah goin' to leave. You comes heah with you army an' ah won't go. Whoeee ... this heah sho' a pretty gal. 'Minds me o' Mist'iss Benay, massa, an' Miz Daisy."

"Elegant kind o' special 'round heah," Fitz explained. "Been part o' our fam'ly fo' many yeahs like she say. She kin sass you back bettah than anyone I evah met, an' you steps on her toes, she whumps you good."

"Now you see heah, Massa Fitz, suh. Don' whump

nobody 'less they got it comin'. Like I said befo', whut we do with all this heah food?"

"Pack it up an' give it to the help."

"Whut's left yo' gets we gots our eatin' done," Clarissa added.

"Sho' goin' to be slothin' tomorrow," Elegant said. "Them niggers eats so much they cain't stan' up by mo'nin', suh."

"Hong Kong will take care of it," Fitz said. "Thank yo' fo' a fine meal, which we goin' to eat soon's you stops jawin'."

Elegant gave a hearty laugh and waddled out. For a few minutes everyone concentrated on the food, helping themselves from the trays offered by the maids. There were six courses. It became necessary to rest after the first four.

"Aimin' to stay in Lynchburg with your brother?" Fitz asked Adalia.

"I don't now, Mister Turner. I came down here because I wanted to teach school. I am a teacher. But when I applied for a job, I was told every position was filled even though I knew there were many openings."

"You kin blame it on our famous Southern hospitality," Clarissa said acidly.

"We've about given up," Captain Morton confessed. "I could force them to place her in a teaching position, if I wanted to exert authority, but Adalia doesn't want that and neither do I. Though I will confess I get damn mad about it."

"I only wanted to do what I could to . . . to bring everybody together again," Adalia said. "There are openings in the North available to me, but Elias suggested I come down here. The idea appealed to me."

"I wanted her with me," the captain explained. "Our parents are dead, and she'd be quite alone up North."

"I hate the idea of going back without my brother," Adalia said softly. "But I'll not stay here and do nothing."

"You objects to teachin' niggers, ma'am?" Fitz asked.

"No." She replied without hesitation. "I never

157

thought of it, but now that I have, I'd gladly teach them."

"This heah," Fitz said, "a mighty big plantation. Used to have mo' than a thousan' slaves. We raises tobacco, an' got me near two hundred niggers wukkin' heah now. Pays 'em well, an' they gives me a good day's wuk. Told 'em jes' the other day, goin' to build a schoolhouse. Kin have it ready in mayhap two, three weeks. Jes' fo' nigger children on the plantation."

"Won't be easy," Clarissa warned. "You thinks you gets snubbed now, wait'll they heahs you teachin' nigguhs."

"You see," Fitz explained, "before the war any white person who taught a black how to read and write was heavily fined. The black who studied was whipped soundly and sometimes even hung. We could not afford to allow any black to be educated because that would give them ideas, and ideas were one thing that could make a slave dangerous."

"Pardon me, Mister Turner," Adalia said, "but for a moment there you sounded more Yankee than Southern."

Fitz threw back his head and laughed. "I didn't even realize how I was talking. Comes from speaking with Northerners. I don't often get to speak that way, and I enjoy it. Now I'll have to explain how all this came about. My mother was a strict New Englander. I was born there and attended Northern schools, including Harvard. My father was a real Southerner, however."

"I'll be damned," Captain Morton said. "Do you think your being from the North is the reason why everyone walked out when we arrived?"

"No. They left because there was a Yankee uniform in the house. Most folks here don't remember that I'm part Yankee. I was even arrested for making treasonable statements when the war broke out. We squelched that very promptly and efficiently. Someday I'll tell you how it came about. Right now, I'm talking too much."

"Mark sho' ain't," Clarissa said. "Mark, you heah?"

"Go to hell," Mark said promptly. Then he grew

beet red. "Miss Morton, ma'am, I apologizes fo' sayin' that."

"Fitz," Clarissa said, "whut's come over the boy?"

"If I say it, he's goin' to throw somethin' at me." Fitz reverted to his Southern speech. "So I'll jes' say he cain't take his eyes off Miss Morton. Fo' that matter, neither kin I."

Mark squirmed a bit and signaled a waitress to bring the next course. Adalia rewarded him with a warm smile and seemed as enchanted with the company as they were with her. The rest of the meal went smoothly. Afterward brandy and cheroots were served to Fitz, Mark, and Captain Morton. Fitz noticed that Mark laid aside the cheroot he always enjoyed after a meal. Clarissa and Adalia went to the drawing room where the orchestra had never stopped playing.

"Wants to warn you again. You teaches nigger childrun, you goin' to be so hated, folks will cross the street they sees you comin'."

"I hope you're wrong because they must learn that some day they'll have to accept us and forget all this bloody fighting. Nobody won this war, Clarissa. Nobody ever wins a war. All war does is bring unhappiness that lasts for years."

"Knows that. You still think you takes the teachin' job?"

"Yes. That's what I'm here for. It means that I don't have to go back north. I hope one day our country will be so united, we won't speak of it as the North and the South."

"That sho' hopin' fo' a lot, but I prays fo' it. An' I helps you all I kin. Wants you to know that there ain't a bettah man in this heah world than Fitzjohn Turner. Reckon I been in love with him since I was a gal, yeahs ago. Nevah had a chance. He marries my cousin Benay, an' they sho' happy till Benay dies o' smallpox."

"I'm sorry to hear that. What of Mark?"

"Well . . . he come heah from N'Orleans some time back. Lived theah with his mama."

"Is Mark's father here on Wyndward?"

"Ain't sho', but thinks he been killed in the war. Mark was a soldier under him an' sees him shot an' then a bayonet. . . ." Clarissa let the sentence fade away.

"Poor Mark. He seems so alone. And so shy."

"Mark ain't shy. No ma'am, he ain't shy. Sometime he kin drive me outen my mind."

"But he was so . . . well . . . uncommunicative."

"That 'cause he in love. All of a sudden he in love."

Adalia seemed startled by that news. "He didn't say anything about a girl."

"Adalia, the boy in love with you. Thass why he so tongue-tied an' kind o' glassy-eyed. Don' think he evah been in love befo'. Not even puppy love, like most o' us goes through. So when he lay eyes on you, that's it. Thinks he kind o' numb gettin' used to the idea he in love. 'Course he may not know it hisse'f yet, but he sho' goin' to if he in your company much."

"Well, I'm sure you. . . ." Adalia began in a choked voice. "I mean, I didn't realize I was the cause of his strange behavior."

"See you lookin' at him kin' o' flirty, Miss."

"I . . . like him." Adalia weighed each word carefully. "I really do. As for love, I've never been in love before."

"You know whut you jes' says, Miss?"

"I said I've never been in love," Adalia replied seriously.

"You said you nevah was in love *befo'*. That mean you in love now. Ain't that right?"

"Nonsense. Absolute nonsense." Adalia gave an indignant toss of her head, but her face flushed with color.

"Won't mention it again, not 'lessen it necessary. Tell you this. Mark got Turner blood an' ain't none bettah. He goin' to be jes' like Fitz an' like his own papa. They fine men. You cain't find any bettah no matter whar you go. An' Fitz a rich man. Not that mean any diff'rence, but jes' say it so you knows."

"That's evident from this house, but it wouldn't

cause me to fall in love. Besides, I'm more interested in the history of this family than I am in romance." She skillfully turned the conversation away from her and Mark. "Mister Turner said he kept one thousand slaves. It's difficult to comprehend. Of course, I know about slavery, but why so many?"

"Keepin' slaves is whut made him rich. Down heah keepin' slaves was a way o' life that had lasted fo' many yeahs. 'Til we lost the war. But Fitz treats 'em fine. Not many evah runs from Wyndward, an' soon's this heah war starts, he sets 'em all free. Sends two of 'em North so his daughter Melanie kin see they gets educated."

"He has a daughter in the North?"

"Married a Northern congressman. Melanie like her mama. Nevah wants anythin' to do with slavery. Hates it, hates Wyndward, an' hates her papa fo' keepin' 'em. Sweahs she nevah wants to see Fitz again. Her husband got killed in the war, an' she blame Fitz fo' that. Fo' his bein' a Southerner. Ain't fair. Fitz loves her an' misses her. Ain't right, but cain't do anythin' 'bout it."

"I'm sure it's a fine family. One with a strange history too. I do like Mark, though we've spoken only a very few words so far. As for love, I . . . don't know if two people could fall in love a moment after meeting."

"Sho' kin," Clarissa said confidently.

"Has it ever happened to you?"

"Fifty times."

Adalia laughed. "I don't believe it. I do believe you read too much into Mark's behavior in the brief time we were together."

"Ain't much diff'rence 'tween like an' love. Reckon bes' you takes your time, but Mark sho' goin' to rush you if you gives him half a chance. That boy nevah knowed many gals, good ones—ladies. A bit rebellious when he come heah."

"I'd certainly like to know more about him." A frown crossed Adalia's brow. "How was he rebellious? Or should I ask?"

"Filled with hate 'gainst his papa. His mama taught him that."

Adalia's eyes widened in astonishment. "Why would she do such a thing?"

" 'Cause Mark's mama always hated his papa."

"Why? Mark doesn't seem full of hate."

Clarissa shrugged. "All I kin say is he got Turner blood in him, like I told you, an' fo' me thass mo' than 'nuff."

Adalia looked intrigued. "Mark did ask me, during dinner, if I'd be interested in seeing the plantation."

"You means now?" Clarissa asked.

Adalia nodded. "Do you think it would be proper? Or safe?"

"Safe?" Clarissa asked indignantly. "You thinks he gonna rape you?"

"I thought no such thing," Adalia said indignantly. "I just thought that since I'll teach here, it would be an opportunity to see the grounds and where the school will be."

"Not certain he could show you whar the school gonna be, but it sho' give you both a chance to knows one 'nother bettah." Clarissa arose, but motioned Adalia to retain her seat. "Knows Fitz got some good brandy an' I'm hankerin' fo' some. I comes right back, or I sends Mark."

Mark returned. "Clarissa wants to talk politics an' business with your brother an' Gran'pa. Mayhap you likes to see the plantation. How we grows tobacco, whar the niggers live. There's two o' them I want you to meet. They's fine people, an' we mighty proud to have 'em livin' heah."

"Mark, I'd be delighted. I have a wrap in the buggy. We can stop by and pick it up."

Mark left Adalia outside at the foot of the veranda steps while he ran to where the buggy was tied up. He returned with a pale lavender shawl that smelled of her perfume.

They walked down the path to the stables first. Mark explained how the plantation had once raised thoroughbreds. He showed her the remains of the race track. They inspected the curing sheds. They walked along the dirt road between the slave cabins.

"Why, Mark," Adalia said, "I understood slaves lived under awful conditions. In shacks with dirt floors and no furniture. But these cabins are really very good."

"Ain't like this on most plantations," Mark explained. "Whut you thought they was like . . . is whut some were like. Some bastahds didn' know any bettah. The slaves couldn' do nothin' 'bout it. They asks massa fo' somethin' bettah, an' he calls 'em no-good sonsabitches."

Adalia looked distressed. "Mark, you do use rather strong language."

"I do?" He glanced at her with a worried expression. "You mean I cusses too much?"

"Well, yes. You see, a gentleman doesn't speak that way in the presence of a lady."

"Reckon I been makin' a real goddamn—pardon, Miss Adalia—wishes I didn't say that. I been makin' a fool o' myse'f. I knows you a lady. Been mostly 'round wh . . . ." He quickly compressed his lips before the word slipped out. His face turned beet red.

"I understand," Adalia said kindly. "Clarissa told me you'd not been around girls. I also know that the war does things to men. Makes them say things they'd never say otherwise."

"Glad you understands," Mark said gratefully. "Sweahs I nevah say anythin' like that in your presence agin."

"Thank you," Adalia said, then added graciously, "I'm sure if you do, the occasion will call for it."

"Then I uses it. Now this heah cabin we comin' to is whar Hong Kong an' his wife Seawitch lives. They been heah fo' reckon fifty yeahs, mayhap mo'. Hong Kong is Gran'pa's driver. That means he bosses the slaves. Used to be slaves. Now they's the folks who wuk heah."

Hong Kong bowed before Adalia. She extended her hand to Seawitch who took it shyly. Adalia wasn't that shy. She embraced Seawitch, and the wrinkled old face was wreathed in a smile.

"Mind I ask whut happened at the big house?" Hong Kong addressed his question to Mark. "Mayhap a hundred an' mo' folks theah in one minute, an' nobody the next."

"Miss Adalia," Mark said, "comes with her brother, who a Yankee officer. Folks gets uppity they sees a Yankee unifo'm in the house. Gran'pa didn' help any when he says the Yankee mo' than welcome in his house. So all the Rebs jes' got up an' left."

"Sho' 'nuff?" Seawitch marveled. "Whut Elegant goin' to do with all that food?"

"You gets all you kin eat. Bettah get up theah fo' your share," Mark advised.

"Mighty proud to have met you, Missy," Hong Kong said. "Yo' goin' back North?"

"Miss Adalia," Mark told them, "is goin' to stay. Gran'pa is 'bout to build a schoolhouse fo' all the childrun heah an' Miss Adalia, she goin' to teach."

"Praise the Lawd," Seawitch exclaimed. "Been prayin' fo' that most o' my life. You sho' is welcome, Missy."

"Thank you," Adalia said warmly. "I'll come by after I start teaching."

Mark led her out of the cabin and back toward the mansion. "That was nice, the way you treats 'em," he said. "They's black, but they sho' is quality folk."

"I could tell that. How many children did they have?"

"None. Happens long ago, when Hong Kong a young buck. Great-Gran'pa Jonathan used to whup slaves they slothed. Hong Kong nevah sloths. But there was an overseer on the plantation who didn' like Hong Kong. One day Hong Kong do somethin' this heah overseer said was wrong. He strings Hong Kong up by his ankles so his laigs spread way apart. Then he takes a big club an' jes' about smashes poor Hong Kong's balls off. Nevah could have childrun. . . . Yo' turnin' your haid away, Miss Adalia. Whut I say to make yo' do that?"

"Mark," she said, "when I come here to teach, would you like to attend a special class. One just for you?"

"Sho' would, but whut I do? Cain't think I says anythin' bad, like I promised I wouldn't."

"We'll talk about that when your special class begins. Now I think we should go back and join the others."

Fitz, Captain Morton, and Clarissa were engaged in serious talk over brandy and coffee.

Captain Morton said, "There will be great difficulties. You see, there are millions of people in the United States. Four million are slaves. Now no one has found yet a way to assimilate that many people into an already free society. The Freedmen's Bureau is establishing offices and stores in the big cities to help. But they're faced with finding work for all those millions of ex-slaves."

"Won't have time," Fitz said promptly.

"Why not, Mister Turner? I'm asking you because I'm quite aware that you know more about this situation than anyone in Washington. The planters are broke. How can they find money to pay the people who are now workers?"

"Won't have to. The niggers will go back to the plantations an' farms whar they were well treated, an' they'll wuk fo' shares. Nevah had money. Some don' know whut it is. If they gets a cabin, some warm clothes, enough food, they'll wuk an' take their share when ev'rythin' is harvested."

"Do you really believe that?" Morton asked.

"Cap'n," Clarissa said, "if Fitz says so, it's so."

"Yes, I'm sure of that. One thing you probably don't know, Mister Turner, is that there will be hard money coming into the South soon. Not enough to pay all those workers immediately, but it will increase. You see, during the war, planters kept on growing cotton. At first, it was to be sold in England and to bring in money to buy guns and powder. But England didn't need that much cotton, and the North was blockading the South's ports anyhow. So the cotton piled up in warehouses. It has kept very well. Up north the mills are hungry for all they can get, and it's already being shipped."

"Heahs some o' that," Fitz admitted. "Didn' know how true it was. Now me, I'm growin' 'bacco, an' mayhap I could sell the stalks it's so much in demand. Cain't see no reason why the South should starve, Cap'n. An' a good thing comes o' all this. Makes the North an' the South begin tradin' an' that takes away some o' the sting o' war."

"Watch out for scalawags," the captain said. "They're coming down here from the North like a swarm of locusts looking for any kind of chance to fleece the unwary. They buy up property at a pittance because the owners need money so badly. They're a bad lot. Don't trust them."

"You forget one thing, Captain." Fitz reverted to the Northern way of speaking. "I'm a Yankee too and, as my mother used to say, tighter than the bark on a tree when it comes to business dealings. In fact, I wish one of them would approach me. Perhaps I could give him a lesson in the art of cheating."

" 'Nother thing," Clarissa said, "one o' them scalawags cheats Fitz, he goin' to get his ass whaled off."

13

At Mark's insistence, work on the new schoolhouse began a week later. Precious lumber had to be bought at four times its actual cost, but Mark persisted.

"Gots to see the childrun learn how to read an write," he told Fitz. "Gots to set a 'zample fo' others."

"Seems to me," Fitz argued, "that we might wait until the fields are plowed an' the seedlin's set. The childrun can help with that, an' we pays 'em too."

"Learnin' mo' important, Gran'pa."

"Yo' knows whut folks goin' to say we does this?"

"I don' care whut they says. Gots to have that school."

Clarissa, listening quietly to all this, raised her eyebrows from time to time, a gesture not lost on Mark.

"Whut fo' yo' makin' faces like that, Clarissa?"

"Ain't makin' faces. Jes' wonderin' whut's come over you, Mark. You been talkin' real nice lately. Nevah heahs a 'sonabitch' outen you."

"Don' have to sweah ev'ry time you talks," Mark said angrily. "Bettah you learn that too."

"Oh, I will," Clarissa said. "Sho' will, 'bout the time I ready to die, an' then I be too goddamn skeered to sweah."

"Mark gets his schoolhouse," Fitz said. "I'm kind o' tired listenin' to both o' you jaw like that. Sends Chickory to town fo' the mail. Whut's keepin' him? Mayhap he learnin how to sloth from Calcutta Two."

"Brought the mail half an hour ago," Clarissa said. "Puts it on your desk like he been told."

"Whyn't somebody tell me?" Fitz said. He left the drawing room for his office, but returned in a few minutes to hand an envelope to Clarissa.

"Whut business you gots with a lawyer, Clarissa? Name o' Jed Tomson on the envelope."

"Nevah heard o' him, Fitz."

"You gets a lawyer, don' get him. He's trash."

She opened the envelope and studied the letter. She looked up at Fitz. "Tell me somethin', Fitz. When you goin' to kill that bastahd who's my papa-in-law? You waits, I'm goin' to do it fo' you. Know whut that sonabitch done? He gots this heah lawyer to write me a letter sayin' I gots to go back to my husband o' I gots to go into court. Reckon the old man gettin' soft?"

"Apperson," Fitz said with an air of disgust, "jes' goes 'round makin' trouble fo' them he hates, an' reckon you right smack on top o' that list, an' me second."

"Kin he make me go back? Horace ain't even a man, fo' chrissake."

"I think you could use that in court, you has to go."

"No, suh, ain't goin' to use that. Make me look like a fool, that whut it does. A gal like me marryin' that pansy."

"I'll see whut I kin do," Fitz said. "How much time the letter say you gets?"

"Three days. He takes me into court on Thursday. I ain't even got me a dress to wear. Cain't even buy one yet."

"I'll go to the bank in the mawnin'," Fitz promised her. "Asks Tallen he kin get me a good lawyer, an' we

168

does mo' than go into court 'cause your papa-in-law say so. We goin' into court, an' you're divorcin' that no-good bastahd. Should o' done it long ago, Clarissa."

Tallen was not optimistic. "Don' know whar in hell we headed, Fitz. Got Northern soldiers runnin' things. Not that they ain't good at it, but seein' Yankee uniforms 'round an' bein' ordered 'bout by them—jes' make a man start boilin' inside."

"Reckon," Fitz agreed. "But you got to 'member they keeps things quiet. Ain't no slaves riotin' an' killin'. Ain't no redneck whites killin' slaves fo' the hell o' it. Things goin' kind o' steady while we gets our feet on the ground again."

"You try tellin' that to anybody you meets on the street. All kinds o' stories bein' told. Like in N'Orleans whar the snooty society ladies theah been turnin' up their noses at all Yankee soldiers. The gen'ral in charge gets mad an' says any woman in N'Orleans who gets too snooty gets treated like any old whore. Don' knows it wuks or not, but it sho' ain't makin' the Yankees any bettah liked."

"Anythin' like that goin' on heah?"

"Not I knows of. Got up Captain Morton an' he acts like a reasonable man, but that don' makes folks like him any bettah. Heahs whut happened at your soiree. All over town."

"Whut they sayin' 'bout me?"

"You a Yankee lover, an' that's worst these days than bein' a nigger lover. An' they says that 'bout you too."

"But nevah to my face," Fitz said with a laugh. "Treats me like I'm a king, I comes to buy somethin'."

"It's your money they respects, not you. Whut makes things worst, a whole army o' scalawags comin' from the North."

"Knows 'bout 'em. You had any dealin's with 'em?"

"Stays away from banks. Figgers a man kin run a bank, he cain't be fooled as easy. But sho', I done some business with 'em. Have to. They buyin' property 'round heah an' payin' nuthin' fo' it. Holds it 'til times gets bettah an' then sells it fo' five times whut they pays."

"You handles the money part?"

"Morgage, quit claims, all that sort o' thing. Somebody gots to do it."

"Knows a lawyer name o' Jed Tomson?"

"Who don't? Wukkin' right in with the carpetbaggers. Finds folks fo' 'em who they kin fleece."

"Knows whar I kin find Colonel Apperson?"

Tallen grew uneasy. "Now, Fitz, knows how much you hates that bastahd, but ain't no time to go 'round bustin' him up. The Yankee soldiers don' like anybody makin' any kind o' trouble."

"Ain't aimin' to. Jes' got some legal business to talk to him 'bout. Was thinkin', you kin get in touch with one o' these scalawags? One who kin squeeze blood outen a rock?"

"Reckon I knows ten or fifteen."

"Mayhap I needs one. Tell you later. How the bankin' business?"

"Fitz, I didn' have your account heah, don' know how I kin stay open. Knows I treated you bad, an' nevah been so sorry fo' it in all my life. I sho' am beholdin' to you, suh."

"Not long as you keeps doin' business with me like you has been. Got me a good profit on my first shipment o' 'bacco. Next yeah goin' to make three times as much. Sees you later, Henry. You ain't told me whar to find Apperson."

"Evah since you burned down his plantation house he been livin' in the hotel. The Alhambra, whar you always drinks when you comes to town."

"Know ev'ry whore in the place," Fitz said with a grin. "Even gots throwed out when I was in that trouble after the war starts. Reckon they let me in now?"

"They puts out a red carpet they has one," Tallen chuckled. "Apperson most always in the bar tellin' folks whut a big hero he was. Colonel Apperson o' the warehouse detail. He nevah mentions that, on'y that he was a colonel."

Fitz walked to the hotel. He could see the town was

slowly recovering from the war days. More stores were open, more vehicles on the streets. Even window displays indicated that shortages were being relieved slowly. Many of the articles, particularly the silver services, had no doubt been hidden during the war years and were now being brought out and sold for whatever they would bring by families destitute enough to sell what they held most precious. The effects of the war were going to be felt for a long, long time, Fitz thought.

The hotel bar was large with an extensive, well-kept bar and tables for card-playing. There were private rooms for ladies, and it was a respectable place.

When Fitz entered, conversations dwindled and all eyes were upon him. Fitz paid no heed. He stepped up to the bar and ordered bourbon, paid for it with a gold piece. He turned around, set his back against the bar, and raised his glass.

"If I been poisoned," he said loudly, "you-all knows who poisoned me."

Nobody laughed or said a word. "Speakin' o' poison, any o' you gen'mun knows whar I kin find Colonel Apperson o' the Warehouse Dragoons?"

"You aimin' to kill him, Mistah Turner?" someone asked.

"That bein' my business, you has to wait an' see. Wants to know whar he is. Right now."

"Got him a gal in the back room," Fitz was told, somewhat eagerly. He thought they were hoping to witness a fight between him and Apperson, and he wondered who they'd cheer for.

Fitz finished his drink, spun another gold piece on the bar, picked up the bottle of whiskey by the neck, and walked across the room to the back area. Colonel Apperson and one of the steady prostitutes were enjoying a drink. Fitz watched Apperson rise slowly in sudden apprehension. The prostitute rose too and backed toward the door.

"Aft'noon, Mistah Turner, suh," she said.

"Molly, nice to see you agin. Whut in hell you doin' with an old man like Apperson? He nevah was any good, an' now he creakin' like a rusty door he gets in an' out o' baid."

"Kin see me any time you wants, Mistah Turner. You sho' don' do no creackin'."

She stepped out of the room hurriedly as if she couldn't believe she'd escaped the carnage she was sure was about to happen.

Fitz approached the table. "Sit down, Colonel. Let's you an' me have a drink. Wants to talk some business."

Apperson seated himself slowly, apprehensively. "Whut kind o' business we got, Fitz?"

"Clarissa business." Fitz poured whiskey into the glasses on the table, taking the one the prostitute had used. "She got a letter from your lawyer."

"Ain't no call for you to start trouble, Fitz. Got my rights. My son back home. Wants Missus Clarissa with him. Aftah all, she is his wife. He gots a right to make her come home."

"Your son," Fitz said, "ain't no husband 'cept to boys. We kin prove that in court."

"Reckon. Don' make no diff'rence to me. Don' give a goddamn whut my son thinks, but Clarissa gots to come back."

"Knows the law," Fitz conceded. "Hate to fight this out in court. How you fixed fo' cash?"

"Ain't seen much cash since the war. Whut you gettin' at?"

"Knows the old Fisbee place? Whar I been livin' 'til Wyndward rebuilt?"

"Knows it."

"You drops all action 'gainst Clarissa, gives me a signed paper sayin' you gives up the right to take her back no matter whut, an' I talks some business 'bout sellin' that farm. Knows you means to go back to raisin' cotton, an' that land sho' achin' to be plowed."

Apperson's eyes gleamed with greed. "You deeds that to me?"

"Sho' will, at a low price."

"Like whut?"

"You ain't said you goes 'long with it, Colonel."

"Ain't sayin' so now either. Don' trust you, Fitz."

Fitz pushed the cork back in the bottle. "Too bad. Willin' to make a nice deal. An' all I asks is you admit Clarissa kin divorce Horace an' theah be no trouble 'bout it."

"You didn' say divorce." Apperson was apprehensive again.

"Was gettin' to it. Well, no use wastin' time."

"Wait a minute. Whut you offerin'?

"The Fisbee place fo' ten thousand. Cash in hand."

Apperson's avarice was now plainly showing. "Ain't got ten thousan'. Ain't got fifty dollahs."

"Too bad, Colonel. Even so, you don' get Clarissa back. Jes' want to make it legal is all, an' make you one hell o' a fine offer. That Fisbee place worth five times whut I offered to sell fo'."

"All you wants is a divorce fo' Clarissa?"

"You heard me."

"You aimin' to marry her yourse'f, Fitz?"

"Wouldn' have her," Fitz said. "Wants her fo' my housekeeper, thass all."

"Mayhap I kin raise the money. You gives me a little time?"

"Very little. An' one mo' thing. Wants you to tell me how you knows the lady we talked 'bout 'fore was caught an' executed."

"Hears it from mo' than one. She daid all right."

"Who saw her die?"

" 'Member Ollie Paulson? He a Reb sergeant. He sees her hung an' tells me."

"Whar did this happen?"

"Up near Green Marsh."

"Thinks there's a record o' this?"

"Don' know fo' sho'. War jes' startin' an' ev'rythin' movin' fast. So Paulson told me."

"Whar kin I find Paulson?"

"Got killed fightin' Sherman neah Atlanta. Heahs the same story from others, but don' know who they were. We talkin' 'bout the Fisbee place."

"You lyin' 'bout this, you sho' cut some time off your life. You knows that."

"Ain't no reason to lie. Now the Fisbee. . . ."

"You'd lie 'cause you a lyin' bastahd, Colonel, an' you knows you're hurtin' me with this heah story."

"Sweahs it the truth. You goin' to talk business o' not?"

"Knowin' you the way I do, reckon I bettah be mighty careful. Kin you get ten thousand?"

"Kin try, you gives me some time."

"Forty-eight hours," Fitz said. "An' you has your lawyer draw up a consent to give Clarissa a divorce right now."

"Meets you heah same time day after tomorrow."

"You bettah, Colonel."

Before the expiration of the deadline Fitz had set, Apperson arrived at Wyndward with a draft from Tallen's bank for ten thousand dollars and a signed agreement that neither he nor his son would contest any divorce action Clarissa might bring.

Mark and Clarissa had joined Fitz, neither saying anything at first.

Apperson said, "You drives a mighty hard bargain, Fitz. The Fisbee place ain't worth mo' than ten thousan', if that. You ain't cheatin' me, Fitz?"

"Takes that as an insult, even comin' from you," Fitz said.

"Told you not to do business with him," Clarissa spoke up. "Ain't nevah made an honest dollah in his whole life."

"You shut up." Apperson roared his wrath. "You gots a mighty big mouth, Clarissa. You always did have."

"Ain't as big as your son's," she countered angrily.

"Keep him outen this heah business," Apperson said. "Gives you the divorce an' glad to be rid o' a whore like you."

Fitz picked up the deed he had prepared. He also picked up the agreement for divorce and handed it to Clarissa. Then he tore the deed paper into pieces and let them fall gently to the top of the table at which they were seated.

Apperson watched all this. His face grew fiery red

and then pale. He tried to speak and made motions with his hands as if trying to seize the deed.

Fitz said, "I does business with gen'mun, suh. I returns your draft fo' ten thousand, but not the divorce paper 'cause we made a deal, an' you jes' broke it all off. Not my fault you did. If you contest this heah divorce action, goin' to make mo' trouble fo' you than you evah knowed. Now take your money an' get the hell outen heah."

Apperson finally found his voice. "Fitz, takes it all back. 'Pologizes to Clarissa. Lost my haid, an' I'm mighty sorry."

Clarissa arose. "I don' wants to look at this bastahd, Fitz. 'Scuse me please."

"Didn' mean to set her off like that," Apperson said plaintively.

"One thing," Fitz said, "you 'members I got two witnesses to this heah deal which ain' no deal. You tell any lies 'bout this, an' I sho' goin' to make you pay fo' it."

"Fitz, you says I gets the Fisbee place. I gives you the money. . . ."

"Colonel, the Fisbee place worth at least fifty thousan'. You stopped bein' the sonabitch you always were, mayhap I let it go through. But when you calls a nice gal like Clarissa, your own daughter-in-law, a whore, then you stops bein' a gen'mun, if you evah was one. So the deal is off. You pays back the ten thousan', an' no mo' to it."

"Fitz, cain't pay it back. . . ."

"Whut you means by that, Colonel? You borrows ten thousan' an' heah it is on the desk. All you got to do is pay it back. Now you kin leave. Kind o' busy these days an' gots no time fo' crazy talk."

Apperson arose, not knowing what else to do. His confusion was pleasing to Fitz. Mark arose, went to the library door and held it open, then preceded Apperson to the front door and held that open as well. Apperson stumbled out of the house and climbed into his carriage. Mark returned to the library where Clarissa had rejoined Fitz.

"Wants to know whut in hell that all about," Mark said. "The colonel looked like he goin' to have a heart attack or a stroke. He wanted the Fisbee place that bad?"

"Nevah wanted it nohow," Fitz explained. "Soon's he hears I'm willin' to sell fo' that low price, he gets ready. Knows how these heah carpetbaggers always lookin' fo' a bargain, so he goes to one . . . or mayhap the carpetbagger gets wind o' this heah sale an' the colonel sells the Fisbee place to him fo' mo' money than the ten thousan'. Finds out how much next time I go to Lynchburg. Mayhap tomorrow 'cause I sho' wants to know how much he was offered."

"But like you says all he gots to do is return the money," Mark argued.

"Son, you don' know Apperson like I do—an' likely Clarissa do. He gets a hell o' a lot mo'n ten thousan' from the carpetbagger, an' 'fore he come heah to close the deal, he sho' spent most o' his profit. Now he cain't pay the carpetbagger back fo' a deal that nevah went through."

"You sho' 'bout that?" Mark asked. "You nevah intended to go through with it?"

Clarissa said, "The colonel in debt so bad they been houndin' him. He gets that money, an' they knows that, they sho' comes fo' it as fast as they kin."

"But how'd they find out?" Mark asked. "This heah deal done mighty fast."

"News like the colonel comin' into money travels fast too," Fitz chuckled. "Sho' gets 'round, an' the colonel sho' pays up or he gets his face busted. Some folks been carryin' his debt fo' yeahs. Durin' the war, nobody dared try to collect 'cause he wearin' that uniform. Now the war over, they lookin' fo' their money."

"You foxed him!" Mark shouted in glee. "Gran'pa, you foxed him."

"Why son, I done no such thing. He insulted Clarissa, an' I do business on'y with gen'mun, like I told him."

"You got the agreement fo' the divorce. . . ."

"Sho' did. Clarissa, tomorrow we goes to Lynchburg, an' you hands that agreement to my lawyer. Pretty soon you be emancipated. Whut you think o' that?"

"Feels like a slave set free. Thass the right name fo' it, Fitz. I been emancipated. Feels like dancin'. Nevah fo'gets whut you done fo' me, Fitz."

"You ain't beholden, Clarissa. You part o' my fam'ly. Now we gets back to the schoolhouse."

" 'Bout time," Mark grumbled. Then he grinned again. "You foxed him. You sho' did!"

"This heah goin' to make him madder'n evah," Clarissa warned.

"Knows that. Knows it might come to my killin' him. Won't spoil my sleep I get to do that. An' when he 'round, keeps my back turned away from him. Mark, you gots any idea how big that schoolhouse goin' to be?"

"Talkin' to the niggers. 'Bout a hundred childrun, reckon."

"That little gal cain't teach a hundred kids."

"I kin help," Clarissa offered eagerly.

"Don' know 'bout that," Fitz said. "Whut you kin teach 'em best, bettah they don' know. Talk about it later."

"One mo' thing, Gran'pa. Adalia comes heah to teach, she goin' to be some hated an' won't be safe she go back an' forth from Lynchburg to Wyndward."

"Her brother runs the city," Fitz said. "Nobody would dare to do anythin' to that gal."

"You says so, but don' mean somebody won't. Want her to live heah at Wyndward, Gran'pa. Clarissa heah to keep her company. Don' wants anythin' to happen to her."

"Thinks 'bout it."

"Wants your answer now. You says no, she ain't comin' heah to teach. Won't let her. Gran'pa, you gots to 'member whut happened to your mama, whut happened to your wife an' whut happened to my papa's wife. They all gets killed. Cain't have that happen again. Not to Adalia. You gots to say she kin stay heah."

Fitz nodded slowly. "You puts it that way, son, reckon she got to stay heah. Yo' tells her she welcome,

177

an' whutevah she wants, you sees she gets. Now you satisfied?"

"Gran'pa, whutevah you wants o' me, you gets. Sweah it."

" 'Members that when you gets uppity an' thinks you kin take me in a fight."

"Nevah wants to fight you long as I lives."

"Tomorrow," Fitz said, "me an' Clarissa goin' to Lynchburg. You stays heah, but next day you takes the carriage an' goes to Lynchburg an' talks to Adalia 'bout whut we 'grees on. Mayhap you take her fo' a ride 'round heah. Show her whut the South looks like."

"I sho' goin' to be happy tellin' her," Mark said.

"Makes sho' thass all you tells her," Clarissa said.

"Don' know whut you means."

"Gal needs time, Mark. 'Members that. Gals gots to think 'bout it, even if they knows whut the answer is. You gives that gal time, heah?"

"You talkin' crazy, Clarissa. Gran'pa, goin' to talk to Toby 'bout the schoolhouse. Clarissa, you sho' says things don' make no sense."

Later, when Clarissa was certain Mark had left the mansion, she turned to Fitz. "Fitz, that gal from up North, she been brought up real nice an' proper. You kin tell that jes' talkin' to her. Now Mark head over heels in love with her, an' reckon she ain't lookin' the other way."

Fitz nodded. "Knows whut you means. How Mark gets borned, kind o' fam'ly he comes from. Raised in his mama's whorehouse, ownin' it fo' a time. Bein' told by his mama to kill his papa when he grows up. That's whut you mean?"

"How you think a gentle gal goin' to like that, Fitz? An' he don' tell, an' we don' tell her, plenty o' folks, like the colonel, they knows an' they tells her quick as they kin."

"Ain't got the heart to do it," Fitz said. "Reckon that gal sho'ly in love with Mark?"

"Says she ain't—yet. But gal who says that sho'ly is an' on'y holdin' out fo' a time."

"When Mark comes heah, wouldn' do anythin' fo'

him. He a pure sonabitch. But growed up since then, an' now he's much like Jonathan. The boy has come to be a great comfort to me. But this gal runs away from him, he goin' to be hard to handle. Wishes they was some other way."

"Don' have to do this day after tomorrow," Clarissa said. "She won' be comin' heah 'til the schoolhouse built, an' even then she goin' to be so busy gettin' the school started, she ain't goin' to have time to think 'bout gettin' married. That'll come later, an' then we sho' gots some thinkin' to do."

"Lucky we kin fo'get it fo' awhile."

"You thinks the colonel goin' to say he fights the divorce, the paper he gives you or not?"

"Clarissa, right now the colonel is so busy hidin' from that carpetbagger, he cain't show his face. Means he stays outen sight fo' weeks, an' thass whut I wanted. 'Fore he gets the guts to come back, the divorce goin' to be all over. You sho' is emancipated."

"Now we kin go to baid we wants to, an' we ain't bustin' no law."

"Nevah thought o' that, Clarissa. Worth thinkin' 'bout too."

"Won't push you, Fitz. Knows how much you still in love with that gal who runs five yeahs ago now."

"She'd daid. Talked to your papa-in-law 'bout it, an' he tells me he heahs 'bout it from mo' than one an' named a sergeant who was theah when it happens. Sees her get hung."

"Fitz, breaks my heart to heah that, but . . . don' fo'get, the colonel the biggest lyin' bastahd in this heah world. You cain't trust him nohow. Not evah."

"Named the sergeant, Clarissa."

"Kin name him too, he don' exist."

"Reckon," Fitz said without a ray of hope. "Looks into it. Fo'gets to tell you. In Lynchburg I sees some new dresses in the big store. Windows full of 'em. You want to go into Lynchburg tomorrow like I said?"

"You goes 'thout me, I sho' nevah sleeps with you again. Mayhap I even kills you. I be ready 'bout six."

14

Fitz pulled the carriage up before the largest store in Lynchburg. He got down and helped Clarissa to the sidewalk. She was facing the store windows, reveling in the merchandise displayed.

Fitz said, "Gots to see Tallen at the bank, gots to see the lawyer 'bout your divorce, gots to talk to Cap'n Morton. Reckon I gets done. . . ."

"Fitz, they sho' 'nuff got Paris gowns. Honest to God Paris gowns!"

"That's nice. Now I comes back an' picks you up an' we has somethin' to eat 'fore we. . . ."

"Fitz," she said softly, "goin' to spend an awful lot o' money you says I kin."

"Spends all you want. You sho' earnin' it. Ain't no limit. Want this heah carriage full o' boxes an' packages when we goes back."

"I'll be ready 'bout—mayhap—four o'clock. Mayhap five. . . . See you later, Fitz."

She took half a dozen swift steps to the door and vanished inside. Fitz grinned, pleased that she was happy.

He put up the carriage at the livery and walked over to the office of his lawyer. There he explained the circumstances of the divorce and handed over the colonel's agreement, without doubting its validity in any way.

That done, he paid a visit to the bank, where he found Tallen. "Sit down, Fitz. You goin' to enjoy this. I been laughin' my haid off all day."

"Colonel Apperson, I hopes?"

"Sho' is the colonel. Like you said, you makes him a damn fool offer fo' a property worth five times whut you asks. Now the colonel owed so much money he cain't raise a dollah. He come to me, beggin' fo' a loan, but you know a bank cain't make a loan 'thout some kind o' security, which the colonel has none. But I happens to mention a carpetbagger who gots lots o' money an' lookin' to buy farms. Pretty soon they comes in heah, the carpetbagger an' the colonel. The carpetbagger gives me sixteen thousan' in cash. I gives the colonel a draft in your name fo' ten thousan'. The six thousan' stays in the bank. Reckon he an' the carpetbagger gots an agreement he cain't touch that six thousan' 'til after the deal is made. But Fitz, they didn' mention that to me. An hour after I gets the money, the colonel comes back an' takes out most o' that money."

"Figgered on that, Henry."

"An' jes' by chance, you knows, all the folks the colonel owes money to is waitin' outside the bank. They say he pays 'em or they takes it outen his hide an' takes the money too. He stands theah handin' it out. Didn' pay all he owes, I finds out later, but 'nuff to keep 'em satisfied."

"Nice o' him to pay his debts," Fitz said.

"Sho' was. But today the carpetbagger comes in heah an' wants to know whar the colonel is. Cain't find him nowhar. Wants to know if I still gots the money, an' I tells him, feelin' sorry fo' him, that the colonel drew out most o' the six thousan' an' jes' disappeared. The carpetbagger say he finds him, he slits his throat. Reckon there be no mo' trouble with the colonel fo' some time. I gives the carpetbagger his ten thousan'—so he on'y lost six thousan'. Feels powerful sorry fo' him."

"Worth all the trouble, Henry."

Tallen removed two glasses and a bottle from his desk drawer. He filled them, handed one to Fitz, and raised his to make a toast.

"Heah's to the colonel's bad luck lastin' fo' fifty mo' yeahs."

Fitz consulted with Tallen on financial affairs and then left to walk to City Hall. There, Yankee uniforms predominated. Fitz was stopped by a sergeant.

"Wants to see Cap'n Morton, Sergeant," he said.

"Your name, please, and state your business."

"Name o' Fitz Turner."

"You may go right in, Mister Turner. No need for you to state your business."

"I thanks you, suh."

"Got orders you see the Captain, or anyone else, any time of the day or night, Mister Turner. Right this way."

City Hall, gone shabby because of neglect, was headquarters for the occupying Yankee forces. The office of the mayor was now used by Captain Morton.

"Fitz," he arose from his desk to advance with outstretched hand, "I'm glad to see you. Very happy. How have you been? And Mark, and Clarissa?"

"Ev'rybody's fine, Cap'n. Got a little business with you, there's time fo' it."

"All the time you need. What can I do for you?"

"Well, we been thinkin', Mark mostly, that when your sister comes out to teach, ain't many folks goin' to like it. An' when they finds out she teachin' niggers, goin' to be worse. The drive from heah to Wyndward is long an' over some lonely roads. We's worried some that harm might come to her drivin' back an' forth."

"I've thought of that too, and it's worried me. We'll have to tell her the danger makes it impossible."

"No! No, Cap'n! Whut I'm goin' to suggest is she comes to Wyndward an' lives theah. Clarissa kin see she's comfortable. We got lots o' room. There's one suite all done in pink that she'd look mighty nice in."

"Fitz, that's a remarkable offer. Of course I'm glad to accept, and I'm sure Adalia will be too. She rather likes your grandson."

"That boy outen his fool haid 'bout her, but that's got nothin' to do with the suggestion I jes' made. It's fo' Adalia's safety."

"Consider it as good as done."

"There's somethin' else. Two things. Is there any way you kin check the rolls an' see if there's a Reb sergeant name o' Ollie Paulson who s'posed to been killed, mayhap 'round Atlanta? Fightin' Sherman."

"I could consult—or have someone consult—Rebel records. We have them. It may take a little while."

"Takes all the time you need. It's kind o' important I finds out if they evah was such a man. Now the next thing, even mo' important, reckon. Got me a son name o' Jonathan. He enlisted in the Confederate Army right after the war broke out. Last I hears he a cap'n too, an' reckon he rose some higher than that. Wants to know if an officer name o' Jonathan Turner is alive or daid. No way I kin find out."

"Perhaps I can. It may take time too because of the red tape, but Fitz, I'm pleased I can be of help to you."

"One mo' thing. Jes' askin' fo' information. Evah since the war ends, seems like I kin do no wrong. I gets into trouble, the Yankees sends me home. Is there some kind of a list sayin' I'm not to be bothered?"

"I can't answer that question, Fitz. I . . . don't know and . . . I can't find out."

The schoolhouse was taking shape. A two-room structure to be fitted with desks now on order. Fitz was sparing no expense to make it a fine school.

"Wonders why," he told Clarissa one evening. "Once the hothaids 'round 'heah sees we hires a Northern teacher that goin' to make 'em mad, an' when they finds out she is teachin' nigger childrun, they goin' to explode. We keeps 'em from burnin' that schoolhouse, we sho' goin' to be lucky."

"Whut if they burns it, Fitz?"

"Build another. Way I sees it, black childrun got to be educated. Way they are, not knowin' a damn thing, they goin' to grow up full o' hate, an' them whut they hates ain't havin' any likin' fo' them. If the white folks cain't abide by whut's happenin', mayhap we kin get the black folks to try an' understand we all lives in the same world. Knows it ain't goin' to wuk, but somethin' has to, an' this is the best I kin do."

"Mighty glad I ain't livin' in Richmond or Lynchburg," Clarissa said. "On'y time I heahs o' this kind o' trouble is from you."

"Hopin' things simmer down some durin' the winter. Takes a long time fo' hate to go away, an' on'y been months since the war over an' the blacks free. 'Course they ain't helpin' any. Lots o' them sloths. Goes to Freedmen's Bureau stores an' gets food an' clothes free. Makes a lot of white folks mad. Ain't no way outen this heah mess I kin see. Don' know whut Washington doin', but cain't be much. Reckon Mistah Lincoln would o' done bettah."

"Used to think the war over, all the niggers runs to the North, but that didn' happen."

"Lots of 'em runs, but in the North they find the same things as down heah. Cain't get wuk 'cause they don' know anythin'. Nevah learned to think fo' themse'ves an' gots no schoolin'. Cain't read or write. Hard to find wuk you so goddamn dumb. An' they ain't treated any bettah up theah. So most comes back. Wishes I knows the answer to this. Kin on'y do a little to help, an' schoolin' the childrun on the plantation is all I kin do even if it gets me in trouble, which it sho'ly goin' to do."

"Well," Clarissa said, "we gettin' old, Fitz. Sho' won't be our problem."

"You wrong theah, Clarissa. Sho' goin' to be up to us. Heahs some folks gettin' real mad an' sayin' they goin' do somethin' 'bout it."

"Whut's that mean?"

"Don' 'zactly know how they thinks, or whut they kin do, but reckon there be burnin' an' lynchin'. Men got no wuk an' blames it on the niggers, sho' goin' to take it out on 'em."

"Mayhap long as the Yankee soldiers stay heah, won' get that bad, Fitz."

"Wonders whut be goin' on right now they wasn' heah. Well, gots to tend to our own affairs, reckon, an' so long we ain't pestered, goin' to mind my own business."

The winter was mild. In early spring, the tobacco seedlings were ready for planting and the slow life of winter grew fast and furious. Fitz added two hundred acres, and Hong Kong was able to recruit more families, which meant added children for the school now almost ready to open.

Tobacco prices were soaring, and Fitz knew the profits would be extensive in the fall. He was financially very sound—and very generous. Clarissa had everything she wanted, even ball gowns, the purchase of which she decried because there would surely be no more balls at Wyndward after the last fiasco.

In April, Adalia came to Wyndward to live. The entire mansion seemed to take on an air of life and liveliness. She was enchanted with the pink suite and overcome by the schoolhouse, which rivaled anything in the cities. She immediately prepared a list of books she required, along with slates, blackboards, crayons, chalk, notebooks, colored paper—it was quite a list. Everything was promptly sent from the North. Fitz had advised against trying to buy supplies in the South. The longer they could keep the school a secret, the better.

It was Mark who suffered the most. Now that the nearness of Adalia was an actuality, his anxiety grew by the day. He was with her as often as possible, but their relationship was only that of friends, if very good ones. He could find no fault with anything she did. He worked hard at getting the school ready. He sometimes rode with her along some of the old trails, as Benay and Fitz had once done.

During the three weeks before the school opened, Adalia took pains to grow acquainted with some of the children, who were extremely shy at first, but soon won over by her warm nature and youthful enthusiasm. She gathered them in a group and talked to them. She could hold their attention in a way their parents never could.

She sensed she was a natural teacher and was impatient to prove herself. Finally, the schoolhouse was completed and would open in three days, on Monday.

Clarissa had helped supervise the women who had offered to wash the windows and do various other duties on Adalia's extensive list. Even Elegant came down to exclaim over the neat arrangement of desks, which were fastened to the floor. On the blackboard at the front of the room, Adalia had printed the day of the week along with the date. Below, she had printed a few simple sentences that stated the name of the plantation on which the children lived, what crops were grown on it, and the name of the school. Mark had insisted it be called "Miss Adalia's Schoolhouse." The name was painted on a board which stretched across the front of the school above the entrance. Much to Fitz's surprise, even Mark displayed remarkable patience, either sitting and watching Adalia carry out the myriad chores necessary for her work, or doing her bidding on anything she couldn't attend to herself.

Fitz was certain Mark had done no wenching since the night Adalia had stepped over the portal of Wyndward. It pleased him that his grandson had shown such restraint. Fitz recalled Jonathan's faithfulness to Daisy for years after her raping by the slave. It was a consolation to know Mark had a lot of the Turner in him. It meant Wyndward would continue to grow. Now if Adalia would only show an interest in Mark so there'd be a wedding and young ones to carry on the name, Fitz knew he'd be content. Not completely, since he'd never known the joy of having Sally as his mate. But it would ease the pain some.

At supper that Sunday evening, Adalia had to be reminded to eat. "I'm so excited I don't know what I'm doing. Their lack of education is a challenge I'm eager to meet. And they're eager to learn. I can't lose. I can't wait to open the doors of their minds. A whole new world will open for them."

"Goin' to change things 'round heah," Clarissa said thoughtfully. "Don' knows how much yet, but bound to do somethin'."

Fitz said, "I don' wants to skeer you, Adalia, but you know well as we do that some folks ain't goin' to like whut we doin'. So I'm goin' to assign 'nuff men to guard the schoolhouse, 'specially by night. The dumb bastahds who'd burn it won't come in daylight. They's creatures o' the night."

"Will it be as bad as that, Fitz?" she asked.

"Cain't say. Jes' takin' no chances."

"I don't understand all this," Adalia said. "I'm trying to, but it's almost like a new world to me. My brother is getting used to it, but I have yet to do so. I just hope it changes for the better soon."

"Ain't no reason fo' you to worry," Mark said in his new, protective way. "Sees no harm comes to you, an' means that."

"Thank you, Mark. I was wondering . . . I'd like to go to the schoolhouse right after supper. Just to make certain everything is in order. I don't want anything to go wrong tomorrow, the first day."

"My Lawd, chile, you spent the whole day theah," Clarissa protested. "Whut you should do is rest. You mus' be plain exhausted."

"I'm not," Adalia protested. "Or if I am, I'm not aware of it. I think a walk to the schoolhouse is just the thing I need. I'd probably sleep better."

"You thinks you sleeps a wink waitin' fo' daylight?" Fitz teased.

She laughed. "Probably not."

Mark's eyes were worshipful as he regarded her. "If you wants to go thah, I'll take you."

"Will you, please, Mark?" she entreated.

"Said I would." He was already on his feet.

"You didn' finish your dessert, Mark," Clarissa said.

"Rather take a walk, right now." He was already leading Adalia from the room.

Clarissa and Fitz remained quiet until they heard the front door close.

"Mark sho' in a big hurry," Clarissa said. "You notice that, Fitz?"

"He always in a hurry he gets to go out with Adalia."

"This time mo' special. Wonder if he goin' to ask her to marry him. Knows he been achin' to do it."

"I hopes he come to us fo' he does," Fitz said. "An' you knows why."

Clarisas said, "Gettin' kind o' worried. Adalia leaves now, we goin' to be in one hell of a fix. I sho' cain't teach all them childrun. Fact, I got to learn somethin' myse'f so I kin teach at all. Times I wish I was back in Richmond."

"Like hell you do," Fitz said.

"I jes' talkin'. I talk too much. An' I worries too much, 'bout other people's business. Bettah I should worry 'bout myse'f." She paused a moment and wrinkled her forehead in thought. "On'y whut I got to worry 'bout fo' myse'f? Feels bettah now. Goin' to have that last slice o' cake, Fitz, to celebrate I got nuthin' to worry 'bout."

Hand in hand, Mark and Adalia walked slowly down the path to the schoolhouse. They passed the cemetery, and Mark brought her to a halt outside the low, white-painted gate.

"Gran'pa comes down heah sometime an' talks to the daid folks. Like they kin heah him. They's all theah. Tells you 'bout 'em someday."

"I would like to know about them, Mark. Is your mother buried there?"

"No. She buried in N'Orleans. That's whut she wanted."

"I see. I think it's a nice gesture for your grandfather to come and talk to them. He must get a great deal of comfort out of it."

"Sho' does."

"Do you ever come down and talk to them?"

"Nevah knowed a one, Adalia. They was all 'fore my time."

"Your father is buried in some battlefield, isn't he?"

"Reckon. Nevah knows fo' sho'."

"Let's go to the schoolhouse," she suggested, "and thank you for taking me by the cemetery."

They entered the main schoolroom, which smelled of newly cut wood and recently applied paint. The desks were all in order. On each lay a pad and a pencil. The covers of the desks lifted to reveal an inkwell, pen, paper, eraser, and a slate. A slightly raised platform had been erected at the head of the room, to give the teacher some prominence.

Adalia went at once to the large desk at which she would preside. Mark stood quietly in a corner, his face more somber than Adalia had ever seen it. She looked up. The light was waning, but there was enough that she could see the anguished expression on his face.

"Mark," she called out. He didn't raise his head.

"Mark, are you ill?" She spoke in a louder voice.

He walked up to the platform, took her arm in a firm grasp, led her to the front row of desks, and sat her down in one of them. He made no reply to her queries and mild protests, but he went up on the platform and stood behind her desk.

"Mark," she said gaily, in an attempt to lift his spirits, "you look just like a teacher."

"Yes'm," he said. "Sho' goin' to teach you somethin', Adalia. Got to tell you this. I don', Gran'pa or Clarissa got to do it, an' hard 'nuff fo' me, let alone them. 'Sides, wouldn' be manly I didn'."

"You're going to tell me something about yourself, aren't you?"

"Aims to."

"You don't have to."

"Knows that, but gots to."

"What do you know about me, Mark?"

"You?" he asked in a startled voice.

"Yes, me! Do you wish me to reveal to you all my secrets? To open my life to you? Mine and those I loved among my own people?"

"Don' care nuthin' 'bout that."

"But you wouldn't ask, would you?"

"Sho' wouldn'. Knows whut kind o' girl you are an' whut kin' o' papa an' mama you got. Knows your brother, an' he a fine man. Ain't askin' you nuthin' 'cause you got nuthin' to tell me."

"And you have?"

He exhaled slowly. "Sho' have. You gots no idea."

"What if I say I don't want to hear it?"

"Tells you anyways."

"Why? Because you're going to ask me to marry you some day?"

"Aims to. That's why you got to know now."

"It's not going to make any difference, Mark darling."

"You cain't say that 'fore you heahs whut I got to say."

"All right. I suppose if you don't tell me you won't ask me to marry you, and I wouldn't like that. Because it would force me to ask you to marry me, and that is not lady-like."

Mark's eyes widened. "You means that?"

The slow, affirmative nod of her head was more convincing than any spoken word.

"Then, will you kindly shut up? Talkin' like that an' I gettin' mo' skeered ev'ry minute."

"I shall listen without saying a word. Just one thing more before you begin. Tell me, Mark, why did you have the walls of this school painted a pale yellow?"

"Paint's hard to get. We could choose 'tween this an' dark brown."

"I see. You may begin."

She settled back, cramped in the small bench behind the small desk. She looked up at him exactly as a kindergarten pupil might look up at her first teacher. A little frightened, but confident and trusting.

Mark clasped his hands tightly, held them before his face for a moment, then lowered them, still clasped.

" 'Members the Fisbee place whar we lived 'fore comin' back to the mansion?"

"Yes."

"That's whar I was born. Comes about like this. My mama lives theah with her papa an' mama an' some uncles an' aunts. Once I heard that Benay—that Gran'pa's wife—say it nuthin' but a pigsty. Thinks I feels bad 'bout that? Hell no! It's whut I was used to. Nevah knowed anythin' diff'rent. Well, Gran'pa's son Jonathan—my papa—stops by one day an' my mama takes him out to the barn, or some place like that, an' he sweahs she rapes him. Didn' say anythin' 'bout fightin' her off.

"You says somethin' now an' mayhap I quits. I'm dyin' inch by inch right now, but I gots to keep on an' it gets worse. I born, Jonathan nevah marries my mama. Don' know she evah asks him—or even gave a damn. My fam'ly went to pieces. Don' know why or whut caused it, but Mama takes me to N'Orleans. She got no money, she as dumb as any o' the childrun you goin' to teach tomorrow. Cain't do nuthin' 'cause she don' know nuthin'— 'cept rapin'. She goes to wuk in a whorehouse, an' that's whar I was brought up. Pretty soon she owns the place an' makes lots o' money. You still wants me to go on? Jes' nods your haid, don' say anythin'.'"

She nodded slowly, without betraying any expression.

"Two times she bring me to Wyndward to see my papa. She tells me I gots to kill him soon's I growed up. Twice I comes heah with her an' puts the muzzle o' a gun 'gainst my papa's haid, but Mama say don' shoot. You askin' in you haid would I shoot him 'cause Mama says so? I kin answer that. I wanted to. But I was to save him 'til I got to be a man, an' all the while he kin worry his haid off wonderin' when I'm comin'. I growed up, I came back to Wyndward to kill him. Gran'pa tells me my papa enlisted. I finds out whar he been sent an' enlisted too, askin' to be sent to the same place. By then he an officer, so I nevah gets near him lessen there's a few hundred others theah too.

"But they comes a day when I'm right behind him. He was with a company on reconnoiterin' duty. Twice I raised my gun to shoot him, but I couldn't pull the trigger. All my life, 'til she dies, I listened to Mama an' nevah questioned she was right or wrong. All of a sudden I know she wrong. She was too damn stupid to know whut she tellin' me to do. An' ten seconds later, after I knew I couldn' kill him, I sees him shot an' ready to be bayoneted. Wasn' a thing I could do. If there was, I'd o' gone to help him. The man I was brought up to kill.

"When Mama dies, I ran the whorehouse—or turned it over to one o' the whores to run fo' me—an' I comes to Wyndward to see whut I could get outen my gran'pa. Sho' found out whut I could get. I could get love an' understandin', an' some kind o' an education. I found out whut it was like to love somebody in return. Thass whut I got to say. Sold the whorehouse. Got the money, lots o' it. Ain't beholden to anybody. Now you kin get up an' walk out o' heah, an' I nevah says a word. You lives heah an' you teaches the childrun heah an' we friends, thass how you wants it. Wants nuthin' to do with me, I go away. Couldn' bear livin' heah with you so close. Loves you pow'ful. So much it hurts."

He stood there in silence now, aware that he was perspiring profusely but not able to lift a hand to brush the beads of sweat off his forehead.

"You heahs anythin' I said?" he asked. "You got anythin' to say? Anythin' to ask?"

"Yes, Mark. Couldn't you have mixed a little brown paint with the yellow to darken this room a bit? No, on second thought, it's perfect this way. As bright and shining as my love for you."

The tenseness slowly left him as her words penetrated his mind, and he stepped down off the platform. She stood up and went to him. They faced each other, their eyes plainly revealing their love.

"You nevah let me know that 'fore," he said softly.

"How could I, when you never even made any attempt to kiss me? All you ever did was look at me."

"Nevah could take my eyes off you. Thought you knew why."

"Maybe I did," she teased. "But a lady can't make advances."

"You still loves me, after whut I jes' told yo'?"

"My dear, handsome Mark, I don't care what your mama was like. I don't care what her people were like. I don't care if you were raised in a whorehouse."

"Nevah slept with any of 'em," he interjected aggressively.

She laughed. "I'm glad to hear that. Let me go on. I don't care if you intended to kill your papa—so long as you didn't. The fact that you couldn't shows you're a Turner. Clarissa said you were. Nothing you've told me makes any difference. Goddamn it, Mark, can't you see

192

it's you I'm in love with. You ... only you and to hell with the rest of it."

"Nevah heard yo' sweah 'fore."

"Nevah did. But this the occasion fo' it." She mimicked his way of speaking. "When you gonna kiss me? I goes clean out o' my mind you don'."

Mark's arms were already enclosing her and drawing her close. "I loves you, Adalia. Loved you from the moment I laid eyes on you. Thought my heart was goin' to burst through my chest wall. Feels like it's gonna do that now."

"So does mine." She stood on tiptoe and raised her face to his. "Kiss me, my darling."

"Still tryin' to believe this comin' true," he said. "Lay awake nights wonderin' how to tell you whut I had to. Thought you'd walk out on me, you knowed. Want to marry you iffen you willin'."

"I'm willin'. We can talk about that latuh. Jes' now my lips achin' pow'fully bad fo' yours."

"Fo' a Reb, you talkin' jes' fine," Mark said. "Loves you, Adalia. Loves you fo' the rest o' my days."

Her arms went around his neck, and their lips met. The kiss was gentle at first, then the passion they'd kept under control for weeks soared, and their kisses became more demanding as their hunger for each other asserted itself.

15

Adalia was too excited to sleep. Her mind was still filled with the magic of those precious moments with Mark when he had first spoken of his love for her and asked for her hand in marriage. She smiled at the thought of their betrothal taking place in a schoolroom that smelled of fresh paint. So far as she was concerned, they'd been seated beneath a bower of roses, enveloped in their heady perfume. She shivered with delight as she recalled his arms enclosing her waist and drawing her close. He'd held her so tightly she had felt his rapid heartbeat, which had throbbed in unison with hers. Her breath quickened again as she recalled their first kiss—his lips closing over hers, gently at first, then more demanding as their ardor grew. Her ecstasy was boundless. She spoke his name aloud in the darkened room, loving the sound of it and adding endearments. She knew she was behaving like a foolish schoolgirl, but she didn't care. She was in love, and she was loved by a man whom she knew would cherish, honor, and protect her the rest of her life.

She was pleased that Fitz and Clarissa not only approved of her, but were fond of her. The fact that Fitz had built the schoolhouse and assured her she could have whatever she needed to carry out her duties as teacher on the plantation was proof. She felt certain her future would be happy and peaceful. She didn't share the concern she'd observed in Clarissa's face when she had come to inspect the building. Though people around here might disapprove and possibly even snub her, they'd come around eventually. Everything was going to be beautiful. She would not only have her marriage with Mark, but the school filled with pupils would take up her time while he was running Wyndward.

So many thoughts were racing through her mind that her head was spinning. She had to settle down and get some rest so she'd be alert when her pupils arrived. The thought warmed her, and soft laughter escaped her.

Once again she spoke into the darkness. "Mark darling, and Fitz and yes, you too, Clarissa, thank you for making me so happy." She turned on her side and, still smiling, fell into a gentle sleep.

Adalia awoke early, bathed, and dressed quickly, selecting a blue and green striped muslin dress, its square neckline trimmed with narrow braid. The front of the skirt was unpleated, all fullness drawn to the back. It was a plain dress, but she knew women in the South had few garments and that those they had were well worn and outmoded. So, though hers was in fashion, it was devoid of frills and furbelows. As was the rest of her wardrobe. There would be plenty of time for those when conditions got better.

Downstairs, Fitz was already at the breakfast table, but when Adalia entered, he arose and kissed her fondly.

"Mark told me last night," he said. "Mighty pleased you goin' to be in the fam'ly."

"So am I, Fitz. I love your grandson. I have for some time."

Fitz chuckled. "Reckon you know he hasn't been hisse'f since the moment he laid eyes on you. Leastwise it's out in the open now an' he'll heah me when I talks to him. Hope the engagement won' last too long. Don' think any o' us could stand it. Least o' all Mark."

"We didn't set a date," Adalia said, her smile wistful. "He told me about himself, though there was no need. It's of no importance to me, though I suppose he feels better now."

"Know it was a load on his mind," Fitz said softly. "Also knowed you had a good haid on your shoulders. Anyways, I don' need to fret now 'bout what's goin' to happen to Wyndward. Hurt real bad sometimes, rebuildin' it an' wonderin' if it would jes' go to seed after I was no longer heah. Now that worry's off my mind."

"What about your daughter? Surely she would be proud to become mistress of Wyndward."

"No! Can say that fo' sho'. Melanie come to hate slavery so much it near wrecked her life an' all the plans I had fo' her. No, she'd nevah come back, an' if I left the place to her she likely nevah have anythin' to do with it. Bad 'nuff 'fore the war, but then her husband got killed fightin' fo' the North an' that made her more bitter than evah. She has disowned me as a father, an' refuses to reco'nize me. Cain't do anythin' 'bout it. I still loves her, but whut good does that do now? Don't change things."

"I'm sorry, Fitz. I wish I could do something to persuade her to change her mind."

"Don' even try," Fitz said. "It would on'y break your heart. An' mine."

"You've never heard anything from Mark's father? I mean, nothing definite."

"Asked your brother to look into it. Reckon he doin' that now, but I got no real hopes Jonathan still 'live. You know, Adalia, Wyndward the finest plantation in Virginny, likely. Used to make a lot o' money an' will again. Got a fine house, once it had a fine fam'ly, but theah ain't much left. Wyndward, fo' all its success an' all the happiness it kin bring—an' did—is beset with tragedies an' troubles evah since it came 'bout. Now my mama an' my daughter would say it happens 'cause we kept slaves. 'Cause it got its start by buyin' human beings, bringin' em heah an' sellin' 'em like cattle. Mayhap they right, but if it's true, ev'ry damn plantation in the South must o' had the same thing happen to it. We all sinners far as Mama an' Melanie concerned."

"I'm sure slavery had nothing to do with what happened here."

"Well, to be honest 'bout it, I think it did. Fo' instance, Mama got killed, Benay died, Jonathan daid, Daisy go outen her mind fo' she dies. Even my papa died on the same ship in which he brought all the slaves. Ev'ry one o' those deaths caused by slavery one way o' 'nother. By damn, so many I clean fo'got the twins. Jonathan's boys. They got blown to bits right after the war starts. Wasn' 'round heah long 'nuff that I kin even 'members 'em, talkin' 'bout all the others."

"Fitz, if you're trying to discourage me, or if you're warning me I might suffer a similar fate, you're wasting your time. I love it here. I want to be a part of it."

"Knows that. Jes' talkin'. Kind o' needs somebody I kin talk to like that. But won't talk 'bout it again. You knows whut you're gettin' into."

"I know I'm in love with your grandson, and I also love you, Fitzjohn Turner. You're just about the finest man I have ever known."

He smiled broadly. "Nice to heah that, Adalia. Reckon Mark comes down pretty soon. Knows he want to take you to the schoolhouse fo' your first day."

"I hope he does."

"Kind o' a fine day fo' me too. Fo' yeahs I been wantin' to give some schoolin' to the childrun heah. 'Course befo' the war, it was 'gainst the law to teach a slave. Still, I got at least one schooled. Real smart boy."

"Good. Frankly, I don't see why those children can't become as well educated as anyone else."

"Well now, don' count on it. All their lives they had nuthin'. No books, no pencils, don' know whut a slate is. Sometime not 'nuff to eat—but not on this plantation. Nevah even learns to talk right. Tries to talk like we does, but cain't do it right so they gots kind o' a language o' their own. You gets used to it, but on'y 'nother 'zample whut they lack. 'Bout all they got is love, but plenty o' that. Heah, they nevah got sold an' taken away. Nevah busted a fam'ly in my life. Cain't sell 'em all, I has to fo' one reason o' 'nother, don' sell any o' them."

"I'm going to work very hard," Adalia promised. "I don't care how many hours I have to spend with them. You were telling me about this man you did educate. What happened to him?"

Fitz smiled slightly. "Reckon I hoped you fo'gets that, but has to tell you the truth. This gal, name o' Nina, brought heah by my papa. Don' know whar she comes from, but she almost white an' so pretty I kin still see her when I close my eyes, an' it been a long time since she dies. 'Fore I marries Benay, I sleeps with this gal Nina. After I gets married, Nina tells me she goin' to have a baby. Thinks it gots to be mine, an' I wants to have it. Benay knows all 'bout this. But I didn' know that a big buck takes Nina one night an' rapes her. An' her child is by him. He was born same time Jonathan born, an' he turn out to be blacker'n midnight. Bornin' him killed Nina."

"That is tragic. I suppose you were bitter."

"Hates this poor child. Hands him to Seawitch an' tells her to let him starve to death, but Seawitch bring him up. Took some yeahs fo' I come to my senses an' finds this boy—named him Dundee—with mo' sense than I gots. Ketches him tryin' to learn, an' I helped him. Sends him North, with 'nother boy I took in. Melanie say she sees they get educated. Last time I heah from Melanie she tell me they both got the schoolin' I wanted fo' 'em, an' they comin' South to do whut they kin to help those who were slaves an' don' know how to live now they's free."

"You are a remarkable man, Fitz. Will you come down and see how I'm getting along?"

"Sho' will. Don' know how many pupils you goin' to have. There's too many, Clarissa comes down to help. Mayhap she cain't teach much, but she sho' kin keep 'em behavin' themse'ves. Heahs Mark comin'."

Adalia arose quickly and went to the door to greet Mark with a kiss. His arm enclosed her waist as he poured a cup of coffee while still standing and drank it without once taking his eyes from her face. She felt her cheeks flame with pleasure, and her hand covered his, which still clasped her waist. Fitz regarded the tableau with satisfaction and a touch of envy, wishing he was once again young, then quickly chided himself for his selfishness. He'd had his golden days; now it was his grandson's turn.

Mark set down the cup, and with a short nod to Fitz and his arm still around Adalia's waist, he escorted her from the house. They moved in silence along the path leading to the school until they came to a heavily wooded area. As he guided her off the road, his arms drew her to him and his lips covered hers. His closeness and his kiss set her head spinning. But he held the embrace only a few seconds before releasing her.

His eyes adored her as he spoke. "Nevah knowed this feelin' befo'. 'Nuff to drive a man crazy, but it beautiful too."

"It's love, Mark. I don't know the words to tell you how happy I am."

"Feels the same way. Knows now why Gran'pa go down to the cemetery an' talks with the folks. He still 'members the glory of those days when they lived. Saw the hurt in his eyes this mawnin' when he was watchin' us. He know he cain't have that again. I knows he glad we got it ahead o' us."

"We'll envelop Wyndward with love and laughter and let your grandpa be a part of it."

"That mighty nice o' you, Adalia. An' now I gots to say it again. I loves you. It's a mighty big love. A pow'ful love. A fo'evah love."

She had to blink to hold back the tears. "You're a poet, Mark darling."

"No," he contradicted, color flooding his face. "Jes' sayin' whut's in my heart."

"I'd like to stay here," she said, suddenly aware of where she was supposed to be, "but I imagine there are a crowd of children waiting to be admitted to the school."

Mark chuckled. "Theah bettah be. Gran'pa be mighty mad he built that school fo' nuthin'. Let's go."

"Are you sure you have the time?"

"I'll always have the time fo' you, Adalia." His hand caught hers, and they resumed their walk along the path.

As they neared the school, she came to a stop. There wasn't a single child in evidence, and though the door to the schoolhouse was ajar, not a sound came from the interior. A piece of level ground, fenced off and cleared as a play area for the pupils, was also empty.

"What do you suppose happened?" she asked in alarm.

"Don' know, but sho' aims to find out," Mark said angrily. "They were all told school starts this mawnin'."

They had reached the building. From it came a quiet murmur of voices, barely audible at this close range. When they stepped inside, the large room was almost full. Each child sat at a desk, hands folded on top of it. They were scrubbed, their hair braided in various arrangements, their faces alight with interest and anticipation. Adalia and Mark relaxed and exchanged smiles of relief.

Surprisingly, in the back were at least twenty adults, all women, who had somehow crammed into the small chairs and wedged themselves behind the desks.

Mark stood aside so Adalia could proceed to her desk. She faced her pupils with some trepidation, but those eager black faces were inspiration in themselves.

She smiled as she said, "Good morning."

There was a chorus of greetings and a few titters. One of the women at the rear spoke up. "We comes so we kin see 'bout readin' an' writin'. Kin we stay, ma'am?"

"Anyone can come. The more, the better. Now we'll get down to business." Adalia removed the dustcover from the desk, folded it, and placed it in the bottom drawer. Later, she'd assign a pupil to come early and attend to that chore. She'd have another cover the desk in the afternoon. She knew the pupils liked being assigned various chores. It gave them a sense of responsibility.

She picked up a large pad from her desk. On the first page was a drawing of the seating arrangement. She would first have to rearrange the pupils so that the smaller ones could be in the front. After that, she would get the name of each boy and girl and place those names in the space that corresponded with their desk. She already had cut strips of cardboard on which their names would be printed and placed on their desks.

Mark, standing at the rear of the room, felt a warm glow of pride as Adalia held up the chart and explained it to her class. She immediately set to work changing the seating. Both children and adults responded eagerly and obediently to her orders and questions. Once Mark was assured that all would go well, he quietly withdrew and walked back to the mansion. He found his grandfather seated on the veranda, taking advantage of the balmy day. Mark sat down beside him.

"Looks like it goin' to wuk, Gran'pa. Reckon I nevah seen folks so ready to learn. Anythin' special you wants me to do today?"

"Might tell Hong Kong to put some boys to wuk cleanin' the curin' sheds. An' looks over the land we thinkin' 'bout plowin'. Thinks there too many trees to get cut down in time fo' plowin'. Mayhap we waits till next yeah."

"Looked already. Cain't get all them trees down in time. Gots almost more'n we kin handle now. Needs mo' hands, an' don' know whar to get 'em."

"Trouble is, the men who used to be slaves ain't got used to the idea they gots to wuk to eat. Too many Freedmen's Bureau stores 'round heah."

"Sho' keepin' lots o' the niggers alive. Reckon we gots to put up with 'em fo' a long time. Gran'pa, open your eyes. Buggy jes' turnin' in from the main road."

Fitz looked up, dismissing the sleepy feeling that had almost overcome him. "Thass Adalia's brother," he said. "Kin see the uniform."

"Wonder whut he wants."

"Reckon he bringin' some news. Asks him fo' some favors some days back. Mayhap he on'y wants to see how the school gettin' on."

"Chickory!" Fitz bellowed, and the boy came running to the veranda. "Take charge o' the Cap'n's buggy. Sees the hoss gets water, it needs some."

"I runs," Chickory said and ran so fast he passed the buggy and had to turn around and follow the vehicle back to the area below the veranda. Captain Morton drew off his gloves as he climbed the stairs.

"Calcutta Two!" Fitz called out. "Brings whiskey an' spring water, an' it bettah be cold or you bends down fo' gettin' your ass kicked."

The captain sat down and lost no time in stating the reason for his visti. "Got some news, Fitz."

" 'Bout that Reb sergeant?" Fitz asked eagerly.

"No, that's a tough one. It's about Jonathan. He's alive!"

"Sho' 'nuff?" Fitz asked anxiously.

"He comin' home?" Mark asked.

"Yes, he's coming home. It may take a few more days, but they're sending him back. It really took some doing. It was necessary that Washington countermand the court-martial."

"Whut court-martial?" Fitz asked.

"Let me give you the details," the captain said. "Jonathan was wounded, as you told us, Mark. But he wasn't bayoneted. They took him prisoner and locked him up. He was never considered for wounded exchange. Incidentally, he was a major by then."

"Whut 'bout a court-martial?" Fitz persisted.

"Jonathan turned out to be a rebellious prisoner who made all the trouble he possibly could."

Fitz shook his head. "Knows whut's the matter. He enlists when he so goddamn mad at ev'rythin' an' ev'rybody he don' know whut he doin'. Lost his twins an' then Daisy dies while he holdin' her hand, thinkin' she gettin' bettah."

"Whom was he angry at?" the captain asked.

"War comes 'bout 'cause o' slaves. War kills his boys. Nigger responsible fo' his wife losin' her mind an' then dyin'. Reckon he mad at ev'rybody, but mostly at the North fo' tryin' to free slaves he hates an' wants to see stay slaves. Reckon he even mad at hisse'f. What he do?"

"For one thing, when the news of Lincoln's death reached the prison, Jonathan tried to get every prisoner to cheer. Got in trouble with the guards, fighting all the time, even with fellow prisoners. In fact, for one attack on guards, he was given a prison sentence of ten years."

"But they lettin' him out 'cause you asked 'em to?"

"Well, hardly that. I wrote about the fact that you are his father, you believed him dead all this time, and that you would make a home for him. I guess it costs a lot of money to keep a man in prison, so it's cheaper to send him home."

"Wouldn' be 'cause my name got him out?"

"Can't say."

"Means you couldn' say if you knew. I'm sorry to heah whut he's turned into, but be mighty glad to have him back."

"Kin you tell me when he gets heah? I'll meet him," Mark offered.

"As soon as I know, I'll send word. There's something else."

Fitz nodded. "Reckon it the school."

"Yes."

"Adalia gettin' right to it, Cap'n," Mark said enthusiastically. "Last I sees fo' I left her theah, even has grown folks 'tendin'."

"What they sayin' 'bout it?" Fitz was more practical.

"Well, the people you employed to rebuild this house knew the school was being built, and word has gotten around that my sister couldn't get a job teaching because she's from the North. They've figured out the school must be for the benefit of blacks. It was pretty good guessing."

"An' whut they aims to do?" Fitz asked soberly.

Though Captain Morton spoke quietly, he looked concerned. "I don't know. But I will assure you of this. If there is any trouble, any attack made on that school, or the pupils, I'll see to it that whoever is responsible will pay for it. I've enough men to back it up even if a mob moves in."

"Mark an' me kin take care o' it lessen a big mob comes. Lets you know that happens. They comes to burn the schoolhouse, somebody goin' to get killed. We stops 'em from burnin' this heah mansion, but didn' do much shootin'. This time we aims to kill. Nobody is burnin' down that schoolhouse lessen they kills us first."

"Ain't goin' to tell Adalia 'bout any o' this," Mark said. "She too happy with bein' teacher theah. 'Sides, no sense frightenin' her."

"I agree," the captain said. "I'm grateful she can stay in this house. There are still some hard feelings about Yankees around here, and I don't want her exposed to any possible danger."

"She stays heah the rest o' her life, Cap'n," Mark said. "Goin' to marry her soon's things change fo' the bettah."

"Congratulations, Mark." Captain Morton shook Mark's hand warmly. "I'm very happy."

"An' I'm very lucky," Mark replied, beaming.

"An' jes' another thing makes our hard-headed neighbors be madder'n evah," Fitz reasoned. "They puts marryin' a Yankee in the same class as marryin' a nigger. Man's got a right to marry anybody he likes."

"I understand most of the South is growing reconciled to defeat and the aftermath of war, Fitz. Except around here, and I think that's because we're so close to Richmond, where the government held its offices during the war. Everyone in this district was too close to the military action. And ... the burning and looting didn't help. We brought some of this upon ourselves."

"War is war," Fitz declared. "Ev'rybody gets hurt. Kindly lets us know soon's you heahs."

"I'll send a man out. Now, may I visit the school and see my dear sister working at last? I teased her about it often enough."

Just as Mark and Captain Morton were about to leave, Clarissa stepped out on the veranda. The captain greeted her graciously and expressed his regrets that he couldn't accept her invitation to join her in a late breakfast.

Mark said, "No time fo' talkin' now, Clarissa. Cap'n wants to see Adalia teachin'."

"Don't blames him," Clarissa said. "Cain't wait to see her myse'f."

Fitz got to his feet. "I'll have a cup o' coffee with you. Got lots to tell you."

"Be glad o' you company," Clarissa said. "Hope it good news."

"Lets you judge fo' yourse'f."

"Some is, Gran'pa," Mark called. He and Captain Morton were already on the path leading to the school.

Fitz smiled agreement, waved him on, and followed Clarissa into the house. He didn't speak until she had been served and he'd taken a few sips of his coffee.

"Jonathan's alive," he told her finally.

She set down the forkful of food she was about to eat and regarded him with astonishment. "Oh, Fitz, that's wonderful."

"Don' know yet how wonderful it is. From whut Cap'n Morton say, Jonathan turns into a bad one. Fightin' ev'rybody, hatin' ev'rythin'."

Clarissa resumed eating. "He'll change once he gets back heah. He be hisse'f again once he gets home."

"Don' be too sho' 'bout that. He madder'n hell when he enlist."

"That was almost five yeahs ago, Fitz."

"Five yeahs he been in prison, an' all the time that hate festerin'. Think he goin' to be worse, an' don' know how we kin change him."

"Needs love, Fitz. We kin change him."

"Goin' to try, thass fo' sho'. Reckon we lucky he's alive."

Clarissa transferred more bacon to her plate. "Makin' a pig o' myse'f an' gettin' too fat. Sees thot Jonathan gets plenty to eat. Mayhap that helps."

"Mo' trouble 'bout the school," Fitz continued moodily. "Damn it, Clarissa, nuthin' in my life but trouble."

"Ain' got trouble, you gets bored," she said. "Keeps your blood runnin' hot."

"Jes' now it seems like it runnin' kind o' cold. Wishes we was back in the old days when all we has to worry our haids 'bout was the next dinner an' ball. An' whut the womenfolk was wearin'."

"Thinks o' somethin'," Clarissa said. "Jonathan come home an' he finds out Domingo married . . . likes that gal

205

an' not even Jonathan goin' to bust her up 'cause he hates all niggers. An' 'cause she married now."

"You sees Domingo an' tells her to stay 'way from him fo' awhile. Tells her the truth. Wants none o' that kind o' trouble 'round heah."

Elegant waddled into the dining room to remove the dishes. She surveyed the empty platter. "Missy Clarissa, you sho' gots a fine appetite."

"It's your cookin'," Clarissa said, smiling benignly as she patted her stomach.

"Jonathan comin' home," Fitz told her.

"Jonathan, comin' home! He 'live? Whooeee... goin' to make him bes' dinnah he evah eats. . . ."

"Hold on," Fitz warned. "He goin' to be changed some, I heahs. Hates ev'rybody 'cause o' losin' Daisy an' the twins. Mayhap the war too. Tells you now, he goin' to hate anybody with a black skin."

"Massa Fitz, when Jonathan no higher'n you ass, whumps him good he sasses me. Whumps him now he sasses me."

"He's kind o' big, Elegant."

"Knows that. Ain't aimin' to use my han' like ah used to. Uses a big fryin' pan now. Ain't goin' to take no guff from him. Ah praises the Lawd he 'live, but he ain' goin' to cuss me out."

Captain Morton and Mark returned from their visit to the school, both looking pleased.

"Adalia got 'em sayin' their ABCs already," Mark said. "They tryin' real hard, an' Adalia a fine teacher. Proud o' her."

"I am too," Captain Morton agreed. "I felt it best that she know the danger of what she is doing. She said she won't let it stop her. Fitz, if there's any suggestion of trouble, let me know at once."

"We cain't take care o' it ourse'ves," Fitz said, "we sho' does that, Cap'n."

"Come back when you kin, suh," Mark said. "Be mighty glad to see you."

"I'll do my best," the captain declared. "But I think it might be wiser if I stayed away from Jonathan. And I hope I'll have word on that other project, Fitz. Do my best."

"Thanks you, suh. Fo' ev'rythin'.' "

They saw him off and then returned to the veranda where Calcutta Two had finally appeared with a round of drinks.

"Jonathan comin' home to lots o' s'prises, Gran'pa. He nevah knows this mansion burns down an' we rebuilds. But thass nuthin' to whut he thinks he finds out he gots a son livin' heah an' helpin' to run the place."

"Has to wait an' see whut he's come to. Thinkin' o' Adalia too, livin' heah," Fitz said thoughtfully. "A Yankee gal goin' to marry his son."

"Reckon he don' give a damn I marries her, but mayhap he gives a damn that Yankee livin' under the same roof. Gran'pa, he make trouble 'count o' that, I ain' goin' to let him get away with it."

"We both won't let him get away with it," Fitz said. "I 'members rightly, it'll take the two of us. Jonathan mighty strong."

Captain Morton sent word that Jonathan would arrive at the depot in Lynchburg on Thursday around noon. Clarissa immediately went to work preparing a room for him. Elegant planned an extra big meal. Adalia was worried about how he would adjust to her presence, while Fitz and Mark worried about Jonathan refusing to come home at all.

Fitz and Mark arrived early in Lynchburg and fortified themselves with a few drinks. They inquired about Colonel Apperson's whereabouts and learned that he had not been seen since the fiasco with the carpetbagger, who was still looking for him, presumably with a gun.

They stood on the depot platform, silent and concerned. A father and a son waiting for a man they might find difficult, but who, nevertheless, deserved all the love they could give him.

Jonathan, in what remained of his uniform, stepped off the train. He looked much older. He was thin to the point of near emaciation. He wore a scraggly beard, and his thick hair seemed long uncombed. But it was his eyes that upset Fitz most. Where once they were alert, they were now lusterless.

"Glad to have you back, son." Fitz extended his hand, though he wanted to embrace him.

"You sho' 'bout that?" Jonathan asked. His voice was harsh and arrogant. Fitz disregarded the arrogance and the question

Jonathan carried a battered carpetbag, but refused to surrender it when Mark offered to carry it. They led him to where the carriage was waiting, and he threw the bag onto the back seat.

Fitz said, "You knows who this boy is?" He indicated Mark.

"Knows him. Last I sees, he runnin' like hell when the Yankees shoots me off my hoss."

"Papa," Mark protested, "wasn't nuthin' else I could do. . . ."

"Nevah mind," Fitz said. "Gots to say though, Jonathan, that your son heah a mighty good boy. An' he don' run from nuthin'."

Jonathan sighed deeply. "Papa, I don' give a damn."

"Sees that. Get in the carriage."

"Rides by myse'f."

"Whatevah you wants," Fitz said. He took the reins and with Mark beside him, drove the carriage to the main road back to Wyndward.

"Got a few things to tell you, Jonathan. You goin' to listen?"

"How kin I help it?"

"The mansion got burned down right after you goes off to war."

"Goddamn Yankees burned it," Jonathan said.

"Son, the war is over," Fitz said.

"Not fo' me it ain't. Nevah fo' me, an' you bettah understan' that. It ain't nevah goin' to be over."

"Gets to that later. An' the Yankees didn' burn it. I did."

"Same thing. They goin' to burn it anyways."

"The Yankee officer say he won't burn it if Melanie ask him not to. He sent her a wireless while we waitin'.

An' she sends back word to burn it. Looks to me like I gots two childrun ain't worth a goddamn 'cause neither one gots 'nuff sense to act like they growed up."

"Papa," Mark said, "ain't no use bein' mad. Wyndward looks jes' like it used to. Clarissa livin' theah, an' she takin' care o' things."

"An' beddin' down with you o' course. When she ain't beddin' down with Papa."

"Gots to tell you," Mark went on, thinking it best to get the entire business over with now. "Gots a schoolhouse back o' the house. Gots us a teacher livin' in the mansion. She teachin' niggers from the plantation."

"Ain't s'prised none."

"She also a Yankee. Her brother a Yankee officer in charge o' Lynchburg."

"You gets her out 'fore mawnin', heah?"

"I'm goin' to marry her, Papa."

"Like hell you are. Whut she want with a bastahd like you? Don' wants you 'round either. You a Fisbee, an' Fisbee blood be stinkin' an' rotten like an old pig pen."

"He gots Turner blood too," Fitz reminded him.

"Ain't no blood kin drown the stink o' Fisbee blood. Get that damn Yankee teacher out, an' you goes with her, heah?"

Fitz said, "Whoa!" and brought the carriage to a stop. He turned around to face his son. "Heard 'nuff outen you, Jonathan. Heah an' now you gots to realize you comin' home at last. We all glad to see you. Thinks you daid all this time. You keeps on like this, an' we wishes to hell you was."

"Papa," Mark pleaded, "Wyndward bettah than evah."

"Daisy theah?" Jonathan demanded. "She waitin' to hold me in her arms an' kiss me? My twins theah, come runnin' to meet me?"

"Reckon not," Fitz said. "Benay ain' theah either. You thinks o' that?"

"Go to hell," Jonathan said.

Fitz's face grew white with rage. "You comin' home, we glad to have you, but the schoolmarm stay an' Mark marries her an' you behaves yourse'f."

Jonathan leaned forward. "You knows whut I been through? You got any idea whut they done to me?"

"They didn' kill you," Mark said.

"Might's well have."

Mark shook his head in despair. " 'Members when my mama tells me to kill you. Wishes now I had. You about the biggest sonabitch I evah knowed."

"You makin' me cry," Jonathan said sarcastically.

Fitz said, "Gives you a choice. You keeps your mouth shut an' you behaves yourse'f or you kin get out right now an' walk. Anywhar but to Wyndward. Spent five yeahs grievin' fo' a man who ain't worth a tear. Fo' whut? You ain't my son. You ain't Mark's papa. You ain't nuthin'! Bettah we nevah find you. Bettah you nevah comes back. So get out, you wants to, an' nevah sees you agin if I kin help it."

Jonathan scowled, but his anger subsided. "Got nowhar to go."

"Got hell to go to you wants. I sho' don' care."

"Papa," Mark pleaded. "I knows it was bad fo' you. But sho' wasn't any picnic fo' any o' us."

"You talkin'! Whut they do to you?"

"Jes' shoots me is all," Mark declared. " Got me a Yankee ball in my hide. Ain't no hero an' you ain't either, but we both did whut we could. Now it's over. All over."

"Told you, not fo' me."

"Makes up you mind," Fitz said. "Ain't waitin'."

"Mayhap I busts you some, Papa," Jonathan said. "Been wantin' to bust somebody good fo' a long time."

"You welcome to try right now," Fitz said.

"You gets outen this heah carriage to bust anybody," Mark said, "you busts me too. This one hell o' a way to have my papa come home. You sho' outen your haid, Papa. You crazy!"

"Wants to go home," Jonathan said in a sullen voice.

"You don't make trouble fo' this Yankee gal. You stays away from the schoolhouse an' you behaves yourse'f." Fitz laid down the conditions.

"Does whut you says," Jonathan agreed.

"Sho' don' trust you none," Fitz said as he picked up the reins. "You my son an' I cain't trust you, but I kin say you starts trouble, you gets kicked out. You get one chance an' no mo'. Knows you been through a hell o' your own, but that don' give you the right to make a hell fo' ev'rybody else. Now we'll go home."

16

When the carriage stopped in front of the veranda, Clarissa ran down the steps. Behind her came Elegant, shouting her welcome.

Jonathan stood like a frozen statue when Clarissa embraced him. She let go and stepped back, clearly puzzled. Elegant, who had noticed nothing amiss, pushed her fat body against him and tried to plant a kiss on his cheek, which was impossible unless he bent down. Instead, Jonathan gave her a push that sent her reeling back.

"Keep your hands off me, you black bitch!"

Elegant moved forward slowly. "You gots no right to call me that, suh. Brought you up, ah did, an' you ain' callin' me no bitch."

She swung her hand and slapped him across the face with an explosive force. He raised his hands, clasped them into fists. Mark lunged, wrapped his arms around Jonathan, and dragged him back a few steps. Elegant, tossing her head, walked back into the house.

Clarissa said, "Whut in hell's the matter with him? He don't belong heah. He belong in a crazy house."

"We all takes it real easy," Fitz said. "Jonathan changed some, an' cain't say it fo' the bettah, but he been through a lot o' heartache an' pain an' we gots to give him a chance to get over it. That understood, I'll apologize to Elegant. Jonathan, you kin do whut you wants."

Jonathan raised his head and looked over the mansion. "Ain't changed none. You sho' it got burned down?"

"Seein' I burned it, I'm sho'," Fitz said. "Wants you to set an' have a drink with me."

"Some other time, Papa. I'm tired an' feels sick. Gots to rest. Gots to go to my room."

"Last door to the left," Clarissa said tartly. "You kin find it fo' yourse'f."

Jonathan shrugged, picked up his bag, and walked into the house. Fitz shook his head in despair. "Mark, calls fo' Calcutta an' get us drinks. Sit down, Clarissa. Gots to tell you whut's the matter with Jonathan."

"Ain't nuthin' the matter with him a good club wouldn't cure, Fitz. You goin' to let him get away with how he's actin'?"

"All I kin do is hope he changes back to the kind o' man he used to be. He needs help. Lots o' help."

"He sho' don' get any from me, he keeps actin' like he did."

"Knows it ain't easy to take, Clarissa, but thass how it is. Mayhap we kin change him. Goin' to try."

"If you cain't do it, Fitz, then whut?"

"Don' know. Mayhap I kicks him out. Mayhap he gets into trouble an' winds up in prison. He don't come down outen his cloud o' crazy anger, don't give a damn they hangs him."

"Gran'pa, he say anythin' to insult Adalia, I sho' am goin' to call him outside fo' a little talk."

"You do, an' you answers to me. Jonathan's sick. Cain't you see he lost so much weight, an' he weak as spring water 'thout bourbon, an' whar the hell is Calcutta Two an' our drinks? That boy sloths bettah'n Calcutta One."

The drinks finally arrived, and Calcutta, after a glance at Fitz's scowling face, left as quickly as possible. Clarissa drank half the contents of her glass in a single swallow.

"We goin' to have trouble with Jonathan 'round heah," Clarissa reasoned. "Reckon he goin' to think the niggers still slaves. You sho' he didn't get a small ball through his haid?"

"Goin' to have a talk with him after supper," Fitz said. "Goin' to lay down some law, an' he obeys or he gets out. I wants my son back, but way he acts he sho' ain't my son. Won't baby him none. Jes' tells him cold whut I 'spects, an' then he kin take his bag an' go off he wants to."

Clarissa's brow furrowed. "Fitz, mayhap he ain't responsible fo' whut he sayin'. Mayhap somethin' happen to his haid."

"Aims to find out. Adalia comin' home pretty soon. Hates to have her see the way he is. Soldier comin' home after five yeahs in an enemy prison, he sho' ought to be thankful he back at all, an' not takin' his hate out on us. Won' stand fo' it."

They drank the rest of the whiskey in thoughtful silence. Fitz finally went to the kitchen to find Elegant perched on her high stool, trying to check the tears that were still running down her fat cheeks.

"Raises him like he my own, an' he call me a bitch," she said bitterly. "Reckon ah shouldn' o' slapped him, but couldn' help myse'f, suh. Jes' couldn'."

"It didn' hurt him any. Mayhap it took some starch outen him an' thass whut he needs. He come to his senses he goin' to come to you an' say he sorry. Fo' my son, I begs your pardon, Elegant."

She pursed her lips in a massive pout and nodded slowly. "Reckon he sick in the haid. Kin fo'give him. You tells him so?"

"I tells him," Fitz said. "Gots to get cleaned up. Leaves it to you to tell Domingo whut Jonathan is like. Be sho' to tell her he sho' changed. Bettah she stay away."

Clarissa and Fitz and a sullen, silent Jonathan were

at the supper table when Mark entered with Adalia. She had been warned, but she bestowed a sunny, warm smile at Jonathan and opened her mouth to utter a greeting. Before she could speak, Jonathan pushed back his chair noisily and stood up.

"Ain't sittin' at no suppah table with a Yankee."

"Then you kin leave an' eat in the kitchen, if Elegant will allow that," Fitz said in anger.

Jonathan walked out. Adalia sat down slowly. "Oh, I didn't want anything like this to happen. Would it help if I followed him and talked to him?"

"Wouldn' if I was you," Mark said. "He on'y make things wuss. Cain't do anythin' with him—not yet. Mayhap later, but he sho' gots to soften some."

"To hell with him," Clarissa declared angrily. "I'm hungry, an' I ain't lettin' him spoil my appetite."

"He must have suffered terribly," Adalia said. "He looks awful. Really ill."

"Thass why I ain't busted him one 'fore now," Fitz said. "Knows he went through mo' than he'll likely evah tell us, but he changes or he leaves. No fam'ly kin put up with someone like him. Adalia, he say anythin' bad to you, tell Mark or me. Don' take anythin' from him."

"He finds he kin get away with things like this," Mark said, "he goin' to get worse. It sho'ly must please him to see others put out over what he say an' do."

The meal, which should have been a joyous one of welcome, was completed mostly in a strained silence. Afterward, Mark and Adalia decided to go for a walk down to the school. Clarissa went to her room, proclaiming that she was tired and disgusted. Fitz found Jonathan in the library, seated behind the desk. Jonathan arose promptly to surrender the chair to his father.

"Wants to talk to you, son. A quiet talk, mayhap a useful one, but a talk."

"Ain't got much to say," Jonathan told him. "Wants you to leave me alone."

"I cain't do that. You lives in my house an' you acts like a gen'mun an' my son, or you gets out. One thing or the other, Jonathan. Now you tells me why yo' acts this way. Jes' sits theah an' talks. Mayhap it'll do you good."

"Says all I wants to say. Told you niggers 'sponsible fo' the war. All that fightin' an' killin' 'cause of 'em. Hates 'em. All of 'em. Hates Yankees. Kin kill any man who tells me he a Yankee."

"Now you see heah," Fitz said. "The slaves had nuthin' to do with any o' whut happened. Not any little bit. They comes outen this worse than they was when it all happens. So you wastin' your hate on somebody you got no right to hate."

"Hates 'em anyways. But hates Yankees mo'."

"Now you tells me why. Right now. Get it off your chest."

"Like Mark say, I gets shot off my hoss, an' this snotty nose Yankee kid ready to push his bayonet through my heart."

"But he didn't, Jonathan. Thass the point. He didn't."

"Got him some wet-nosed officer who stands theah an' look down on me an' says to this heah boy, 'You sticks him with your bayonet. Don't kill him. Jes' lets him have a taste o' Yankee steel 'fore we takes him to the hospital.' An' that boy pushed the bayonet nice an' slow through my shoulder like I be nuthin' mo' than a hunk o' daid beef he carvin' fo' his suppah."

"Still, they didn' kill you. That soldier had a right to kill you. Mayhap you on the other end o' that bayonet, you send it through his heart."

Jonathan arose abruptly. "Cain't talk to you no mo'. You don' understan' whut I'm talkin' 'bout. You too goddamn righteous to know whut I'm tryin' to say. Goin' to baid. Mighty tired."

Fitz bent his head and said nothing. He heard Jonathan go upstairs. When Mark and Adalia returned from their walk, they found Fitz still seated in the library.

"Cain't do a thing with him," he told them. "An' don't wants no mo' bad talk. You sits down an' tells me 'bout how the schoolin' went."

"Fitz," Adalia said, "those children seem hopeless until you get to know them. Their ignorance is appalling. Some may never learn, but white children are the same in some instances. There are those who are going to be quite intelligent once they master the art of learning and get interested in it. Most are interested now. For a few minutes, I felt helpless, as if there was nothing I could do, but then I came to realize the grown people were just as childish as the children. It's not their fault they understand so little. They never had a chance to understand anything."

"Make no mistake 'bout that," Fitz said. "I know it fo' a long time."

"Adalia thinks she kin do much fo' them," Mark said. "Think so myse'f."

"Thass whut I been hopin' to heah."

"I won't do wonders," Adalia said, "but I'll do my best, and I know there will be some positive results."

"Good. Day you comes to Wyndward a happy one fo' all of us."

"Thank you, Fitz. Mark, I'm very tired. I'm going to bed so I'll be fresh and ready to go in the morning. I've never had a more exciting challenge in my life, and I'm more anxious than ever to bring those children and yes, the adults too, out of the misery of living without the ability to absorb what's going on."

"Whut you really has in them pupils," Mark mused, "is barren ground you goin' to make fertile."

Fitz nodded approval. "Likes your thinkin', son. Knows you an' Adalia be a great help to each other."

"Helps her all I can," Mark said. "Mighty proud o' her."

"When you gonna get married?" Fitz asked.

Adalia spoke up quickly. "I asked Mark to please be patient until I got my school going. When I marry, I don't want to have them on my mind."

"I told her, Gran'pa, I lets her have them on her mind now," Mark said pointedly. "But when we marries, she have to show me she 'preciated my patience."

Amalia gave him a chiding glance, but her laughter mingled with Fitz's. Mark joined her as she got up.

"I goin' to turn in too," he said. "Arguin' with Papa made me tired, reckon, an' knows it won't be much diff'rent tomorrow."

"Reckon not," Fitz said soberly. "Lock your door, Amalia."

Her face shadowed. "Mark already told me to."

Mark said, "My papa still actin' up?"

Fitz nodded, but made no further comment. After a while he arose and walked down to the quarters where the slaves used to live. He knocked on the door of Hong Kong's cabin. Hong Kong greeted Fitz cordially.

"Evenin', Seawitch," Fitz said. She was seated in a rocker, industriously patching an article of clothing.

"Evenin', suh." She started to get up, but Fitz motioned for her to remain seated.

"Heahs you gots trouble with Jonathan," Hong Kong said, his tone solicitous.

"News sho' travel fast 'round heah," Fitz said. "Sho' is trouble. Reason why I comes down."

"Elegant tell us," Seawitch said. "She cryin' her poor heart out."

"Don' blame her none. Jonathan come back so full o' hate, he don' know whut he doin' or sayin'. Wants you to be careful you meets him. Reckon he got no bettah friend in all this heah world than you two, but ain't no tellin' whut he goin' to do when he meet you. Best you stay outen his way if yo' kin. Leastwise fo' a few days. Mayhap he calms down. Don' count on it, but we's hopin'."

"Poor Jonathan," Hong Kong said. "Reckon he gots too much sorrowin' in his life. Losin' he two fine boys, losin' Missy Daisy. Reckon it a wondah he didn' lose his min'."

"Way he actin' now, reckon he has. Some way we gots to bring him back. Turn him 'round. Wyndward needs him. We ain't gettin' any younger, you an' me an' Seawitch. Jonathan actin' like he crazy, goin' to wreck this plantation in one season. Wouldn' s'prise me he gets to whar he take somebody down to the whuppin' shed."

"Suh, he does, an' ev'ry nigguh on this heah plantation walks."

"'Cept you an' Seawitch," Fitz said with a low, almost harsh laugh.

"We don' walks, suh. Nevah."

"Knows that. You kin think o' a way to make that boy—boy hell, he a full-growed man now—if you kin, make him change. Gots to be some way."

"Looks fo' it, suh. Wants to see him like he used to be. We thinks a lot o' him."

"I do too, when he not near me. When he is, I wants to choke him."

"You sets awhile?" Seawitch invited.

"Reckon not. Wants to take a walk an' cool off. Was goin' down to tell the folks he back, but not tonight. Don't wants to tell 'em whut kind o' a fool he turn out to be. Good night."

Fitz took his walk, skirting the cemetery. He walked for an hour and slowly the anger left him, replaced by wonder of how a man such as Jonathan could change that much, even after what he must have undergone. But for all his walking and thinking, Fitz found no way to help his son. All he could do, he told himself, was to tolerate him and hope. After all, he had hoped for five years that Jonathan was not dead, and a miracle had come about. Perhaps the same kind of miracle would change him.

Clarissa couldn't sleep. Her mind was too full of Jonathan and the grave disappointment he was to Wyndward. She tried to find some logical reason for the way he acted. Not even five years of imprisonment could have done that to him. Other soldiers had endured it and persevered, returned without more than normal rancor, the kind that would quickly go away when matched against a happy homecoming.

She had no idea how long she'd been awake. She'd turned down the lamp and then blown it out at least two hours ago. She had heard the normal sounds of a household preparing for bed, but now everything was deathly quiet.

She heard the doorknob turn, very slowly with the intent of making the least possible amount of sound. The door clicked as it opened. She felt a cool breeze sweep over her. Then the door closed with a similar click. Clarissa lay on her back, looking up at the darkened ceiling.

She said, "Come in, Jonathan."

He was beside the bed. She threw off half the covers, and he slipped in beside her. He was naked. She turned on her side, touched his cheek tenderly.

"You goin' to rape me, Jonathan?" she asked softly.

"Clarissa, I ain't been this close to a woman in five yeahs. I tried to sleep, but all I could think of was bein' with a woman. Wants you. Don' fight me, Clarissa."

She laughed in a low, throaty voice. "I old 'nuff to be your mama, an' if you see anythin' you wants in me, I kin on'y say I kinda proud. You don't have to rape me. Pesterin' mo' fun an' lasts longer."

She moved to lay her head on his bare chest. She heard him take a long, deep breath. Clarissa didn't speak again. Not for a long time, and then they both lay on their backs.

"Will say this, Jonathan," she said. "Five yeahs away from a woman sho' didn' do you any harm. You better'n evah."

"I been through so much," he said. "So damn much. I almost died. It took them a week to get me to a doctor, an' all the time I had a bullet wound an' a bayonet wound festerin'. An' I gets put in a dirty old hospital. Layin' next to Union soldiers. They gets the best. They gets medicine fo' their pain. I gets nuthin'. Reckon on'y the good Lawd let me pull through. Or mayhap I was too goddamn ornery to die. So I fooled 'em. They said I was goin' to die, an' I didn't."

"Talk some mo'," Clarissa urged. "Gots to get some strength back 'fore we finishes off the evenin'."

"They puts me in a cage on wheels, an' they takes me to a fed'ral prison. Soon's they get the spancels off me, one o' them bastahds hits me 'cross the face 'cause I sassed him fo' not seein' I had a docter. He knocks me cold with a gun butt, an' they locks me in a cell. No window, no nuthin'. An' I stays theah fo' three months. Thinks that's how long it was. Thinks it three centuries. Feeds me stuff not fit for a pig. But they nevah gets me to beg. Reckon they gets tired o' havin' me theah so they puts me in a big room with mayhap three hundred pris-oners."

"You poor boy," Clarissa said gently, encouraging him to talk. Fitz hadn't been able to get a word out of him. His own son had drawn only a blank in attempting to learn his story. But he was talking it out now, and she had to get him to keep on.

"Reckon time nevah went by so slow. Started losin' weight fo' the food they hands me. Jes' plain slop. An' they calls me names an' say they thinkin' 'bout shootin' me."

"Bets you sassed 'em back," Clarissa said.

"Fought 'em. Man lays a hand on me, I fights back. Hears Lincoln gets shot, an' I yells fo' the man who shot him to get the biggest medal in the world. Then I heahs jes' some crazy actor did it. I got some o' the other prisoners, an' we all cheered 'cause he daid. Nevah saw anythin' make them so mad. Know whut they done? Stripped me, tied me to a post, an' whupped me. Ev'ry time they swung that whup, they asks me how I likes it an' how a slave felt when I whupped him. Nevah cried out once."

"You're a brave man, Jonathan. You're a true Turner, thass whut you are."

"They even puts me 'fore a court-martial fo' bein' so happy 'bout the death o' Lincoln. They says I'm the worse troublemaker in the camp, an' I tells 'em thass a compliment. They says when other prisoners gets sent home after the war, I stays fo' ten mo' yeahs. Ev'ry time they sends a big batch o' men home, they makes me stand by the door an' watch 'em go. Near drove me outen my mind, but nevah says a word."

"They sho' ain't goin' to fo'get you," Clarissa said, patting his arm lightly.

"Says to myse'f, I gots to stay alive, gots to show 'em I'm bettah than they are. Wasn't easy. They has some nigger guards fo' awhile, an' they gives me pure hell. Reckon I nevah fo'gives the whole goddamn nigger race. Cain't stand to look at 'em."

"Elegant on'y happy you comes back," she said gently, wondering if his anger toward her had lessened.

"She black, an' I don' sees Elegant. All I sees is black."

"You hates the Yankees jes' as much."

"Mo', reckon. That gal heah in this house, I lays awake wonderin' if I goes to her room an' rapes her good."

"Jonathan, you rapes her, you lays a hand on her, Fitz will kill you. An' if he don', you son will, an' if he don', I will."

"Lets her be, reckon. What kind o' boy Mark turn out to be?"

"None bettah. You kin be proud o' him."

"Cain't be that good with a bitch of a mama like Belle."

"Whutevah Belle was, whutevah that whole rotten fam'ly was, Mark ain't like them. He smart an' full o' ambition. Done as much wuk 'round heah as Fitz or anybody else. An' ain't skeered o' nuthin'."

"Could take him down I wants to."

"Mayhap, but you sho' goin' to know it. Your papa took him when he first comes heah an' feelin' like he bettah'n anybody else. But when it's over, your papa was busted up much as your son. Anyways, they wouldn't let you fight one of 'em. You'd have to fight both of 'em, an' you'd come out worse than anythin' the Yankees gives you."

"Whups me like I some old slothin' nigger. Heah, you kin feel the scars on my back. Go on, feel 'em. Thass from the whup."

Clarissa obeyed, then said, very softly, "Wonders how many slaves got scars like that? Mayhap a million."

"They's niggers, I ain't."

"You through talkin'?" Clarissa asked.

"Fo' now, reckon."

"Whut I wants right now don' take jawin'."

Afterward, they slept, but when Clarissa awoke in the morning, she was alone in bed. She turned her face to the pillow and wept. Not for herself, not for her surrender to Jonathan, but for him, and what he had gone through. At least, now Fitz would know and perhaps soften his anger toward his son. She dried her tears, got out of bed, and washed her face. She dressed, attended to her hair,

222

and went down to an early breakfast because she knew Fitz would be there and quite likely alone.

He looked up as she entered the dining room. "Kind o' early fo' you, ain't it?" he asked. "But good mawnin' to you anyways."

"Had a good night," she said with a sly smile.

"Whut you gettin' at, Clarissa? Knows whut you considers a good night."

"Jonathan came to visit."

Fitz whistled softly. He filled her coffee cup and passed the scrambled eggs, the bacon, and the grits.

"He come to you by hisse'f?"

She nodded. "Figgered he might. Needed me, o' any other woman. An' he talked. How he talked, like a man who ain't talked fo' yeahs, an' reckon that be mo' true than false. They gives him a hard time, Fitz. Near kills him. Even whupped him like he a slave. Feels the scars on his back. Don' blame him fo' bein' mad."

"It's over," Fitz said. "No matter whut happened, time to fo'get."

"Reckon he nevah will. They got down into his soul, reckon. Gets nigger guards, an' they torments him, way he says. Nevah gives me many details, but kin 'magine whut he went through."

"Says it now an' says it again. Ain't sorry fo' him. Think that worse than gettin' killed? Millions was. Millions! On both sides. In war, don' look fo' any diff'rence in men. They gets wounded, they dies, they gets taken prisoner. Jonathan lucky to be alive, an' he ought to be grateful fo' that if nuthin' else."

"He sho' ain't grateful. Goin' to take yeahs 'fore he changes. You gots to handle him careful, Fitz."

"Handles him like I handles anyone else. He don' like it, he kin go away. Who the hell he thinks he is? Somebody special?"

"Don' know. You mad he comes to me?"

"No. Thinks it mighty nice o' you to take him."

"Be good to the boy, Fitz. Deep inside you knows he your son an' loves you. On'y he cain't realize that. Not yet. Comes a time an' he will."

"Kind o' worried whut he does to Adalia. He say anythin' 'bout that?"

"Thinks o' rapin' her but comes to me instead."

"Son o' no son, he rapes her an' he dies. Sweahs I kills him."

"Told him you don't, Mark will, an' Mark don't, I will. Says he ain't goin' to go near her."

"Good. Had me plenty worried. That boy wants somethin', he goes an' gets it even if he has to fight fo' it. Was wonderin' if I should send Mark an' Adalia away."

"They're safe here. From Jonathan anyways. Cain't say 'bout the bastahds 'round heah who cain't get used to the idea a nigger needs to know how to spell 'cat' an' add two an' two."

"Goin' to do my best not to pay too much attention to Jonathan. Jes' let him come an' go like he pleases. Ain't goin' to ask him to do any wuk. Needs a rest anyways an' a chance to get fattened up some."

"Fitz, tells you somethin' you don't get mad."

"Won't get mad."

"You son ain't as weak as he looks."

17

Jonathan began spending more and more time in Lynchburg. There was a great deal of work in the fields, but Fitz kept silent, reasoning that his bringing Jonathan into daily close contact with the black workers might have resulted in his dislike for all blacks getting out of bounds. And at this time, Fitz couldn't afford to have a single man leave.

The tobacco crop promised to be one of the best Fitz had ever grown, and demand was greater than before the war. Hong Kong managed to keep the workers in line, sometimes by simple persuasion, other times by threatening the laziest of them with being fired and losing their cabins and allowances.

At school, Adalia's work was progressing far better than she had hoped. The children learned quickly and quite easily. Most of the adults, who persisted in attending class, did not do as well, though a few showed definite progress, spurred on by the strong desire to learn.

She and Mark were making plans to marry, perhaps

in the spring. Adalia had hoped to enlist the services of another teacher, but her efforts for this purpose were met with silence or contempt.

Except for Jonathan's dereliction, everything was almost too quiet to suit Fitz. He was growing worried about it. He knew animosity toward him still prevailed. The townspeople didn't object to borrowing on his money, and they were careful not to offend him, but there was an aloofness which Fitz could not penetrate. He resented it, but was helpless to change it.

The underlying problem, which he was unaware of, came to light during one of his visits to the bank. Henry Tallen was reluctant to talk to him about it, but circumstances compelled him to.

"It's about Jonathan," Tallen said. "He's been comin' in heah demandin' money. Reckon he gamblin' some an' drinkin' a hell of a lot. Sho' goin' to get in trouble he keep on. Last week, he gets drunk, finds a Confederate flag somewhar, an' marches down the street with a lot o' his drinkin' friends behind him singin' 'Dixie.'"

"Got a mind o' his own, Henry. I cain't do anythin' with him."

"Folks laughed an' encouraged him, but you know, Fitz, he wasn't doin' that jes' to make folks laugh. He was tauntin' the Yankee soldiers. Town is full of 'em, an' they don' take kin'ly to a Reb actin' like the war still goin' on. Wonders why they didn' lock him up."

Fitz thought he knew why. Captain Morton was personally bending over backward to avoid causing Fitz any heartache.

"Henry, you give him no mo' money. An' I goin' to fix it so he gets no mo' credit. Don't know whut in hell he doin' with all that stuff he buys, but I gets some mighty big bills to pay fo' his carryin' on."

"Goin' to make him awful mad, Fitz."

"Don' care 'bout that. Had 'nuff o' his crazy ways. War over a long time now, an' bettah he gets his feet on the ground 'fore it too late an' he goes all the way to hell."

"Well, at least Colonel Apperson ain't 'round heah

to help Jonathan spend you money, but Bibb sho' is gettin' his share."

"Been skeered o' that. I thanks you fo' tellin' me. Business gettin' any bettah?"

"Some. Takes time, but we ain't goin' backwards anyways. An' ain't much trouble goin' on. The Yankee soldiers keepin' things quiet. Hates to think whut goin' to happen they pulls out."

"Goin' to try an' find Jonathan now. Takes him home. He comes peaceful or he comes fightin'. Gettin' so I don' care which."

Fitz found Jonathan at the saloon they both used to frequent in those better days when Jonathan was happy. He was seated at one of the round tables in the middle of the large room, and at his side Bibb was enjoying drinks poured from a bottle no doubt paid for by Jonathan. There were others too, hangers-on, mostly favoring Bibb in whatever he did. They were an unruly, unreliable group of men, most of them as ignorant as the slaves they once kept. Fitz stood behind Jonathan.

"Goin' back to Wyndward, son. Wants to come along?"

"Ain't nuthin' I cares 'bout at Wyndward," Jonathan said without looking up. "All you got theah is a school fo' niggers run by a Yankee who says she goin' to marry my son. Like hell she is."

"You comin' o' not?"

Bibb raised his head. "Your son doin' no harm. Let him alone."

Fitz said, "Don't like the kind o' company you keeps, Jonathan."

"Drinks with who I pleases, Papa. Do like Bibb say, leave me alone."

"This sonabitch comes to burn Wyndward—after we gets it rebuilt. He evah tell you 'bout that?"

"He kin burn it fo' all I cares," Jonathan said.

"Made a mistake," Fitz acknowledged. "I hung this bastahd by his feet when I ketches him an' should o' hung him by his dirty neck. Next time I will. You heahs that, Bibb?"

"Heahs it. Thinks you gettin' crazy, Fitz. Don't

227

know whut you talkin' 'bout. Burnin' an' hangin' an' all."

"Keep your mouth shut, Bibb, or so help me, I closes it fo'evah."

Some of Bibb's cronies were moving closer, forming a loose ring around the table, in a position to interfere violently if Fitz tried to reach Bibb.

"You thinks Bibb your friend?" Fitz asked Jonathan. "You 'members how you gets to go into the army when the war starts? This heah friend o' yours got you drunk an' talked you into enlistin'. You comes heah feelin' mad at ev'rythin' an ev'rybody. Mad at yourse'f. Ain't blamin' you fo' that. Your sons killed, Daisy dies, an' reckon your whole world fallin' apart. But Bibb gots you into the army 'cause he knows that would hurt me. Hurt Wyndward, 'cause we sho' needed you them days when food was so short. He's the man you now call your friend."

"How he lies," Bibb said with a loud, derisive laugh. "Reckon ain't much he wouldn' do to get you back under his thumb. Don't know whut in hell he talkin' 'bout."

Fitz reached for Bibb, seized him by the collar, and hoisted him to his feet. Jonathan jumped up and grabbed at Fitz. The other men began moving closer.

Fitz let go of Bibb and pushed him back into his chair. He faced Jonathan, his eyes were blazing in anger.

"You takin' his side?" he demanded.

"Goin' to bust you good you lays a hand on him again. Heah me, Papa?"

"Heahs yoo. Ain't fightin' my own son jes' to give these bastahds heah somethin' to laugh 'bout. But you comes back to Wyndward an' 'fore you gets in the house, you goin' to apologize to me fo' whut you jes' said, or you has to fight your way in. An' don't think I cain't take you."

"Why don't you try it now?" Bibb shouted. "Jonathan, you heahs whut he says. You lettin' him talk that way?"

Jonathan turned to face his father. Fitz knew he was in a dangerous dilemma. If he beat Jonathan, it would be like Bibb to urge his cronies to take part in the battle. Yet Fitz was not inclined to back down. This was a show-down between him and his son.

Jonathan might have weakened. In all probability, as he told himself later, he certainly would have. He didn't have to make the decision, however. The impending fight was stopped by a sharp command from a Yankee ser-geant, leading four rifle-armed men.

"Mister Turner," he addressed Fitz, "is there trouble you can't handle?"

"No, suh," Fitz said. "Jes' havin' an argument with my son."

"Sounded like a noisy one," the sergeant said. "Do you wish us to escort you from this place, Mister Turner?"

"Reckon I'm ready to leave, suh."

"I've warned the people who run this saloon to be a little more careful about trouble. This is the last warning. Next time the place will be closed down."

Fitz turned toward the bar. "You sends me a bill fo' whut my son spends in heah, an' I pays it, up to now. From heah on, he gets no mo' credit, an' the same goes fo' any other place in town."

Fitz walked out. Someone yelled a caustic "Yankee lover," but Fitz paid no heed. His heart was too heavy for any anger. He thanked the sergeant and his detail and went to his hotel. He passed up the blandishments of the lobby prostitutes, but did provide himself with a bottle of whiskey.

In his room, he sipped the whiskey until it made him drowsy, all the while faced with this problem of a once-dutiful, loving son, who had been changed by the war. Now he would have to write Jonathan off as a liability, when he needed him so acutely to help run the plantation. He damned the war and all its ramifications as he finally lapsed into an alcohol-induced sleep.

The next morning Fitz made the purchases he had intended to and then drove back to Wyndward alone.

He told Clarissa and Mark about it while Adalia was in school. She had enough to worry about.

"He hangin' 'round with Bibb, an' that bunch o'

scalawags always with him. He drinkin' hard, spendin' money like the reckless fool he is. Still full o' hate an' darin' me to do somethin' 'bout it."

"Whut yo' aimin' to do, Gran'pa?" Mark asked.

"Not one damn thing. Told him if he come back I meets him outside an' beats his brains out 'lessen he apologizes fo' the way he talked. Reckon didn't mean that, but I was mad an' tryin' to make some sense out o' all this. I cut off his credit so he kin now make his own way. Mayhap that learns him somethin', though I doubt it. Cain't do anythin' but wait an' see whut happens. Hopes he wake up soon an' realizes whut he doin' to hisse'f."

"You cuts off his credit," Clarissa said, "he comes back. Wait an' see."

"He hangs 'round Bibb, he goin' to get in bad trouble fo' sho'," Mark commented.

"Knows it. But Bibb ain't cottonin' up to Jonathan 'cause he like him. He a friend 'cause Jonathan got money an' treats Bibb an' all those bastahds who sides him."

"Most of all," Clarissa said, "Bibb knows he hurtin' you, an' he sho' lookin' fo' anythin' that kin get Jonathan in bad trouble. That's when Jonathan finds out who his friends are. But I'll keep his room ready case he comes back."

It required a week for Jonathan to relent. Clarissa sent Chickory down to the fields to tell Fitz.

"Is he in the house?" Fitz asked the boy.

"No, suh! He sittin' on the grass, suh, an' lookin' kind o' sick I thinks."

"Walk back with me," Fitz said. "How you comin' 'long, Chickory?"

"Fine, suh. Real fine."

"You goin' to school like I told you'?"

"Yessah. On'y in the mawnin', suh. Gots to do my chores in the afternoon, suh."

"You learnin' anythin'?"

"Yassah. Learns I comes from Africa, suh."

"Your people came from theah. You born heah, an'

you goin' to be an American citizen you gets a little older."

"Sho' 'nuff?" The small black face looked up at him eagerly.

"Mayhap by the time you grows up, it'll be diff'rent. Mayhap we gets used to the idea you ain't no slave, but a useful citizen. Mayhap, but ain't got much faith in it after seein' whut goes on in Lynchburg."

Chickory left Fitz when they neared the house. Jonathan, laying on his back on the lawn, looked up at his father's tall frame standing above him.

"Well?" Fitz asked.

"Wants to come back, Papa."

"You seems to be back."

"You says I got to fight you 'fore I goes in." He managed to get to his feet. "I'm ready, suh."

Fitz shook his head. "Way you looks, you couldn't fight anybody. Takes it back. You kin come home."

"Rather fights you, Papa. You said if I didn't apologize to you, I gots to fight."

"You kin follow me in o' not, as you pleases, Jonathan. I ain't in the mood to whup you this mawnin'."

Fitz walked into the house. Jonathan followed him, his manner meek. He barely nodded to Clarissa who stood at the dining-room door, trying not to reveal her dismay at Jonathan's bedraggled appearance. Fitz went to the library, and when Jonathan followed and finally sat down, Fitz closed the door.

"Whut made you come back?" Fitz asked bluntly.

"I'm hungry, Papa."

"Whut's the matter with your friends? Like Bibb?"

"Ain't got 'nuff to feed themse'ves."

"You means they don' spend anythin' on you, but when you could buy anythin', they was your good friends."

"Reckon, suh."

"You comes back you wuks in the fields. You stays away from Lynchburg, an' you drinks like a gen'mun. Not like the kind o' riff-raff you've been drinkin' with."

"Does whut you says, Papa. Means it."

231

It was only with difficulty Fitz concealed his surprise at Jonathan's mollified behavior.

"You treats Adalia like the lady she is, an' Mark wants to marry her you gives them your blessin'."

"Promises, Papa."

"You hungry, you goes to the kitchen an' asks Elegant to feed you. An' you apologize to her fo' whut you did when you comes home."

"Yes. Papa. I does what you says."

"All right. Fo' today you don't have to do no wuk. You lookin' kind o' sickly. Thinks you bettah get some rest in baid. Clarissa keeps your room ready."

"Papa, wants to wuk hard. Wants to fo'get the war an' whut happened to me. Don't thinks I kin do it, but I kin sho' try."

"Up to you, Jonathan. You kin be a man again, you tries to be, or you kin join the riff-raff whut men like Bibb belongs to. Make up you mind on that."

Later, Fitz paid a visit to the kitchen.

"Jonathan acts like a gen'mun he come to get food?" he asked.

Elegant nodded. "Sho' did, suh. Tells me he sorry fo' whut he said. Thinks he means it?"

"Do you have doubts?" he asked.

"Don' know, suh. Likes whut he say, but when he says it he nevah looks me in the face. Man hangs his haid, cain't look you in the eye, that ain't good."

"So you noticed that too. Well, we'll make the best o' it fo' the time bein.' He had a bad time o' it, Elegant. Real bad."

"He kin look you in the eye," she said grimly. "He kin do that if he means whut he say. Sho' kin if he means it."

In the morning, Fitz watched with interest as Jonathan ate a hasty breakfast and then reported to Hong Kong in the fields. He'd never done that before. When Jonathan went into the fields, he was in charge. Perhaps he'd forgotten how to care for tobacco plants. Perhaps he wished to learn all over again, but the way he acted was unusual. Even Clarissa commented on it.

232

"Kind o' wondered he comin' to see me last night, but he nevah does."

"That boy too damn weak to handle a woman like you, Clarissa. Been hellin' 'round an' drinkin' too much. Not eatin' right, gettin' no sleep, losin' all that weight. Kin wear a man down, that kind o' life. Gets his strength back pretty soon, an' you sho' goin' to see him in you baid agin."

"Don't knows I wants him, Fitz. Whut's wrong with him? Meets him this mawnin' in the hall, an' he polite as kin be, but 'fore this he grabs me an' pesters me some. Not this mawnin'. He ain't like he used to be."

"We'll give him ev'ry chance. He my son. Cain't fo'get that. Gots to do whut Benay would o' done. Fo'gives him fo' whut he done befo' an' now he gots a chance to prove hisse'f."

Later in the day Fitz wandered down to the fields and watched Jonathan hard at work, helping Hong Kong lay out a new field for plowing. He was sweating, he looked better than he had since he'd come home. Fitz began to hope.

Adalia added to his hopes when she came into the library after school was out. She was quite excited.

"Jonathan came into the schoolroom this afternoon and stood listening and watching. He didn't say anything, but I think he was impressed. I'm so glad he's back and improving Fitz."

"Kind o' s'prised he did that, but grateful fo' it."

"I must admit he frightened me when he first came in. He didn't approach my desk, and he didn't try to talk to any of the children. He just watched. He needs good food. He's so thin he's almost emaciated."

Fitz nodded agreement. "If food will change him, my worries are over."

Jonathan joined them at supper for the first time since he had come home. He held Adalia's chair and smiled as she looked up at him gratefully.

Clarissa said, "Look at him. Been in the sun one day, an' he gettin' tanned a'ready."

"Been out o' the sun too many yeahs," Jonathan said. "Goin' to get all I kin of it."

233

"How'd the wuk go?" Fitz asked.

"Well, kind o' rusty yet, but it comin' back. Hong Kong did most o' it, but we goin' to have a new field out theah come spring. Goin' to be ready to plow."

"Needs it," Mark said. "Cain't grow 'nuff to fill the orders we kin get."

"Used to drive me kind o' crazy," Jonathan said. "The guards would smoke cheroots, an' the smell got clear under my skin. On'y thing gives me comfort, they were the cheapest an' worst cheroots I evah did smell."

"Got boxes of 'em," Fitz told him. "You know whar they are."

"Goin' to have me one after suppah, Papa. Lookin' forward to it."

Supper was barely over, it was still daylight, when somewhat to Fitz's horror, he saw a buggy drive up with Captain Morton handling the reins. Jonathan's reaction to a Yankee uniform worried him. But he would have to face this some day, and it might as well be now.

Fitz said, "Jonathan, a Yankee officer-jes' drove up. He is Cap'n Morton, an' he Adalia's brother. We treats him like a gen'mun, an' he's all o' that."

Jonathan arose, crushing out the cheroot he had been enjoying. "You will kin'ly excuse me, suh."

Fitz moved forward and seized his elbow. "You ain't runnin' out. Cap'n Morton is as fine a man as I evah knowed. It was he who got you outen that prison. We asked fo' his help, an' we got it."

Jonathan tried to pull away, but Captain Morton was inside by then. He embraced his sister, kissed Clarissa on the cheek, shook hands with Mark, and approached Fitz and Jonathan.

Fitz said, "Cap'n, this heah Jonathan. You helps him get out o' that prison, an' we sho' grateful."

"It's a shame you were held as long as you were, Major. Yes, I know what your rank was. I know it couldn't have been very pleasant. . . ."

"Don' use that word to me," Jonathan said coldly. "You knows whut you Yankees did to me? You knows whut kind o' slop we gets? You knows we gets whupped an' busted? You knows anythin' whut went on up theah in the Northern prison?"

"Yes," the captain said quietly. "I do know, and I deeply resent and regret it. Things we don't approve of happen during a war. But there was Andersonville too. I assume you heard about it."

"What's that?" Jonathan asked suspiciously.

"A Confederate prison where many Northern soldiers were held in open stockades, and many of them died. True, the prison was administered by someone not capable of handling the job, but that doesn't soften the impact of the terrible things that happened there. We were no better. I admit that, and I'm sorry about it, but the shoe fits on your side too, Major."

Jonathan's face was pink and then white. He turned quickly and walked out of the room. Fitz heard him pounding up the stairs. Adalia went to Mark, who held her closely while she wept. Mark's expression was one of anger. Clarissa broke the embarrassed silence.

"I seen goddamn fools in my life, but he the worst."

"No, Clarissa," Captain Morton said. "He went through too much. Some of it he brought on himself by his rebellious attitude, but still he was held too long and conditions at that prison were not good. I can easily forgive him, and I hope sincerely that he gets over this."

"It was the uniform," Mark said.

"Uniform o' not, he had no right to act like he did," Fitz said. "Had some hope fo' him today, but now wonders if he evah gets bettah. Have to wait an' see."

Captain Morton said, "Fitz, can we talk?"

Fitz nodded and led the way to the library. Captain Morton sat down and accepted a glass of brandy.

"Fitz, I have had every available record checked on the Rebel side and even ours. There is not and never has been any such person as Ollie Paulson. Certainly not around the regions where he was supposed to have been fighting Sherman. In my opinion, he never existed."

Fitz nodded. "I thanks you fo' helpin' me."

"I hated to bring you this news."

"Hated? Cap'n, you jes' made me as happy a man as

I kin be under the circumstances o' my crazy son. Goin' to ask another favor. Seems like all I kin do is ask you favors."

"Nonsense. You know I'm glad to do what I can."

"Kind o' hard to understan' whut I goin' to say next. Jes' 'fore the war starts, I meets a gal name o' Sally. Now I falls in love with her right off. 'Cept fo' Benay, my first wife, nevah meets a gal so pretty an' so warm an' kind. Thinks she fall in love with me too. Brings her heah to live. Jonathan's twin sons, kind o' runnin' wild, an' Sally tamed 'em down some. But Sally say she heah to help settle the estate o' some rich woman she care fo' 'til she die. Goes to Richmond lots o' times on business. Nevah thinks 'bout it. You trusts who you loves, Cap'n."

"I'm aware of that, Fitz. Go on."

"War starts, an' Sally run. Leave me a letter sayin' she loves me an' hate to tell me she a Northern spy. Kin you 'magine that? She in Richmond to get all the information she kin. But skeered they comin' fo' her, an' she has to run. Nevah knows she gets through the Rebel lines. Didn't seem possible to me she did fo' the Rebs had closed the border an' were theah in force."

"There was a great deal of espionage going on. On both sides," the captain said. "You never heard from her again?"

"Nevah. But a Reb colonel, who hates me as I hates him, told me he heared Sally was caught an' hung. Say he heard it from mo' than one person, but 'members Ollie Paulson saw her hung an' told him 'bout it. Now this heah colonel hates me so much I thinks he lied 'bout it to make me feel bad. Reckon he made up that name, an' he don' know a damn thing 'bout Sally or whut happened to her. So I kin believe again she got through, an' she alive."

"You want me to see if I can get any word of her, Fitz?"

"Mighty big job, but sho' would 'preciate it. Cain't do it myse'f. Don' know which way to turn. Her real name is Elizabeth Rutledge, an' think she kind o' an important woman up North. Likely in Washington."

"Elizabeth Rutledge. A fine name, Fitz. Perhaps I'll be able to find her. I know many people in Washington, and tomorrow I'll write them. I'll also try to examine files pertaining to spies and check all records of hangings. There were some not recorded. Whether by intent or carelessness, I don't know, but I do know several Union spies were executed. Can't say if I ever heard there had been a woman among them."

"She alive, I gots to find her, Cap'n."

"I wonder why she never got in touch with you. After all, the war is over and even while it was going on, letters could get through from one side to the other."

"Reckon she think I hates her fo' whut she did. Deceivin' me, lyin' to me, usin' me, in fact. That nevah mattered. Nevah will. But she the kind o' woman would think I don' want to see her again an' she would nevah come to me feelin' that way. Even if she nevah does, I kin sleep bettah knowin' she's alive."

"I'll get right at it, Fitz. You should have told me to help you with this before."

"You done 'nuff. An' whut reward you get? My son insults you. Got to beg your pardon fo' that."

"Forget it, Fitz. The war is over, and your son will realize that one day soon. Frankly, the prisons on both sides were terrible. In the heat of war, some tend to forget their enemies are also human beings. Especially in this war, between one people, all of us alike."

"Thanks you fo' that. After whut jes' happen, you still gives your blessin' to you sister an' my gran'son?"

"With all my heart. He's a fine boy."

"Thinks they gets married come spring."

"Good. I'll be here," he smiled, "if your son allows me to attend."

"By then, suh, he either fo'gets this heah war or he finds 'nother place to live. An' now, how things in Lynchburg? You havin' much trouble theah?"

"Some, Fitz. I hate to admit it, but there are some who swear they will never agree that the South was beaten. Mostly they're men with few skills, just hangers-on who love to make trouble for others. I've been soft on them because those are my orders, but there are times

237

when I feel like turning my guns against them. But then, sometimes, I think I'd rather shoot the carpetbaggers who prey on people who need help so much they are actually willing to be fleeced."

18

The shrill screams of terror wakened Fitz and every-one else in the mansion. He was the first downstairs, clad only in his underwear and carring a pistol. Elegant met him in the hall. She was carrying a lamp, which was shaking as much as she. Fear was evident in her eyes, and her voice quavered as she spoke.

"Ah's skeered, Massa Fitz. Don' know whut the hell's goin' on."

"I'll find out damn fast. Go upstairs an' stays with Clarissa an' Adalia. 'Magine they're skeered too."

"Yassuh." She was already climbing the stairs, hold-ing her nightdress up to her knees, revealing bony legs that amazingly supported her ample body.

Fitz ran out into the cool night to find the black workers in a state of great confusion and fear. They had come to the mansion in their terror, and at least thirty or forty of them, both men and women, were huddled in a croup. Hong Kong, wearing only pants, emerged from the darkness as Fitz hurried toward them.

Fitz's presence calmed the group somewhat, and

Hong Kong helped too. They were finally able to make some sense out of the chattering that went on. One husky man seemed to have more courage than the others, though his eyes were still bulging in fear.

"Haunts, Massa Fitz," he managed. "Haunts comes ridin' their hosses an' says we all goin' to die."

"Ghosts?" Fitz asked in awe. "They ain't no such thing."

"Massa, suh, asks anyone heah, suh. They wakes us. They carryin' to'ches an' say nex' time they burns us out."

"All right," Fitz said, "calm down now. Whut makes you think they were ghosts?"

"Haunts comes in they buryin' shrouds, don't they? Comes an' goin' to kill us all."

"Hong Kong, you makes anythin' o' this?" Fitz asked.

"Heahs riders, suh. An' nobody rides in the middle o' the night lessen they's up to no good."

"You heahs that? Seawitch too?"

"Wakes us, suh. Right after that we heahs eve'ybody yellin' an' screamin'."

"You didn' see anybody? Any ghosts?"

"No, suh, but sho' was somebody 'round heah ain't got no bus'ness heah."

"Get yourse'f calmed down," Fitz said tersely to the man who had assumed spokesmanship for the group. "Tells me jes' whut you sees."

"They all in white. Like they was buried an' wakes up, suh. An' they tallest riders I evah seed. Ten feet tall, reckon."

Mark, who had joined Fitz, was far more skeptical than his grandfather. "Might's well think ghosts be ten feet tall as believes in ghosts."

"Somethin's wrong heah," Fitz said. "All these folks wouldn' agree to whut they saw if they didn' see somethin'. Kind o' crazy, but somethin' sho' happened."

Jonathan joined them, carrying two lanterns. "Whut's goin' on?" he asked.

"Ev'rybody heah say they sees riders look like ten-feet-tall haunts ridin' in the night an' yellin' they goin' to kill ev'rybody. Somethin' like that."

"Papa," Jonathan said, "I wakes up 'bout half an hour ago. Thinks I heahs the sound o' riders, but then thinks I dreamin' it. Goes back to sleep, 'til I wakes now to the screamin'. Reckon they tellin' the truth."

"You believe ghosts ten feet tall ridin 'round heah?" Fitz asked.

"Don't know whut was ridin' heah, but sho' knows they was somebody."

"Well, ain't nuthin' we kin do tonight," Fitz said. "Reckon ev'rybody kin go back to sleep."

The blacks slowly returned to their cabins still fearful but not knowing what else to do. Fitz, Jonathan, and Mark walked toward the house.

Mark said, "My God Almighty, I fo'gots 'bout Adalia."

"No need to fret," Fitz said. "Sends Elegant to stay with her an' Clarissa."

"That a relief. Sho' hates to have my gal sees me like this," Mark said, looking down at his bare legs.

Fitz regarded his grandson. "Don' blame you. Sho' ain't very impressive. 'Magine she be too skeered to notice though. Ev'rybody else be. Mayhap with good reason."

"Thinks I should dress an' go comfort her?" Mark asked with concern.

"Not jes' now. I needs you mo'n she do. We gots some talkin' to do. Whut time is it, anyhow?"

"When I wakes to all that screamin', I lights my lamp," Jonathan said. "Bedside clock say it near half past three."

Fitz said, "I didn't take time to light mine."

Jonathan snickered. "Damn good thing one o' us thought o' lanterns. We'd break our damn necks out heah."

"Mark an' I done all right," Fitz countered. "Anyways, Hong Kong carried lanterns. An' seein' it near fo' o'clock, needs a drink mo' than sleep. Reckon we bettah do some thinkin' an' talkin' 'bout this."

The three men went into the library where Fitz lit the lamps and poured brandy in glasses which Mark had fetched. Mark began to laugh.

"Whut's so damned funny?" Jonathan asked.

"Jes' look at us. Gran'pa on'y gots underwear on; Papa, you gots on'y britches. An' me—got a shirt but no britches. The niggers sho' skeered, or they laughs themse'ves to death lookin' at us."

"This ain't no time fo' jokes," Jonathan said. "Thinks there's somethin' mighty wrong an' mighty important goin' on, an' we bettah find out whut it is."

"Seems to me," Fitz said, "somebody aims to scare the workers half to death. Don't know why lessen they wants 'em all to quit wuk so we loses this heah crop. An' reckon you knows who could be to blame fo' that."

"Bibb?" Mark asked.

"Bibb ain't got the brains fo' anythin' like this," Jonathan said. "Mo' like Colonel Apperson."

"Is he back?" Fitz asked quickly. "You heahs anythin'?"

"Heard his name mentioned once o' twice, like he back, but ain't seen him, Papa."

"Cain't think o' anyone else hates us 'nuff to do this. Reckon I gettin' old. Yeahs past I'd o' killed 'em long ago. They tries anythin' like burnin', sho' goin' to pay 'em a call."

"Papa, you sho' gettin' old," Jonathan agreed, but not unkindly. "Things changin'. You keeps tellin' us that, but you don' pay attention to it yourse'f. Yankees runnin' things now. Killin' ain't as easy to get away with any mo'. Even if you a friend o' the cap'n in charge. No way he kin let you get away with it, you kills Bibb or Apperson."

"Ways o' doin' it," Fitz said. "We talks 'nuff fo' tonight. Mayhap we kin get to the bottom o' this crazy business in the mawnin'."

He arose and led the way upstairs. But Fitz didn't sleep. He was mystified and worried about this new puzzle of ten-foot-tall ghosts. It made no sense, but all those blacks hadn't been dreaming, nor had they made up this story from some far less mysterious event. They were telling the truth, and they were frightened. Even Hong

Kong, after he had heard what was said, showed some degree of apprehension. Fitz wondered if this episode was unique to Wyndward, or if other plantations had been visited by these same creatures.

His theory that they might learn more in the morning, certainly came true. Mark had breakfasted with Adalia and answered her questions as best he could about what had happened during the night. Her sober features showed she regarded the matter with grave concern. Mark insisted on accompanying her to the school to make certain nothing had been done to it. They'd no sooner left than Fitz and Jonathan sat down to their breakfast. They were soon joined by Clarissa.

"Whut the hell goin' on last night?" she asked. "Thought the goddamn world comin' to an end with all the screamin' an' hollerin'."

Fitz's account of the night's events was interrupted by Mark, who burst into the dining room in a state of high excitement. He placed a large, square piece of heavy white paper on the table.

"Finds this nailed to the schoolhouse door. Some o' the smart childrun already skeered an' Adalia skeered too. She stayin' with the childrun."

Fitz read the crude message, printed in red paint:

THIS SCHOOLHOUSE CLOSES DOWN IN FIVE
DAYS OR WE WILL BURN IT DOWN.

"Whut the hell?" Clarissa said in astonishment.

"Gran'pa, whut's it mean? It's signed KKK. Whut's KKK?"

"Don' know. Sho' aims to find out."

"You thinks they means it?" Jonathan asked.

"Thinks the niggers sho' saw the ghosts, ten feet tall an' all. Thinks we goin' to have trouble we don' find out who did this."

"How you aims to find out, Papa?" Jonathan asked.

"Goin' to Lynchburg today an' talk to Cap'n Morton. We mayhap needs his help, an' I don' wants to heah any objections on your part, Jonathan."

"Ain't said nuthin'."

"You comin' to it. Time you gets over the war, son. 'Cause it sho' over, an' you cain't bring it back."

"Some things nevah over, Papa. Knows I cain't make you understan' this. Won' even try no mo'. But warns you, gots to go to Lynchburg or Richmond ev'ry so often. Stays heah all the time, I goes crazy."

"You comes an' goes like you wants," Fitz said. "You doin' fine lately. Sho' needs your help, but fo' the next few weeks won' be much to do' til we tops the plants an' fills the curin' sheds."

"Reckon you goin' to Lynchburg today, I goes with you an' stays a couple o' days. You says I kin."

"You gets ready in half an hour. Mark, gets Chickory to bring the carriage 'round. You find all the money yo' needs in my desk. Help yourse'f, Jonathan."

"Thanks you, Papa. Ain't goin' to drink an' gamble like I did. Knows bettah now."

"Stay away from Bibb," Fitz advised.

"Was thinkin' 'bout that. Mayhap I sees him an' finds out whut I kin, 'thout him knowin' it."

"Papa, that a good idea," Mark approved.

Fitz nodded. "Yes, reckon it might help. We knows whut he's up to, we kin get ready fo' it. An' do whut you kin to find out whut in hell KKK means."

"An' whar you kin find ghosts ten feet tall," Mark added.

"Mo' an' mo'," Fitz said, "I thinks this sho' ain't nuthin' to laugh at. Mark, wants you to stay close to the schoolhouse. Don' let Adalia know how much we's worried. I be back 'bout suppah time, but if I ain't don't wait fo' me. Jes' tells Elegant to keep somethin' warm. Bettah get ready, Jonathan. Wants to find out whut this is 'bout quick as I kin."

In Lynchburg, Fitz and Jonathan put up the carriage at the livery. Jonathan left his father close to the saloon where the trouble had started days back.

"Bettah I ain't seen with you, Papa. Lets Bibb think you an' me sort o' busted up."

"Does whut you thinks best, son. Got business at the

bank an' with the Yankees. You comes home when you wants. 'Course you gets knowin' whut Bibb up to, or you finds out whut KKK means, you bettah come back."

"Soon's I knows anythin', Papa."

Fitz first went to the bank to discuss finances and enjoy a drink of bourbon with Henry Tallen.

"Things improvin'," Tallen informed him. "Not fast, but slow an' steady. No' hard money comin' in from the North. Folks beginnin' to borrow a little mo', an' there seems to be a small improvement in savin's. 'Course, whut you got deposited heah keeps this bank goin' real fine. I certainly 'preciates it, Fitz."

"Tell me, Henry, you evah heahs of somethin' called KKK?"

"Not's I knows of. Whut's it 'bout?"

"Don' know. Got me a note warnin' me to close the schoolhouse fo' the black childrun on Wyndward, or it be burned. It's signed with those initials, KKK."

"New one on me. Sounds like a joke o' some kind."

"Ain't no joke, Henry. You heahs anythin' 'bout whut them three letters means, let me know fast as you kin."

"Yes, sho' will. Don' make any sense to me now though."

"Let's hope it nevah does. Sees you later, Henry. I thanks you fo' the bourbon."

Fitz next made his way to City Hall, where the same Yankee guards were on duty. He was immediately escorted to the mayor's office, now used by Captain Morton.

"Fitz," Morton greeted him, "it's good to see you again. How are things at Wyndward?"

"Middlin', suh. Got somethin' on my mind mayhap you kin clear up. Last night the niggers on Wyndward gets woke up in the middle o' the night an' tells me they sees ghosts, ten feet tall, ridin' through the plantation. Yellin' they goin' to burn ev'rythin' down."

Morton showed greater interest than Fitz had anticipated.

"This mawnin', Adalia an' Mark goes to the schoolhouse an' finds this heah paper tacked to the door. Don' know whut it means, but sho' makes it plain they goin' to burn down the schoolhouse. On'y thing, they sho' is goin' to leave Wyndward with fewer ten-feet-tall ghosts than when they comes."

Fitz handed over the large piece of paper. After reading it, Morton handed it back.

"It's a serious matter, Fitz. They've not showed up in Virginia until now. You bring the first news of their presence here, and it worries the devil out of me. Let me explain. It began last Christmas eve in Tennessee, a town called Pulaski. The War Department has been sending us information about it ever since. KKK stands for Ku Klux Klan."

"That sound funnier than the initials," Fitz commented wryly.

"Nothing funny about it. Seems a small group of veterans were looking for something to do. Just for the hell of it they covered their horses with bedsheets, draped themselves with more sheets, and at night paraded through the town. We think it was just a joke, a prank. Still we can't be sure. What happened was that the Negroes thought they were seeing ghosts on horseback. They were terrorized. Somebody got the idea this was a way to hold them in line, and a large number of men joined the Klan."

"Ain't no joke they rides 'round whar they ain't wanted an' says they goin' to burn down schoolhouses."

"It certainly is not a joke. The thing got out of hand, and the KKK became a threatening organization bent on keeping the one-time slaves down. And to punish whites who admired the North, or who sympathized with the ex-slaves too much. They say their mission is to protect the whites."

"Burnin' down property ain't protectin' anyone, Cap'n."

"They have already hung Negros who committed crimes against whites. They hold some sort of trial to satisfy their consciences and then string up their victims. Let a white woman, for instance, make a claim a Negro insulted her, or touched her, and they make him an example. Sometimes by vicious flogging, sometimes by hanging. We regard them as very dangerous."

"Reckon somethin' gots to be done 'bout them 'fore they gets too big."

"It's too late for that. They are too well organized and too influential. We don't even know who they are because, when a man joins, he swears never to betray the members of the local chapter, nor to reveal any of the secrets they operate under."

"Seems to me you kin see who they are, they runs 'round tendin' other peoples business."

"Fitz, they wear gowns made of bedsheets, or anything else they can find that's white and covers the entire body and hides their faces. And they wear high, peaked hats."

"Makin' them look ten feet tall," Fitz nodded. "That's how my niggers described them, an' I thought they were crazy."

"These riders move around by night. The blacks are scared to death when they first see them, which is what the KKK wants. They know they must be feared to gain their goal. Nobody seems to know what that is."

"But if you strips the bedsheets offen 'em, you sho' knows who they are."

"It's not been done yet. We do know how they came to name themselves the Ku Klux Klan though. There might even be some well-educated members in the group that started this business. At least someone knew his Greek because the Greek word for circle is *kýklos,* and the Klan gathers in circles. They make a point of it. So they named themselves Ku Klux and added the Klan, probably because it sounds like a close association. A fraternal club of sorts."

"Cap'n, they ain't goin' to keep their members secret too long. Men crazy 'nuff to belong to an outfit like that ain't got sense 'nuff to keep their mouths shut. They goin' to do some braggin' 'fore long."

"Each member only knows a few others. They have it well set up, Fitz. They give the officers fancy names, likely to influence the lesser members. The man who heads the outfit is called the Grand Wizard. Under him are Grand Dragons, then Hydras, Furies, Cyclops and when it comes to the lowest of the order they have a very fitting title. They call themselves Ghouls."

"I be damned," Fitz said. "Anybody else tells me this, I thinks they gone outen they minds."

"No, Fitz. We get information on them as soon as it is established. This is a very dangerous organization because it takes the law into its own hands. And its secrecy makes it very hard to pin anyone down. They've been operating mostly in Tennessee and Kentucky, but we've been afraid it was going to spread. They are a clan of haters. Right now they hate all blacks and are convinced they should survive as slaves only. Since they've been set free, the Klan now intends to govern them by fear, keeping them from improving themselves, keeping them down as much as slavery did."

"That's why they don't care fo' the school at Wyndward. We teachin' the niggers to bettah theyse'ves. To get 'nuff learnin' to mayhap be as good as some of the whites. You takes a white trash now, he so stupid even a nigger like Calcutta One an' Calcutta Two a mental giant in comparison, an' them two niggers the dumbest I evah sees."

"That's why the KKK warned you the schoolhouse will be burned down. What of Adalia? I surely don't want her in danger."

"Ain't goin' to be, even if I has to close the school."

"That would surely break her heart."

"Didn't say I'm goin' to close it. Won't do that 'lessen they's no other way. They comes ready to burn, they cain't be any law says I cain't fight 'em off."

"The message says you have five days. So, with your permission, I'll send a number of my men to Wyndward. Send them secretly, two or three at a time so their presence won't be noticed. Then, if these nightriders do come, they'll be given a reception they won't forget. I'd like to stop this movement in Lynchburg right in its tracks."

"You sends 'em, I sees they's fed an' made comfortable as I kin."

"Don't even let your workers know. Remember the Klan is expert at intimidating people."

"Kin see that. An' you gets my word no harm comes to Adalia. Sends her away first, she likes it o' not."

"Good. You can expect my men to begin reaching your place two days before the deadline. I suggest you house them secretly. Not in your mansion, but perhaps in some of the empty cabins. Heaven knows you have enough of them. That would be best. They'll pretty much take care of themselves, and they'll know what to do."

"Goin' to be theah with 'em," Fitz said. "Wants to see how these poor brave men who hides behind bed-sheets, likes the s'prise we gots waitin' fo' 'em."

"Let's hope it will be a surprise. They keep spies everywhere, and as we have no idea who they are, most of the time they get information useful to the Klan."

"Jonathan lookin' 'round some now. Mayhap he gets somethin'. Lets you know if he does."

"Fitz, we regard this as so serious that if we find the Klan hangs anyone, black or white, and we find out who was responsible, who gave the order, we'll hang him after a fair trial. Which is more than they grant those they kill."

"Goes back now an' gets things ready fo' your men an' fo' the plantation. I thanks you fo' tellin' me all this. Whutevah I kin do to help bust up these crazies, jes' lets me know. Me an' Mark an' Jonathan knows how to fight."

"I'm sure you do. And I'm very happy Jonathan is coming around."

"He get over the whole thing 'fore long. Once he start improvin' like he done already, the rest o' it comes fast. Don' worry 'bout him no mo'."

Fitz believed this information so important that he returned to the bank and apprised Henry Tallen of the situation. Then Fitz developed a real hunger, so he delayed his departure for home by having a rather elaborate supper served to him at the hotel.

Daylight was waning rapidly when he turned his horse along the road back to Wyndward. He'd looked for

Jonathan in the city, but had seen no trace of him. The horse knew the way and required little guidance, keeping up a steady trot that covered the ground at a satisfactory pace.

Fitz had time to ponder, and the more he considered this new problem, the more concerned he became. Such a secret outfit could be highly dangerous. It seemed impossible for one member to climb out from under his bedsheet and give sufficient information to be useful, in a broad sense. As Captain Morton had said, each member knew only a very limited number of other members and when he joined, submitted to this need for strict secrecy.

Fitz was only halfway home when darkness covered the countryside, so he pulled off to the side of the road, got out of the carriage, and slipped beneath the vehicle to hang the lantern under the front seat. He was fumbling in the dark to find the hook when he heard the first shot. A bullet struck the carriage somewhere. Fitz scrambled from under the carriage and lunged for the brush at the side of the road. Another rifle shot broke the silence. The horse gave a wild, shrill scream and broke into a gallop, dragging the carriage behind him.

Fitz stayed where he was. Unarmed, he could not offer resistance, so he hunched down behind the heavy brush and remained very quiet. He could hear movement close by. He estimated that there were perhaps five or six men. Oddly, in the face of all this danger, he wondered if they were wearing bedsheets and peaked hats.

One came very close as he prowled the darkness looking for Fitz. Fitz could have reached out and dragged the man down, but that would only bring all the others. He could only combat them by silence and wait for an opportunity to slip away.

It didn't seem to be forthcoming. They were still moving about. The dry brush, crackling under their feet, gave them away. Apparently they knew this for they began calling out to one another. Fitz lay on the ground, still clutching the lantern.

He couldn't hear what they were saying, and they seemed to be careful about not giving him any inkling of who they were, why they were trying to kill him, or how they expected to find him in the darkness. Of course they knew he was there, for he couldn't move with any more silence than they. There'd been no rain in several weeks, and the ground was bone dry. Branches and twigs were like tinder.

Tinder! Fitz wiped perspiration from his face and decided to take a gamble. He reasoned it wasn't much of a gamble either, for merely staying where he was, waiting for a chance to get away, would only lead to his capture. He had to take some form of offense. Without a weapon, that seemed impossible, but perhaps the lantern would solve the problem. Fitz fumbled in his pocket for matches. He found them, removed the glass chimney of the lantern, and turned the lantern upside down to allow the maximum amount of kerosene into the wick.

He took a long breath. The hunters were coming closer. This would be his only chance. He scraped the match and applied it to the wick. The whole lantern seemed to be afire. Fitz rose and hurled it in the direction of the hunters.

The dry tinder sprang into fire as the flaming lantern hit the ground. In less than a minute fire began to spread. Fitz heard someone yell a warning. He turned about and began to run.

The crackling of the flames hid the noise made by his hasty departure, and the fire was moving so fast that those who hunted him had to look to their own safety. Fitz reached the road, ran across it into high grass, and dropped to his knees. No one came after him. Three or four minutes later, he heard the sound of horses being ridden fast. From where he was crouched down, he saw four men emerge from the flaming forest. They looked ten feet tall in their peaked hats, and they were robed in white.

Fitz had caught his first glimpse of the Ku Klux Klan.

He cursed them as he walked down the road, watching for any signs of their return. A quarter of a mile away he found his horse and carriage. The animal had stopped and waited patiently. Fitz quieted him down, got into the carriage, and drove home. He didn't stop in front of the mansion as he usually did, but continued on to the stables. The man in charge emerged to take over the horse.

Fitz said, "Help me look him over. They was a bit o' shootin' on the way back, an' the hoss bolted. Wonders if he was hit anywhar. Too dark to see fo' now."

The groom brought a lantern, and they both checked the horse. There was no sign of a wound, but the groom discovered that there was a gouge in part of the harness. The bullet must have struck there, passing over the animal but frightening him into bolting. Fitz was grateful there was no wound. He walked back to the mansion. Mark was on the steps waiting for him.

"Whut happened?" he asked. "You drove by kinda fast."

"Gots a lot to tell you an' Clarissa an' Adalia. Goin' to tell Hong Kong later. We gots a problem, son. Bad one. On the way back some o' these ten-feet-tall ghosts shot at me. Set the woods on fire to get away. Cain't help it. No other way to get out. Hopes the fire don't spread too far."

"Sees it from upstairs," Mark told him. "Wonders whut it was. So the niggers didn't 'magine seein' the ghosts."

"They saw 'em, an' they sho' ain't ghosts. Some o' them goin' to be 'fore I gets finished with 'em. We gots plannin' to do, son, an' we gots to be mighty quick about it."

"Fetches Clarissa an' Adalia while you gets washed up."

"Meets you in the drawin' room in ten minutes."

19

They formed a close circle in the drawing room. Fitz, Clarissa, Adalia, and Mark. Fitz told them everything he had learned about the Klan, emphasizing the danger of such an organization.

"Now this heah is not to be told to anyone. Your brother, Adalia, is sendin' soldiers heah. They comes two at a time, an' they goin' to live in the overseers' cottages. We gots five days to close up the school. On the fifth night they goin' to hide in the school. Any o' these bedsheets comes, they goin' to get shot right from under them high hats they wears. After that, it goin' to be up to us to see the school don' get burned down."

"But they surely will come a second time," Adalia said. "The soldiers can't be there all the time."

"You're right 'bout that. But they comes once an' 'nuff of 'em gets shot or caught so we kin see who they are, mayhap we kin make 'em tell us 'bout the others. Cap'n Morton tell me it won't be easy to get 'em to tell us 'cause they on'y knows some others. But we gets 'nuff talkin', mayhap we skeers 'nuff to bust up this heah part o' the Klan anyways."

"Wants to be in theah with the soldiers," Mark said.

"No, you cain't do that, Mark. Gots to look like ev'rythin' goin' on 'round heah as usual. They kin hide easy close by, an' if they sees all o' us wukkin' as we always done, they goin' to think we don' believe whut that warnin' said was goin' to happen."

"Wishes Jonathan was heah," Clarissa said. "Somethin' like this mayhap makes him think a little bettah 'bout whut's goin' on."

"Jonathan stayin' in Lynchburg to see whut he kin learn," Fitz explained. "They takes him fo' a red-hot rebel, an' mayhap they even asks him to join the Klan. Now that would settle it. With his help, we kin destroy the whole lot of 'em. Come to think on that, I sets a pretty good fire to get away from them. Mark, wants you to go upstairs an' see if you kin see any fire still burnin'. There is, we bettah do somethin' 'bout it."

Mark hurried out of the room and ran upstairs. Adalia was doing her best to analyze the situation.

"Fitz, I think we are in real danger. Even if you manage to stop, or even disperse, the local chapter of the KKK, there are others all over the South to take their place."

"You sho' gettin' me skeered," Clarissa said.

"I'm scared too," Adalia admitted. "Not so much for myself as for the children. What if they come to burn us out by day and the children are in school?"

"Long as the soldiers heah, we kin handle 'em. After that, we does whut we kin—an' we kin do plenty, Adalia. No reason to be skeered. I gets any idea we cain't handle 'em, we closes the school an' sends you back to Lynchburg 'til this business settled fo' good."

"I'll tell you one thing it won't do," she said. "It is not going to stop Mark and me from getting married."

"Take mo' than the Klan to stop us," Mark declared confidently as he entered the room. "Cain't see no fire, Gran'pa. Reckon it burned out."

"Glad o' that," Fitz said. "Well, you-all knows whut you're facin'. Any word o' this gets out, even to the niggers, sho' goin' to spoil ev'rythin'. Gots to make it look like we don' suspect a thing. Gots to make 'em come, an' then they gets taught a lesson they ain't goin' to fo'get day after tomorrow."

Two days later the soldiers, in civilian clothes, began to arrive after dark. They went at once to the cottages where the overseers used to live. There was room enough for them. They brought field rations so that not even Elegant was aware they were on the plantation.

On the third day, Jonathan came home, riding horseback, for he intended to return immediately.

"Papa," he said excitedly, "knows whut KKK means."

"Knows it myse'f, son," Fitz told him. "You' knows who belongs to it in Lynchburg?"

"No, suh, but thinks mayhap Bibb know somethin' 'bout it. Kind o' braggin' 'bout whut they been doin' in Kentucky."

"They comin' heah," Fitz said, "but they sho' goin' to get a s'prise. Yankee soldiers ready fo' 'em."

"Heah, on Wyndward?" Jonathan asked.

"They heah an' mo' comin'."

"Wishes I could be heah, but goin' back. Thinks someone from outen the state comin' to recruit men fo' the Klan. Papa, goin' to try an' get myse'f recruited."

"Son, they sho' kills you they finds out why you joins."

"They won't find out, Papa. They thinks you throws me out o' Wyndward, an' I don' see you no mo' an' nevah goes back heah. Thinks I ain't got over whut the Yankees done to me."

"Have you?" Fitz asked swiftly.

"No, suh, ain't nevah goin' to get over it, Papa. Ain't the kind o' liar to say I am, but it don't bother me much any mo'. An' I be damned if I stands by an' lets somethin' like this heah Klan get so big an' bad the war jes' 'bout starts over again. Want to do whut I kin to destroy the Klan."

"You wukkin' from inside sho' gives us a bettah chance. Don' likes the idea much, but you say you kin handle yourse'f, sho' thinks it goin' to be a big help."

"Lets you know soon's I heah anythin', Papa."

"How you goin' to do that? You tells 'em you nevah comes heah any mo'?"

"Gots to find some way."

"Goin' to send Chickory back with you. Gives him money to find a good place to stay, an' he meets you wharevah you wants. You sends any word by him. Goin' to see he kin get a hoss to ride whenevah he wants it. That way he kin carry your messages."

"Kin have him ride the saddle with me, Papa. Reckon I bettah get back too, so you calls Chickory an' we goes."

"He'll be ready in ten minutes." Fitz called for Calcutta Two, to have him bring drinks and send Chickory in.

Twenty minutes later, with Chickory's thin body astride the saddle in front of him, Jonathan set out for the trip back to Lynchburg. No one else had known he'd returned. Mark was in the fields, Adalia was at school, and Clarissa was sleeping late. It was best that if Jonathan succeeded in infiltrating the Klan, only he and Fitz should know it, for fear that even a slight slip of the tongue on the part of anyone else would give Jonathan away.

Soon after dark, the soldiers would slip down to the school, quietly enter, and remain out of sight until just before dawn when they would return to the cottages.

No one at Wyndward slept well during those five days. The expectation of a burning in the middle of the night was on the minds of everyone. But there was no shooting, and nothing occurred to give cause for alarm. The soldiers remained for two more days before the project was abandoned and declared a false threat.

"Would o' bet anythin' they was comin'," Fitz said during the group meeting.

"Gran'pa," Mark said, "wonders somebody heah on Wyndward finds out the Yankees waitin'. Heahs the Klan got spies ev'rywhar they kin place 'em."

"Wouldn' s'prise me none," Fitz admitted.

Clarissa said, "Thinks myse'f the Klan nevah means to come heah. On'y means to skeer us."

"Hopes you right, Clarissa," Mark said. "Mayhap you are. They sho' didn't come."

"Jes' the same," Fitz said. "From heah on, I sleeps in the schoolhouse."

"We changes ev'ry other night," Mark offered.

"Fine. Cain't do much sleepin' waitin' fo' 'em to come. Goin' to lay out guns in the hall near the front door. Anythin' happens at the school, we all goes down an' start shootin'. Knows you ain't used to guns, Adalia, but all you got to do is point the gun at the sky an' pull the trigger. Mo' noise you makes, the bettah. An' I given' Hong Kong mo' rifles so he kin hand 'em out. They comes burnin,' they goin' to pay one big price 'fore they done."

The first night Fitz stayed in the schoolhouse, he laid out four loaded rifles, some ammunition, and a handgun. He seated himself at Adalia's desk, high enough on the platform so he was able to see out of the windows. Fitz had no doubt but that they could reach the schoolhouse without his knowing it. There was too great an expanse of wooded area, the nights were dark, and it was impossible to see anyone creeping toward the building. But if they got there, Fitz was prepared to greet them with plenty of gunfire and to hold them until help came from the mansion and from Hong Kong and his selected men, well armed.

Fitz experienced not being able to determine when someone approached the schoolhouse. Halfway through the first night, the door suddenly opened. Fitz seized a rifle, aimed it, and luckily held his fire.

"You in theah?" Clarissa asked.

"Damn you," Fitz said. "Skeered the hell outen me, an' you damn near got shot."

"Couldn't sleep. Thinkin' too much. Worried some, an' anyways wanted to be with you. They comes, two o' us bettah than one."

"Got a grownup's chair heah," Fitz said. He carried it over beside the desk. "Make yourse'f comfortable. Reckon I'm glad fo' your company."

Clarissa settled herself, adjusting the robe over her

nightgown. "Heahs anythin' I don' knows 'bout, Fitz?"

"Whut I knows I tell you, Clarissa."

"Heah anythin' 'bout that sonabitch papa-in-law o' mine?"

"Henry Tallen at the bank say he thinks Apperson back, but ain't sho'. He is back, he keeps out o' sight. Some folks lookin' fo' him, 'specially the carpetbagger who lent him money."

"Is they any way he kin get me back?"

"Clarissa, he nevah could make you go back, an' now we gots a paper in his writin, saying he nevah tries to get you back. An' you divorced from Horace, so you gots nuthin' to worry 'bout."

"He skeers me anyhow. Nevah did get to tell you why he wants me back. Say it's to keep house fo' him. He lives in a hotel. He wants me to keep house in baid. Wants me fo' his private whore. Nevah tells you 'cause thinks you gets so mad you kills him."

"Jes' one mo' reason why I should o' killed him, Clarissa. Think he gots 'nuff juice to be any good?"

"Reckon he likes to beat me mo' than sleep with me, but wants that too. Oh, when I sees him in that uniform struttin' like he next to God, I hates him so much wonder why I nevah kills him myse'f."

"Well, your worries 'bout him are over. But sho' am worryin' 'bout this heah Klan."

"Whut's Jonathan doin', nevah comes home? Whorin' an' gamblin' an' drinkin' like he done befo'?"

"Likely," Fitz said.

"He evah comin' home?"

"Up to him. I cain't order him 'round no mo'."

"Reckon he 'bout forty some yeahs old now," Clarissa mused. She gave a sharp laugh. "Bettah I don' talk 'bout him bein' old. You an' me, Fitz, we sho' ain't young no mo'."

"We didn't have to keep our eyes an' ears open, I'd show you how old I am."

"You aimin' to make me horny, you sho' doin' it." She paused, suddenly serious as she hurried to one of the windows. "You heahs anythin', Fitz?"

He joined her, peering into the darkness. "Been

258

listenin'. Mayhap your ears sharper'n mine. Was it riders you heahs?"

"Reckon. Mo' than one if I heahs right. Don' see nuthin' out theah. Mayhap I gettin' a little crazy an' listenin' too hard."

"You take the west window. Take a rifle with you. We kin watch three sides of the schoolhouse anyways. You sees anyone comin', sing out once an' then start shootin'. Mark, Adalia, Hong Kong...they knows bettah than to sneak up on us, so give 'em on'y one chance fo' you shoots."

Clarissa made her way between the desks to the west window, where she took up a position with her face all but glued to the windowpane.

"Reckon these heah bastahds makes mo' trouble fo' us than they worth," she grumbled.

"Whut you talkin' 'bout now?" Fitz asked from across the room.

"You an' me was havin' the beginnin's o' a nice conversation."

" 'Bout whut?" Fitz asked, almost absent-mindedly.

" 'Bout provin' to me you ain't old. You fo'gets that, reckon you don' have to prove it any mo'. You cain't, 'cause you sho' gettin' on."

"We talks 'bout that some other time, Clarissa. Right now we stops jawin' an' listens fo' anythin' outside."

Clarissa saw the first glow of fire. She cried out shrilly, "Fitz . . . they got the mansion burnin'!"

Fitz, rifle in hand, revolver stuck under his belt, raced out of the schoolhouse. There was some kind of a fire up the slope where the mansion stood, and he cursed himself for not having put some sort of guard there too. Perhaps what they were really after was the mansion.

Clarissa, puffing and unable to speak, joined him as he came to a stop. The mansion was not on fire, but directly in front of it on the nicely cropped lawn, a huge cross, at least ten or twelve feet high, was afire. The entire cross seemed to be one mass of flame. They stood quietly watching it, bewildered and mystified. Clarissa finally managed to speak. "Whut in hell is that?"

"Looks like a cross somebody fired up."

"Whut's it mean, Fitz?"

"Ain't got no idea. Kind o' pretty though, ain't it? Got to mean somethin', but damned if I know whut."

"Thinks this the work o' the Klan?"

"Cain't think o' anybody else do a thing like this. Smell that smoke? The cross is soaked in oil. That's whut makes it burn so fast an' so bright."

"Ain't pretty to me. Thinks it means somethin' bad."

"Soon's I find out whut it means, tells yo'. Sho' aims to find out quick as I kin. Goin' to talk to Cap'n Morton 'bout it."

"Know whut I wishes?" Clarissa asked.

"Wishes I had my hands on the bastahd doin' all this."

"Wasn't whut I was goin' to say. I wish Cap'n Morton comes heah an' brings his whole goddamn Yankee army with him. An' stays heah 'til we fo'evah safe."

"Sees Mark an' Adalia out on the veranda. Elegant too."

"Let's go an' see whut they thinks."

"I'm goin' back to the schoolhouse. They sets this fire an' we don' even know they 'round heah, they sho' kin get to the schoolhouse we spendin' our time lookin' at the burnin' cross. You go see whut Mark an' Adalia thinks."

Fitz turned and trotted down the slope toward the schoolhouse, rifle ready for prompt action. The Klan might have been trying to distract anyone who guarded the schoolhouse so they could reach it without danger and throw in their firebrands.

But nothing happened. No one came out of the gloom. Fitz took up his former post behind the teacher's desk. Clarissa didn't return. Just before dawn Fitz fell asleep with his head on the desk, but one hand remained closed around the rifle.

He awoke before the children came and was outside to meet Adalia coming down the path.

"Oh Fitz, you've been up all night," she said.

"Mawnin', Adalia. Yep—an' the schoolhouse still standin'."

"What in the world was the meaning of that fiery cross last night?"

"Somethin' to do with the Klan, reckon, but ain't positive. Whut it means, I don' know."

"Mark thinks it's some kind of a warning."

"Comes to my mind too. Has to be that. You heahs anythin' last night befo' the cross burns?"

"Nothing, and I'm a very light sleeper. Mark took the cross down. It was pointed at the base so two men could have driven it into the lawn very easily. And it was covered with old rags which had been soaked in some highly combustible fluid. Some kind of oil."

"Figgered that."

She glanced at the three rifles he carried. "You look well armed, Fitz."

"Cain't always get time to reload. You gots 'nuff guns, you don' have to, an' you drives 'em back faster."

"My kids are coming," she said. "I'll see you at supper. And Fitz, thank you for all you are doing for me."

"Doin' it fo' myse'f. They burns the schoolhouse, next they goin' to burn the mansion. No call to thank me, Adalia, but nice to heah you say so anyways."

She stood on tiptoe and kissed him on the cheek before she ran down the slope, waving to the group of children rapidly nearing the schoolhouse. Fitz grinned happily and went on his way to the mansion. Mark came out to meet him.

The cross, not burned through, lay on its side where Mark had left it. Fitz paused to examine it.

"Whut you thinks, Gran'pa?"

"Klan done this fo' sho'. Got any idea whut it means?"

Mark shook his head. "Goes to some trouble to do this an' takes chances settin' it up in the middle o' the night. I heahs 'em, I sho' 'nuff stahts shootin'. Took mo' than one man to set it up."

"Needs some breakfast, Mark. Wants to have a cup o' coffee with me?"

"Told Elegant sees you comin' so ev'rythin' ready."

Elegant was fussing at the breakfast table. "Massa

Fitz, suh, whut in hell kind o' religion say they gots to burn a cross?"

"Ain't no religion, Elegant. Believe me."

"Cain't you do somethin' 'bout all this fussin'? Skeers me, it does, suh."

"It don' do me any good either, an' stops it if I kin. How many eggs you gives me?"

"Two, suh."

"Gets me two mo'. Had a bad night an' hungry."

He and Mark sat down at the table and discussed the situation while Fitz ate.

"Wishes Papa heah," Mark said. "Needs all the help we kin get. I stays at the schoolhouse tonight."

"Seems to me he was doin' fine. Whut made him change his mind an' leave?"

Fitz studied his grandson for a moment between buttering his fourth biscuit. "Made up my mind not to tell anybody, but you his son and my gran'son, an' if I cain't trust you, cain't trust anybody. Tells you the truth. Jonathan gone back to Lynchburg an' says I throws him out again. An' he goin' back to his old habits o' hatin' ev'rybody the war touched. But whut he really doin' is aimin' to join the Klan. He gets in, he gets to know the important folks, an' when we goes after 'em, we knows who to look fo'."

"Wonders why he changes so fast an' don' come to me an' tells me anythin'."

"Be sho' to keep whut I told you a secret. He gets in the Klan an' they finds out he a spy, they sho' kills him quick."

"Knows that. You kin trust me."

Elegant arrived with two more eggs and another portion of fried potatoes.

"You keep eatin' this way, suh, an' you gets fatter'n me."

"Wouldn' mind. You kind o' good-lookin."

She giggled and left them. Fitz ate without speaking for a time, and Mark remained silent while he searched his mind for some reason why anyone would go to the bother of making a heavy wooden cross, preparing it to burn briskly and brightly, and risk being shot when installing it and getting it afire on someone's front lawn.

"Funny thing, Gran'pa," Mark mused. "I thinks the burnin' cross ain't bad to watch, but skeers the hell outen Adalia an' Clarissa. Skeers Elegant an' Calcutta Two like nuthin' I evah sees. They thinks the end o' the world comin'."

"Thass whut it meant to do. Skeer folks so they does whutevah the Klan say. If it was the wuk o' the Klan."

"Goin' to cut it up myse'f. Cain't call on the niggers to do it, thinks it skeers 'em too much. Now you goes to baid. Clarissa theah already. Not in you baid," he added hastily.

"You doin' some good thinkin' lately, son. An' the best thinkin' you evah did was ask Adalia to marry you. Wyndward needs someone like her, an' mayhap it lucky too."

"Don' understan' that, Gran'pa."

"Wyndward starts with a man from the South an' a woman from the North. Reckon we had 'nuff o' that 'fore we has this damn war. Good night. Keep your eyes open. Ain't past 'em to come by day."

"You wakes to shootin' if they comes," Mark assured him. "I stays right heah. Not even goin' to the schoolhouse."

20

Mark, sitting alone on the veranda, reached for the rifle at his side as a buggy turned down from the main road. As it drew closer, he saw that it carried two men. Black men, but as the buggy neared the house Mark thought he had never seen more assured and confident blacks. And when the buggy stopped and they got out, Mark's confusion grew even greater.

One was fashionably dressed. A neat blue-serge suit, white shirt, and black tie topped off with a derby set at a precise angle. The other wore a washed-out, thin blue shirt with a button missing at the neck. His trousers were ragged at the cuffs and held up with a length of rope. While the well-dressed man wore patent leather shoes, the other was barefoot. They approached the veranda confidently.

Mark stopped them with a gesture of the rifle. "You kin wait right theah," he said crisply. "Whut you wants heah?"

The fashion plate smiled and spoke in Northern style, not at all like a Southern Negro.

"I'm not certain who you are," he said. "But I assume Mr. Fitzjohn Turner still owns Wyndward."

"You knows Mr. Fitz?"

"Ever since I was born, sir. May I ask who you are?"

Mark scratched his head. "Kin' o' funny talkin' to two niggers like they was my brothers. Reckon you knows whut you wants. Mr. Fitz sleepin'. He was up all night."

"Then, if you don't mind, we'll wait."

"Suit yourse'ves. You kin sit on the veranda steps. We been havin' some trouble heah lately, an' don' 'zactly trust many folks."

"I do see you had visitors." The one dressed like a slave pointed to the burned cross, which Mark had not yet cut up.

"Sho' did," Mark said with growing suspicion. "Whut made you say that?"

"Seems to me the Wizard and the Dragons and the Ghouls have been here."

"You knows 'bout them?"

"Oh yes. We know the Klan all right."

"Why you tellin' me this?"

The poorly dressed one squinted at Mark. "Now let me see. You can't be Jonathan, of course. Fitz had no other sons, but Jonathan. . . . You must be Jonathan's son."

Mark laid the rifle across one of the chairs. "Come up heah an' sit. You knows that, you sho' 'nuff ain't part o' the Klan."

They both laughed loudly. "The day the Klan takes on anyone with our color, my friend, will be the day the Klan expires."

Mark said, "You two gots me talkin' to myse'f. I'm goin' to wake Fitz. Time he got up anyways."

"You would do both of us a great favor, sir," the one wearing the derby said.

Mark backed away toward the door, somewhat uncertainly. The rifle still lay across one of the chairs. He picked it up with an almost apologetic air. Then he ran up the stairs, entered Fitz's room, and shook him awake. Fitz sat up, sleep leaving him at once.

"Whut's happened?"

"Don' know whut's happened. Downstairs two niggers waitin' to see you. Knows all 'bout you. Knows 'bout me. Talks like they comes from a Northern college."

Fitz bounded out of bed, ran into the bathroom, popped out again. "You tells 'em I'm comin' right down. An' tells Elegant we got company fo' suppah. You treats 'em two real nice, heah."

"Yes, suh, Gran'pa, treats 'em fine," Mark said, still mystified. He went to the kitchen.

"Gran'pa say we gots company fo' suppah. I thinks thass whut he said. We gots nigger company fo' suppah befo'?"

"Whut you talkin' 'bout, boy?" Elegant eyed him impatiently.

"Two niggers on the veranda. Fitz comin' down an' actin' like they old friends. . . ."

Elegant rudely bumped him out of the way as she hurried to the veranda.

"Hi . . . yeee," she screeched. "Dundee! Dundee an' Two Bits! You comes back! You comes back agin!"

She enveloped the well-dressed one in an affectionate hug that left him breathless. She then turned her attention to the other, hugging him as well before she stepped back and regarded them with a puzzled look.

"Dundee, you comes all dressed up. Two Bits, you looks like hell. Ain't no nigger dressed like that any mo'."

"We found that out," Two Bits said. "I'm going to have to change."

"Now see heah," Mark broke in. "I got to know who in hell yo' are. Cain't 'member seein' you 'fore, but you sho' knows ev'rybody on Wyndward."

"This heah Dundee," Elegant explained. "Born heah same night your papa was borned. His mama your gran'pa's wench. Dundee a fine boy. Got mo' brains than any nigger heah. An' Two Bits, he comes heah when he a young man. Your gran'pa buys him fo' two bits. That's how he gots his name."

Fitz came hurrying down the stairs. Elegant looked into the house and called to him, "Look who's come back, suh. It be Dundee an' Two Bits."

Mark stood aside while Fitz embraced Dundee and held him as if he were his son. Then he turned to Two Bits and drew him close too. When he stepped back, he was obviously appraising both of them.

"Dundee, you looks like you comes outen a bandbox. Two Bits, you looks like you comes outen jail. Whut in hell this means I don' know. An' don' care. Sit down." He raised his voice. "Calcutta Two, comes heah quick."

Calcutta was as confused as Mark had been when he saw two blacks seated like guests on the veranda.

"Calcutta seems to have changed," Dundee said.

"He's not Calcutta," Two Bits added.

"This Calcutta Two," Fitz explained. "Calcutta One was murdered. 'Members Apperson? When the war starts, he made a colonel. Comes heah to take all the horses. Calcutta skeered o' him an' runs. The great colonel rides after him, yells fo' him to stop an' Calcutta runs faster'n evah. So the colonel rides him down an' cuts his haid off with his sword 'cause he wouldn' stop."

"Poor Calcutta," Dundee said.

"Now this heah Calcutta Two," Fitz went on. "He sloths mo' than Calcutta One, an' he drinks mo 'too. So you fetches whiskey an' spring water fo' all o' us, an' you runs, heah?"

"I runs. Yassuh, I runs." Calcutta Two disappeared.

Mark said, "I'm still waitin' to learn whut this heah all 'bout."

"Sit down, son," Fitz said. "Tells you. Dundee raised heah an' sho' one smart boy. Two Bits. . . ."

"Mr. Fitz," Two Bits interrupted, "I prefer to be known as Jubal now, if you don't mind."

"Course," Fitz said. "I begs your pardon, Jubal. Now Mark, Jubal come later, an' he mighty smart boy too. 'Fore the war starts, I sends 'em North to my daughter Melanie. Tells her to see they gets educated an' leaves money fo' it. Thinks o' them often an' nevah knows how they gettin' on. Way you looks, Dundee, you gets to be a successful man. Jubal, way you looks, you sho' gots to be backslidin'."

"We can explain that," Dundee said. "But first, how have you been, sir?"

"Real fine, Dundee. You brings any word from Melanie?"

"No, sir. I'd like to tell you what happened to us."

"Waitin' to heah it. You two talks like Northern gen'mun."

"And what a time they had teaching us to talk this way," Jubal said with a broad grin.

"Well now," Fitz said, "it's nice to heah that kind o' talk agin, an' I'm goin' to talk that way too, b'fore I get entirely out of practice. Please tell us what happened after I left you in Washington."

"Your daughter did as you requested. She found us a nigger hotel where we stayed for a long time. She found us work. Good, solid work for a fair wage. She would not send us to college until we had studied enough to qualify. When we were ready, she got us into a fine college where we were fully accepted and taught."

"We applied ourselves, sir," Jubal added. "How could we do anything else after what you and your daughter did for us."

"Go on," Fitz urged. "You're bringing back a lot of faith I thought I lost."

"We graduated. . . ."

"Dundee cum laude," Jubal said. "I didn't make that. Dundee's too bashful to tell you himself."

"Now that you're free men and there's no longer any slavery, what do you intend to do with yourselves?"

"You solved that for us years ago, Mr. Fitzjohn."

"I did?" Fitz looked puzzled.

"You told us, and your daughter, that we were to be well educated so that when the war was over, we could return to help the men and women who were once slaves and, being set free, wouldn't know what to do. That's why we're here."

"Good! Good . . . that's excellent. Have you any idea of how to go about it?"

"Yes, sir," Dundee said promptly.

Calcutta appeared with a tray of drinks, which he served with some degree of hesitation to Dundee and Jubal. He made a fast retreat before Fitz could yell at him again. His tray was also well supplied with spilled whiskey.

"I was saying," Dundee raised his glass, "to your health and to yours, Mark."

Mark automatically raised his glass, thinking this was the first time in his life he had ever drunk with a Negro and that these two talked like professors.

"About what we intend to do," Dundee said. "I'm going to teach school and give what advice I can. Train promising students for college. We have a school now up North for young black people."

"You came to the right place," Fitz said. "Got us a schoolhouse down near the quarters, and the teacher is a wonderful girl from the North. Her brother is a military Yankee commander of Lynchburg, and she's engaged to marry Mark."

"No wonder they burned the cross," Jubal exclaimed. "You, Mr. Fitzjohn, have committed about every crime the Ku Klux Klan lists."

"You know about the Klan," Fitz said with a sigh. "You also probably realize how well they're going to accept you two."

"We surely do," Jubal said. "That's why I'm dressed the way I am. I'm going back to Lynchburg and try to get a job where I can possibly learn something about the Klan. I doubt I could serve the black people any better than to help destroy the organization which fosters hate."

"You'll be taking an awful chance," Fitz reminded him.

"Knows that, massa, suh," Jubal broke into the old slave way of speaking. "Knows whut they does to po' nigguhs like me, but firs' they gots to ketch me."

"You haven't forgotten," Fitz said.

The screen door squealed. Clarissa came onto the veranda, drawn by all the voices. She came to a dead stop, staring at the two Negroes with whiskey and water, which they raised in a salute to her as they got to their feet. Then she gasped and headed for Dundee.

"By damn," she cried out, "if it ain't Dundee. Lookin' like a duke o' somethin' mighty important."

She held out her hand. Dundee reached for it. Clarissa said, "Whut the hell!" She embraced him warmly. "Sho' kissed many a white bastahd nowhar near as good as you. An' this heah gots to be Two Bits."

"Jubal now," Fitz told her.

She embraced and kissed him too. Fitz yelled for Calcutta. "Brings Missy Clarissa whiskey. Bettah yet, brings her two an' all o' us 'nother one."

Calcutta disappeared promptly. Fitz smiled at Dundee and Jubal. "If I spoke to him in Northern, he wouldn't know what I was talking about. Well now, you two are certainly welcome to stay as long as you like. We have plenty of room here."

"Thank you, sir," Dundee said, "but we can't waste any time. There is much to do."

"I have to go back to Lynchburg," Jubal said. He glanced inquiringly at Fitz. "It's all right to speak out?"

"Of course. Clarissa is one of us."

"I'm glad. I have to go back and begin working on the project of learning what I can about the Klan. They have been very active in Kentucky and somewhat in the Carolinas, but this is the first group in Virginia—that we know of. I am to report what I learn to certain authorities in Washington who are quite concerned about the Klan."

"You have an official status then?" Fitz asked.

"No, sir. This is voluntary on my part. I wouldn't have it any other way."

"If you need money, either of you, I can supply any amount you require."

"We're most grateful, sir," Dundee said, "but we saved quite a bit and we earned more after graduation. We're in good shape, sir."

Clarissa had been listening to the dialogue. Now she turned to Mark. "You ketch all they talkin' 'bout in this heah foreign language?"

"Cain't say I does," Mark said. "No, ma'am, sho' is difficult to understan', an' thass a fact."

"Mark," Fitz said, "it a good idea to takes Dundee down to the schoolhouse so he kin see how Adalia gettin' 'long."

"I thanks you, suh. An' Mistah Dundee, I shows you

the prettiest gal you evah laid you eyes on. An' a school-room full o' childrun learnin' ev'rday."

Calcutta Two arrived in time to supply Mark and Dundee with fresh drinks, which they happily carried down the path to the school.

Dundee said, "Mark, please let me see Hong Kong and Seawitch first. They brought me up, the only parents I ever knew. I missed them. I've thought of them a great deal. I studied hard so they'd be proud of me."

"Sho' ain't outen the way. You sees Melanie fo' you leaves Washington?"

"Yes, but you notice I did not say anything to Fitz about it. I am sorry to say that now she detests him, can't even bear to hear his name mentioned. You see, she lost her husband in the war."

"Heard that. Nevah knew Melanie, but thinks she mighty uppity she cain't see her papa nevah was any diff'rent than any other plantation owner. An' the war over. She ought to stop sorrowin' fo' her husband' an' come back to her papa. Gran'pa loves her mo' than anyone else on earth. 'Cept fo' a woman who is daid."

"Benay was a wonderful lady, Mark."

"Don' means Benay. Fitz has nevah stopped lovin' her, but he falls in love again with a woman who was a Northern spy an' had to run when the war broke out. She got caught, an' they says the Rebels hung her."

"I'm sorry to hear it," Dundee said. "Fitz deserved the love of another woman."

Mark knocked on the door of Seawitch's cabin. She opened it promptly.

"Mawnin', suh." She looked at Dundee, and her wrinkled face broke into a wide smile. "You is Dundee? 'Course you is . . . my Dundee. . . ."

He embraced her and held her until she stopped weeping. She dried her eyes, then looked at him more critically. "You sho'ly rich to dress like that. Whut you been doin'? What you been? Mistah Mark, suh, 'preciates you goes to the fields an' yells fo' Hong Kong. He goin' to be some s'prised."

Mark nodded and left them. He had an idea they wanted to be alone for a few moments. He hailed Hong

Kong and, without giving a reason, told him Seawitch wanted him in a hurry.

Hong Kong recognized Dundee from a distance, broke away from Mark, and began running. He whooped it up as he neared his foster son and greeted him as affectionately as Seawitch had. Mark waited some distance away, giving them the privacy they deserved.

Dundee told his foster parents briefly about his education and his ambitions to help the ex-slaves as soon as he got organized. He told them Two Bits, now calling himself Jubal, the name of his father, was at the mansion, and they were to hurry up there to greet him as he could not remain long.

After that, Mark and Dundee went down to the schoolhouse, approaching it from the rear and in so doing, passing the cemetery. When Dundee hesitated, Mark came to a stop.

"Go ahead," he said. "Gran'pa always talks to them. I think they'd be glad to heah from you."

Dundee spent a few moments at the grave of his mother, his head bent in prayer. He paused at the graves of each of the others before he rejoined Mark. When they entered the schoolroom, all activity ceased. The children grew silent as this important, well-dressed black man looked at them critically.

Mark said, "Adalia, this heah is Dundee. Mayhap you heahs o' him from time to time. He jes' comes back, with Two Bits, who used to be a slave heah also. They been in the North all durin' the war. They was goin' to college an' got educated. Now they comes back heah to do whut they kin helpin' the folks who were once slaves."

Adalia shook hands with Dundee. "You are the most welcome news I've had since I came down here. Mr. Dundee, they need help. All you can give them."

"Thank you, Miss Adalia." Dundee bowed his head slightly. "It's even more amazing to me that you, a white woman with a fine education, are devoting your efforts to teach these children."

"Will you address them, please? Let them see what they can become if they try hard."

"My pleasure," Dundee said. He stood tall on the

platform, and every student gave him their attention, their features a mixture of admiration and puzzlement, for here was a strange sight indeed: a black man, talking like a Northerner, expensively dressed, and obviously very much a success.

Dundee said, "You children are too young to remember me, but I was born here on Wyndward. I was a slave, as your parents were, until I was manumitted by Mr. Fitzjohn. He knew I wanted to be something more than a slave so I studied. I studied even when a slave caught studying might be hung, and certainly whipped. Yet it was worth the risk. Mr. Fitzjohn found me out, but instead of punishing me, he helped me. He placed himself in considerable peril in doing so because whites were also punished if they helped a slave to learn to read or write. He sent me to a Northern college, and I graduated. Now I am back to do what I can to help young people like you. To help you become educated as I was. You can do it if you try. And trying means you must study hard, obey everything your teacher tells you to do. And you must hope. That's the main thing. Hope and work and pray. You have a long way to go, a long, hard road to travel— sometimes a dangerous one—and my prayers will go with you."

"That was beautiful," Adalia said. "Thank you, Mister Dundee. And thank you, Mark, for bringing him to the school."

"I wish I could stay longer," Dundee said. "But there is much to do, and the quicker I get started, the better."

"I agree," Adalia said quietly. "Good luck, Mister Dundee. I'll pray for your success. What you have in mind is going to take a great deal of courage."

"I hope mine matches yours, Miss Adalia," he replied soberly. "You should give some thought to the danger you have placed yourself in starting this school for my people. Mark should also."

"We're aware of that now," Adalia replied. "And we're prepared to fight for what we believe in. Aren't we, Mark?"

All Mark could do was give a slow, affirmative nod.

He was overawed by Dundee's poise and manner of speaking. Also, he was filled with pride at the determination in Adalia's voice. She was so beautiful and so well educated, he wondered how he'd had the presumption to ask her to marry him. Certainly, he'd been aware from the moment they met that she was different. Yet he'd never thought of her as his superior. Now he knew she was, in every way.

He already realized how lucky he was to be a part of Wyndward, but not until moments ago did he feel a growing awareness of the responsibility that went with it. He'd always been mindful of the high standards and sense of fairness his grandfather displayed, and at first he'd resented it. His way of getting even had been to call his grandfather "old man." Fitz had tolerated it for a while, then gotten sick of it. Mark rubbed his chin reflectively as he recalled the sting of his grandfather's fist against his jaw. After the trouncing he'd got, his resentment had changed to grudging respect. Gradually, as he observed his grandfather's behavior and listened to his reasoning, he knew the older man stood tall among men and was looked up to by them.

He knew now he wanted to be able to stand beside his grandfather and feel his equal, yet he knew he wasn't. He'd not thought of that before Dundee came. Now it was all he could think of and he knew, with a trace of despair, there was only one way he could be worthy of Wyndward. It had taken Dundee's arrival to make him cognizant of it.

On the way back, Dundee's features were thoughtful as he observed the fields where men were at work. Mark, for the first time, had an awareness of his lack of education. He'd noticed how easily Dundee had conversed with Adalia and how her face had lit up as she heard him speak and learned the reason for his returning to the South. Mark wondered if his lack of knowledge would ever be a source of embarrassment to Adalia. He knew at this moment it was to him, and he was perplexed as to what he could do about it. He could read and write fairly well, but could he mix with people who knew their way about and could speak with ease wherever they went?

Both his father and his grandfather had a college education—but he was needed at the plantation. Yet his grandfather had stated that one day he would be master of Wyndward, and it would be a matter of pride to be a gentleman in every way—which meant he must be better educated. He was at a loss.

Dundee spoke and pulled Mark out of his troubled reverie. "How everything has changed and how lucky I am."

"Whut you means?" Mark asked, still too filled with his own uneasy thoughts to make sense out of Dundee's observation.

Dundee smiled reflectively. "I used to hoe those fields. Hong Kong set me to work helping to raise corn and all I could think of—when I was old enough to think and know what a slave was and that I was one of them—was that we slaves meant no more to our masters—Mr. Fitz excepted—than the stalks of corn we grew. It was childish, but I regarded myself as no more than an ear of corn, grown on the stalk only to be harvested and sold. I told myself that was how it was with slaves, and that was what gave me the incentive to become something better. I never thought I'd make it, but your grandfather saw to it that I did."

"Nevah grew up with slaves," Mark explained, "so I don' know too much 'bout it, but knows slaves were bought an' sold—mayhap like ears o' corn. I used to think mo' like cattle."

"Yes, that's how we termed it too. Now it's over. It can never happen again. Never! No matter what people like me must go through, we have to remember that. Tell me, is your grandfather really well? He seems changed a bit. Probably worries too much."

Mark laughed. "Dundee, you older than me, but even you thinks Gran'pa changes. Whut you sees is he gettin' older. That's all. Older, but he kin fight like a wildcat an' he so damn strong he licks me so bad I nevah fo'gets. Nothin' the matter with him 'cept the yeahs, an' he don' pay no 'tention to 'em."

"I hope he keeps that attitude. It won't be easy with the Klan gunning for him."

"Comin' to know that. Says they goin' to burn down the school."

"They're capable of it. They're even capable of burning it down with all the children inside. The trouble is, their group has been taken over by radically inclined people who don't have the ability to judge what is right and what is wrong. Frankly, most of them are more stupid than my people were. This gives them an opportunity to assert themselves. To show power and ruthlessness. You must never forget, they can be deadly."

When they returned to the mansion, Jubal was ready to leave, and Dundee joined him.

Jubal said, "As soon as I learn anything about members of the Klan, I'll let you know. It may take some time, but I'll find a way."

"I'll be working with teachers and people who sympathize with the ex-slaves," Dundee said. "I'll live in Richmond, but I'll also be traveling about. I'll keep in touch whenever I can."

Hong Kong and Seawitch were there to see them drive off in the buggy. Fitz turned back to the mansion.

"If I never do a worthwhile thing again in my life, I'll rest on what those two men have become with my help. And yours too, Seawitch. You and Hong Kong raised Dundee. You can be proud of it."

"Yassuh, I'se proud," she said. "Don' know whut I feels like cryin' fo', but I sho' does. 'Minds me o' Nina, his mama. Loved her too."

21

Clarissa was the first to turn back to the mansion and the veranda where three filled glasses set on the porch railing. She eased herself into a cushioned rocker, reached for her glass, sat back, and sipped it contentedly.

Mark sat on the top step, using the pillar to support his back. He appeared to be looking down the drive as if still watching Dundee and Jubal depart in the buggy, but they were no longer visible.

"You wants a drink, Mark?" Fitz asked. He had settled himself in the chair beside Clarissa, and he too was sipping his drink.

"No thanks, Gran'pa."

"Settin' on the rail waitin' fo' you," Clarissa said.

"No thanks, Clarissa," Mark said. He was still staring off in the distance.

Fitz studied his grandson more closely. "Hot day. Had a long walk back from the school. How come you don't wants a drink?"

"Jes' don't, thass all," Mark answered without turning around.

"You sho' you feels all right, Mark?" Clarissa asked, her voice rising in concern.

"Feels fine," he replied.

"What's on your mind then?" Fitz asked. "Somethin' wrong you don't wants a drink."

"Wonderin' when Dundee learn to read," Mark said.

"Don't know 'zactly when," Fitz mused. "I lets him have the books. A nigger preacher helps him with book learnin' too. After he held services fo' slaves."

"Whar Dundee study an' keep his books?"

"In the stable loft. Kept 'em hid theah."

"Talks like you kin, when you wants," Mark observed.

"You papa kin talk Northern too when he wants. He went to college," Clarissa said.

"You college-educated too, Gran'pa," Mark said quietly.

"That's right."

"So is Adalia."

"Whut the hell eatin' into you, Mark?" Fitz asked impatiently.

"Nuthin', Gran'pa. I goin' down to school. Time fo' it to be out. Wants to be with Adalia."

Before Fitz could question him further, Mark was striding around the side of the house to the path.

"Whut the hell's wrong with him?" Clarissa asked.

When Fitz made no answer, she moved forward so she could study his face. His glass was tilted at a angle and was in danger of spilling onto him. She thought how much Mark looked like Fitz, except for Mark's blond hair. And where Mark's face had held a troubled look, Fitz's was thoughtful, almost pleased.

"I said," Clarissa repeated, raising her voice for emphasis, "whut the hell's wrong with your gran'son?"

A smile touched Fitz's face. "Reckon he growin' up."

"I says he growed up all the way since you took him under your wing."

"Cain't grow up all the way 'thout bein' educated."

"Whut the hell you talkin' 'bout?" Clarissa asked testily.

"I sayin' my gran'son a Turner all right," he replied. "Yes, suh, he goin' to be all right. He doin' plenty o' thinkin' now. Glad Dundee an' Two Bits called."

"Thought Two Bits got to be called Jubal now."

"Does," Fitz agreed. "Jes' fo'gets."

"That drink goin' to spill in you lap you don't drink it. I'm drinkin' mine. Jes' wish I knowed whut the hell's goin' on."

Fitz took a hefty swig of his drink, then spoke. "I'll tell you, but if you opens your mouth, I'll sho' close it."

"I knows how to keep my mouth shut when I has to," she said, giving him a sharp glance. "I's part o' Wyndward now. Leastwise, hopes I am. Sho' tries hard 'nuff."

"Yes, you does, Clarissa," Fitz agreed kindly. "An' I 'preciates it. Knows Benay would want you heah. Knows I do. You is part o' it. So you listen well an' fo'gets whut I tells you. Dundee upsets Mark."

"Whut you mean, upsets?" Clarissa asked, her interest now thoroughly aroused.

"You notice how good Dundee speaks? Two Bits also. But Dundee smarter."

"Talks Northern," she replied tartly. "Cain't understan' it half the time. Don't even knows the words Adalia say sometime."

"Real nice talk," he replied. "Though I likes Southern myse'f. Used to it now. Feels mo' comfortable with it."

"Whut that gots to do with Mark?"

"Fo' the first time, he realize he ain't got an education."

"He kin read an' write," Clarissa said defensively.

"Perhaps not's good as he'd like to. An' don't fo'get, he got hisse'f an educated woman. Adalia talk real good, an' she highly educated."

"She's beautiful too," Clarissa said. "With her fair hair an' Mark's, they looks like a god an' goddess."

Fitz almost choked on the drink he was swallowing. "Whar the hell you learn talk 'bout gods an' goddesses?"

"Adalia," Clarissa said smugly. She finished her glass, set it on the railing, and reached for the one left for Mark. "She watchin' Mark one day comin' up the drive an' I with her. She say, Clarissa, don't he look jes' like a god with his fine figure an' his blond hair?"

Fitz nodded slowly. "Thinks I knows whut Mark up to."

"Whut?" Clarissa asked, pleased that she'd impressed Fitz.

"Won't talk 'bout it now. Tells you later when I feel it's time. Jes' don't mention whut I tell you."

"You ain't told me a damn thing," Clarissa said angrily.

Fitz yelled for Calcutta Two to bring more drinks and settled contentedly back in his chair.

"Sho' was a pleasant s'prise to see Dundee an' Two Bits today," he said.

"Jubal," Clarissa corrected. "Sho' brought back old times, but I like these times bettah. Bettah fo' me anyways. One thing fo' sho'. Ain't been a dull day."

"I tells you right now," Fitz said, "ain't goin' be many days 'round heah that'll be dull. While Mark an' Dundee goes down to the school, Two Bits tells me whut he knows 'bout the Klan, an' they says they goin' to burn ev'rythin' heah. They goin' to do it even if we shoots half o' them."

"Goin' to sleep in my clothes from now on," Clarissa vowed. "Wants to be ready to run if I kin. Whut's the diff'rence anyways? Ain't nobody cares I sleep in my clothes or with nuthin' on but my skin."

"Got mo' to think 'bout than pesterin'," Fitz said. "An' mo' I thinks, mo' I believes the Klan wukkin' 'gainst me, means either Bibb or your damn colonel behind it. They burns the first cross heah, they makes the first threat to us. Ain't jes' a matter o' the Klan hatin' me fo' teachin' black childrun. Mo' personal than that. Bibb an' the colonel wants me busted or daid. An' that's whut I wants fo' them. Up to Jubal an' Jonathan to see whut they kin do 'bout the Klan."

"I didn't tells 'em. I may tell Jonathan later if I think it needful. Let 'em go 'bout learnin' whut they kin by themse'ves."

"Fitz," Clarissa said, "wonders why they nevah comes to burn the schoolhouse like they says?"

"Don't know:"

"They sho' comes to burn that goddamn cross, didn't they?"

"Yes," Fitz agreed thoughtfully. "Reckon I nevah considered that."

"Whut I wants to know is how they finds out the Yankee soldiers heah to meet 'em when they comes to burn? An' how they knows ain't no Yankees heah when they comes to burn the cross."

"On'y thing I kin say, they gots somebody heah on Wyndward sendin' 'em word. Or they gots men out theah in the woods watchin' us with telescopes an' field glasses. Gots to be one o' the other. Cain't be nuthin' else."

Mark waved a farewell to the two students who were racing across the schoolyard to the path that led to their cabins. They had stayed to wash the blackboard, clap the chalk out of the thick erasers, and perform various other chores when the school day was ended. The children vied with each other to perform these tasks, so Adalia assigned different people to do them each week. As a result, the schoolroom was spotless, attesting to their diligence, pride, and efforts to outdo one another.

Mark entered the room quietly, not to spy but in the hope that Adalia's back would be turned. He always liked to stand and just watch her. He was still in awe of her loveliness and femininity and lady-like qualities. He loved the sound of her voice and the way she had of suddenly turning, then pausing as their eyes met. Without even touching, they would mentally embrace. He was fortunate. She was busily engaged in printing the next day of the week and its date on the freshly washed blackboard.

He noted the desks which were highly polished. Each one had an inkwell and the name of the pupil,

281

printed in large letters and propped up. He realized Adalia was a born teacher, one who loved her profession and gloried in molding the minds of her students.

He switched his attention back to her. She was tall and slender with a waistline his large hands could encompass without difficulty. She dressed simply, but always managed to pretty up the plainness of a dress with a touch of lace or a silk flower. Always a feminine touch. The more he admired her, the more convinced he became that he could never marry her. Adalia deserved better.

He walked quietly up the side aisle, now that his mind was made up as to what he must do. Just as he reached the front, she became aware of his presence and turned in that quick way of hers.

"Mark," she exclaimed happily. She set down the chalk and went to him, her arms extended.

He made no attempt to draw her to him, so she let her hands rest on his shoulders and studied his somber features. "Aren't you going to kiss me? You looked as if you wanted to."

"I wants to," he said soberly. "I wants to so bad I hurts. But I ain't goin' to kiss you again, Adalia. Ain't nevah goin' to even touch you."

She lowered her hands to her sides. "Don't you love me?"

"That's jes' it. Loves you so much I won' let you waste yourse'f on me."

"I think you've lost your mind," she said sternly. "You asked me to marry you. We pledged our betrothal in this very room. Now you're saying you don't want me. Mark Turner, you're a very fickle man. I suppose you've met someone else."

"Ain't no one but you, Adalia. Nevah will be. Love gots nuthin' to do with it."

"What else matters?" she asked, her eyes flashing angrily.

"Education. I ain't got none. I don' speak right."

"You're a Turner. You're just like your grandfather."

Mark backed off and pointed a finger at her. "That ain't so, an' don't you say it is. Gran'pa's got a college education. My papa's college-educated. I can read an' write, but not good as I'd like to. I cain't talk like Dundee an' made me sick inside an' 'shamed 'cause a slave—a former slave—talks bettah'n me. Thinks bettah too, an' the reason is 'cause he's got book learnin'. He's college-educated too."

Adalia wanted to go to him, to comfort him, but she knew better. His inner agony was revealed in his face. It had been difficult for him to express himself—humiliating—but he had to do it.

She said, "Your grandfather would send you to school."

Mark nodded. "Knows that. But cain't leave him heah. Not jes' now. Theah bound to be trouble heah, an' this my place now."

"Suppose I married you, and we went North so you could go to school."

"Cain't marry you ignorant like I am."

"You can, Mark," she disputed. "Don't turn your back on me, darling, please. I love you too much. I don't care if you haven't had an education."

"You would one day," he said thoughtfully. "Then I'd hate myse'f. I'd embarrass you sho' as hell. Theah—you see. A gen'mun wouldn' say that."

"He certainly would," she replied spiritedly. "I don't want you to turn into a prissy prim."

Despite the gravity of the situation, Mark had to smile.

"What are you laughing at?" Adalia demanded.

"Not laughin'," he replied. "Jes' thinkin' o' me bein' a prissy prim. Don't think that the right name fo' me."

"You're adamant you won't go North to school now."

"I'm adamant," he replied.

"Ever hear that word before?" she asked.

"Nevah."

"Then you learned a new word." She folded her arms across her bosom and looked directly into his eyes. Before he could shift his gaze, she said, "Look at me, Mark Turner."

"I'm lookin'," he said with a sigh.

Her mouth widened in a slow smile. "You're looking at your teacher. I'm going to tutor you."

"Couldn't let you. 'Sides, would be embarrassed if the folks at the house knew."

"No one will know but you and me," she replied. "You must manage to come here every day after school. I can teach you easily. A variety of subjects. I'll be your teacher until you are able to go away to school."

"Won't leave you heah with the Klan."

"You needn't go until that trouble is over with."

"Not lookin' on it endin' in a hurry."

"No matter. The more time I have to tutor you, the more you'll know when you go North to take examinations so they will know how far your education has advanced."

"Ain't had much," Mark sighed.

"Sometimes you learn a lot by being around intelligent people."

Mark's face flamed. "People I was 'round in my mama's whorehouse knew jes' one thing. But they knew that good."

Adalia's delicious laughter seemed to fill the room. Though Mark loved hearing it, it sent shafts of pain through him.

"Whut's so funny?" he asked.

"Just thinkin'," she replied, slipping into his way of speaking. "Just thinkin' that one day I'll know that just as good as they did, an' you can do the teachin'."

Despite himself, his laughter mingled with hers. She extended her arms, and he drew her close. Before his lips could close on hers, she leaned her head back and spoke with quiet firmness.

"No kissing until you say you'll be my student."

"I'll be the best student you evah had. Promises that."

22

After supper everyone congregated in the drawing room. Clarissa and Adalia had sherry; Fitz poured brandy for himself and Mark.

Calcutta, who had apparently been doing his loafing somewhere at the front of the house, came in to announce that someone on horseback was coming.

"On'y one comes," he said. "But comin' mighty fast, suh."

Fitz set down his glass and hurried to the veranda in time to see the slight figure of a black boy slide from the saddle of a sorry-looking plow horse.

"Chickory," Fitz said, "whut you doin' this time o' night?"

"Gots lettah fo' you, suh."

"Let's have it," Fitz said. "Whar you gets this hoss?"

"Livin' with a fam'ly got hosses fo' wuk an' lets me take one."

"You tells 'em whut fo'?"

"No, suh. Says ah wants to ride an' gives 'em a quartah to ride the hoss."

"Good. Gives you five silver dollahs fo' yourse'f, you nevah tells you wukkin' fo' me."

"Sho' won't, suh, an' I thanks you, suh."

"Wait heah, case theah's an answer to this letter."

Fitz returned to the drawing room. "Chickory brought a message from Jonathan." He broke the seal and scanned the contents himself first. Then he read it aloud.

"Jonathan say they goin' to be a Klan meetin' at the farm o' Roger Sims. Goin' to mayhap hangs somebody. Clarissa, go out an' tells Chickory to go back. Mark, you an' me, we gets dressed in dark clothes, takes guns, an' see whut we kin do."

"Mark, be careful, darling," Adalia implored.

"Sho' will, honey."

Clarissa returned before Fitz left the drawing room. "Clarissa, you fetches Hong Kong an' go down to the school an' makes sho' nobody comes to burn."

"I'm going too," Adalia said.

"Rather you stays heah in the mansion. Sees anyone comin', go out the back door, runs to the school an' tells Clarissa. You kin trust her to keep you from harm. She mighty near bein' a dead shot an' kin hold anyone off fo' a good while. Gots to go now. Watch yourse'ves."

The Sims farm was two miles to the east, well off the main road. A small cotton-raising farm on which was a medium-sized house, a barn that slanted slightly to one side, and three small sheds, one of which had already collapsed for want of care.

Fitz and Mark left their horses a quarter of a mile away, concealed in heavy brush through which any intruder would not be likely to cross. Their pockets heavy with cartridges, rifles loaded and ready, they made their way to the farm.

Before they reached the edge of this forest growth, they heard the sounds of many people talking, shouting, and moving about. They also came across a score of horses, two buggies, and a carriage left at the side of the narrow dirt road to the farm. The Klan was already in operation.

Fitz and Mark dropped to the ground, hugging it with their bellies as they crawled forward to find a good observation spot. On the fringe of heavy brush they watched a score of Klansmen in robes and peaked hats going about on whatever nefarious business had brought them here.

Held at gunpoint by three Klansmen, Sims, his wife, and a lanky, long-haired son were obviously terrified. Two Klansmen carried a kitchen table out of the house, others brought a few chairs. The group now assembled around them. Three men were busy setting up a cross for later burning. All faces of the Klansmen were hooded except for eyeholes.

"Whut they up to?" Mark whispered.

"Reckon they goin' to hold a trial. Thass whut they wanted the table fo'. They sho' hides pretty good under the sheets. Now will you look at that! They draggin' two niggers from inside the house. Reckon they the ones goin' to be judged."

"Whut if they hangs 'em? Kin we do anythin'?"

"Not 'lessen you wants to hang alongside 'em. All we kin do is watch, an' this ain't the best place fo' it. If we could reach the barn an' get into the loft, we sho' got fine seats fo' this show."

"They sho' sees us we try that, Gran' pa."

"You right, but we sees a chance, we takes it. Now they gots the big buck facin' the table. Wishes I could heah whut's goin' on."

"Don't see no rope hangin' from that tree," Mark commented. "Don't mean nuthin', reckon, seein' they kin throw a rope over the branch in no time."

The Klansmen moved in closer for the ceremony, which was now beginning.

Fitz said, "We moves fast to the left we kin get to the far side o' the barn an' gots on'y a short clear space to run. They so busy now, thinks we got a chance."

"Goes first," Mark said.

He led the way, broke from the brush, and ran

toward the barn. No one seemed to notice. Once Mark was inside, positioned to cover him, Fitz broke away from the brush too. He found the door open, with Mark standing nearby to close it once he was inside. They didn't take time to speak, but looked for the ladder to the loft.

Mark went up first after handing Fitz his rifle. He made his way to the loft door above which hung the projecting beam used in hauling hay. It was partly open. Mark opened it a little more and got a fine view of the proceedings almost below.

He signaled Fitz, took the rifles Fitz passed up to him, and, with Fitz at his side, crouched beside the loft door. They could even hear some of what went on.

Seated behind the table, a Klansman in a red robe seemed to be in charge. One of the bucks stood before him with his head bowed, hands clasped before him in the old stance of a slave. Whatever he had been charged with, the trial seemed to be over and the Klansman judge was meting out a sentence.

"We ain't listenin' to any mo' o' your lies. Knows you stole from your massa. . . ."

"Gots no massa." The Negro finally found the courage to defy them. "Ain't no mo' massas."

"You ain't doin' yourse'f any good lyin'. You tells us you did it, an' we don't string you up."

"Nevah stole anythin' in my life. Tellin' you the truth I am."

"I say you guilty. One o' you men fetch a rope."

The prisoner backed away a step or two, and terror grew on his face. He lowered his head again, clasped his hands.

"Suh, I steals like you says."

"Now that's bettah," the red robed man said. "Fo' tellin' the truth you kin go. In a minute. Men, line up."

The Klan members quickly formed a double line with room between for a man to walk.

Mark said, "Damn, they goin' to make him run a gauntlet."

"Whut the hell that?" Fitz asked, peering down at the assembly.

"He gots to go 'tween the lines, an' he gets busted ev'ry step he takes."

"Poor bastahd," Fitz said. "Feels like shootin' 'em all."

"We sho' daid you try it. These heah sonabitches lookin' to kill somebody."

"Whut we gots to do, if we kin, is get one of 'em an' takes the sheet off to see who he is. Knows most o' Bibb's scalawags. Mayhap I kin recognize one of 'em."

"We could sort o' ask him who the others are, Gran'-pa."

"He gets away he tells who we are, an' then the Klan sho' come to visit. Don't wants that we kin help it. Whutevah goes on heah tonight, son, we kin do nuthin' 'bout. Don' get your dander up. Nuthin' we kin do. 'Cept watch an' be able to tell whut we saw later."

The black seemed to have no idea what the double line of men portended. He thanked the red-robed one when he was told he could go. As he turned around, he was expertly maneuvered between the lines. Then he knew. He gave a loud yell and started running. Every half a dozen steps he was tripped and when he fell, kicked until he screamed in pain. Someone would hoist him to his feet, and he would manage a few more steps before a blow to the head sent him sprawling and the cruelty was repeated. By the time he reached the end of the line he was crawling, making mewing noises. A six-foot, two-hundred-pound man in the pink of condition, reduced to the status of an animal. And all the while the robed men cursèd him and laughed uproariously when he finally was forced to crawl.

"Damn them!" Mark muttered.

"The nigger lucky they didn' string him up. Reckon he nevah did whutevah they says he did. Still he's alive, an' that's somethin' after these bastahds gets through with you."

"Time comes," Mark muttered, "goin' to have me some o' them down theah to bust up good. Right now I could kill 'em all."

"Somethin' else comin' up."

The far younger prisoner, not more than sixteen or seventeen, was dragged before the red-robed leader. Sims, who owned the farm, was also shoved over to stand beside the Negro.

The red-robed judge, serving also as jury, spoke to them in a stern voice. Fitz thought he had heard that voice before, but he couldn't identify it.

"Mistah Sims, suh, we charges you with hidin' this heah rapist in you house. We charges your wife with helpin' hide him."

"Does whut you wants, you don't touch my wife," Sims pleaded frantically. "She ailin' an' she done nuthin'."

"Did you hide this nigger who rapes?"

"Wuks fo' me. He comes home. Don't know whut he been doin'. Ain't hidin' him. Wuks on the farm fo' food an' to sleep in the barn. He rapes, I don't know it."

"Yo' must o' s'pected he up to somethin'. A man came by 'bout two hours ago lookin' fo' this heah nigger, an' you says you ain't seen him."

"Nevah seed him. Mayhap he was in the barn. Don't know 'bout that."

"You should be given fifty lashes, but you an old man an' dumb as a mule, so you on'y gets six. Next time you favors a nigger, you gets hung. Tie him fo' lashin'."

Sims was dragged to a small tree in the front yard and quickly roped to it. His shirt was torn off his back. One of the robed men produced a lash, a length of thin rawhide, tipped with metal. The kind of a whip Fitz kept at Wyndward, but never used, though his father had been generous with it. It could cut a man's back open and leave him in agony for days.

The man with the whip tested it by flicking it at Sims' bare back. Even this caused a howl of pain. Then he settled down to inflict the prescribed punishment. Six times the lash struck and blood spurted.

"Ain't feelin' too sorry for that man," Fitz whispered. "Saw him use a whup like that on his slaves an' laugh while he did it."

"Jes' the same, days like that gone fo' good. Whut they goin' to do with that poor boy they gots tied?"

"Hangs him, reckon. Talks 'bout rapin' an' that means hangin'."

"We gots to sit heah an' see that done, Gran'pa?"

"'Lessen you wants the same rope 'round your neck. These bastahds kills 'cause they likes to, an' they sho' get somethin' to like they sees you at the end o' the rope. Told you, nuthin' we kin do."

The trial began. A scraggly-looking woman of at least sixty was brought forward. From the way she walked and, later on, spoke, she was apparently half-drunk.

"Asks you, ma'am, evah sees this heah boy 'fore?"

"Puts me down an' rapes me he did," she replied with a simpering laugh.

"Not even a nigger in the heat would rape that old whore," Mark muttered. "She say anythin' they asks, an' they sho' told her whut to say befo'."

"You sho' this the boy?"

"Reckon knows whut a rapin' nigger look like."

"Yes, I believe that true. Now after he gets on top o' you, he put a knife to you throat an' tells you there's any yellin' he cuts you?"

"Sho' did," she said eagerly. "Hangs this rapin' man an' heals my poor eyes has to watch him rapin'."

"Boy, you heahs whut she says. Got anythin' to say?"

"Massa, suh, ain't raped nobody. Sweahs I ain't."

"You hears whut she say. You thinks a white woman lyin'?"

"Didn' rapes nobody, suh. Sweahs it. Nevah sees her befo' in my life."

"You lyin', an' anythin' we hates is a liar. You rapes this heah poor woman, an' you laughs while you rapin'. Nigger like you ain't fitten to live. You gets hung."

The boy didn't crumple with this news. Apparently he'd been expecting it and had braced himself for the ordeal that was to follow. He didn't plead for his life, and he made no condemnation of the ugly woman who was now laughing at him.

"Get the rope ready," the red-robed judge ordered.

"Gran'pa, we cain't jes' stay heah an' watch him get hung."

"Don' know whut we kin do."

Below them they saw the boy led toward the barn. A man threw a rope that curled around the projecting beam two feet from Fitz and Mark.

"Put the rope 'round his neck," the red robe ordered. "Then cut his hands loose. Wants to see him thrashin' 'bout while he dies."

The boy was placed below the noose, untied but heavily guarded. The noose was brought down and fixed around his neck. Neither Fitz nor Mark could see how he was reacting, but no cries for mercy came from him. He was no longer in view unless they leaned well out, which would give them away.

Several torches had been held high for the ceremonies. Sims, a dead weight in the arms of his terrified wife and son, was being dragged to the house. The red-robed leader held up his arms.

"Light the cross. Let this rapin' man see it. Last thing he evah goin' to see. When the fire dies, hoist him up an' he dies with the fiery cross."

Fitz grasped Mark's arm as the younger man began to raise his rifle. "Not yet," Fitz whispered.

"We goin' to cut some o' them down, Gran'pa. Gots to."

"Mayhap. Got an idea. If it wuks, I'll be s'prised, but knows we gots to do somethin'."

"Tells me whut I kin do."

"They must have the boy guarded, but all the others gatherin' 'round the cross. Reckon when it burns, they goin' to watch it an' when the fire dies, goin' to return an' see the boy hoisted up to strangle."

"Not while I gots a gun, they ain't," Mark vowed.

"Seems like I always gets caught in somethin' like this," Fitz grumbled. "Now you does whut I says, an' no talkin' back. They cuts the boy loose so they kin see him kick. Means his hands an' feet now free. When they hoist him up, mayhap that rope, right theah whar we kin reach it, ain't goin' to be strong as they thinks."

"'Specially it gets cut down to a few seconds," Mark said with a soft laugh. "Got me a big knife fo' that kind o' cuttin'. Think it safe I reaches out now?"

"They puttin' out all the torches so they kin see the burnin' cross bettah. Kind o' dark 'round the barn now. Soon's the fire starts up, you kin cut the rope. Be sho' not to cut it through. Leaves on'y 'nuff so it breaks when they raises him."

"Thinks he kin get away?"

"All the men in a circle 'round the cross. Reckon they does that whenevah they kin. Mayhap on'y two men guardin' the nigger down below. They hoists him 'fore the others leave the cross, mayhap when the rope breaks he kin run fo' it 'fore they knows whut happen."

"Gran'pa, I cuts the rope now. We gets the hell outen heah an' hides in the brush. They tries to take the boy, mayhap we kin start shootin'."

"No shootin'," Fitz warned. "We got to be sho' they nevah knows whut happened when the boy drops an' runs. He don' make it, we do nuthin' mo'. At least we gives him a chance."

Mark laid the rifle down gently, took a heavy folding knife from his pocket, and opened the largest blade. He tested it with his thumb and found it razor-sharp. He crawled forward. The base of the cross burst into flame, rising fast to the cross itself. There was enough light from it for Mark could see what he was doing. He reached out, drew the blade across the rope, and kept gently sawing at it until he knew the rope would never hold up the condemned boy.

He crawled back to Fitz's side. "Thinks it goin' to let 'em hoist him up a little 'fore it breaks."

"It bettah break, or it be you hangin' him. Now we gets out o' heah."

They crept across the loft floor and went down the ladder making very little sound. Outside, the robed men had gathered in a circle around the burning cross and were singing. It was some kind of a hymn, but Fitz wasn't familiar with any church music and Mark knew even less. To Fitz, it seemed sacrilegious. But it did cover any sound they might make.

They were free of the barn now, crouched near a corner of it, contemplating the open space between the barn and the brush. Peering around the corner of the structure Fitz saw that two men were holding the boy's arms while they watched the proceedings around the burning cross.

Fitz said, "Now!"

Mark sprinted across the cleared space while Fitz kept his rifle half raised. If either of the guards saw Mark, Fitz was prepared to shoot them both. They were too intent on the ceremony around the cross. Fitz began his sprint, and when he reached the brush, he dived headlong into it. The fire was dying down now. The singing had stopped. All the Klansmen turned toward the barn to watch the condemned man die.

The red-robed one must have given a signal or called out an order that Fitz didn't hear. As Fitz and Mark watched, scarcely daring to breathe, the two guards grasped the end of the rope and stepped back. The noose tightened around the silent prisoner's neck. Then he was hoisted up quickly. About four feet off the ground, the rope parted and he came down, landing on his feet.

Startled as he must have been, his reflexes were fine. He didn't bother to take the rope off his neck. He went into a long-legged run that carried him into the gloom before his executioners were aware of what had happened.

"Gran'pa," Mark said, "the Lawd was sho' on that boy's side."

"The Lawd an' us," Fitz said. "Hopes he got 'nuff sense to keep runnin' 'til they nevah gets him. Anyways we gave him his chance."

"Bettah we gets out o' heah," Mark advised.

"Goes fo' our hosses. We gets to them 'fore the Klan stahts leavin', we mayhap gets us one o' them. Sho' wants to see whut one looks like."

"Gran'pa, they ain't even goin' after the boy."

"Whut they been doin' is 'gainst the law. That boy goin' to tell somebody sho', an' they knows it. They's got to be long gone 'fore Yankee soldiers comin'. The boy

294

don' mean nuthin' now. They lookin' out fo' their own skins."

They ran for the spot where they'd left their horses. By the time the Klan was leaving the area, Fitz and Mark were in the saddle, waiting just beyond the heavy brush that lined the road from the farm.

The Klan came, headlong in retreat, the red-robed leader in front. Well behind were the buggies and the carriage, and at the very rear a man on horseback seemed to be watching for pursuit.

As he passed by, Fitz and Mark rode out, spurring their horses. They caught up with him. As the sound of hoofbeats behind him became apparent, he turned to look back. At that moment, Fitz, holding his rifle by the barrel, swung it as hard as he could.

The sound of the impact was loud enough to make Fitz and Mark ready to make a run for it, but no one ahead seemed to have heard anything. Fitz and Mark dismounted. They gave the Klansman's horse a resounding whack on the rump, sending him galloping down the road. Mark knelt beside the prone man. He looked up.

"Granp'a, he daid. Must o' busted his neck when he fell."

"Way I swung that rifle butt, reckon his neck was busted 'fore he fell. Drag him into the bushes whar we kin light a match an' see who he is."

The sound of the retreating Klansmen was rapidly fading as Mark pulled the body into the brush. They knelt, and Mark lit a match as Fitz pulled the hooded peaked hat off the robed man.

"Reckon we sho' guessed right, son. Don' know his name, but sees him often 'nuff with Bibb."

"Reckon the one in the red robe was Bibb?"

"Cain't say yes o' no. Sort o' recognized his voice, but he could easy change it some. Or the damned thing over his haid changes it fo' him. But this man sho' one o' Bibb's crowd."

Mark blew out the third match he'd struck. "Whut'll we do with him, Gran'pa?"

"Leave him heah. Let somebody try an' figger out

whut happen to him. Think that black got away all right."

"Hope so. Mighty lucky we was in that loft. Reckon to his dyin' day he goin' to say he was saved by the Lawd."

"In a way," Fitz said, "reckon he was."

"Gran'pa, Wyndward kind o' close to this heah farm. Mayhap one o' them night riders thinks o' that, an' they rides to see if we theah."

"Means we rides 'round the mansion 'fore we goes in. Sees anybody we jes' waits."

"Lessen they pesters Adalia. They does, an' I shoots some o' them fo' sho'."

"Let's go an' see."

As they neared the mansion, keeping hidden from the front, they saw no signs of anyone. Lights gleamed in the windows, and nothing seemed amiss.

The schoolhouse was dark. Mark turned his horse in that direction. Fitz followed him. As they neared it, Fitz gave a loud whistle. A light appeared in one window, and Clarissa appeared at the door, a rifle at her shoulder. She lowered it as the riders came into her view.

"Anybody comes?" Fitz asked without dismounting.

"Quiet heah, Fitz. You finds anythin'?"

"Sho' did. Reckon safe to leave the school now. Climb up behin' me, Clarissa, an' we rides to the house."

Mark said, "Comes soon as I gets some men to guard the school. Wouldn't s'prise me some o' that bunch o' scalawags comes ridin' fo' mo' excitement."

"Don't think so. Right now they too busy fixin' it up so they kin say they someplace else."

Still, Mark rode off to assign guards to the school. Fitz, with Clarissa holding on tightly from behind, rode back to the house.

Clarissa said, "Gettin' close to you, Fitz, makin' me kind o' horny."

"Well, you gets over that real fast," he said. "Sho' ain't in no mood myse'f. Not tonight."

"You gettin' to spoil ev'rythin' lately, Fitz."

"Mayhap. Been gettin' told I gettin' old so much lately, mayhap I am. But we sho' has all the excitement we needs fo' one night. Means Mark an' me."

"You busts a few o' them, hopes."

"Mo' than that. We confused 'em so, reckon they don' know whut happen. They gets mo' confused when they finds one o' their kind got hisse'f killed tonight, an' no way o' tellin' how. Or who did it."

"Makes a bargain. Won't pester you none tonight, you tells me all 'bout it."

"Don't see Adalia 'round. Hope she all right."

They dismounted. As they walked toward the veranda, the door opened and Adalia stood ready. Before they were inside, Mark rode up fast, slipped out of the saddle, and ran up the steps to take Adalia in his arms.

"Been mighty worried," he said.

"I'm all right, darling. Talk about being worried. I've been chewing my fingernails. Are you all right?"

"Tells you 'bout it."

In the drawing room, with Mark and Fitz well supplied with brandy, Fitz told the story of their adventures.

"I'm proud of you, Mark, for helping that boy escape," Adalia said.

"Reckon them bedsheet-wearin' skunks kind o' confused tonight," Clarissa commented.

"We owe something to Jonathan," Adalia said. "He sent word about that Klan meeting."

"He must be havin' a great time, if they tellin' him whut happened," Fitz said.

"He'll sho' be valuable if they takes him into the Klan," Mark said.

"Jonathan pretty smart man," Fitz said. "If anybody kin get in, he will. Mayhap he heahs o' mo' meetin's like tonight. Give me lots o' pleasure breakin' 'em up."

"I wonder if my brother knows all about the Klan," Adalia said.

"He knows, Adalia," Fitz told her. "Ain't much he kin do 'lessen he know whar there's a meetin', like we did. Too bad there ain't goin' to be a real big meetin', an' we heahs of it in time to gets the cap'n to send in his soldiers. Takes somethin' like that to bust up the kind o' club the Klan is."

Clarissa arose. "Ain't late, but kind o' tired. If the Klan comes heah lookin' fo' you, Fitz, wakes me so I kin shoot a few o' the bastahds."

Fitz glanced at Mark and Adalia seated side by side on a small sofa. Mark had set his untouched glass of brandy down on the table and had an arm around Adalia's waist. She was holding his free hand between both of hers. Neither were aware of Fitz or Clarissa.

Fitz felt more than a trace of concern about Adalia's safety, yet he knew better than to suggest she return to Lynchburg where she'd be close to her brother and also have the security of the Union Army nearby. He wished she and Mark would marry, but he abandoned the thought just as quickly. Mark had the Turner pride, and just now he didn't feel Adalia's intellectual equal. He wasn't either, but he'd shown good sense tonight and revealed himself to be a man. Fitz hadn't fully realized until tonight how comforting it was to have Mark. At least the Turner line would be carried on. He wondered how Jonathan felt about the boy, or if he ever gave a thought to the fact that Mark was his son. Fitz saw Mark try to draw Adalia closer. But she gave an almost imperceptible shake of her head. Fitz knew what that meant—she was embarrassed by his presence.

He yawned audibly. "Reckon a old man like me ought to be in baid an' get some rest. Been one busy night. 'Scuse me, Adalia—Mark."

Mark didn't even hear him. Adalia slipped free of Mark's arm and went to Fitz. She stood on tiptoe and kissed his cheek.

"Good night, Fitz dear."

He was touched by the gesture and rested his hands lightly on her shoulders. "You skeered heah?"

"I won't let myself be," she said quietly. "I have work to do, and no one's going to stop me—not even the Klan."

Fitz wished he were as certain, but he gave her an admiring smile and a nod of approval. He bent and kissed her brow, surprising even himself at his show of affection. At the same time, it seemed as if a burden had lifted from his heart.

"Guess," he said softly, "you be the daughter I always wanted an' nevah had. Glad somethin' seemin' to wuk out heah. Night, Adalia. Night, Mark."

He looked over to his grandson. To his surprise, Mark was standing, and had been doing so since Adalia had gotten to her feet. He was already observing the social graces. Fitz patted Adalia's shoulder lightly, turned, and left the room.

Adalia turned to Mark. Her arms raised, she went to him. He drew her close, and their hearts pounded madly in unison as their lips touched. Mark broke the embrace and stepped back.

When he spoke, his voice was uneven. "Wants you so bad, Adalia, wonders sometime how I kin stand it."

"I want you too, darling," she said quietly. "I don't know what to do about it except get married."

"Cain't marry you 'til I gets educated," Mark's tone was resolute now. "Loves you too much fo' you to marry an ignorant man without book learnin'."

"Character is just as important," Adalia reasoned. "You certainly displayed that tonight—along with courage."

"Gots to," he said quietly. "Gran'pa got it, Papa got it, an' I gots to have it."

"You already have it," Adalia spoke as firmly as he.

"I'm skeered fo' you heah," Mark said. "Thinks mayhap you should go back North. You could teach theah jes' as well. Plenty o' niggers theah needs learnin' as well as heah."

"My place is here with you," she replied quietly. "I didn't tell you before, but I spoke with my brother. He's greatly concerned about conditions here."

"Whut do you mean?" Mark asked quickly.

"He says he'll get orders someday soon to pull out. There'll be no protection here or anywhere once the troops leave. And they will."

"My sweet Adalia, they gots to go sometime, an' we

cain't stop it. We stays heah an' takes care o' Wyndward. It's part o' my life now an' soon be part o' yours. Time the Yankees leave, things goin' to quiet down. They don't, not much o' this city trouble reaches out heah to Wyndward, an' if it does, Fitz knows how to take care o' it."

"What if the Klan grows stronger and stronger? My brother said there are an awful lot of men who'd be glad to join it."

"Reckon so, but won' last. Cain't, 'lessen it gets organized bettah than it's now. Any men who ride wearin' bedsheets an' with their faces hidden, sho' ain't much in the way o' real men."

"Yes," she agreed. "Their methods are cowardly."

"Sho' you don' wants to leave? I won't lie. I'm plenty worried 'bout you bein' heah an' runnin' that school like you is."

"I love you, Mark. What I'm doing doesn't take the courage you proved you have tonight. You're brave and a man of principle. You saved a life—probably two if that second Negro recovers from the severe beating he received."

"Pure luck, Adalia. Nothin' but pure luck. Fitz an' me could o' been too far off to help. They could o' used a tree branch to string that boy up, an' all we could o' done was jes' watch the poor boy die. On'y thing Gran'pa an' me done was bein' whar we could help."

"I'm also worried about Jonathan."

"No need to. He one o' us."

"I know that, but when he was here, he couldn't abide me because I was from the North. He hated everything concerning the North. He frightened me."

"Knows his ways must o' hurt you, Adalia. Sorry 'bout that. He changed, that's true. But think o' whut he done fo' us. Findin' out 'bout the Klan meetin' so we could do somethin' 'bout it."

"I realize from what Clarissa and you told me, Jonathan went through an awful time. He may never get over it. But, as you say, he did send that warning message tonight."

"Leastwise he didn't change so much he joined the

bedsheets," Mark mused. "I think Papa comes 'round one o' these days."

"I hope so," Adalia said fervently. "I want him to accept me."

"Don' worry your pretty haid 'bout it," Mark said. "My biggest worry now is to keep my hands to myse'f."

"You can put them around me," Adalia said, giving him a winning smile.

"Don't dare," Mark said worriedly. "They be all over you. Don't wants to pester you. Not 'til I gots the right. Cain't sleep, that's fo' sho'. Reckon I takes a walk."

"I can't sleep either," Adalia said. "Would you laugh at me if I asked whether you'd like another lesson?"

"You serious?" he asked in surprise.

"Completely," she said firmly.

"I'd love that, Adalia. I wants a lesson whenevah you gots the time."

"I'll make the time, Mark darling. You just find the time. I know how busy you are here."

"No mattah how busy, I wants book learnin'. I wants my education. I wants to marry you, an' that's the on'y way I will."

"Then let's go to the library. We won't disturb anyone. I'll teach you how to conjugate the verb *amore*."

"Whut the hell that?" Mark asked in amazement.

"*Amore* is the Latin verb meaning to love. In private schools, children in the fourth grade are taught Latin."

"I bettah learn English first," Mark said. "Whut kind o' language is Latin?"

"It's a dead language," Adalia said. "The Romans spoke it. You'll learn about them in history class."

"Mayhap I bettah takes a walk," Mark said worriedly.

"You will," Adalia said quietly. "Directly to the library. The way I'm going to work with you is to give you general lessons in several subjects. It may be a little confusing at first, but one day they will all come together. Latin will teach you a lot about words. It will help increase your vocabulary."

"Don't see how," Mark said, thoroughly mystified, "but if you says so, I'll learn it. Learn anythin' you says I needs to."

Adalia had no trouble finding a book of Latin. Mark found paper and pencil in his grandfather's desk, and they sat there side by side. He worked diligently with Adalia for two hours. At first, it seemed like a lost cause, trying to say those strange words, but he soon became intrigued by them.

It was Adalia who called a halt to the lesson. She was fighting sleep. Mark put out the lamps on the desk, and they went upstairs, their arms around each other. At the landing, they exchanged a good-night kiss, and without the slightest hesitation, each headed for their rooms, too tired to think of anything but a bed on which to lay their weary bodies.

23

Strangely, the next two weeks were serene. So much so that Fitz felt a growing uneasiness. He had expected at least one person would stop by, whether out of a spirit of neighborliness or a pretense of it, in the hope they might learn if he had been aware of the activity that took place on the Sims plantation. There had been no more forays by the Klan. At least, no word of any had been sent by Jonathan. The death of the man Fitz had killed was never reported. Mark, out of curiosity, even paid a visit to the spot where they'd left the body and discovered it had been removed, probably by the Klan and disposed of in some secret grave. If the man had any relatives, they no doubt had been warned to be silent.

Mark spent any spare time he had with Adalia. When Clarissa questioned Fitz, he told her he supposed since they were young and in love, they preferred their company to anyone else's. She didn't look convinced, but compressed her lips tightly to hold back the comment she undoubtedly wanted to make.

Nonetheless, Fitz was worried lest this new serenity

lull them into a false sense of security. He had an uneasy feeling trouble was brewing—if not for him, then for someone the Klan felt needed a lesson. However, he didn't voice his fear to Mark. Especially since he had nothing but his own intuition to go on.

In the fields, work was progressing well but at a hurried pace these days, for the plants were being stripped and the leaves hung in the curing sheds. It was painstaking work, for Fitz insisted on perfection in every leaf. That was the way he had attained his reputation for turning out the finest and most valuable leaf in Virginia.

The seasonal slaughtering was also going on and the smoke sheds rapidly filling with hams. It was a bountiful season on Wyndward, the kind the plantation used to enjoy in the days when life was without the problems brought on by secession and war.

Fitz still thought frequently of Sally. Apparently, Captain Morton's friends had been unable to find any trace of her. It convinced Fitz that it had been a malevolent lie on Colonel Apperson's part when he said he'd heard she was dead. He'd done it only to torment Fitz, but Fitz now began to believe her death to be a fact.

He had received no further message from Jonathan, but that was to be expected. It wasn't easy to penetrate the Klan, especially by someone as close to Fitz as Jonathan was. Two Bits had disappeared somewhere among the black population of Lynchburg. Fitz had heard once from Dundee in a letter mailed from Richmond. Dundee was running a small office where he gave free advice and sometimes small amounts of cash to ex-slaves in trouble. Fitz wondered where he got the money and assumed it must come from Washington. Dundee seemed satisfied with what he was doing and the progress of his mission.

Clarissa spent her time managing the mansion. She had become quite proficient and took pride in carrying out the duties and obligations. Adalia's school was prospering. Almost too well, for more and more students were enrolling, many from other plantations. They rode or sometimes walked to Wyndward for the privilege of getting an education. It had reached the point where something would have to be done. Her classes were too large, and she was working too hard. Fitz wondered if it would be possible to hire a second teacher. He doubted a Northern lady would come down. A Southern lady would be either contemptuous of such an offer or too fearful of reprisal from the Klan to accept.

Fitz knew there was nothing he could do about it just now, so he put the thought out of his mind. He was too grateful for the continued peace and quiet. After the burning of the cross at Wyndward, followed by what he and Mark had witnessed at Sims' place, he'd expected continued harassment, with the Klan possibly concentrating their violence first on the destruction of the school.

There was no question but that the school was prodding many people into doing something about it. The idea of teaching black children to read and write was anathema to them. Teaching those children like the whites were taught was a source of growing resentment. The Klan gave several interviews to the newspaper about it, castigating Fitz for permitting the school to exist. But the school was on private property, being run by private means, so there seemed to be no legal way of exterminating it.

Underlying all this quiet was a slowly forming potential for trouble. Some of the Southerners, strangely not the veterans, still fought the war in speech and sometimes in violence. The Klan openly solicited membership, and those people were eager to join. Under the anonymity of the Klan they could prey on their enemies and take their revenge against anyone who had either not favored the war or was too happy it was over, even in defeat.

Captain Morton was ready for an outbreak. He had beefed up his company with fifty extra soldiers who were of help in patrolling the streets and keeping every means of communication open.

No attacks were made on the military, as if those who resented this Northern presence knew better. Captain Morton had gained a reputation for being fair but strict if necessary.

None of this underlying anger reached Wyndward, but Morton was aware of it. He was worried about a Klan meeting scheduled in the park on the outskirts of the city, the largest meeting yet. There'd been rumors filtering in that the black population resented the Klan to the point that they were making plans to openly resist, given an opportunity. A big Klan meeting would be a tempting target. But Captain Morton hesitated in sending an extra large force to maintain order for fear it would be opposed and called an unnecessary form of reprisal against the South. He did, however, keep an entire company of men at the ready without leave, not even six-hour passes.

He took command on the afternoon of the Klan meeting. He rode the streets around the park on horseback, issuing orders for his men to close in and maintain strict order.

The white men came in numbers that frightened Morton. His force would be outnumbered twenty to one at least. Still, the meeting seemed to be orderly enough. There were fiery speeches, some of them aimed at Morton's command and at the North, but that was no violation of the rules the captain had set down.

The trouble didn't begin until the meeting was almost ready to close, when three symbolic crosses were to be set afire and a bar dispensing free beer would be opened. Morton had ordered it kept closed until then.

The blacks materialized like ants coming out of the ground. They came from everywhere. Down the streets in unorganized parades, out of buildings where they must have been hiding. A sweep of two hundred or more was running full tilt down a slope of the park, straight at the still-unsuspecting whites and the Klan members in their robes.

When the blacks were suddenly discovered, chaos broke loose. Some of the whites had guns, which were promptly brought into play. Several blacks fell to the ground, some dead, some seriously wounded. But the Negroes outnumbered the whites and knew it. They could suffer losses. The fighting grew intense. Stones, rocks, clubs of every description, and a number of razor-sharp knives were used until the ground was littered with dead and dying. Some blacks, mostly whites.

Captain Morton had already assembled his men for

a charge through the fighting. A white-haired man ran up to Morton's horse.

"Cap'n, you keeps you men from any shootin', heah?"

"Get out of the way," Morton shouted. "If you interfere, I'll have you locked up."

The white-haired man drew himself up. "I am a colonel of the Confederate Army, suh, an' I ordah you not to ride into that crowd."

"The Confederate States no longer exist, Colonel. Your standing is of no interest to me."

"You asks anyone 'bout Colonel Apperson, suh, an' you finds out I am a 'spected man in this city an' I carries a great deal o' influence."

Morton's laugh was one of surprise. "I have heard of you, Colonel. You're a fraud and a liar." Morton raised his arm high. "Pass the word," he told a lieutenant. "No shooting unless things get too hot. But use clubs and rifle butts at will. We are going to disperse this bunch of lunatics. You lead the charge."

It was like a military operation. A bugle sounded charge, and the line of mounted soldiers started forward, followed by a hundred more on foot. The crowd was penetrated and sent reeling back. The horses quickly broke up groups of fighters. The men on foot ably swung their rifles and cleared passages through scowling, fighting people. It required half an hour to reduce all the fighting to some degree of order. Most of the blacks had fled, for they knew that whatever punative steps were taken would be directed at them.

Finally, only one fairly large group remained. Morton rode up to them. Their leader, a silver-haired merchant, pleaded with his followers to stop fighting. Morton noted that there were six black men on the ground, held there by whites who had their feet on necks and backs.

"All right," Morton said, "you disperse now. It's over."

"Captain," the merchant said, "We have six prisoners. They were armed with knives, and we have witnesses who saw them stabbing and murdering here."

Morton looked over what had been the battlefield.

Some men were limping off, some were carried, and some lay without moving. From where he stood, Captain Morton counted eleven presumably dead. All but three were white.

"Do you see what I mean, Captain?"

"Yes, I do see. You have witnesses to give evidence these prisoners were seen using knives?"

"Ten witnesses to each prisoner, Captain."

"Very well. They're to be taken into custody."

"Custody hell!" Colonel Apperson had managed to make his way to the group. "I say hang 'em now. Right away! Knows they're guilty so whut's the use of a trial? Hang 'em so the other niggers knows they cain't do this, the murderin' bastahds."

Morton said, "Sergeant, take possession of the prisoners. If there's any interference, make whatever arrests necessary. There will be no hanging. I want that strictly understood. There will be a prompt trial, and if these men are found guilty, I shall order them properly punished."

The crowd was now openly defiant. "You goddamn Yankees puts 'em in jail. Hang 'em! Break their necks."

"I warn you," Morton called out. "Stay out of this, all of you."

"You sho' ain't heared the last o' this," Colonel Apperson roared out his wrath. "You may have won the wah, but you ain't takin' over the kind o' law we lives by."

"Colonel, if you don't get the hell out of here I'll lock you up too. You have five minutes to clear this park."

The men went off, sullen and resentful. The elderly merchant was among the last to go. Apparently he wanted to wait until the others were beyond hearing what he had to say.

"All right," Morton told him, "move on."

"One moment, Cap'n. Means no harm. Ain't tryin' to disobey you ordahs. Means to say you handled this well, an' I 'preciates it, suh. But it won't end heah, suh. By no means. They goin' to try an' take those six niggers out an' hang 'em."

"Thank you, sir," Morton said. "I'll take proper

precautions, and you might pass the word along, if you hear of any plans to try this, that any such attempts will be met with gunfire. I mean to have my way about this, sir. I'm not bluffing."

"Reckon you ain't, suh. Tells any who will listen. Won't be many. Whole city's 'gainst you on this."

"Then the whole city will be placed under martial law if such an attempt is made. Good day, sir, and thank you again."

Morton returned to City Hall. The six prisoners were already in cells. Morton went down to the cell room to talk to them. He stopped before each barred door.

"Did you use a knife during the riot?"

"No, suh," each man replied promptly. "We gettin' blamed fo' it 'cause we close by when they decides to get some o' us fo' hangin'. Done nuthin', suh, 'cept try to rip the hoods offen them men wearin' Klan robes."

Each of them concurred in one way or another. Morton ordered the main cell door locked. Four soldiers were to guard it twenty-four hours a day.

In his office, Morton began preparations for protecting the prisoners. The city was quiet, but ominously so. Smaller crowds had gathered again when Morton had withdrawn his men and the bodies of the victims had been carried off. There was growing resentment, lots of grim talk, and threats from almost every throat.

Morton sent for his staff of officers. "Sergeant Gaffney, you are to contact headquarters at Richmond and ask them to send two companies of troops as quickly as possible. Report to me when you get the news about when they can be expected to arrive. The rest of you, listen carefully. An attempt will be made to take those prisoners from their cells and hang them. It's not a feeling in my gut—it's something I know. Every man is to remain on duty until relieved, and heaven knows when that will be."

"You intending to try these blacks?" a lieutenant asked.

"I do not, Lieutenant. I intend to try to send them out of here, to the North where they can be fairly judged."

"Might be better if we let them have the blacks," a sergeant suggested.

"Sergeant, you know you didn't mean that. We must keep the prisoners from harm and see that they are fairly tried in an atmosphere of non-violence. If we take them into court here, they'll never make it."

There were further plans, more orders, until Morton was satisfied that he was doing everything possible. Word came that reinforcements wouldn't arrive until late the following day. It was only the middle of the afternoon. Morton's worries increased.

He placed a troop on alert, compelling them to remain close by their mounts, which were to be saddled and ready for instant duty. Then he returned to his office and wrote a terse document stating all the facts of the riot and incorporating the possibility that an attempt would be made to free the prisoners and execute them. He wrote that he would resist that to his own death. He named Colonel Apperson as a troublemaker, detailed the activities of the Klan and its growing dominance over the countryside.

It was late afternoon when he finished. He asked for reports from his patrols and learned that the streets were quiet and there seemed to be no trouble of any kind.

He had placed this report on file when a corporal knocked, came in, saluted, and handed Captain Morton a folded piece of paper.

"A black boy handed this to one of the sentries," he said. "It seems to be important, sir."

The note consisted of two lines, crudely printed.

KLAN RIDING TO WYNDWARD NOW.
ALL BUILDINGS INCLUDING THE SCHOOL WILL BE BURNED.

Morton stood up, buckled on his pistol, and gave sharp orders. "Corporal, send in Lieutenant Taylor on the double."

Taylor reported two or three minutes later. Morton was picking up his gloves.

"There's an attack pending on one of the biggest

plantations. Klan work. You will be in charge here. I'm taking half our company to ride to Wyndward. You are to guard the prisoners. If there is any attempt to take them, resist to the best of your ability, but don't do any shooting. Things are bad enough now."

"Yes, sir. It won't be easy if we can't use our guns."

"I know that. But the whole state is stirred up enough, and we can't risk any more antagonism. Do the best you can. When I return, we'll secretly transfer the prisoners to another city. That's all."

At the head of a strong force of men, Morton rode out of town and along the road to Wyndward. He rode at top speed, worried that this might be a trick to get him away from the city. Or it might be an authentic warning of an attack on Wyndward. Morton was well aware of what might happen there. He knew any attacking force would concentrate on the school first, and his sister was there. It was impossible for Morton to disregard the anonymous warning.

Nearing the plantation, he deployed his men, sending some to circle the mansion and the schoolhouse. The rest would ride straight to the big house.

Clarissa was the first to see them coming and shouted to Fitz. They both rushed outside and stood on the veranda. The line of troops was bearing down at full gallop.

"Whut the hell's goin' on?" Fitz asked.

"Sho' glad they's got Yankee blue on their backs 'stead o' old bedsheets," Clarissa said.

"Must be somethin' mighty important to bring half the army. Stay close in case I gots to send word to Adalia at the school an' Mark in the fields."

Captain Morton halted the advance by raising one arm. He rode up to the veranda and dismounted. Fitz went down the steps to meet him.

"Any trouble here?" Morton asked.

"Not's I knows of, Cap'n. Whut's goin on?"

"We had a riot. Blacks charged a meeting of the Klan. There were deaths and a lot of fighting. We have six blacks locked up, charged with murder, and I see now

I was sent here on a false report that Wyndward was under attack by the Klan."

"To get them six fo' hanging'," Fitz said. "Bettah ride back, fast as you kin. Ain't no trouble heah, an' we sho' goin' to be ready fo' it, comes now."

"Yes, I know. And Fitz, when this is over, ride in. I have some news about that woman in Washington you were trying to find."

Fitz was so stunned by that casual remark he just stood there as if transfixed. Morton remounted, gave the order, and the troop galloped away.

"You heah that?" Fitz asked Clarissa.

" 'Bout Sally? Heahs it, Fitz. I hopes it somethin' to help you find her. Ought to wish it wasn't, but knows how much in love you been all this time since she runs."

"Go down an' fetch Mark. Hurry! I'm goin' to get ready to ride to town."

"Fitz, liable to be too much fightin' theah."

"Don' care 'bout that. I'm leavin' in fifteen minutes. Stops by the stable an' has a buggy brought out. Don't waste any time."

Fitz went upstairs, changed his clothes, and packed a small bag on the hunch he might have to stay in town over night—or even begin an urgent journey to Washington.

Mark returned as Fitz ran down the stairs. "Wants me to go along, Gran'pa?"

"No. You stays heah jes' in case the Cap'n was right 'bout an attack. Give some o' the blacks rifles an' post 'em 'round the place. Makes sho' Adalia safe an' sees Clarissa don' get too rambunctious."

Clarissa ran through the house from the back door, pausing only long enough to announce that she had alerted Hong Kong as well.

"Waits fo' me, Fitz," she shouted as she ran up the stairs.

"Hold on now," Fitz called her to a stop. "You stayin' heah."

"Like hell I am. Waits fo' me, or I nevah fo'gives you."

Fitz made a hopeless gesture. "Too much goin' on at

one time, Mark. Don' know whut's real an' whut ain't. Thinks Morton gets sent heah so them prisoners could be taken."

"He must o' left some o' his soldiers to guard 'em."

"Mayhap. Reckon he got 'nuff to keep a mob off, but Cap'n Morton got mo' sense than most. Cain't tell whut orders he gives the men he left. But if too many come fo' the prisoners, the soldiers know they cain't stop 'em no matter whut. Ev'ry damn thing up in the air. Gots to find out whut's goin' on, an' mostly gots to see whut Morton got 'bout Sally. Hopes it means she's alive."

Clarissa came down, still buttoning the dress she'd changed into. Fitz had one more thing to do. From a gun case in the library, he took down two rifles and a box of ammunition. He handed one to Clarissa.

"You comin', you goin' to make yourse'f useful, anythin' happens."

"Good luck, Gran'pa," Mark called out.

Fitz waved a hand. When Clarissa was aboard, he whipped the horse.

"You takin' a chance," Clarissa reminded him.

"Like whut?"

"Mayhap they waitin' in the woods 'til the soldiers goes away 'fore comin' outen their holes to attack."

"Thinks not. The Klan wants to hang the prisoners mo' than they wants to burn Wyndward. That kin wait, the prisoners cain't. Mo' likely they after them, an' the note Morton got was a fake. We soon finds out."

"Fitz, you knows whut I thinks o' you. Over the yeahs we been friends an' we been enemies. Hates you an' you hates me, but we young an' crazy in them days. Growed up now, an' we sho' friends fo' life. Reckon I been in love with you fo' yeahs an' yeahs, but too goddamn stupid to know it. An' yet, here I am prayin' Cap'n Morton got some news 'bout Sally so you kin find her quickly. Wishes you had nevah met her an' wishes you finds her an' you brings her to Wyndward."

"Beholden to you fo' sayin' that," Fitz said. "Thinks mo' o' you than anyone else."

" 'Cept Sally."

"Well, yes, that's the truth. Don't know whut's in

sto' fo' us, all this trouble, but whutevah it is, you shares it with me. An' that's fo' sho'."

"Cap'n didn' say whut kind o' news he had?"

"He in too much o' a hurry to say anythin' mo'. Soon as things settles down, we finds out. Won't get back fo' dark. Don' like that. Not these days. Does the best we kin. An' who evah said this damn beast was a fast hoss?"

When they reached the outlying streets of the city, they both knew there had been grave trouble. Not a soul could be seen. Closer to the center, the same conditions prevailed except that more and more soldiers were about. Two of them stepped into the street, rifles leveled, and stopped Fitz.

"Can't go any farther, sir," one told Fitz. "Everybody ordered off the street."

"Got business with Cap'n Morton. My name is Fitzjohn Turner."

Both men lowered their guns and moved back. "You may go, sir. We have orders to admit you."

Fitz thanked them and touched the whip to the horse. Clarissa hung on as the buggy began to move fast.

"You didn' ask them whut happened?" she said.

"Don't have to. Thinks you sees whut happens soon's we gets to City Hall whar the jail is."

"Cap'n must o' guessed you wouldn't wait an' gave the order you kin pass."

"Reckon," Fitz said shortly. "One mo' minute an' you sees."

He turned the buggy down the main street. Nearing City Hall they came upon the grisly sight of six bodies swinging from six different lampposts. More soldiers came into the street to stop Fitz, and once more he explained and was allowed to proceed. He and Clarissa left the buggy and hurried into City Hall, again being stopped along the way but not for long.

They found Captain Morton in the mayor's office along with several of his officers. "I'll be with you in a minute," he greeted Fitz. "Figured you'd not wait."

He turned to his men and gave orders for the bodies

to be cut down and turned over to relatives for later burial. He ordered that Colonel Apperson be found, placed under arrest, and brought before him.

"Apperson!" Clarissa said in horror. "He heah?"

"Very much here, Clarissa." Morton dismissed his men and turned his attention to Fitz and Clarissa. "During the riot he came up to me, told me what I could and could not do, and acted as if he were my superior officer. I've since learned that he came back a few days ago and has been industriously engaged in bettering his reputation. A man he owed a lot of money to has gone back North, so I guess Apperson thought it was safe for him to return."

"Cap'n, you said somethin' 'bout Washington. . . ."

"Yes, I've some news. When they bring in Apperson, I'm going to dress him down properly, and if he oversteps in any way, I'll lock him up."

"This heah news, Cap'n. . . ."

"Yes . . . the news. Fitz, they tricked me in going to Wyndward. One of the oldest tricks in existence, but I fell for it. My sister is with you on Wyndward for one thing, and I regard you as a very good friend and, quite likely, a relative after your grandson marries Adalia."

"Cap'n, knows all that. Cain't you see whut's mo' important to me?"

"I know. You saw the bodies, of course."

"Sees 'em."

"My lieutenant told me a thousand showed up right after I rode out. They threatened to wreck the place, to kill all the soldiers if they had to, but they were going to get the prisoners. I wanted no more bloodshed. I did my best to protect the prisoners. Quite possibly they were guilty, but that was not for me to judge. I gave orders if the situation became too grave, my men were to stand aside. I may be censured for that. I may even be dismissed, but if that mob used force on my men, there'd have been a hundred killed, and hatred for me and my men would build to proportions we couldn't handle."

"Cap'n, 'preciates all you an' your men went through. Wishes it nevah happens, but fo' God's sake, will you tell me 'bout Sally?"

"All right, Fitz. I'm not eager to tell you. In fact, I was trying to get the nerve to tell you the news was not authentic and thus worthless. The people I contacted in Washington made all sorts of inquiries and got nowhere until . . . one of them saw a notice in the society page of a Washington newspaper. He sent me the page. I'm sorry, Fitz. Here it is. Judge for yourself why I've been so reluctant."

Fitz took the page with growing fear. As he read the article, Clarissa leaned over his shoulder, reading it too.

"Oh Fitz," she exclaimed. "Oh Fitz . . . goddamn it!"

Fitz placed the page on Morton's desk. "I thanks you, suh, fo' whut you did."

"What I did was destroy any hope you had of finding this woman, that's what I did, Fitz."

"Goin' to marry someone else," Fitz said tonelessly. "Gots to admit she sho' waited long 'nuff. Nuthin' I kin do now 'cept try an' fo'get her."

"Mayhap there's a mistake," Clarissa attempted to soothe Fitz.

"Says right theah—Rutledge-Miller betrothal an' weddin' to take place in two mo' days."

"Still says might be a mistake," Clarissa persisted.

"You nevah sees Sally. Well, that ain't the best sketch I evah sees in a newspaper, but it sho' 'nuff looks like Sally so there's no mistake."

"Hell with the sketch. Got to be a mistake, Fitz. You tells me over an' over she in love with you."

"Five yeahs ago," Fitz said dismally.

"She the kind o' woman you says she is, she ain't goin' to stop waitin' fo' you."

"Whut do you call this? A notice she marryin' a man name o' Miller. All I kin do is hope she gets to be mighty happy."

"You a stupid, boneheaded fool you don' go to Washington right away an' finds out fo' yourse'f. Fitz, you gots to go."

"Damn you, Clarissa, don't tell me whut I gots to do 'bout Sally. You thinks I'm goin' theah an' mayhap when the preacher say anybody heah who says she cain't marry

I stands up an' says she in love with me? Use you damn brains fo' a change."

"Fitz, you gots to admit I'm a woman."

"Kin think o' a few other things you don' let me alone."

Morton broke into the argument. "Fitz, you could go up there. It's certainly not far, and you have plenty of time. See for yourself. It isn't necessary that you approach her, or let her know you're in town. I know you wouldn't want to destroy her happiness with this other man. But you have your own peace of mind to live with the rest of your life. Go and see. What if there is a mistake? What if she waited for you and then decided you wouldn't seek her out because you thought of her as a spy who tricked you?"

"Thinks she daid. All this time thinks she daid. Reckon I'm the biggest fool o' all. I should o' gone up theah long ago, but . . . but skeered she thinks o' me as a Johnny Reb an' hates me fo' that."

"Fo' your age," Clarissa grumbled, "you don't know nuthin' 'bout women. Reckon Calcutta One an' Calcutta Two knows mo'. You don't go to Washington right away, goin' myse'f, an' I sho' tells this heah lady somethin' she nevah heerd befo'. Fitz, I knows whut the trouble with you."

"Knows you bettah keep you mouth shut," he said angrily.

"You skeered to go. You skeered you finds out she in love with somebody else. She the kind o' woman you says she is, she cain't be in love with anybody else an' nevah marries another man even if you goes outen her life fo'evah."

"We goin' back to Wyndward," he said. "Cap'n, I thanks you. Reckon no man evah did as much fo' me."

"I wish I had better news, Fitz. And I wish this problem with the Klan and everybody else would clear up. Please let me know if there is anything more I can do."

"Cap'n," Clarissa stormed at him, "ain't you goin' to tell him to go an' see fo' hisse'f?"

"I did, Clarissa. It's Fitz's business, not ours."

"No wonder I nevah wants to get married again. Not that I evah was—not to a man—but figgers men so goddamn dumb they don' even know whut a woman is like."

"You sho' goin' to find out whut a man is like you don' come along," Fitz said. "We takes too much o' the cap'n's time now. Come on, Clarissa. We kin talk on the way back."

"Talk 'bout whut? You skeered to go to Washington?"

He grasped her elbow and piloted her out of the office by force. They walked down the corridor to the main entrance. They were halted by a sentry who told them to wait a moment. There was some trouble on the street just outside.

Fitz cursed under his breath. He wanted to get out of here. He didn't know what he wanted to do, but whatever it was, he did not wish to make any decision here. Then he heard a voice that seemed familiar.

"Wait heah," he told Clarissa and walked out onto the wide steps leading to the building. Four soldiers were having an argument with a very large black man who spoke to them without a trace of Southern accent, confusing the soldiers even more.

"Fo' God's sake," Fitz said aloud. "If it ain't Two Bits."

He went by a protesting sentry and joined the mild fracas with enough force to free Jubal from the grasp of two soldiers.

"This heah a friend o' mine," he said. "Vouches fo' him. Two Bits, whut in hell you doin'?"

"Mr. Fitzjohn, you are in serious trouble. They know you're in town, and they're already going into ambush to get you on your way home."

"Who? The Klan?"

"Yes, the Klan. They have decided you must be disposed of."

Fitz said, "Takes this man to see the cap'n. You hears whut he says, an' likely true. Cap'n ought to be told. Man's name is Jubal Turner."

Clarissa, puzzled by the whole thing because for she'd not been close enough to hear Jubal, followed them back to Captain Morton's office. There, Fitz introduced Jubal, explained who he really was, and let him do the rest of the talking.

"I've been doing my best to stay as close to Klan meeting places as possible," Jubal said. "I just heard several of them talking and your name was mentioned, Mr. Fitzjohn. They are going to be waiting for you."

Morton said, "Do you vouch for this man's honesty, Fitz?"

"Sho' do. Knows him fo' yeahs. Sends him to college in the North. You hears how he talks."

"Yes indeed. I realize he's an educated man even if he looks like somebody released from jail day before yesterday. Jubal, you may leave by the back door. Good luck. If you need any help, let me know. Fitz, you and Clarissa drive back as if you know nothing about this plot. I'll have men following you and I'll have an ambush of our own set up. Now Clarissa, you don't have to take part in this, but they might wonder why Fitz is going back alone."

"Wouldn' miss it," Clarissa said. "Mayhap I gets a chance to kill one o' them bastahds, but if I does, won't be a Klansman I'm think' o' killin'. Jes' another man. Period. Anotheh stupid, skeered man."

Fitz couldn't think of a suitable reply.

He kept the buggy moving well. It was dusk, but not dark enough to light the lantern under the seat. If the Klan was in ambush, it was possible they'd strike so fast and so hard that the troops riding some distance behind wouldn't be able to reach the scene quickly enough.

"You got both rifles cocked an' ready?" he asked.

" 'Course I has. An' keepin' my eyes an' ears open. Fitz, knows I gets you mad, but don't blame me too much. Swears if that gal loved you the way you says she did, she ain't changed any mo' than you changed. Go to Washington. Go fo' my sake if nobody else's."

"I'm goin'," Fitz said. "We gets outen this heah mess, leaves soon as I kin. You right 'bout seein' fo' myse'f. She gets married an' I sees it happen, then I knows it over an' I comes back heah an' does the best I kin."

"Now you talkin' like Fitzjohn Turner, suh. We comin' to the road that goes through the forest in a few minutes. Figger that's whar they waits."

"Thinks so too. Slide that rifle 'cross my lap. We gots to keep 'em off 'til the soldiers gets heah. Won't take 'em mo' then two o' three minutes. Keepin' the buggy goin' slow so the soldiers kin ride slow too 'thout makin' much noise. They starts shootin', you duck down. Won't do much good a stray bullet finds you, but at leas' you ain't givin' 'em a target to shoot at."

"Go to hell. I ain't duckin' down fo' no crazy men wearin' bedsheets."

Fitz could almost feel the tension closing in. Another hundred yards and they'd enter a portion of the road overshadowed by tall trees with heavy brush alongside. Beyond this point, it was all open country to Wyndward. They had to strike here.

Fitz slowed the horse even more to give the soldiers time to move closer. He let the reins go slack and picked up the rifle.

Men came out of the brush. There were eight or nine of them. They emerged in a group. Their identities were concealed under the white sheets and pointed hats.

Fitz opened fire at once, and Clarissa's rifle joined the barrage. The gunshots would bring the troops on the double, but meantime Fitz had to stave off these men. One was down, one was kneeling and holding onto his middle, but the others were firing revolvers as they rushed toward the buggy.

Fitz cut down another. In the distance, he could hear the yells of the soldiers and the pounding hoofbeats of their horses. The firing had alerted them. They would be on the scene in half a minute.

All but one of the remaining Klansmen hesitated and finally broke for the brush, not caring to make a stand against the troops. But one man kept coming at a dead run. Fitz had fired fast and indiscriminately. His rifle was empty while this man in his Klan outfit kept coming and yelling wildly at the top of his voice.

Then he stopped yelling and seemed to be lifted off his feet by an invisible power. A big splotch of red showed below the peaked hat he wore. He went down heavily. Clarissa lowered her rifle.

Fitz leaped off the buggy, ran to the fallen man, and tore off the peaked hat. Bibb had been shot squarely between the eyes. Fitz looked up. Clarissa was still in the buggy, leaning out to get a better view. The soldiers arrived and were riding through the brush in search of those who had run off.

Fitz said, "Goddamn you, Clarissa!"

"Whut I done?" she asked as he strode toward her.

"It's Bibb! You kills him. That bastahd was fo' me to kill."

"Fitz, you sittin' theah tryin' to load you rifle, an' he comin' like a mad bull, with that pistol in his hand. He was aimin' to kill you no matter whut."

"He was mine! Told you that fo' yeahs. That sona-bitch has to die, it's me whut kills him."

"Next time, I lets him shoot you first."

"Nevah min'. I could o' taken him."

"The hell you could."

"Damn it . . . well, he daid. Reckon makes no diff'rence who sent him to hell. But he was mine, damn you."

"Pretty good shootin', you asks me, Fitz. Whar'd I get him?"

"Right between the eyes. Sho' was good shootin'. I . . . Clarissa, I asks you pardon. Reckon nuthin' you could do but kill him. Wanted him fo' myse'f, but reckon I cain't have ev'rythin' I evah wants."

"When you goin' to Washington, Fitz?"

"Tomorrow. Cain't fight you any mo'. Mayhap you right, but sho' goin' to break my heart I sees her walkin' down the aisle with 'nother man."

"Bettah you heart breaks now than later, Fitz. You cain't spend the rest o' your life hopin' an' prayin'."

321

"Sho' been doin' 'nuff o' that. Reckon Sally thinks I hates her fo' foolin' me an' fo' bein' a Northern spy. Knows now should o' tried harder to find her, but damn, I thinks she daid. Now got one mo' bone to pick with you."

"Reckon it won't be the last."

"Apperson tell me she daid, an' he lie 'bout that. Goin' to kill him an' don't wants you buttin' in. He mine. Gives you Bibb, but Apperson mine."

"Not if I see him first, Fitz. You fo'gets whut that man did to me."

"I say he mine. You 'members that. Now let's go home."

24

For the first time in more than five years, Fitz stepped off the train in Washington and found it a new city. Of course, he reasoned, the war had brought many more people to the Union capitol to engage in the war effort, but, remarkably, there were new buildings, streets were paved, sidewalks installed where there had been none. All this accomplished during a bloody, terribly expensive war. To Fitz, it was just another example of why the shattered, bankrupt South had lost and why its defeat had been inevitable.

He checked into the finest hotel, bought the newspaper in the lobby, and searched it for any further mention of the wedding to take place the following day. He found no reference to it.

He cleaned up after the sooty train ride, had dinner in the hotel, then went outside and flagged a carriage. He gave the last address of Melanie, hoping she might still be there despite the death of her husband.

During his midday meal, he'd made a sudden decision to try and see her. If she would see him, she might know something about Sally. Or, with luck he didn't anticipate, she might have softened her attitude toward him. He dismissed the carriage and walked up to the door of the house where she'd lived. A small brass nameplate indicated she had not moved. He pulled the bell.

A maid moved the curtain aside and looked out at him questioningly before she opened the door. Apparently, Melanie had not seen his arrival, or she'd have instructed the maid to slam it shut in his face if her feelings toward him had not changed.

"Is Missus Hayes at home?" he asked.

"May I ask who is calling, sir?"

Fitz said, "If I tell you, she won't see me and, as her father, I believe I have the right to see my own daughter. So it won't be necessary for you to announce me."

He brushed past the startled girl, made his way through the house, which was familiar to him, and sat down in the drawing room. The maid had followed him, unsure whether to call her mistress or the police.

"Now you may announce me," he said with a disarming smile. "And you may tell her if she refuses to come down, I shall search the house for her."

"I'll tell her," she said.

"Never mind. I hear her coming down the stairs. She must have heard and recognized my voice. Thank you anyway, and I apologize for pushing you aside as I came in."

Melanie entered the room and signaled the maid to leave. She walked slowly across the room and seated herself on a thickly upholstered sofa. Fitz regarded her with wonderment as he watched her move with that grace he found so appealing. She was wearing a beautiful satin tea gown, which rustled with her slightest movement.

"Before you order me out of here, let me say one thing, Melanie. When I was here five years ago, I thought you resembled your mother to a remarkable degree. Which meant you were beautiful enough to take my breath away. Now, five years later, I find you even more attractive and still resembling your mother. Are you going to welcome me?"

She stared at him, saying nothing.

Fitz sighed. "It will be like that, eh? Just the same, my lovely daughter, I am going to tell you a few things so you may keep up with the family. Some of it will delight you. That is, if you can register delight, or even feel it. You're like a marble statue, but I hope not as cold. Are you even listening?"

She said nothing, but made no attempt to rise and leave. That, Fitz thought, was encouraging at least.

"I have come to Washington on a private matter not concerning you, but I have thought often of you. I wanted to see how you were, discover if your attitude toward me had changed. Our last communication was a wireless message sent you by a Yankee officer who was mulling over the question of burning Wyndward—or not burning Wyndward. He said he would be influenced by your opinion of what should be done, you being a well-known Yankee, your husband being an important man in Washington. Your answer to the officer was for him to burn it. Now, I ask you, was that a nice thing to do? A beautiful house where you were born, where you were loved and cherished. However, the Yankee officer did not burn the mansion."

He noted a look of restrained surprise on her face.

"I burned it," he said. "Before that message was sent to you, I doused the place with kerosene. You see, I knew what your answer would be. Well, Wyndward has been rebuilt, exactly as it once was. No changes. Clarissa—you remember her, of course—is the housekeeper and a good one. Jonathan managed, years ago, to get a Fisbee girl pregnant. Her child was born in a New Orleans whorehouse. The boy grew up there. At present, he's living with me. His name is Mark Turner and he is a remarkable young man.

"As for your brother, Jonathan enlisted in the Rebel army, he was captured and imprisoned. He was treated brutally, which is neither here nor there as far as you and I are concerned. However, he's back, embittered and a changed man. I think you recall his twin sons were killed early in the war, his wife died, and Jonathan is not the brother you once knew. Am I boring you, my daughter?"

There was no change in her expression. Still, she didn't get up and leave as he expected.

"Wyndward is coming back. The blacks are now paid for their work. We have built a school on the plantation to which all the black children attend. It is governed by a Yankee girl who is engaged to marry Mark. You'd be proud of this girl. She hated slavery as much as you did. Now there is no longer any slavery. You do not have any sound reason to hate me. Of course, I have often grieved at the death of your husband. He was a fine man with a brilliant future. This, I suppose, you blame on slavery and therefore on me, so I won't go into it. I do have one extremely important favor to ask of you. I do not expect you will grant it or even utter a sound, but, by God, it'll surprise you."

He waited again for some response, but she gave none.

"Just before the war another woman came into my life. I knew her as Sally. She professed to be in the South on business. We quickly fell in love. She moved to Wyndward to try to straighten out Jonathan's twins. I adored her then, I do now. Sally's real name is Elizabeth Rutledge. She now lives here in Washington. She used another name because she was a Northern spy. You ought to like that. Me, a Southerner, harboring and being in love with a Yankee spy. Well, she had to run or face arrest. I thought she'd been caught and executed. I was told that was what happened by a notorious liar I should never have believed. Are you interested, Melanie?"

He gave a short, harsh laugh. "You are. I know that, but you're double damned if you'll allow me the satisfaction of admitting it. I'll make this brief. I'm tired of talking to a dummy. I learned recently that she is to marry a man named Miller tomorrow morning. I came to look upon her loveliness for the last time. To me, it will be like attending a funeral. I wrote you about her, asked your help in finding her, and you returned the letter unread. A very cruel thing to do. But then, you can be cruel, Melanie. I hoped you might receive me at least graciously and tell me if you knew this woman. I know so little about her. No, I am not going to interfere with her marriage. That would be the most reprehensible thing I could do. I only wanted to know more about her. And to look at her for a last time."

He leaned forward with a slight smile on his face. "You may gloat now. You may give a lusty cheer. I am to be deprived of the woman I love. You might have prevented that if you had read my letter. So, Melanie, you have now paid me back for all the imagined cruelties I inflicted upon you—like keeping slaves, getting rich by the sweat of people who worked or were whipped. Yes, you've paid me back. I consider the slate now clean, and you may go to hell for all of me. One more thing—Dundee and Jubal returned. They're doing what they can to help the former slaves. I back them fully in this."

He arose and stood looking down at her. "Jes' to remin' you whar you comes from, I will now speak the way I speak at Wyndward. I don' care you nevah comes back. I don' care if I evah sees you agin long as I lives. Your mama would o' been ashamed o' you as I am ashamed. From now on, I have no daughter Melanie. Reckon nevah did have. Now you kin sit heah, lookin' beautiful an' worthless. But at Wyndward theah's happiness an' joy. You wouldn't like that. Good-bye, my daughter, an' I use that word fo' the last time."

Fitz walked briskly from the room, trying to contain the anger surging within him. He passed the still-startled maid and slammed the door on his way out.

He never saw Melanie bow her head and cry softly for a few seconds, then in torrents of tears. She held her hands tightly to her face in a vain attempt to stem them.

Fitz walked the street for a time with quick, angry strides, doing his best to rid himself of the mixture of rage and sorrow inflicted upon him by an unreasoning daughter.

A four-mile walk quieted his nerves, steadied his brain, and he was able to think rationally once more. He had lost Melanie, but then he'd never had her affections anyway, so there was no reason why he should dwell on it.

327

He had lost Sally and he could do nothing about it, but he was determined to see her once more, if only from some hidden position outside the cathedral.

Thinking about that, he asked directions and walked there. He looked for some vantage point where he might be close enough for a good look at her. There were not many such places. The area around the church entrance was open, a stately looking square dominated by the imposing church.

On impulse he walked into the cathedral and came upon a vestryman engaged in tying ribbons along the aisle to the altar.

"Afternoon, sir," Fitz said. "I presume you are decorating for the Rutledge wedding tomorrow."

"Oh yes. Are you a relative?"

"Well—no. But I knew the bride."

"Lovely lady. It will be a large formal wedding. She is very prominent in Washington society."

"So I heard. And yes, she is a lovely lady. Ah yes, so very lovely."

The vestryman gave him a curious look. "Will you be attending, sir?"

"Like to be. Do you anticipate a full church?"

"Capacity, sir. The Rutledge family is well known and the groom's family as well. I wouldn't miss it."

"Thank you. Formal, you said?"

"Yes indeed. Quite formal."

Fitz nodded and walked out. He had made up his mind to see her at as close a range as possible, not to sneak about hoping she would not see him. He wished to carry away an image of her to last him a lifetime. And the best way to accomplish that was to attend the wedding, to take his place in a pew and watch her march down the aisle. He needed full dress. He hailed a carriage and had himself driven to the finest haberdashery in town. There, by dint of earnest persuasion and the passage of a considerable sum of money, he was promised full dress by morning, in time for the wedding.

Fitz returned to his hotel. He had little further interest in Washington. The well-dressed people, the profusion of vehicles drawn by spanking horses, the stylishly dressed women: they were all a blur to him. He stopped at the hotel bar and seriously considered getting drunk.

He decided against it. He might oversleep, and, even if he didn't, he'd not have the clearest vision through bloodshot eyes. And this vision, he knew, must be absolutely clear. Anyway, he could get drunk after the wedding.

He slept uneasily that night and in the morning took special care in shaving and bathing. When the fashionable men's store opened, Fitz was there. They'd measured well, worked the tailors all night, and now fitters were putting on the final touches.

Finally, Fitz surveyed himself in the full-length mirror and was satisfied that he would look as fashionably dressed as the groom. The trousers were striped and his shirt ruffled, but not unduly so. There was a gray vest piped in black, a morning coat, the tails accommodating his height well. A cravat was the finishing touch except for new, brilliantly polished shoes. There were white gloves too, and a top hat of silk.

The wedding was at noon, and Fitz had timed it well. He took a carriage from the men's store to the cathedral. It was already well filled, flower-bedecked, the pews filled with friends and well-wishers. Sally's social standing as Elizabeth Rutledge was certainly important, for her friends were obviously wealthy and no doubt very influential. The women's gowns and hats were the latest in fashion.

"Which side of the aisle, sir?" an usher asked.

"Bride," he said. "Will you please permit me to sit on the aisle if possible."

"Yes, sir." The usher seated him about halfway down the church aisle, in full view of the altar. Fitz wasn't concerned that Sally would recognize him. As she came down the aisle, he would turn away slightly. Once at the altar, she'd be facing it until after the ceremony, and when she was leaving on the arm of her husband, Fitz would not be there. He wished only to see her. To have this last opportunity to see the woman who had captured his heart and held his love during the five or more years since they'd last been together.

He didn't blame her for not waiting. After all, what did she have to wait for? When he never tried to find her, she must have believed it was because of the way she had deceived and deserted him. He could, however, blame himself for believing she was dead. Colonel Apperson was going to answer to that, although Fitz realized how foolish he'd been to blame him. He had been convinced she was dead before Apperson had rendered that awful lie.

The church was almost filled. The organ burst into sound with the lovely strains of Mendelssohn's Wedding March, and the chattering came to a halt. A woman beside Fitz turned around as everyone arose. The bride was coming down the aisle.

"She's beautiful," the woman exclaimed in an awed whisper. "Enchantingly beautiful."

The march beat like a hammer against Fitz's nerves. He took a long breath and closed his eyes for a moment because he actually began to feel dizzy. When he opened them, the bride, on the arm of an elderly man, had passed.

Fitz told himself that was a good time to leave. His eyes were smarting, and he blinked several times to hold back the tears. Why prolong the agony? He remained standing after everyone else sat down and became suddenly aware of how conspicuous he was. He sat down quickly instead of walking out.

A tall, handsome man, graying at the temples, moved to the side of the bride. There were four bridesmaids, in pink. They moved up. The ceremony began and Fitz couldn't leave. Nor could he take his eyes off the bride.

He saw her turn toward her new husband, lift her veil, and accept his kiss. Then she turned to face the congregation, and Fitz almost cried out. It was Sally. No doubt of that, but she'd changed. Her hair was almost white and she seemed to have put on weight, though her rare beauty predominated. Still, there seemed to be a difference. The bridesmaids now gathered around the bride. One of them looked out over the congregation and waved to someone she knew.

Fitz came to his feet. He stepped into the aisle. With slow steps he walked toward the altar. All six feet of him in impeccable attire, he drew considerable attention. Especially since he moved with a set purpose toward one of the bridesmaids.

She, in turn, saw him with a glancing look, began to turn away, and then turned back. Her face grew white for a moment, and then with a happy cry she ran down the aisle toward Fitz.

She stopped three feet from him. He had come to a halt as well. Slowly she raised her arms toward him.

"My love!" she said in a clear, loud voice and went into his embrace.

He didn't speak because he was incapable of it. Someone tapped him on the shoulder. The bride came between him and Sally to kiss him on the lips.

"You must be Fitz," she said. "Oh, this is the happiest wedding day any bride ever enjoyed."

Someone shook his hand. He thought it might be the groom, but he wasn't sure. Not sure of anything. Not even sure he was here.

"Fitz, my darling. Fitz . . . how did you know? When did you come? Oh, please kiss me. As hard as you can so I know you're really Fitz. Fitz . . . it's been so long."

"I thought," he said. "I thought . . . "

"Never mind what you thought. Oh, Fitz, we have to find somewhere to talk. To let you hold me. To hear me tell you I have years of love stored up and now that you're here, I can give it."

"I didn't know. I don't really know how I came to see you . . . being married . . . "

"That was my older sister, Fitz. My sister! I've waited for you. I would have waited the rest of my life. But I don't want to have to wait that long for a kiss."

There were so many people pressed around them that Sally stepped away from Fitz and made an announcement in that clear, sweet voice that shook Fitz to his ankles.

"Ladies and gentlemen, dear friends . . . I wish to introduce Mr. Fitzjohn Turner of Wyndward plantation in Virginia. And if the war ended for no other reason, then it ended for this."

She kissed him. Someone began to clap, and it was

taken up until Fitz managed to smile uncertainly and bow awkwardly. He was kissed and his hand shaken while Sally clung to his arm, letting her head gently move against his shoulder. She cried a little.

"I won't be going to the reception," she said to someone. "Not right away."

"Looks to me like you'll be giving one yourself before long," someone said.

The clergyman embraced Sally, shook Fitz's hand. "It is apparent to me," he said, "that you two people require privacy. May I offer you the use of the small chapel reached through that door?"

He pointed. Fitz took Sally's hand and led her to the door. Beyond it they found a small, intimate chapel. They sat down on the nearest pew. Fitz hadn't let go of her hand, and he held it still.

"You," he said, "are the most beautiful sight in the world. I still can't believe this is real. I'm afraid I'll wake up."

"I love you so," she said.

"For the first time in my life," he said, "I'm utterly at a loss for words. I don't know where to begin."

"How did you happen to be here, darling?"

"It's a long story. I thought you were dead. I was told you had been captured and executed. I tried in every way to confirm that story, and I never could. I tried not to believe it. The war burst forth in all its ugliness, and there was no way to reach you if you were alive. I prayed I might get a letter. Something that would give me hope. Put an end to my constant wondering."

"And I . . . lived with the awful thought that you hated me for what I'd done. I deceived you. I ran like a coward."

"You were no coward. It was the only way to save yourself. Besides, I'd never have let you stay. The war in those days, when it first started, was brutal indeed."

"Did you hate me?"

"Never. I hurt from missing you, but I never hated you for running or for being what you were."

"Can't we forget what I was? What I did to you? No," she answered her questions. "I'll never forget. The deceit I practiced on you will haunt me the rest of my life."

"I never heard that. But I just hope the love I have stored up for you will help you forget."

"Thanks, my darling. I don't deserve you, but I want you terribly—madly—and for the rest of my life. I'm utterly shameless. I want the opportunity of proving I love you."

"The best way is to marry me," Fitz said. He was still shaken by the turn of events and still unsure that it had really happened, but he felt his sanity was gradually returning.

"Yes, Fitzjohn Turner, I will marry you." Her eyes glowed as they held him prisoner.

He said, "I've stored up those words for so many years they almost hurt saying them. Sally—what's the matter with me? That's not your name."

"Elizabeth," she said. "Frankly, I prefer Sally, but there might be some confusion. Please call me Liz. I like my friends to call me that. I want you, my love, also to call me that."

Fitz's head moved slowly from side to side in wonderment. "I even closed my eyes when the bride passed because I couldn't bear to look into your dear face and know I was going to lose you. Of all the stupid idiots, I'm the stupidest."

"Fitz, how did you find out?"

"I asked a Yankee officer who had friends in Washington to see if he could find out if you were dead or alive. Someone sent him a clipping from a newspaper announcing the wedding."

"No wonder you were confused. At the time I thought it quite lacking in the proper presentation, for in no place was my sister's first name used. And the sketch didn't come out well. Oh Fitz, if I had been in your place I would have suffered ten deaths. You really believed it was me. We bridesmaids arrived early and entered the church through a side door so I didn't see you. But then, it was wonderful how it happened. I turned and there you were, handsomer than ever, looking just like a bridegroom, standing in the middle of the aisle while my senses told me my eyes were deceiving me, that it could not possibly be you. I forgot where I was, what I was doing. Tell me, did I make a fool of myself?"

"I don't know. I'm sure you couldn't have. I couldn't think either. All I could see was you. And if we were both foolish, how wonderful it was we didn't know enough to feel the slightest embarrassment."

"Fitz, open your arms to me, hold me very close, and tell me what's happened on Wyndward. Tell me all the details, and I pray none are sad."

"There was sadness, " he said. "A great deal of it." He held her close, slowly passing a hand over her hair. He talked for a long time, omitting nothing, answering her questions patiently and in detail.

"What an awful war," she said when he finished. "What an awful, terrible war."

"Maybe I'll sound crazy," Fitz said, "but I think it was a silly war. The slaves would have been ultimately freed. The South would have had to set them free. But then—how long would it have been? To people like us, probably not too long. Twenty or forty years. But a slave would think centuries had passed. The North had nothing to fight for except to preserve the country's unity. The South had much to fight for, mainly its pride. There's as much pride down there as there are cotton plants. And, probably even more important, that way of life. The like of it will never again exist. Perhaps it never should have existed, but . . . it was worth fighting for. At least several million people thought so."

"I came to love the South," Liz said. "It broke my heart to find myself working against it, trying to prevent this war from happening. It was an adventure for me at first. Then it grew serious. I hoped I might be helping to prevent the war from even breaking out. Can you see how immature I was? Five years of war! Five years of a loneliness I sometimes thought I couldn't bear."

"You had no trouble getting through the lines?"

"Yes, it was dangerous. It took us almost a week before we reached safety. We lived in the fields and the forests. We were hungry, and I don't think I was ever so dirty in my life. Or so frightened. All the while I wondered how you were feeling about the way I had cheated, deceived, lied."

"It only worried me sick knowing you might be captured."

"Fitz, let's go to the reception now. Would you mind? And I'll probably look happier than the bride. I know she's not one whit happier than I."

"I'll be glad to go," he said. "I need some people around me to steady myself. To make me realize I'm not dreaming."

"Fitz, you're speaking Northern. Please tell me you love me, Dixie style."

"Loves you sho'. Loves you with all my heart. Ain't nevah goin' to let you go. Takin' you back as Mistress o' Wyndward. Takes you back whar you will be loved an' cherished. An' that, lady, is a fact."

They left the chapel hand in hand like two lovers. They found a carriage, and Liz gave the address. Then they settled back against the plush seat, and neither paid heed to the fact that Washington was a live and bustling city.

"Was that your father giving away your sister?" he asked.

"My father and mother are both dead. That was a darling uncle. Fitz, I'm quite wealthy. If you suffered any losses. . . ."

"All that happened to me is that I found something more valuable than money. I found you again. I don't care if you're rich or poor. I don't care if I'm rich or poor. Because no matter what, I'm rich. There's no measure of wealth in this world compared to what I have now."

"And forever," she said.

Liz's sister had made a full explanation of the unusual display at the cathedral, and Fitz and Liz were met with shouts of joy, wishes for their happiness, and at least twenty direct queries as to when they were going to be married.

The daze that had afflicted Fitz soon left him, and he enjoyed meeting and mixing among all these people and getting to know Liz Rutledge a little better. And yet, he and Liz were both glad when it ended, when the bride and groom made their escape in a carriage, and the house settled down.

Now they could talk, they could plan. The past and lost years were talked out and set aside first.

"I want to marry you as soon as possible," Fitz said. "That means tomorrow, if it can be arranged."

"It can be. I want that too because then we shall never again be without one another."

"I'm not too sure you should come to Wyndward just yet. There is nothing in this world I wouldn't do to bring you there at once, but . . . there are happenings. An organization calling itself the KKK is growing fast. It's composed of a great many radical types who think that in the guise of secrecy they can protect the South. You know how those kind of people think. Keep the ex-slaves from raping and looting and killing. They've done little or none of that. Not around where we live. But this group—the intials are for the Ku Klux Klan—is partly composed of people addicted to violence. They hate everybody but themselves. They've hung blacks, whipped whites—there really isn't anything they won't do."

"You spoke of the school for black children. This Klan must hate that."

"I'm afraid they may burn it down. Given a little time, I may be able to break the Klan, or its local branch. What worries me is what they'll do if you come down there, even as my wife." He slipped into his Southern dialect. "A Northern spy! Why ain't nuthin' any lower an' makes no diff'rence she a mighty good-lookin' woman, she a spy. A Northern spy!"

"Would they have to know, Fitz?"

"Already know. A Colonel Apperson knows, and there's nothing in this world he'd rather do than make more heartache for me. We've been enemies for years. I could directly blame him for the death of Benay. I've sworn a hundred times to someday kill him. But . . . there's been so much killing. I don't know if I could do it. After all, I'm not young. And with age I've developed better sense, but when I see that man I lose all reason. May I suggest something?"

"Whatever you like, Fitz. I know you consider all facts and make wise decisions. I leave it up to you."

"Marrying you is the greatest purpose of my life. I want us to be married at once. Quietly, so the word won't travel too far. I'll go back to Wyndward and make it safe for you. I'll do this as quickly as I can and then send . . . the devil with that . . . I'll come for you."

"Darling, so long as I know you're safe. So long as we belong to one another. As you say, we're not young lovers, though that's the way I feel. We can sacrifice a few more weeks because in the end we'll have all the happiness we've missed."

"Thank you for seeing it my way."

"We'll be married in that little chapel. I feel that's where we met after all the years. I can arrange attendants. It will not be in any newspaper, and word will not reach Wyndward."

"You're wrong there, my dear Liz. When I get back, Wyndward willl hear of it, but it won't go beyond there. If I can somehow be rid of Colonel Apperson, I feel it will be safe for you. The only real danger comes from the Klan, and I believe Apperson is not only the secret head of it but is fomenting as much trouble as he can. Leading these idiots gives him a sense of power. I'll do what I can as fast as I can, but above all, I wouldn't want anything to happen to you. Not even if it's just unpleasantness. When you come to Wyndward, you'll bring all that happiness with you."

'We'll be married tomorrow, Fitz, but you won't be going back right after the ceremony, I hope."

"The whole Union Army couldn't drive me away, Liz. We may not be too young, but a honeymoon will erase some of the years. In all my life, even with Benay, I don't think I've ever been as happy. And if Benay knew the circumstances, she'd be just as pleased. It's been a day."

"It surely has, darling Fitz. It surely has."

"Just one more thing. Something odd happened to me during the war. After the Union forces took over, if I found myself in some sort of mess, everything seemed to work in my favor. I was arrested and held once until a general set me free without asking questions. I came to have the feeling that someone—with plenty of influence—was acting as a sort of guardian angel, that orders had been issued I was to be given preferential treatment. Were you responsible for that?"

She laughed her light, silvery laugh. "I thought you might suspect. I did it to save you any embarrassment and . . . if you decided it might be me, you'd . . . come for me. Of course, with the war on, I know now how impossible it would have been. I did do my best for you. And I do have a certain amount of influence."

"I didn't think it was my imagination, or my terrific personality. Thank you, Liz. There were a few times when I needed help and you were there, even if I didn't know it for certain."

She leaned closer and kissed him lighly. "You will have to give me this evening to myself. A girl does have to make preparations for the most important day of her life."

25

Fitz was somewhat surprised to find only Clarissa waiting for him at the depot. She's certainly changed since she got away from her father-in-law. Her features, in maturity, revealed a serenity that had never been evident in her youth. Or could it be that she had finally found contentment? She'd done an excellent job in furnishing Wyndward and had proven herself competent in the running of it. It had to be because she liked it. Certainly, she knew the attraction that had existed between them had been only physical and was over. Perhaps fulfillment in that, though brief, had mellowed her.

She hadn't yet caught sight of him so he had a chance to observe her further. She wasn't aging. She had dressed for her meeting with him and made a fetching picture in her violet print muslin dress. Her bonnet matched and was trimmed with some kind of flowers that had a silken sheen. Fitz couldn't help but smile at her decorous posture. She looked the picture of primness, and he had to repress a smile as he recalled their moments of unrestrained and enjoyable intimacy. That was over now.

Clarissa knew it and he knew it. But he appreciated the fact that she had come to greet him and had made herself attractive for the occasion.

She saw him the moment he started to move toward her. His arms extended in unfeigned welcome, and she rapidly closed the distance between them. He gave her an affectionate kiss, then held her away from him. "Gots to be mighty careful way you kisses me an' pushes up 'gainst me like that. Likes it, I sho' do, but you now talkin' to a married man."

"Fitz, you found her!"

"Sho' did. Tells you 'bout it on the way home. Whar's Mark?"

"Skeered to leave Wyndward fo' even a little trip like this. We had some trouble. They came, the bastahds in their goddamn bedsheets, an' tries to burn down the school. But Mark 'spected it might happen, an' he gots twenty o' so niggers posted near the school, all with guns. They sho' sent them ten-foot-high haunts runnin' fo' their lives, but two of 'em gots to one o' the overseers' cottages an' sets it on fire."

"Damn them!" Fitz said vehemently. "No damage to the school or anythin' else?"

"Keeps 'em away. Done some shootin' myse'f. Don't knows whut damage I done, but Mark an' Toby Morgan runs down two of 'em an' yanks off their robes 'fore others come to rescue 'em."

"Mark knows who they are?"

"While they gots the two tryin' to get 'way, Hong Kong come by an' know 'em."

"Good! Mayhap we kin do somethin' 'bout that. Adalia strong 'nuff to take this sort o' thing?"

"That little gal stronger'n you think. Was yellin' fo' a rifle, but wasn' any left to give her. Don' worry 'bout that gal. Goin' to be mighty nice havin' her married to Mark. An' now you goin' to bring your new wife back. Makes it kind o' even again. You, Mark, an' Jonathan takin' orders from me, Sally, an' Adalia. Goin' to like that."

"Sally's right name is Elizabeth. We call her Liz. She bettah lookin' than evah."

"Gots to be careful she comes," Clarissa said with a note of sadness. "We sho' ain't gettin' in baid no mo'.'"

"You sho' right 'bout that." He picked up the suitcase, and they walked to where the carriage was waiting. Fitz took the reins.

"Reckon I don' mind much," Clarissa said, with a trace of sadness. "Bein' in baid with you, I mean. Ain't got much left. How 'bout you, bein' a bridegroom gettin' up to sixty?"

"Ain't as old as I looks, reckon," Fitz said with a laugh. "You kin ask Liz, you gets 'round to it."

"Well, cain't say I wouldn' recommen' you, Fitz. When she comin' to Wyndward?"

"Cain't say. You knows she was a Northern spy, an' that sho' ain't goin' to make her welcome heah whut you might call warm. An' there's the Klan, damn 'em. They'd nevah sit still over somethin' like that. A Union spy marryin' a half-Southern, half-Northern man like me. Thinks gots to quiet down some first. Liz knows whut I'm talkin' 'bout, an' she thinks it best to wait some. 'Sides, Washington ain't so far I cain't go theah often."

"Mayhap not as often as you thinks, this heah Klan sets out to burn ev'rythin' on Wyndward. Been thinkin' some on it. Seems like the Klan fixin' to get you mo' than anyone else. Lots o' plantations 'round heah, but they comes heah most often."

"Mayhap you right. Whut you thinkin' 'bout it?"

"Mayhap somebody way up in the Klan got it in fo' you."

"You gots somebody in mind?"

"Bibb sho' daid, an' that leaves my papa-in-law. Wouldn' be hard fo' him to take charge o' the Klan 'round heah. Bein' a Reb colonel an' a big-talkin' man, the kind o' damn fools joinin' the Klan would think of as a fine leader. An' if he takes command o' the Klan, first thing he goin' to do is burn Wyndward if he kin."

"Reckon the two o' us thinkin' the same thing, it gots to be true."

"Whut kin you do 'bout him, Fitz? Sho' gots to do somethin'.'"

"They burns a cottage on Wyndward, mayhap we

341

burns somethin' the Klan got, they thinks twice 'fore they tries agin."

"Whut's Colonel Apperson got to burn? He lives in a hotel. Evah since you wiped out his plantation."

"You gets me thinkin' too hard on that, Clarissa, an' mayhap I jes' burns the colonel. 'Members when he sends one o' his slaves to Wyndward an' tells him to go 'round meetin' ev'rybody. On'y thing, this heah slave gots smallpox, an' it go all through Wyndward like the colonel knew it would. Benay takes care o' the sick slaves an' gets it herse'f. After she die, I goes down to the colonel's plantation house, an' I burns ev'ry damn thing that kin burn. Now, reckon I gots to finish him off."

"Should o' done it yeahs ago."

"Knows that. Won't be easy now. Liz, well she ain't one fo' killin. Mayhap she knows it gots to be done, but she ain't goin' to like it, an' cain't say I blames her. Killin's got to stop. Ain't like it used to be."

"Feels the same way, Fitz. Mayhap we gettin' soft. Mayhap we gettin' some sense. But you gots to get rid o' the colonel one way or 'nother 'cause he nevah goin' to stop lookin' to make trouble fo' you."

"We have to wait an' see. Any word come from Jonathan?

"Nuthin'. Mark was wonderin' 'bout that too."

"Jonathan mayhap got hisse'f into the Klan, an' he gots to be mighty careful. Reckon he sends word when he kin. Knows he kin send Chickory with a message. Wishes this thing over with. Wants to settle down an' live nice an' quiet fo' a few yeahs. Whut Liz wants too, an' reckon you ain't 'gainst it."

"Sho' ain't. How they treats you in Washington? You bein' a Johnny Reb."

"Nobody mentioned it, but then bein' close to Liz an' after she tells 'em 'bout me, reckon they don't think o' me as an enemy. Seems to me, they don't have much hate up theah."

"Why should they? They wins the goddamn war."

"Make sense. Nevah knows how folks goin' to act anyways. But gettin' time we all begin's wukkin' together agin. North needs cotton, an' the South needs ev'rythin'."

"First they gots to stop sendin' down these goddamn shifty carpetbaggers, lookin' to cheat ev'rybody they kin. An' the missionaries—calls 'em Gideonites—they comin' down to give religion to the black folk an' to white folk too. They sort o' lumps us all together, but hell, we gots religion down heah mo'n they gots up North. An' the niggers got mo'n the white folks North o' South. Ev'rybody gets to hate the carpetbaggers an' the Gideonites. Ought to mind their own business an' do their wuk up North whar they belongs."

"Goin' to take some time to get things smoothed out again, but it comin'. Bound to."

When the carriage turned down the road to Wyndward, Fitz felt, as he always did, that he was coming home again. The sight of the mansion and the sprawling farmlands always greeted him in this manner. It was the only way of life he knew, and he wouldn't have traded it for any other in the world. Now it would soon be even better with Liz here, bringing with her the long-abiding love she had shared with him.

Elegant was loudly critical of the fact that Fitz had not brought his bride home. "Ain't nobody goin' to harm that lady," she vowed. "Any sonabitch tries, an' I kills him daid. Bein' married an' leavin' you wife back theah in Washin'ton ain't right. Reckon she be safer right heah, even with all them bastahds ridin' 'round in the sheets they nevah used in baid. Whut's it comin' to, you cain't bring your wife home?"

"She'll be heah 'fore you knows it, Elegant, an' she sends word she sho' lookin' to your cookin'. Say she nevah fo'gets it."

Elegant beamed. "When she comes, makes the fines' suppah you evah eats in your whole life. Goin' to start plannin' it now. You tells me when you goin' to fetch her."

Adalia greeted Fitz with a hug and kiss and a thousand questions. But it was Mark who went into the more serious aspects of what could be expected.

In the library, with the door closed, he talked freely

and wasn't afraid to express his feelings. Fitz felt a warm glow of pride as he listened to Mark quietly relate what had happened.

"Cain't seem to think how we kin win this heah war, Gran'pa. There's too many of 'em, an' folks backs 'em up some. On'y ones tryin' to run 'em down is Cap'n Morton, an' he ain't gettin' far."

"Goin' to talk to him soon as I kin. Now tells me 'bout burnin' the overseer's cottage."

"Comes to burn the schoolhouse, but sho' ready fo' 'em. Keeps a strong guard all 'round the place, an' when they gets heah, we send's 'em runnin'. On'y thing, one o' 'em throws a firebrand into the cottage while he runs by. We gets him an' one other man. Figgered on hangin' both, but thinks twice on that. 'Fore the war wouldn' think once 'bout it."

"Whut you do to 'em?"

"We whales the hell outen 'em an' says we goin' to have the law on 'em."

"Clarissa say you knows who they are."

"Hong Kong knows 'em. Gots their names on your desk, right in front o' you."

Fitz studied the slip of paper. "Knows 'em both. Got small farms, but mostly they sloths an' gets nowhar. Kind o' folks used to whup on slaves jes' to hear 'em yell. Soon's it get dark, we show 'em how we feels, an' mayhap the rest o' 'em learns from that. 'Bout nine tonight we rides, jes' you an' me."

Armed with rifles and two large cans of kerosene, Fitz and Mark stopped first at the drab, little-cared-for cabin of Ben Cordor who never owned more than three or four slaves and worked them half to death. An insignificant person, a failure, and a sly, cruel man Fitz had detested for years.

Ben looked out of the window when Fitz banged the door with the butt of his rifle. He then dropped the curtain quickly and pretended he was not at home. Fitz stepped back and kicked the door open. Ben appeared, holding a shotgun. Mark leaped past Fitz, grasped the shotgun by the barrel, and deflected its aim. He tore the gun free and slammed the butt of it against Ben's head, which sent him reeling back.

"Howdy, Ben," Fitz said.

"Keep away from me," Ben shouted defiantly. "You keeps away, o' the Klan hangs you, Fitz. Sweahs they hangs you."

"Gots to ketch me first," Fitz said genially. "Whar your wife?"

"Left me. Been gone fo' near a yeah."

"You lives alone heah?"

"Sho' do. Whut you wants with me?"

Mark exploded into a hearty laugh. "He burns you cottage, Gran'pa, an' wants to know whut you wants."

"Ben," Fitz said, " 'fore the war, you should be swingin' from a tree branch by now. Times change, no mo' lynchin'."

"Yo' bettah not touch me. Like I said, the Klan. . . ."

"Know whut I thinks o' the Klan? They comes fo' me, they comes shootin' 'cause that's the way I meets 'em. An' they kills somebody on my plantation, I kills a Klansman. They burns down anythin' on my property, I burns somethin' on theirs. Like your house. You gots money heah, o' anythin' valuable, gives you two minutes to get it. Mark, spread that oil 'round the place."

"Fitz," Ben suddenly realized the purpose of Fitz's visit, "you cain't do this. You cain't burn me out."

"Well now, you jes' go an' stand outside an' see if I cain't. Catches you red-handed burnin' my cottage. Now I burns your house. On'y fair."

"An' if you squawks," Mark added, "mayhap we fo'gets ain't no mo' hangin'. You two minutes runnin' out."

"I'll have the law on you. . . ."

"Whut law?"

"The Klan. . . ."

"Told you whut I thinks o' the Klan. You gots one minute left."

"Fitz, whut kin I do, you burns me out? Fitz, you cain't."

"Time's up," Fitz said. He seized Ben by the wrist and dragged him out.

Mark soon followed, pausing at the door to drop a burning piece of paper into a pool of oil.

In five minutes the ancient, ramshackle house was a ball of fire. Finally, there was nothing but charred ash and a chimney.

Fitz said, "Ben, you kin tell your Klansmen whut happen. You kin tell 'em next time they burns anythin' anywhar I heahs of, somebody under one o' them bedsheets, gets burned out. You lynches somebody, a Klansman gets strung up. Don' care who it is, but whut the Klan does, they gets back, fire fo' fire, lynchin' fo' lynchin', an' you damn lucky you ain't swingin' right now."

Fitz and Mark left Ben standing in front of the ruins of his home, a bewildered man. They rode directly to the home of Marvin Holt, four miles away. There they found Marvin and his wife as arrogantly defiant as Ben had been. Fitz wasted no time with them.

"You burns one o' my cottages, Marv, an' you caught doin' it. You hidin' under a bedsheet. Now me an' Mark, we ain't hidin'. We jes' looks you straight in the eye an' tells you to get out o' this house 'cause we burnin' it down. Ben Corder's place already a heap o' ashes."

"Marv," his wife said, "you kills this heah bastahd right now."

Marvin looked at two rifles casually aimed in his direction. "You kills 'em," he said. "I ain't lookin' to get killed myse'f. Fitz, you sho' makin' a heap o' trouble fo' yourse'f. The Klan goin' to burn you out an' kill you an' all o' your fam'ly 'sides."

"They aimin' to do it anyways, so figgers I might's well gives 'em a reason. Take your wife an' get out. Mark, you knows whut's to be done."

The odor of kerosene changed the minds of the Holts. Marvin's wife continued to curse Fitz, but her husband wisely dragged her out of the house. He had made no protest, for he knew without a shred of doubt that Fitz meant exactly what he said.

Like Ben, Marvin and his wife stood and watched their house burn to the ground. Fitz and Mark were long gone.

Marvin said, "Nevah wanted to wear one o' your

346

bedsheets anyways, but you says I gots to. See whut it brought us? The hell with the Klan an' to hell with you an' your big ideas."

Mark rode beside Fitz on their way home. "They goes to the police, whut goin' to happen, Gran'pa?"

"Don't know. They goes to Cap'n Morton, nuthin' goin' to happen. They goes to the sheriff, mayhap he come to see us. Mayhap he won' 'cause likely he belong to the Klan too, an' he got mo' brains than I think he has, knows he's next if he does anythin' to us. On'y way you kin handle these people skeered to show they faces. You gives 'em back whutevah they did to somebody else, 'specially you. Mayhap we discourages 'em not to come callin' at Wyndward again."

"Hope it wuks, Gran'pa."

"Gots to be a showdown, son. Sooner it happens, the bettah. Gots to get things quieted down heah. Liz wants to come an' live heah, but I won't bring her 'til I knows it safe."

"You wants the Klan to come? Gots to tell you, there's two o' three hundred belongs to it now."

"Ain't no way we kin avoid a time when either they takes over the law o' folks like you an' me drives 'em outen their sheets an' lets 'em know that they dressed that way don' means nuthin' to folks like you an' me. From now on, makes sho' there's 'nuff men 'round the school, day an' night. Gives the wukkers extra money fo' helpin' guard Wyndward."

"You sho' a tough old coot, Gran'pa. Likes you fo' that. Hopes I gets older, I gets tough as you."

"Have to, you wants to keep Wyndward goin'. You thinks somethin' worth fightin' fo', you fights. Mayhap comes a day you don't have to, but this damn war makin' enemies among ourse'ves. An' this heah Klan, 'bout the worse enemy we evah had. How the niggers actin', you wants 'em to help keep this heah plantation goin' an' not gettin' burned out?"

"S'prised me, Gran'pa. Figgered they don' care whut happens to a place like this, but they all tells me they willin' to fight hard to keep it. You kin depend on 'em. They sho' on our side."

"That's good. We sho'ly goin' to need 'em if the Klan come callin' again. Wishes we'd hear from Jonathan 'bout whut's goin' on. Bettah fo' us we knows whut they plannin' to do."

"Worries some 'bout him," Mark said.

"Why? Whut makes you worry 'bout your papa?"

"Well, he comes home he so full o' hate it crawlin' all over him. Don' care the mansion gets burned, hates the schoolhouse, hates me, an' thinks Adalia some kind o' devil fixin' to wreck the South."

"You papa had a hard time, Mark."

"Sho' he did, an' I don' blame him fo' bein' so mad, but all of a sudden he ain't mad no mo'. Man on'y changes that fast he gots a good reason to."

"Comes to his senses," Fitz argued. "That's all there was to it. Jonathan ain't no fool. Knows Wyndward mighty important to him."

"Sho' didn' act like it when he comes home."

"Son, he your papa. He my son. Gots to stick with him. Gots to make him glad to be home. Wants him like he was when he an' Daisy heah. Had good times an' he 'members that."

" 'Members Daisy all right," Mark said. " 'Members whut happened to her. You says he carries on mighty bad when she dies, befo' he goes off to war. You goin' to say any man would, but reckon not as bad as he did. Makes him hate slaves, hate you an' ev'rybody. Makes him join the army. Sees him when we movin' 'round fightin' the North, an' he like a crazy man we loses a battle. When we wins he yells he haid off in happiness. Times I thinks he crazy, outen his haid. An' now, he worse than befo'. Hates to say it, but I sho' don't trust him."

"Cain't go along with whut you're thinkin' 'bout Jonathan. Say he wants the Klan busted much as we does."

"That's whut he say," Mark was unconvinced. "But like you says, we gots to trust him. Knows I wants to, he bein' my papa."

"Then fo'gets whut we talked 'bout. An' don't mention this to Clarissa or anybody else."

It was a restless night for Fitz. There was some

substance to what Mark had talked about. A man so filled with hate as to be almost crazed by it has to be regarded with suspicion if he changes as fast as Jonathan had.

Yet, Fitz couldn't bring himself to believe that Jonathan would do anything to jeopardize Wyndward. Jonathan *was* Wyndward. It would be his before long. Fitz measured time in years, and many of his own years were used up.

He was lonesome too for Liz Rutledge. It was a cruel thing to do. Marry a woman and leave her miles away because it was dangerous at Wyndward. This aura of peril had to be eliminated. Until it was, she could never come to live here. How that was to be done was beyond Fitz except for his idea that violence met with violence might stop the Klan. Certainly tolerance wouldn't. He planned to talk to Captain Morton about it in the morning.

Even with this decision made, his sleep was light and left him tired the next morning. He ate an early breakfast alone and sent Calcutta Two to the stables to drive the carriage to the door.

He was in Lynchburg by midmorning and first paid a visit to the bank. Henry Tallen was in a somber mood.

"Fitz, gots us a new kind o' war. Talkin' 'bout the Klan."

"Burns one o' my cottages," Fitz told him. "Rides in wearin' their bedsheets an' tries to burn the schoolhouse. To do that they had to fight Mark an' the blacks wukkin' fo' us. Bastahds who has to hide under sheets sho' don't have much in the way o' guts."

"Trouble is, there's too many of 'em."

"Sho' knows that. Way I sees it, Henry, men comes back from five yeahs o' fightin', instead o' sayin' they mighty lucky they comes back at all, they comes back mad 'cause they lost the war. Ain't nothin' they kin do 'bout it. Cain't fight the North no mo'. But they kin fight the niggers, they kin burn an' kill mayhap any whites they don't like. Mayhap even a way o' gettin' rid o' someone who stands in the way."

"Cain't argue that, but whut we goin' to do?"

"Mark runs down two o' the men who burned my cottage. Last night me an' Mark pays 'em a visit. We burns their houses to the ground to see how they likes it. An' they comes burnin' again to my place, I'll do some mo' burnin' myse'f. Cain't sit still an' lets 'em walk over me. Don't intend to."

"Hope it wuks. Fitz, who you think run this damn business?"

"Colonel Apperson," Fitz replied readily.

"Well, mayhap. Reckon he gots somethin' to do with it, but this is too big fo' the colonel. Think somebody smartuh'n him runs it."

"Mayhap you right. Bein' mostly on Wyndward I don't gets to heah much o' whut goes on. Whut makes you think theah somebody bigger'n the colonel?"

"Joel Colfax thinks so. Talks to me 'bout it mo'n once an' makes speeches sayin' so."

"Who he?" Fitz asked with a frown, as he searched his memory for the name.

"Comes heah from Richmond few weeks ago. You knows 'fore long the South gots to send men back to Congress. The North goin' to be mighty fussy who come, an' he bettah have a clean record. Well, nobody runnin' fo' office yet, not fo' Congress anyway, but Joel, he gettin' a haid start. Campaignin' fo' an office don' exist yet fo' the South."

"Nevah heard o' him."

"Mighty fine talker. Folks like him, an' he sho' runnin' down the Klan."

"Mayhap bettah fo' me to meet him. Thinks it kin be arranged?"

"Why not? You sho'ly one o' the most important men 'round heah. Kin find him at the hotel. Lookin' 'round fo' a house so he kin bring his fam'ly from Richmond. Goin' into the cotton factorin' business from whut he tells me."

"He borrowin' from the bank?"

"Not much, but be mo' when he finds the house he wants. I studied up on him through Richmond, an' he pay his bills on time. Reckon he got plenty o' money. We trusts him, heah at the bank."

"I'll try to find him," Fitz said. "Seems like an interestin' man. Some say there's two o' three hundred in the local branch o' the Klan. Thinks that 'bout right?"

"Mo' than that. Men joinin' ev'ry day. They gets too pow'ful, an' they sho' goin' to make a lot o' trouble. Wishes I knows who they are. Makes me sick to my stomach to think I sittin' heah talkin' to a man an' he belong to the Klan."

"Goin' to look up this Joel Colfax. Needs all the help I kin get."

"So does Joel," Tallen said with a thin laugh. "Threw eggs at him last week, he makin' a speech, but he keeps right on an' dares who threw the eggs to step out lessen he was a yellow dog. You kin guess how many stepped out. Tells him mo' than once, he bettah be mighty careful. The Klan sho' don't mind killin' an' maimin' folks they don't like."

"Pays to be careful," Fitz agreed. "How things goin'?"

"Gettin' bettah. Makes me sick when I thinks o' these damn fools makin' all this heah trouble fo' you an' they comes to the bank to borrow money. Some gets it, an' it your money they borrowin'. This town so poor my bank wouldn't be heah 'thout all the money you put into it. Keeps tellin' folks that, but all they say is it got to be Northern money or gold you buried somewhar 'fore the war start."

"Mighty glad you puttin' the money to good use, Henry, even if the folks who borrow it don't like me. Kin stand up under that 'thout bowin' my haid. How Cap'n Morton gettin' along?"

"Ain't nobody tanglin' with him. Whut he say he mean, an' thinks he ketches any Klansmen causin' damage, that Klansman goin' to be mighty sorry he evah join that goddamn outfit."

"He's a fair man, Henry. Blue uniform o' not, he ain't talkin' out any hate fo' us."

"Likes him myse'f. Nevah tells him that. Sho' loses plenty o' business I cottons to him."

"I likes him, an' I don't min' sayin' so outloud. 'Course I ain't beholden to the whole town fo' their business like you. Ain't blamin' you any. Goin' to see him now. Mayhap I looks up this heah Joel Colfax 'fore I goes back. Oh yes, you heahs anythin' 'bout my son Jonathan?"

"Not lately. Fo' a time he was drawin' on your money an' spendin' it on this friends an' gamblin' . . . jes' goin' to hell. He heah in Lynchburg again?"

"Sho' is. Kind o' coolin' off after the war. He wants fo' anythin', you sees he gets it. Knows I cuts him off befo', but that's over with."

Fitz had left his carriage at the livery where he always did business, so he had to walk down to City Hall. There, he again promptly passed through the guard system. Captain Morton welcomed him warmly.

"How did you make out in Washington?" he asked. "I've been thinking about that as if it was my girl who was lost there. Adalia keeps me advised, but I haven't seen her in some time."

"You is shakin' hands with a married man," Fitz said with a wide grin. " 'Member that newspaper clippin' say she goin' to be married to 'nother man? The bride was Liz's sister. Don't knows this 'til after the ceremony. I was sittin' in a pew halfway up the aisle. Then I sees Liz, she one o' the bridesmaids. I gets so excited an' so filled with happiness, knows whut I did?"

Morton laughed. "I can readily imagine."

"I runs down the aisle, takes her in my arms, an' kisses her. Right in front o' all them guests. They didn't mind. Welcomes me like an old friend. Next day we gets married, but she stays in Washington. Sho' ain't safe fo' her heah."

"A wise decision, even if it must have been a hard one to make."

"Knowin' whut was goin' on heah, wasn' so hard, Cap'n. Any complaints 'bout a couple o' burnin's lately?"

"No. I've heard none. Were you involved?"

"The Klan comes an' burns one o' my cottages, so I rides to whar two o' these heah Klansmen lives—Mark tears off they hoods so we knows who they were. Goes to see 'em an' burns their houses down. Ain't 'zactly lawful, but whut they doin' ain't either."

"They're getting more and more powerful. I'd take drastic action against them if I knew who they were, but they have a very tight system."

"Reckon Colonel Apperson at the head o' this part o' the Klan."

"I've heard rumors of that too, but you can't hang a man on the strength of rumors. Bring me some solid evidence, and I'll lock up any troublemaking Klansman until he's a hell of a lot older when he gets out."

"Heah o' a man name o' Joel Colfax?"

"Yes. He's been to see me. He's been making speeches against the Klan, and they've been threatening to burn a cross on his front lawn. Trouble is, he hasn't got a front lawn. He hasn't moved his family here yet. But the Klan manages to frighten him. Not enough to make him stop, however. I don't quite know who he is, but he talks and acts like a preacher."

"Politician," Fitz corrected him.

"No wonder he talks so much. What's he running for?"

"Congress, as soon as Southern states are allowed to send people to Washington. He wants to be ready."

"He'll make it, if his voice doesn't run out on him. I rather like the man because he's absolutely sincere."

"Reckon we needs someone like him. And Adalia doin' fine too. Mark tell me most o' her pupils kin read an' write already. Some o' 'em grown people too. Will say this, the South needs a few thousand mo' like her."

"I'm pleased to hear that. I was against her coming down, but Adalia can be very stubborn when she wants to be. She insisted, and now I'm glad she did. Of course, we can thank you for whatever success she's had. Without your help, nothing would have developed for her."

"No, cap'n, it's fo' me to thank her. The blacks on my place are mighty happy they wuks theah. I pays 'em well, gives 'em nice places to live, an' there's plenty o' food. But bettah than all that put together, they knows there's white folks who is tryin' to help 'em. Means a lot to 'em. They already fights fo' Wyndward when the Klan comes."

"I'm sure that gives Adalia a warm feeling. When I see her, all she talks about is marrying Mark. How much trouble is that going to make for Wyndward, Fitz, Mark marrying a Yankee? And you already married to one."

"No mo'n it makes 'cause she teachin' black childrun. Don' give a damn anyways. Come out to see us when you kin. You always welcome."

"Thank you, but with conditions as they are now, I don't dare leave this office. I wish the Klan had never happened. Things were coming along very well until they appeared from nowhere."

Fitz took a slow walk down one of the main streets, alert for any sign of Jonathan. He reached the hotel and went into the bar. There he inquired for Joel Colfax.

" 'Bout dinnertime, Mr. Fitzjohn," the deskclerk told him. "Mistah Colfax kind o' regular with his meals, an' he takes 'em in the dinin' room heah."

"Heahs he a fire-an'-brimstone preachin' man."

"Don' knows he a preacher, but there sho' is lots o' fire an' brimstone. Goin' to get his haid knocked off, he keep talkin' like he does."

"That'd be too bad," Fitz said. " 'Specially if he talks sense."

26

Fitz could have picked the man out without the help of the headwaiter. Joel Colfax occupied a table alone, set apart from the others as if he was afflicted with a disease that might spread on close contact.

Fitz judged him to be about sixty, not too much older than himself. He was a big man, in height and build. His face was slightly fat and quite florid. He wore long sideburns but no whiskers, and Fitz would describe him as a handsome, attention-getting type of individual, a forceful, intelligent-looking man. His thinning hair was still straw-colored and his blue eyes were alert.

Fitz said, "Begs your pardon, suh. I'm Fitzjohn Turner of Wyndward plantation. Wants to talk to you."

"Mistah Turner, suh." Colfax came to his feet and extended both hands, taking Fitz's in one and covering it with the other in a cordial welcome. "I've been hopin' to meet you, suh. Mighty glad you comes by. Sit down. Let me order you suppah, suh. I insist on it, suh. Whut you

355

drinkin'? Or whut you drinkin' your bourbon with, suh? Knows a bourbon drinker on sight.'

"Spring water," Fitz said, already fascinated by this almost overpowering man. He could be a very strong force in the fight against the Klan and a fine possibility for political office by dint of appearance alone.

Colfax ordered a duplicate of his own meal and waited until Fitz was served to finish his drink. Later they enjoyed thick cuts of beef and vegetables. More drinks were promptly served, and over them they began their first real conversation.

"The Klan, suh," Fitz said, "been raisin' hell at my place. Tryin' to burn me out an' damn near gettin' away with it too. Burned one cottage."

"Too bad. Sympathizes with you, suh. The Klan is a nasty outfit o' murderers an' theives hidin' behind their damned sheets. Sho' goin' to keep makin' trouble fo' you 'cause you gots a Northern gal teachin' the niggers. Might's well have committed ten murders, suh. The Klan would think the teacher worse than the murders. Kin I be of any help to you, suh?"

"Not right now, but we gets our haids together some other time, mayhap we kin think o' some way to bust the Klan wide open. You knows Colonel Apperson?"

"Wishes I did so I could spit on him. Man rises in rank an' serves his country well, makin' a fool o' hisse'f runnin' the Klan heah in Lynchburg. Swears I'm goin' to find a way to get the law on him. He don't get me first, with his Klan doin' the dirty wuk."

Fitz finished his steak and laid aside his napkin. "Wishes I could talk longer, suh, but gettin' dark an' that's when the Klan does its best wuk. Likes to get back 'fore they finds out I'm in town an' waylays me. Tried that befo' an' sweahs I'll fo'get it sooner'n they will. You is welcome to come out to Wyndward fo' a long talk an' mayhap some plannin' any time you likes. Or I comes heah whenevah you says."

"Needs your support, suh. We sho' goin to get together soon. You heahs from me."

They shook hands. Fitz felt that at last he had an

356

ally and a worthy one. Colfax was no dreamer, no talker with nothing behind his words. He seemed as much a fighter as Fitz was.

Once again, in the gathering dusk, Fitz looked for Jonathan as he walked to the livery. The man outside the stable had fed and watered the horse and now harnessed him. Fitz paid the livery man and picked up the reins. He heard no sound, but someone climbed into the back of the carriage with remarkable speed. Fitz reached under his coat for the gun he carried.

"It's Dundee, sir," the voice came from the back seat. "Please don't let on there is someone back here. I'll keep out of sight until after we leave town."

"All right, Dundee. You ain't hurt o' sick?"

"No, sir, neither one. At least not sick in body. In mind is something else again. Thank you for letting me go back with you."

"How'd you know I was in town?"

"I saw you walking down the street. I've been hiding in a vacant store."

"Hidin' from whut?"

"The Ku Klux Klan, Mr. Fitzjohn."

"Bettah keep quiet 'til we out o' town. Stay down."

Fitz drove at an ordinary pace through the city, but increased speed when he reached the more rural areas, where the road narrowed and was mostly bordered by brush or forest. Finally, Fitz brought the carriage to a stop in a cleared area not far from Wyndward.

"Come up front, Dundee, an' let's have a look at you." He reached down to grasp Dundee's hand as the black clambered onto the front seat.

"Thank you, sir," Dundee said in his meticulous English.

"You sho' welcome. Now tells me whut this is 'bout, Dundee."

"I went to Richmond to set up an office where ex-slaves could come to me for advice. It worked very well until I was warned to close the office and get out of the city. I refused to do either, and they came in one night and ransacked the office, burned all my files, and broke

357

every stick of furniture in the place. That was enough of a hint for me. Next time they'll break me as they did the furniture."

"Ain't nobody wouldn' say you were anythin' but wise. Go on."

"They didn't give me a chance to leave town. They began closing in on me. They sent people to watch eating places where I could buy food, and they kept watch on the rooming house where I lived. I had to walk out of the city, and when a freight train came along, I hopped it. That's all I could do."

"Whut happened in Lynchburg?"

"I don't exactly know, and I have some bad news. At least I think so. Jubal and I agreed to keep in touch. He was in Lynchburg trying to discover what he could about the Klan. I set up my office. We wrote regularly. But when I came back to Lynchburg, I couldn't find him and when I went to the address to which I'd directed my letters, I was almost caught by two men I will swear were waiting for me."

"You think Jubal in trouble?"

"I have to think that. Why wasn't he home where he said he'd be? Why were men stationed at his address waiting for me to come along? I think they either killed Jubal or are holding him somewhere."

"We'll look into that fast as we kin." Fitz squinted at Dundee's face. "Even in the dark I kin see you looks sick. Sho' you ain't?"

"I'm tired, sir. Very, very tired. I haven't slept five or six hours in a week. An I've been afraid all that time. Yes, I'm afraid. Against one or two men I wouldn't be, but this organization is spreading all over the South. There are several hundred in Lynchburg and at least a thousand members in Richmond. They thrive on hate, and they have to show how much they hate blacks and others. I understand carpetbaggers and scalawags are now included. They have to show they're doing something about them too by killing a few every now and then."

"We havin' our share o' trouble with them on Wyndward. Tells you 'bout it tomorrow. Right now you bettah get in back again an' get some sleep. Wakes you up when we gets to the plantation. Ain't far now."

"Yes, sir. If I don't get some sleep I'm liable to fall out of the carriage."

Fitz let Dundee reach the back of the carriage before going on. The man promptly fell into a deep sleep, untroubled by the swaying and jouncing of the carriage over the rutted dirt road.

Fitz stopped at the front of the mansion and started for the house, expecting Dundee to join him. When he didn't, Fitz went back to the carriage. Dundee was still deep in sleep. Mark ran down the steps and watched in amazement as Fitz hauled the still-sleeping Dundee out of the carriage.

"It's Dundee," Fitz explained. "He sho' beat. Been runnin' fo' days. Gots to get him in baid. Tomorrow he tells us whut it's all 'bout. Told me some, mayhap most, but theah likely be mo' once he wakes up."

Dundee was a big man. Despite Mark's objections, Futz swung him over his shoulder and carried him into the house, under the startled eyes of Clarissa and Adalia. Mark ran up the stairs ahead of him, and by the time Fitz arrived, there was a bed ready. They took off Dundee's coat and shoes, loosened his necktie, and covered him. He never opened his eyess. Fitz left the room, followed by Mark. Mark closed the door, and they went downstairs to the drawing room where they joined Clarissa and Adalia, already seated and awaiting them.

Fitz said, "Makes this short an' sweet. Gots to get some rest myse'f. Didn't sleep very good last night. The Klan runnin' wild in Lunchburg an' reckon they goin' strong in Richmond. Dundee helps ex-slaves 'til the Klan drives him out. Been lookin' fo' him, an' reckon they passes the word to be on the lookout fo' him in Lynchburg."

"If the Klan in every city is hooked up as well as Richmond and Lynchburg seem to be, we sho' in a mess o' trouble all over the South," Mark observed.

"Ain't much question 'bout it, Mark. Dundee hides in Lynchburg, lookin' fo' a way to come back heah. Sees me an' waits in the livery fo' me."

"Whut 'bout Jubal?" Clarissa asked.

Fitz shook his head. "Don't know fo' sho' whut happened to him. Dundee tries to reach him, but he got to whar Jubal lives, there's men waitin' fo' him, so he slips 'way. Reckon Jubal been caught, an' if he ain't daid, they holdin' him fo' some reason."

"What in the world are we going to do?" Adalia said. "Can't my brother act against them?"

"Could if he knows who they are," Fitz explained. "The Klan is a secret organization. On'y a few knows one 'nother. On'y way to find out whut they up to, somebody has to join 'em to keep track o' whut they plannin'. Hopes Jonathan doin' that. Mayhap Jubal is busy too an' that's why they after him. Gots to find Jubal. He's too valuable a man to sacrifice."

"If they kills him," Mark said quietly, "I goin' to do some killin' myse'f, Gran'pa."

"Mark, please don't say that," Adalia cried out in alarm.

"Has to do somethin' like that," he said. "Gots to be done 'fore they runs the whole South."

"Mark sho' right 'bout that," Fitz said.

"Heah anythin' 'bout my ex-papa-in-law?" Clarissa asked.

"On'y that he likely headin' up the Klan in Lynchburg."

"Then it sho' goin' to fall apart," Clarissa said. "The colonel cain't run anythin'."

"Hear there's someone else over the colonel. Cain't say fo' sho', but heahs it from folks who got ways o' knowin' 'bout things like that."

"A large part of it is my fault," Adalia said. "Teaching black children seems to be in the same category as committing murder, as they see it. Perhaps if I quit and go back North, it might stop."

"It won't stop," Fitz assured her. "There's a hundred other things they don't like. Seems they fightin' the war all over, but this time they ain't fightin' Yankees. They's fightin' the South."

"Gots blacks watchin' the schoolhouse," Mark said. "Hong Kong an' twenty men patrollin' the whole plantation. Gettin' so we ain't got time to do any wuk 'cept tryin' to guard the place."

"Ain't anythin' bein' done 'bout it?" Clarissa asked Fitz.

"Not much. Meets one man, name o' Joel Colfax. Evah heahs o' him?"

"Not me," Clarissa said.

"He likely comin' heah to see us. He goin' 'bout preachin' 'gainst the Klan."

"Reckon his life ain't worth a shinplaster," Clarissa said.

"He won't be an easy man fo' them to take," Fitz explained. "Got plenty o' brains an' sho' ain't a weaklin'. Mayhap we kin do some good with his help. First we gots to find out whut happened to Jubal, an' if they holdin' him, we gots to see how we kin get him loose an' outen their hands."

"I hope Colfax can help," Adalia said. "I'm really becoming quite frightened. Not so much for me as for all of us."

"We gots to be careful from now on," Fitz warned. "Cain't take no mo' chances. Wants somebody with you, Adalia, all the time. We nevah lets the schoolhouse go unguarded. An' we gots to hide Dundee. Ain't no way they kin find out he heah on Wyndward—I hopes. They finds him, they tars an' feathers him if he lucky. They kills him if he ain't. Mark, wants you to be in charge heah all night. Makes sho' Hong Kong's boys patrols well. I takes over daytimes with your help, Clarissa. Fo' now I gots to get some sleep too. Been a busy day."

After Fitz left the room, Adalia set her pretty jaw at an aggressive angle. "Mark, I'm not going to leave. I will not give in to them, and I shall continue to teach. The children are coming along too well to just drop the whole thing because a lot of stupid men say we must."

"That gal o' yours," Clarissa addressed Mark, "got mo' gumption than I gots. When you ain't with her, I will be. An' from now on, I don't go anywhar on this plantation 'thout a rifle under my arm."

"We'll all be doin' the same thing," Mark said.

"An' hopes if the Klan comes, my ex-papa-in-law

comes leadin' 'em. He does an' anybody else shoots him, I sho' goin' to have a fit. Wants him fo' my own."

"Soon's Gran'pa wakes up," Mark said, "goin' to tell him I gives orders to slow down all wuk in the fields an' at the curin' sheds. No sense raisin' bacco that's goin' to get burned up if we don't be on guard. Damn it, nevah had this heah kind o' trouble when the war goin' on. The Yankees comes, we knows they comin', an' they don't gets heah wearin' bedsheets so we can't see who they are. Bettah we gets some rest now too. 'Cept fo' me. You heahs whut Gran'pa says. I'm in charge at night so I orders you to go to baid. You first, Clarissa, so's I kin say good night properly to Adalia."

"Trouble with gettin' old," Clarissa said on her way out of the room. "Ain't nobody says good night to me. Not properly, like you says, Mark."

Mark joined Adalia on the small sofa where she'd been sitting. "I'm sorry this has to spoil ev'rythin', darlin' Adalia. Makes me sick you can't enjoy Wyndward fo' whut it is. An' you gots to be skeered all the time 'bout the schoolhouse an' the kids. Sho' ain't right, but we goin' to do whut we kin to change that. Mayhap someday soon Wyndward gets nice an' peaceful again."

"Please don't do anything rash," Adalia begged. "I don't want anyone hurt."

"We knows pretty well how to handle things. Gots to 'member, the kind o' jackasses joins the Klan, ain't got much in the way o' guts. Ten o' them ain't feared o' one man—lessen he got a gun. Well, we all got guns an' we kin use 'em. 'Sides that, gets too bad we kin send fo' your brother an' the Yankee soldiers. Looks bad fo' us, but really ain't that bad. Now let's stop talkin' 'bout unpleasant things an' talk 'bout you an' me."

"I'd like that," she said. "I'd rather let you hold me and kiss me and keep me from thinking about anything else."

"Sho' kin oblige," Mark said. He drew her to him and their lips met in a gentle kiss. It was sufficient to dismiss the dire troubles that beset them. Yet Mark still marveled that he could contain his passion when he loved Adalia so much.

The next morning Elegant grumbled about serving Dundee at the same table with the rest of the family. "Ain't right," she said. "Ain't nevah goin' to be right. Makes fo' nuthin' but trouble. Now you eats plenty, Dundee. You lookin' skinny as a runt hawg. Bringin' mo' biscuits."

Dundee smiled. "Too many blacks think as Elegant does. They still can't realize they are free. It's one of the things we're trying to put a stop to, but it's harder than getting the white folks to accept us."

"Takes time," Adalia said. "Much time. Years of time, but it has to happen. It must! Lots of men died to make it possible."

"It would be well," Dundee said, "if you taught your students to stand on their own feet. If I can help, Adalia, I'm at your service."

"Dundee goin' to stay heah fo' some time," Fitz said. "Anyone come heah, he hides an' we ain't seen him fo' weeks. Mark, you goes to baid now, like we agreed. I takes over."

"Takes Adalia to the schoolhouse first," Mark said.

After they left, Clarissa announced that she intended to sit on the veranda with a rifle at her side, to keep watch. "Cain't do mo'n that, but fo' an old lady, got pretty good eyesight. Wants to know soon's I kin when somebody come down the road."

"You do that," Fitz said. "No matter all this goin' on, gots to tend to plantation business. Dundee, you stays in the mansion. Bettah not even lets the niggers see you 'round heah. Less they know, the bettah."

"I'll do my share of watching," Dundee said. "At the same time I'll try to think of some other way we can break up this Klan."

"Gives you some field glasses. You watches from the upstairs front room. 'Tween you an' Clarissa, reckon we don't get visitors we don't want. Let me know at the first sign o' dust."

Fitz went to work in his office. The house seemed to grow quiet, yet he had a constant feeling of foreboding. He knew the odds were against them in what they were fighting and wished he was thirty years younger. Not only was Dundee in peril, Adalia threatened, and the plantation at risk, but their whole way of life was in the balance. A very successful Klan could alter the entire Reconstruction program and set the South back as many years as the war had. It might even bring on the return of Yankee troops in greater force.

The security Fitz had longed for was still far off. He had looked forward to the marriage of Mark and Adalia; to Jonathan industriously engaged in the growing of tobacco with Clarissa moving about keeping things in order; and, finally and most joyous for him, Liz coming to Wyndward to take her rightful place as its mistress.

All was now postponed, and it made Fitz angry and frustrated. The very people his family would try to help had turned against them and anyone else who wanted to get the South going again. There certainly had been nothing like this included in what everyone hoped for, up until the birth of the Klan.

It was coming on time when the tobacco crop would go into the curing sheds, but so far, no harvesting had been done. The thought worried Fitz, for Wyndward would then be the most vulnerable, as all hands would have to take part in the harvesting. It could not be done in easy stages. Leaves had to be stripped as fast as possible to catch them at their peak. And Fitz knew he would sacrifice the entire crop rather than send out inferior tobacco.

Early in the afternoon a sharp whistle from Dundee announced someone approaching. A few moments later, Clarissa also saw the buggy. As it turned down the lane to the mansion, she stood up, steadied the barrel of the rifle against one of the veranda pillars, and kept the buggy in the sights of her gun.

Fitz came out to join her. "Looks like Cap'n Morton an' 'nother man. . . . It's Mistah Colfax. Told you 'bout him."

Clarissa lowered the gun. "Hopes they gots some news 'bout Jubal."

Fitz went down to welcome the pair as they got out of the buggy. Colfax held Fitz's hand in a strong grip while he stood looking about with astonishment.

"Mistah Turner, suh, had no idea you gots a plantation big as this. An' this sho' the finest house I've seen in a long time."

"Thank you, suh. Cap'n, how are you, suh?" Fitz extended the hand that Colfax had finally released.

"Fine, Fitz. Mister Colfax and I have discussed the situation in Lynchburg, and we came here hoping you might add something to help solve this problem."

"Come inside an' we talks it over. Mistah Colfax, this heah is Clarissa. She a relative o' mine, an' she stayin' heah."

Clarissa was openly elated at seeing a gentleman close to her age at Wyndward, and she regarded him with unfeigned interest. Not since before the war had a visitor of Mr. Colfax's type appeared here. She knew also that she was the hostess of Wyndward—at least until Liz's arrival—and so, lost no time in attending to her duties by extending her hand graciously and curtsying deeply. It had been some time since she'd been called upon to curtsy, but her corset helped support her and she managed it gracefully. Her eyes were warm and inviting as she regarded Colfax. He bowed in a courtly manner, kissed the back of her hand, releasing it as he straightened, but gave no evidence he was cognizant of her obvious interest. She turned and led the way into the house, continuing to the drawing room.

Fitz yelled for Calcutta Two. When he appeared, Fitz ordered four drinks. There was no need to order Calcutta Two not to sloth today—four glasses would spill more whiskey on the tray than two.

"Mr. Colfax and I have been trying to find some way to fight this Klan before it takes over Lynchburg," Captain Morton said.

"An' Richmond as well," Colfax added. "The movement is gettin' stronger theah too. We hopes you might have somethin' in mind, Mistah Turner."

"Or you, Miss Clarissa," Captain Morton said. "We're not discounting a woman's viewpoint."

"On'y thing I gots to offer is you gets rid o' the man runnin' the Klan, an' mayhap the others goes home. I mean Colonel Apperson. You tells me to shoot that sonabitch, an' I sho' mighty happy to do so."

"It might be a way at that," Colfax said with a laugh. "But we have to find some way to offset the harm they doin'. Now I told the cap'n that in Richmond I did some preachin' 'bout it, an' I suggested to the people who heard me that ev'ryone donates somethin', even a small sum o' money. Nobody has very much, but the amount don't matter. I base it on the theory that if they gives money, they sho' gots their hearts in whut we tryin' to do. Thinks mayhap I tries this in Lynchburg. Cap'n Morton ain't so sho' I should go that far."

"Why not?" Fitz asked.

"Like Mistah Colfax says," Clarissa added, "folks gives money, they shows how they feels, an' helps bustin' up that bunch o' men ought to be spendin' mo' time usin' the sheets in baid an' not usin' 'em fo' clothes."

"Then I begins preachin' tonight," Colfax said. "Whut cash we collects won't be 'nuff to do much good, but we'll sho' find a use fo' it one way o' 'nother. Whut else kin we do?"

"The Klan holds big meetin's, burnin' their damn crosses an' such," Fitz said. "Mayhap we busts up the meetin's we kin discourage 'em some. Might even put a few bullets over their haids to lets 'em know we ain't foolin'.'"

"I can't order my soldiers to do anything like that," Morton said.

Fitz nodded, feeling a deep exasperation coming over him as everything suggested led to frustration.

Calcutta Two brought the drinks, and everyone ceased their planning to devote their attention to quenching their thirst.

"Fine whiskey," Colfax commented. "An' Mistah Turner, you gots one o' the finest houses I evah did see. Miss Clarissa, if you decorated this room, you shows mo' talent fo' it than anyone I evah met. It's a beautiful room."

"You kin see the rest o' the house you likes, Mistah Colfax," she said. "Be proud to show you 'round."

"I'd like that. My wife is goin' to join me soon as we

get the town settled down an' I feels she be in no danger. I would 'preciate any suggestions I get from the other rooms in case we decides to build."

"Goin' to be hard keepin' Dundee out o' sight," Fitz said. "Might's well brings him down."

Clarissa's face grew pink. "Oh, Fitz, fo'got 'bout him."

"Makes no diff'rence," Fitz said. "We all friends heah, an' we all lookin' to bust the Klan. Dundee feels the same way. Please fetch him, Clarissa."

"No need. " Dundee's voice came from the reception hall. "Been listening." He entered the room. Colfax came to his feet and extended a hand.

"Knows this heah man. Doin' fine wuk in Richmond. Hear him talkin' to the ex-slaves an' tellin' 'em to behave themse'ves."

"Name o' Dundee," Fitz said. "This heah Mistah Colfax, Dundee."

The white man and the black man shook hands warmly. Dundee accepted an invitation to sit down. Calcutta Two received shouted orders to bring more drinks for all.

"I've heard you address several crowds, Mister Colfax," Dundee said. "You are a born spellbinder, sir."

"Thank you, Dundee. Does the best I kin. You sho'ly ain't from the South."

"Dundee born heah. Right on this farm," Fitz explained. "Befo' the war he goes North to college an' comes back one mighty smart man. Tryin' to help the niggers best he kin."

"I shall offer my help whenever you need it, Dundee," Colfax said. "I wish we had a thousand mo' like you."

"Thank you, sir."

"We gots 'nother boy who goes to college along with Dundee," Fitz said. "Last we hears, he in Lynchburg tryin' to learn whut he kin 'bout the Klan."

"I hope he learns a great deal," Colfax said.

"Cain't say. Ain't heard from him. Dundee, you ain't thinkin' anythin' mo' kin help us find him?"

"No, Mr. Fitz. Jubal and I were going to do what we

could to help our folks in the South. There was bound to be a great deal of confusion here, especially among the blacks who had been slaves and were suddenly free men and women. But the first thing we encountered when we came to Virginia was the advent of the Klan, and until we can send that back to the hellhole it came out of, there won't be much we can do."

"This man Jubal—there's been no word from him?" Captain Morton asked.

"None, Cap'n," Fitz replied. "Worries me some."

" 'Zactly how did he hope to go 'bout gettin' information 'bout the Klan?" Colfax asked.

"I don't know, sir," Dundee replied. "I suppose he was going to dress and act like an ex-slave looking for work, trying to get something to do at places where the Klan gathers."

"That would place him in considerable jeopardy," Captain Morton said. "If he makes one slip. . . ."

"Jubal wasn't given to making any slips," Dundee said. "He wasn't well known in Lynchburg. He came here from another city when Mr. Turner bought him as a slave. He worked on the plantation until we were sent North. I doubt he was in Lynchburg more than once or twice in his life. Even that often would surpise me. So he wouldn't be recognized."

"Were you to contact him?" Colfax asked.

"Not if it involved any risks," Dundee said. "I did write to him at an address he furnished. I suppose he received my letters—two of them—but he never responded, and when I came searching for him, I couldn't find a trace. Yet he would cover his steps well, so it may be he's not in any trouble."

"Let's pray he ain't," Colfax said. "Now I suggest 'sides gettin' small donations, I keeps makin' speeches an' tryin' to convince good folks that the Klan ain't goin' to do the South any good, on'y harm. Best we kin do is see the Klan gets as little support from folks as possible. Throws 'em out, bound to make heroes outen 'em. Best we kin do is hope some gets ashamed an' some leaves. Now that would be a help. Mayhap their wives won't lets 'em use the bedsheets any mo'."

"Thank you, sir," Dundee said. "There are many things we can do if we are allowed to, even in the face of the threats the Klan seem to offer every chance they get."

"Mister Dundee," Colfax said, "it would not be advisable fo' you to return to Lynchburg an' out of the question fo' you to go back to Richmond. My advice is fo' you to remain heah whar you kin be protected an' whar you safe from Klansmen."

"Yes," Dundee said. "If I'm permitted, I will try to help Miss Adalia at the school. I want to do something more than hide."

"She sho' could use some help," Clarissa said.

"Jes' watch out," Colfax warned.

"If you do go to Lynchburg and you run into trouble," Captain Morton said, "I'll pass your name along to my men stationed around City Hall, and you can count on them."

"That's good to know, Captain, and I thank you."

The second round of drinks arrived, and the conversation grew lighter in tone, centering on tobacco and Wyndward's crop. After a while, Colfax accepted Clarissa's invitation to inspect the mansion, and they went off together.

"Seems like a man surely dedicated to getting rid of the Klan," Captain Morton said.

"He's been working hard in Richmond," Dundee told them. "He has the power to make people listen."

"I understand he intends to run for Congress when the South again joins the North in Washington," Morton said.

"He ought to make a mighty good legislator," Fitz agreed.

"I'd hate to debate him on any subject," Morton commented. "He has a winning personality and is a persuasive speaker."

"He sort o' took Clarissa's eye," Fitz said with a grin.

"I noticed that," Morton said. "He's married, but . . . it may be some time before he brings his family from Atlanta. That's where he originally came from."

"Clarissa sho' ain't goin' to do him any good," Fitz laughed. "Bets you she gets him to make a date to see her in Lynchburg."

"I won't take that bet," Morton said.

"Nor I," Dundee chuckled. "I've known Miss Clarissa for a long time. She knows how to handle men."

"Sho' does," Fitz said in a brief moment of memory.

"Suppose," Morton said, "we give ourselves a little time to think about ways and then meet in my office in a few days."

Fitz nodded. "Fine with me, suh."

"I wish I could get word from Jubal," Dundee said. "I'm growing more and more worried about him."

"I'll instruct my men to keep an eye out," Morton promised. "I can offer this as a note of urgency. We'd better have the Klan in check before all Union troops are withdrawn from the South. The Klan would run rampant if it ever got a chance."

"It may not," Dundee said. "I think Southern folks will soon realize that the Klan is no more than a gang of hooligans looking for excitement and trying to find it under the guise of helping the South and protecting it from ex-slaves and Northern scalawags."

Colfax entered the pink bedroom suite and looked about in amazement. "Nevah in my life, Miss Clarissa, have I seen anythin' like this."

"Meant it fo' Fitz's daughter who live in Washington, but she don't like it heah on Wyndward. So lets Cap'n Morton's sistah use it. She livin' heah while she teachin' school fo' the black childrun on Wyndward."

"There seems to be no end to whut Mistah Fitzjohn is involved in. You are related to him, I think he mentioned."

"Fitz's first wife, name o' Benay, my cousin. Sho' ain't no blood relation."

"I see. I presumed you might be 'cause Mr. Fitzjohn sho' a handsome man, an' I thinks beauty sort o' runs in the fam'ly."

"Well now," Clarissa beamed. "Sho'ly takes that as a compliment, suh."

"You're a beautiful woman, Miss Clarissa," he said. "You sho' cain't be a spinster."

"In a way, mayhap. I used to be married to Colonel Apperson's son Horace. But that ain't 'zactly like bein' married."

"I don't understand, Miss Clarissa."

"Horace like to go to baid with boys, not gals."

"I see. I'm sorry 'bout that. You sho'ly deserves bettah. Now I ain't a man goes 'round flirtin' with other women, seein' I'm married myse'f, but ain't no sin if I asks you to suppah in Lynchburg whenevah you kin make it."

"Mistah Colfax, ain't no man asked me to suppah, 'sides Fitz, in so long cain't 'member the last time. I sho' accepts."

"Fine. Jes' the two o' us. You know, Miss Clarissa, I could o' fallen in love with you when I sees you fo' the first time downstairs. You a woman fo' my taste an' sho' knows a handsome one I sees one. Gots to warn you, I'm a passionate man myse'f."

"Mistah Colfax!" Clarissa exclaimed in what she hoped was a shocked voice.

"Believes in bein' honest, Miss Clarissa."

"Believes in it myse'f, suh. Nevah been a wallflower. Kin prove it."

She moved up to him and slowly slipped her arms around his neck. Ardor and desire lit up his eyes. She kissed him and at the same time pressed close to him.

"Miss Clarissa," he said huskily, "when kin you come to Lynchburg? An' tells Mistah Fitzjohn you stayin' with a friend all night?"

"Cain't say, suh, but sho' aims to do it. You hears from me, Mistah Colfax. Reckon you kin pester a gal real good."

"You waits an' see," he said eagerly. "Don't be too long."

She nodded. "Best we go downstairs 'fore they wonders if we gone to baid heah."

"I'd sho' like to but don't wants to get Fitz mad at me. We gots important wuk to do. How that school comin'?"

"Bettah than we evah expected. The kids learnin' mighty fast. An' I heahs nigger childrun too dumb to learn anythin'. Provin' it ain't so."

"Very interestin'. But you have to be careful 'cause if the Klan heahs 'bout it, they might come in force."

"Already comes," she confided. "An' leaves fast as they comes. Next time sho' be plenty who won't leave 'cause they nevah goin' any place again. Keeps the school guarded at night."

"Whut 'bout daytimes?"

"The bastards who wear bedsheets an' masks don't come out by day. Like rats, they goes 'bout by night when they kin sneak up on a man."

"You has a fine insight on things, Miss Clarissa. Befo' we goes down. . . ."

He held out his arms, and she moved into them readily for a prolonged kiss and a tight embrace that left them both gasping for breath. Then they returned to the drawing room, quite composed, and Colfax praised Fitz's house once again.

Dundee, Fitz, and Clarissa saw them off. Dundee made his way to the shed directly behind the schoolhouse where he felt safest. Fitz took Clarissa's elbow and guided her back up the veranda steps. They stood watching the buggy vanish in a cloud of dust.

"Ain't sayin' nuthin'," Fitz commented, "but Mistah Colfax comes downstairs, he sho' breathin' kind o' hard. But then, walkin' downstairs takes a lot outen a man."

"Go to hell," Clarissa said promptly.

"You rubbin' up 'gainst that man? You knows he married."

"Fitz, he ask me to suppah an' I accepts. Ain't had an offer like that in so long I jes' kisses him, thass all."

"Knows the way you kisses. Likes it myse'f. Ain't blamin' you none, but don't 'spect he goin' to marry you. He a kind o' preachin' man an' sho' ain't goin' to divorce his wife."

"Goddamn it, Fitz, a gal don't has to marry a man to enjoy suppah with him. Whut's wrong with that? You thinks we goin' to make love mayhap on the restaurant table?"

"Reckon not. You needs a man anyway. All I kin say is good luck."

"Thanks you, Fitz. You knows whut a woman is like."

"Yes," he sighed, "an' when I thinks o' Liz in Washington, knows whut a man is like too."

27

Fitz and Clarissa stood on the fringe of a good-sized crowd listening to Colfax orate in a manner that hadn't been heard in the South since before the war. He had selected his place well. As Fitz had done before, with Mark as his audience, Colfax had chosen the old slave market. He stood on the concrete auction block while he spoke.

"We o' the South," he said, "gots our honor to preserve, an' we sho' ain't doin' it lettin' this heah Ku Klux Klan do their will whenevah they feels like it, on whoevah they hates. There's been mo' than one murder by them devils in white sheets. I say if they gets the upper hand heah, ain't nobody goin' to be safe. Knows nobody in the South gots much money these evil days, but asks you to give whut you kin so we gets a chance to bust this organization 'fore it buries some o' us."

There had been more before Fitz and Clarissa arrived and there was more afterward. Colfax surely had the ability to hold his audience.

"That man kin speak o' carrots an' potatoes, an'

they listens to him," Fitz observed. "Heahs he goin' to run fo' Congress soon's it gets legal. Ain't nobody I kin think o' who could beat him."

"Havin' suppah with him tonight, Fitz. You don' mind ridin' back to Wyndward—alone. Mights be . . . kind o' late we gets through eatin' an' don' wants to keep you heah jes' to drive me home."

"Now Clarissa, you knows I gets to baid early so I won't wait. An' might be bettah you gets to baid early too . . . mayhap in the mawnin'."

"Fitz, you knows I gots to do this, an' sho' ain't so bad with a man like Colfax. Don' 'spect nuthin' from him, an' he don't 'spect anythin' from me."

"Knows that. Both o' you 'spectin' nuthin' sho' goin' be a dull night. You mind stayin' heah 'til he gets through? He been eyin' you evah since we got heah. Got business at the bank an' with Cap'n Morton an' when I finishes, I'll be goin' back. Tomorrow, I either comes fo' you o' sends fo' you."

"On'y way I kin thank you is to wish Liz comes to Wyndward soon as she kin."

" 'Preciates it, Clarissa. See whut you kin find out 'bout Apperson, if there's any way his name come up. Kind o' think he takin' over the Klan an' that means he sho' comin' to Wyndward. The mo' we knows 'bout him, the bettah."

"He comes an' you gets your hands on him, lock him up 'til I gets back so I kin shoot him."

"He comes, ain't goin' to be nuthin' left fo' you to shoot at."

Fitz observed again that while Colfax's masculine appeal attracted an audience, it was his commanding manner and forceful way of speaking that held them. Fitz didn't blame Clarissa. She'd been living the life of a spinster for a long time now, which was not in keeping with her flamboyant personality. She'd kept it under wraps. He reasoned it would be good to let her have her fling, then she'd settle down again.

Colfax was hastily winding up his speech. Though no one in the audience noticed, he glanced in Clarissa's direction often. Though his speech was no less persuasive, it was obvious to Fitz his mind was on a rendezvous with Clarissa.

Fitz left to visit Henry Tallen at the bank and Captain Morton at City Hall. Neither visit was very productive. All he learned was that Colfax was to confer with them soon and he would be notified.

Tallen was highly impressed by Colfax. "That man kin stand in pourin' rain an' gets an audience. Been bankin' fair-sized sums heah, collected from those who listens to him. Say he goin' to use it to fight the Klan. He keep on, mayhap we kin buy those bastahds off."

"They'd take the money," Fitz said, "an' buy new bedsheets. Wouldn' trust 'em in any way."

On the way back to Windward, riding alone, Fitz had a rifle beside him, cocked and ready. There was a handgun under his belt, and he kept a wary eye out. The Klan hadn't been very active in a few days now, and it worried him. Any times of inactivity on their part meant they were planning their next moves and watching for a chance to put them into operation. That they'd be directed at Wyndward seemed more than possible. The Klan had to destroy Wyndward first to keep their reputation for ruthlessness intact. Fitz had been expecting more burning crosses on his lawn for some time.

At Wyndward, everything was peaceful. With the curing of the tobacco leaves at their peak, it became necessary for Mark to be there often and longer than he liked. Still, nothing had happened in days. Adalia dismissed her classes as usual in midafternoon, then sat at her desk preparing the next day's lessons. The students who vied for the assignments of washing the blackboard, dusting the desks, filling the inkwells, sweeping the floor, and clapping the erasers free of chalk attended to their chores. When they finished, she complimented and thanked them. After they left, she returned to her work, checking and marking papers. She made notes of some students who could be tutored by others. For those who were moving along faster than others, she planned more advanced lessons.

She and Mark met secretly for lessons whenever

possible. Mark had proven himself a willing student and was applying himself diligently. He was fascinated by what he was learning, and Adalia was delighted at the speed with which he was acquiring knowledge. They both wished there was time for more extended studies.

She'd finished her bookwork and absently covered her desk with the dustcloth, for her thoughts were on Mark. She did not see two men come boldly across the open space from the forest. They looked like two harmless visitors from another plantation.

When they entered, Adalia looked up and then came to her feet in alarm. One of them closed the schoolhouse door and the other came toward her in a lunge that almost knocked her down as she tried to back away from him. He caught her in his arms, brought one hand across her mouth.

"Wants to know whar the nigger name o' Dundee hides. Knows he heah. You tells me, or I breaks your pretty neck. Takin' my hand off you, but if you yells, I busts your face in. Heah me?"

She had ceased struggling—there was no point to it. She was held firmly and couldn't make any noise. Even if she could there'd be no one close by to hear except for Dundee, who was in the small shed just outside the schoolhouse.

The hand came away from her mouth. "I don't know anything about anyone named Dundee," she said.

He slapped her hard across the face. "You lyin' an' you knows it. He heah an' we wants him. Whar is he?"

While the man spoke, his hand was hard against her mouth again. She bit him so hard he cried out in pain, but he didn't let go, except to suck some of the blood from the laceration. Then, before she could cry out, the hand was over her mouth again.

"Asks once mo'. Whar that high an' mighty nigger?"

The hand came away from her mouth. "I don't know," she said.

He maneuvered her against the wall, reached down with his free hand, and lifted her dress. Then he pushed up against her.

"Know whut's goin' to happen you don't tell? Goin' to take you right heah, standin' up. Goin' to take you an' then turns you over to my friend watchin' by the door. Mayhap goin' to give you a baby. Wants that? Likes it, I sho' do, an' you tells me whut I wants to know or I takes you. Ain't askin' again."

Adalia sagged limply in his arms, hoping he might believe she had fainted, but that didn't work. It wouldn't have mattered to him if she had fainted. He was now so aroused that he would go through with his threat even if she told him what he wanted to know.

She prayed that Mark wouldn't come along. These men were armed with heavy sidearms. The one at the door had his gun swinging down near his hip, ready to be raised and fired instantly if anyone came by.

She was going to have to let him have his way. But she intended to fight with all the strength she had left. She tried to knee him, but that didn't work. She attempted to bite his hand again, but he was prepared for that. He pressed harder against her, his free hand busily exploring her body.

The man at the door suddenly cried out, "The nigger runnin'!"

Adalia's captor let her go, but only long enough to hit her sharply on the point of the jaw. While she sagged to the floor, he joined his companion. They raced across the cleared space in hot pursuit of Dundee, who was running hard but wasn't sure he was going to escape.

The pair were closing in on him. He veered to the right and headed for the forest. Once there, he might elude them. But saving himself was of less consequence to him than having saved Adalia from these two men. He'd heard them and broken from his hiding place, making enough noise to arouse their attention.

He thought he was going to make it. The forest was fifty feet away.

Two men stepped out from the wooded area. Both had rifles. In terror, Dundee tried to turn away from them, but it was too late. One swung his rifle and struck Dundee across the face. As he sagged toward the ground, the other man sent his rifle butt crashing down on Dundee's head. He fell. The men who had been pursuing him now helped to pick him up, and then all of them disappeared into the forest with him.

Adalia sat up with a cry of pain. For a moment she wasn't certain what had happened. Then memory came back. She got to her feet and ran out of the schoolhouse. There were no signs of Dundee or the two men. She ran along the path toward the fields. Two workers saw her and came to her assistance, then went racing off to find Mark when she told them what had happened. Mark came at once, running as fast as he could.

She didn't break down until his arms were around her. "Two of them," she said. "They were . . . horrible. They wanted Dundee and . . . and . . . they were going to . . . assault me. Dundee must have heard them. He was in the outside shed, working on a speech he was going to make tomorrow at the school. I don't know just what happened, but . . . when I thought I was completely at their mercy, the man at the door saw Dundee running."

"Were they Klansmen?" Mark asked.

"I don't know. They were not robed."

"Would you know 'em again?"

"Yes! Oh yes, I'd know them. Especially the brute who held me."

"Your face is bruised. Are you in pain? Did they hurt you anywhar else on your body?"

"No. Before they went after Dundee, one of them struck me so I wouldn't raise an alarm."

"How long ago?"

"I'm not sure. I was unconscious from the blow. I don't think it was very long, but they must have captured Dundee. Mark, he made noise to let them know he was running so I'd be saved from them."

"I'll take you back to the house. I don't think Gran'pa is back from Lynchburg yet."

"I'm all right. Just . . . just shaken up and my face hurts some. Poor Dundee. What will they do to him?"

"Nuthin' if we can get to him first. Gran'pa is sho' goin' to do somethin', an' I'll be with him."

"Please try to save him. I owe him so much."

"We all do. Now lean on me, you likes, or I kin carry you. . . .

"No, darling, I can walk."

"Seems like I cain't do anythin' alone. Wishes Gran'pa gets heah quick. You evah sees those two 'fore?"

"No, Mark. They were ruffians. Cruel men. I think they might have killed me if . . . I had continued to refused to tell where Dundee was."

"Tells you this, they sho' ain't goin' to live much longer. Damn, even Clarissa ain't heah to help you."

"Mark, I'll be all right. I'll be safe in the house. Elegant will help me, and there are guns. If those two come again, I swear I'll shoot them."

"Ain't likely they comes back. They gots whut they came fo'. Now we gots to find out whar they took Dundee an' whut they goin' to do to him."

"I hate to think," Adalia shuddered. "I . . . oh Mark, what makes these people so obstinate and brutal? Why don't they realize the war is over and they'd best serve the South by finding work and settling down?"

"They ain't the kind to do that. They wants to show how big they are. Goin' to show 'em whut bein' skeered is like. Damn it, why ain't Gran'pa comin'?"

Though it was after dark when Fitz turned down the drive to Wyndward, he immediately sensed something was wrong. The mansion was alight, every room was bright. Before he could pull up, Mark ran out to meet him.

"Whut's goin' on?" Fitz asked as he got down from the carriage.

"Hell to pay, Gran'pa. Thinks you nevah gets heah."

"I'm heah. Whut happen?"

"Two bastahds, sho'ly from the Klan, comes an' near rapes Adalia while they tryin' to make her tell whar Dundee hidin'. Sho' knowed he was heah. Dundee heahs 'em talkin' to Adalia, knows whut they tryin' to do to her, an' he makes noise as he busts out so they chases him an' lets her go. Don' know they gets him o' not, but reckon he nevah had much of a chance."

"He daid, you thinks?"

380

"Sends Hong Kong an' some men to look 'round case they kills Dundee. They can't find him, but they sees some blood on the grass jes' befo' the forest an' signs o' mo'n two men hidin' theah. Reckon they jes' took Dundee away, but reckon they goin' to kill him."

"Adalia knowed the men who comes fo' him?"

"Nevah saw em' befo'."

Fitz sat down on a veranda chair and hollered for drinks. "Gots to think this out. Right now cain't think o' anythin' to do. Don't know why they takes him. Don't know whar. Don't know who we kin turn to fo' this kind o' information. Sho' gots some thinkin' to do."

"Gran'pa, we cain't jes' set heah an' jaw."

"You tells me whut to do, son. Whar we starts? Mayhap we searches all o' Lynchburg? Or rides to ev'ry little farm an' big plantation an' looks fo him? You tell me."

Mark sat down heavily. "You right. Reckon I gets so mad, don't think right. Was disgusted with myse'f 'cause I cain't thinks whut to do. But they were goin' to rape Adalia an' swears I finds out who done that, I kills him."

"He makes a fuss you doin' it, I holds him fo' you. How'd they know Dundee was heah? We jes' gots to hidin' him."

"Cap'n Morton. . . ."

"You kin rule him out."

"My papa knowed he was heah, didn't he?"

"They lookin' fo, Dundee, Jonathan sho' knowed this is whar he'd be, but ain't no reason why he tells the Klan."

"Lessen he a member now."

"Even so, Jonathan an' Dundee borned the same night, grows up together. Mo' like brothers . . ."

"'Til my papa got to hate all niggers. Pow'ful hate he got, Gran'pa. Reckon Dundee no mo'n 'nother nigger to him."

"I say no! Jonathan might hate ev'ry other nigger in the world but not Dundee. Come to think o' it, we ain't heard from Two Bits either. Don' like this, son. Bad fo' Dundee an' likely fo' Two Bits, but ain't a damn thing we kin do. Don' means no disrespect when I calls Jubal by name I give him, but keeps fo'gettin'.'".

"Colfax knowed Dundee was heah."

Fitz nodded slowly. "Colfax 'gainst the Klan. Makin' speeches sayin' it one bad outfit. He raises money to fight the Klan. Told me he was plannin' to run fo' Congress. He belong to the Klan, he sho' won't have a chance."

"If they knows he belongs to the Klan," Mark said. "They all hides under their goddamn sheets."

"Goin' to see Colfax soon's we kin decide whut to do."

"Whar Clarissa?"

Fitz gave a bitter laugh. "Right now thinks she in baid with Colfax. Goin' to have suppah an' knows sho' 'nuff whut's on Colfax's mind. Ain't 'gainst it. Clarissa know whut she doin', an' she a pow'ful passionate woman, even at her age."

"We jawin' too much. We ain't doin' anythin'."

"Like I says, tell me whut to do an' we sho' goes an' does it. Reckon things goin' to happen, they happens fast, an' we gots to act fast. So right now we has some bourbon, then we eats a good suppah, an' we ready when comes need fo' it."

Calcutta Two arrived with the drinks. Mark drank his swiftly. Fitz sipped his slowly.

Mark said, "Cain't sit heah doin' nuthin' when the bastahds who manhandled Adalia runnin' loose an' Dundee mayhap already hung. Gots to do somethin'."

"Nobody else sees these men who comes fo' Dundee? On'y Adalia?"

"Nobody else I knows of, Gran'pa."

"Then Adalia is of no help. Whut we goin' to do is nuthin' rash an' crazy. We cain't afford to make a mistake heah, son. But tonight we rides to Lynchburg, an' we tries to find Jonathan, even if we has to let ev'rybody know he been spyin' on the Klan. We talks to Cap'n Morton—mayhap he know somethin'. Or kin do somethin'. That don't wuk, I'm goin' to make a call on Colonel Apperson, an' he goin' to be told if anythin' happens to

Dundee or Jubal, case they got him too, it ain't goin' to make no diff'rence who responsbile. I kill Apperson 'thout waitin' fo' proof o' anythin'."

"Reckon we rides in now, Gran'pa."

"You takes it easy, Mark. Rushin' 'round gets you nuthin' but a headache. Like I said, we has our drinks an' we eats a good meal, an' then we tries to do whut we kin."

"You thinks they goin' to kill Dundee?"

"Whut else they takes him fo'? One thing still in our favor. If the Klan goin' to kill him, they goin' do it at a big meetin' whar they burns their damn crosses. Dundee a fine 'zample o' whut a nigger kin do if he got a mind to get all that learnin'. So Dundee gots to be a 'zample, an' they goin' to get all they kin out o' killin' him. We looks fo' a Klan meetin' too."

"Gran'pa, they holds their meetin's in secret. How we goin' to find whar it be?"

"You for'gets, a Klan meetin' out o' Lynchburg goin' to be a big one. The Klan lookin' fo' mo' members, an' this heah one way o' gettin' 'em. Now you calm down. We goin' in to have suppah."

Adalia came down for the meal. Fitz gathered her in his arms and comforted her.

"Jes' don't judge all Southerners by whut happened," he said. "No matter whar you goes, you finds men like the kind joins the Klan. They stupid men with no brains an' led easy as a lamb."

"I know, Fitz," Adalia said. "I know only a small fraction of Southerners are capable of such a thing. We have the same kind in the North, but all I'm afraid of is that their kind will draw so many to the Klan that it will become like another government."

"Ain't goin' to happen," Fitz said. "Swears it won't. Now Mark an' me goin' to Lynchburg tonight an' see whut we kind do 'bout findin' Dundee. Reckon we does, it goin' to be a miracle, but we gots to try. Wants you to stay heah, in the house. Elegant stays with you, an' I sees that there be men outside, so ain't nobody goin' to harm you."

"I'm not afraid. Just be sure to leave guns. Elegant says she'll shoot the—uh—her favorite word—sonsa-bitches—if they come."

Fitz laughed to reassure Adalia, but knew that Elegant could, on occasion, say exactly the right words, but maybe not quite the terms Adalia, for instance, would use.

They ate a hearty meal under Elegant's approving eye and were enjoying a large serving of cake when they heard the fast approach of a vehicle. Fitz and Mark hurried out to the veranda. Clarissa, driving a buggy, pulled up and jumped down in a hurry. Fitz ran to meet her, knowing she had important news of some kind.

"You sho' in a hurry," he said. "Mayhap you wore Mistah Colfax out o' juice so he dies?"

"Fitz, ain't no time fo' fool talk. Wait'll we gets in the house. Sho' got news fo' you."

Fitz led her into the dining room with Mark follow-ing. Clarissa, out of breath and in a state of great excite-ment, nevertheless took one look at the cake and cut herself a large slice.

Fitz said, "Befo' you begins, you has to know that the Klan comes heah an' kidnaps Dundee, among other things."

"That's it!" she exclaimed. "Fitz, that's whut I figgered. Somethin' like that."

"Fo' Gods sake, tell us whut you talkin' 'bout," Mark begged.

"Please," Adalia added. "You've no idea how im-portant this is if you have any information."

Clarissa drank some of the coffee Adalia poured for her. "Reckon whut I gots to say goin' to make you think o' me as a old whore, Adalia, but gots to say it. When you leaves me in Lynchburg, Fitz, Mistah Colfax come to me. Now he a real Southern gen'mun, bowin' an' kissin' my hand an' tellin' me how beautiful I am. But he also say it too early fo' suppah so best we goes to his hotel so we kin talk in private. Knows whut he wants sho' wasn't jes' talk. Ain't sayin' I didn't want the same thing. You gots to understan', Adalia, we old folks gots to take it whar we finds it. Ain't nobody goin' to wink at us an' kind o'

384

hint whut they wants. Old folks don' waste that much time."

"Clarissa, will you tell us whut in hell you knows," Fitz said. "Ev'ry minute you wastes mean Dundee closer to bein' killed."

"Makes it short. Colfax an' me, we stops at the bar an' has a few drinks. He buys a whole bottle, an' we goes to his room. Right 'bout then I thinks this heah polished gen'mun ain't no gen'mun at all. Don't wants to baid down with him, but cain't see any way out. So I pours him mighty strong drinks an' takes it easy myse'f. All the while he pawin' me an' takin' my clothes off an' talkin' dirty as he kin. Braggin' some too, he goin' to be the most important man in the South. Gon' to Washington an' raise hell theah an' make lots o' money. I stays with him, I goes to Washington too. He kin fool his wife easy. He keeps gettin' drunker an' drunker, an' pretty soon he say we gots to go to baid 'cause somethin' important might come up an' he has to go off. 'Bout then a man comes. Colfax steps into the hall with him. I tries to listen but cain't heah nuthin'. His glass o' bourbon 'bout empty, so I fills it again an' adds no water. He comes back mighty excited. . . ."

"This man comes to see him. Whut time was that?" Fitz asked.

" 'Bout six, reckon. Mayhap jes' after five."

"Go ahead," Fitz said.

"He talkin' half crazy he come back, prancin' 'round like he a little boy an' got a toy he been wantin'. Braggin' mo' an' say he gots to leave soon's he kin, but gots time fo' me an' the baid. All this time he so excited he kept on drinkin' an' don't seem to know he gettin' mighty drunk. Say he got an important meetin' tonight an' cain't be later'n nine so we gots to baid down. 'Bout then he baids down. Falls right into baid an' starts snorin' like an old sow. Knows somethin' goin' on, so I looks 'round the two rooms he keeps at the hotel. Knows whut I finds, Fitz?"

"You tells us an' fast," Fitz said.

"Colfax preachin' fo' money to fight the Klan, but that sonabitch a big man in the Klan. Finds his robes an' funny hat. They sho' ain't bedsheets, but mighty fine cloth, an' they purple an' gots dragons embroidered over the front."

"Knows whut we gots to do now," Fitz said to Mark. "Runs down an' brings back two o' the fastest hosses. We rides faster'n a buggy kin take us. You gets back, I be ready. We takes guns . . . I'll have 'em. Now you gets the hosses fast as you kin."

Mark went off. Fitz got up from the table and assembled two rifles and two pistols. He also took along a huge Bowie knife in a scabbard. He donned gloves and a jacket, and before he left, he kissed Adalia.

"Don' worry none. Now we knows whut to do, an' we sho' ain't goin' to get hurt."

He turned to Clarissa and kissed her hard on the lips. "Fo' you theah ain't one thing you craves you ain't goin' to get." He paused watching the warmth begin to glow in Clarissa's eyes. "Cept fo' one thing," he added.

"Knows whut you means, but you kin talk 'bout frustrated women an' reckon I kin give lessons in it. Jes' mighty glad I kin be o' help."

"Reckon things goes right, you kin say you saved Dundee's life. An' mayhap we busts this heah Klan in Lynchburg so it nevah come back. Sho goin' to open the eyes o' many a man thinkin' 'bout joinin' the Klan. Now you takes charge heah. Get guns ready fo' shootin', keeps all windows an' doors locked an' an eye out 'case they come heah. Mark an' me will come back soon's we kin."

He hurried out to wait for Mark.

28

Fitz and Mark rode out into the night, side by side. Fitz managed to make himself heard above the pounding of the fast-driven horses and the stream of air whizzing past their ears.

"Clarissa gets Colfax drunk. Takes her mayhap two hours to ride back, so reckon he didn' wake up yet, or at least not long ago. From whut Clarissa says, he talk 'bout an important meetin'. Cain't mean anythin' but a Klan meetin'. Man comes an' talks to him, an' after that, he gets mighty excited. Thinks this heah man come an' tell him they gots Dundee. So now the meetin' goin' to be held, an' Dundee goin' to be the big attraction."

"How we finds the meetin' place?" Mark yelled back.

"Knows whar Colfax is. Ain't no meetin' 'thout him bein' theah. So we waits an' follows him. Ain't no other way. We says prayers 'bout now he too drunk to wake up 'til after we gets theah."

"How we goin' to find out he wakes up o' not?"

"Think o' somethin'. Now keep your mouth shut an' ride."

Fitz dug his heels into the belly of his horse. The pace increased. They reached Lynchburg shortly before nine o'clock. If Clarissa hadn't left Colfax so dead drunk, Fitz would have guessed they were too late, but now he believed there was a chance Colfax had not yet left the hotel. When they reached the city, they tied their horses to a hitchin rail not far from the hotel.

Fitz said, "Mark, reckon Colfax don' see as much o' you as he did o' me, so you goes into the hotel an' buys a newspaper. You sits whar you kin keep your eye on the stairs, an' you watches fo' him. I waits outside."

"Gran'pa, he see me, I sho' goin' to kill him I has to."

"You lets him see you, an' Dundee a daid man sho'. Ain't no time to talk o' killin' 'til we gets to that Klan meetin'. Then we sho' gots plenty o' bastahds to kill, we has to. Now you goes in theah. Goin' to take a chance an' ride over to City Hall to see Cap'n Morton, 'case we need his soldiers 'fore we gets through. Colfax comes out, you follows him. Don't wait fo' me, but soon's you knows whar he goin', come back to the hotel whar I'll be waitin'."

"Bettah hurry, Gran'pa. Wants you heah he comes down."

"Be back real fast. An' Mark, you sees your papa anywhar 'round heah, don't talk to him, don't look at him. Cain't be sho' whut he really doin' an' don't wants to do anythin' to worry him."

"All right, Gran'pa. Get goin'. Colfax might come any minute."

Fitz mounted and rode to City Hall, only a four-minute ride. He was admitted to Captain Morton's office immediately.

"Cap'n, got no time to 'splain things. Knows they goin' to be a meetin' o' the Klan tonight. Don't know whar, but you gots any way you kin look fo' the light from their burnin' crosses?"

"If it's not too far out of the city, Fitz, there's a tower . . . high enough. . . ."

"Got time on'y to say they kidnaps Dundee today, an' reckon at this heah meetin' they goin' to kill him. 'Cause you sees the fire, asks you come fast as you kin. Cain't say no mo', but things sho' happenin'."

"I'll have a watch set up right now, Fitz. Don't stick your neck out too far. The Klan has gotten very dangerous to cross. And I haven't found a way to destroy it."

"Mayhap we finds a way tonight, suh. Hopes so. Tells you all 'bout it later. Fo' now, kin on'y say Colfax is the Grand Dragon."

Fitz ran out to the street, mounted his horse, and rode back. He saw no sign of Mark outside so he ventured a few steps into the hotel lobby. Mark was seated in a big chair facing the stairs, with a newspaper held before his face. Fitz backed out of the hotel, crossed the street, and found a doorway that would conceal him fairly well. All he could do now was wait, and pray that Colfax had not wakened long ago.

Almost an hour dragged by. Fitz gave a start of excitement when he saw Colonel Apperson with a man who was a stranger to Fitz enter the hotel hurriedly. He moved across the street in case Apperson saw and recognized Mark. If there was trouble, Fitz meant to be in the thick of it. But apparently Apperson hadn't seen Mark, for there was no sign of Apperson when Fitz looked into the lobby. This time Mark saw Fitz and signaled to him that he was alert. He also gave Fitz a knowing look and a single nod of his head to indicate that he had also seen Apperson.

About half an hour went by. Fitz grew restive. Everything depended on the next few minutes, and so much could go wrong. If Colonel Appearson came out alone, Fitz intended to follow him and leave Mark behind to pick up Colfax's trail if he emerged.

To Fitz's relief, the three men came out of the hotel and walked briskly toward a carriage half a block away. Apparently it was Apperson's. Colfax carried a thick bundle under his arm, no doubt the purple robe of a Grand Dragon. Colfax would be in charge of the Klan meeting.

As they stepped into the carriage, Mark emerged

from the hotel. He hurried to where their horses were tied and when Fitz joined him, was already in the saddle, eager to get started.

The carriage had pulled away, but Mark had it in view as they prepared to follow.

Fitz said, "I rides first an' you stays behind, but nevah outen my sight. They goin' far, an' jes' one rider keeps behind 'em, they gets suspicious so I drops back an you rides up front an' I follows you. Understan' all that, son?"

Mark said, "Understands, Gran'pa."

"Ride then; 'fore we cain't see 'em no mo'."

Fitz rode at a brisk pace and soon spotted the carriage. It was moving fast, as if they were late, which was quite possible. Fitz felt like taking the rifle out of its saddle scabbard, pulling back the hammer, riding hard to the side of the carriage, and shooting down both Apperson and Colfax. It was a foolish idea.

After about a mile of travel through the city, they reached the countryside. Fitz dropped back, and Mark rode ahead to take up the watch on the carriage.

Mark decided he was closing in too fast. But as he pulled up, the carriage came to an unexpected stop. Mark could not bring his horse to a halt without arousing their suspicions, so he kept the animal at an ordinary trot and passed the carriage, thankful it was an especially dark night. He was worried as he wondered what he'd done to make them suspicious.

Apparently, he had not aroused them. They had stopped only to light the lantern below the carriage. But Mark was too far ahead now. It all depended on Fitz, who had to be well back.

Fitz was. He'd seen Mark ride too close and he dropped back farther so if Colfax and the others saw Mark, at least they'd not see the other horseman behind them. He was riding faster now, trying to bring the carriage into sight again. He saw no sign of it, so he rode even faster, and found Mark at the side of the road waiting for him. Fitz dismounted and ran over to his side.

"They go on by?" he asked.

"Gran'pa, I made a damn fool outen myse'f. Had to ride past 'em an' keeps goin', or they sho' ready to suspect. But they nevah comes by me. You sees 'em?"

"Not a sign. Means they turned off somewhar. You sees a side road?"

"Nevah had time to see nuthin'."

"We rides back to look fo' the road they must o' taken. Oh Lawd, we cain't fail now."

"Mayhap others comin' if it's a big meetin'."

"If we earlier, would say we might see somebody come along, but takes time to wake Colfax up, an' he an' Apperson sho' mighty late. Still, the others must be wharevah the meetin' place is. Let's see now. They needs a big cleared field fo' this sort o' thing. Whar's there a farm o' a plantation got a big cleared space? Watson's too small, an' he'd shoot any sonabitch comes along in a bedsheet. There's one plantation . . . ain't been used since 'bout halfway to the end o' the war. The owner gets killed in the war. Used to be a road, mayhap kind o' grown over . . . ain't sho' I kin find it. Tell you whut, you bein' young an' spry, we finds a good, tall tree an' you shinnies up to the top if you kin. Look fo' the light from a burnin' cross. Cap'n Morton in town got men lookin' fo' the same thing. The cross mayhap big 'nuff fo' the light to be seen fo' long time an' even from far off."

Mark didn't waste time talking about it. He walked his horse along the road, reversing directions until he saw a tree that seemed tall enough so he'd have a clear view for a mile or two. Leaving Fitz to hold the horses, he climbed the tree quickly. Perched on a high branch and clinging to it, he turned his head, scanning the darkness for the first sign of fire. Although they had failed in following Colfax, at least they were not too far away from the destination of the two Klan officials.

When Mark spotted the first glow, he came down the tree quickly and joined Fitz. He pointed. "In that direction, Gran'pa. Sees the fire from the cross. Gots to get theah fast. They ain't goin' to wait long 'fore they brings out Dundee."

They discovered the old road. The entrance to it had been hidden by an overgrowth of thick branches from trees on both sides. There were enough signs, however, that a large number of vehicles had passed between these trees recently.

They rode as far as they dared and then tied their horses and went the rest of the way on foot, carrying the rifles, with the sidearms stuck under their belts and their pockets heavy with more ammunition.

They came to the old plantation, led on now by sounds from the assembly. A large area was still clear, and the Klan had gathered there. There was light enough from the cross for Fitz and Mark to move easily, though with the greatest caution.

The cross was not a large one. But as they watched, a second cross was prepared. Fitz could smell the oil doused on the rags tied to the wood. There seemed to be some excitement there too, for they could hear angry voices, muffled, but the tone plain.

"If they follows whut they most always do," Fitz whispered, "they goin' to raise that cross, set it on fire, an' then they marches in a big circle 'round an' 'round, 'till the fire dies."

"Gran'pa, cain't see too well, but thinks there's a third cross."

"That's strange," Fitz said. "Nevah hears o' them burnin' three."

"Reckon this heah a most important meetin', an' they burns three," Mark commented.

"Might be. Gots to get in closer. Cain't see 'nuff way out heah."

"When Cap'n Morton ridin' out?"

"Soon's his men see the fire. Mayhap this small cross don't make 'nuff light to be seen in the city, but that big one sho' 'nuff goin' to make plenty o' fire. Get down on your belly, an' we crawls close as we kin."

Moving in that manner, they were unable to watch what was going on. But being this close, and in a cleared area, they had to depend on tall grass to hide them, so they kept their heads down.

The bigger cross had been fired now, for the darkness was retreating before the light of the flames. There was a piercing scream that rang through the night. Fitz raised his head quickly.

"Oh Christ," he said in horror. "Mark . . . they got somebody tied to that burnin' cross . . . "

Mark gasped in horror. "Dundee . . . ?"

"Mayhap. Don't know. Poor man yellin' his haid off. Flames goin' to get him any second now. Look . . . light's gettin' stronger at the top o' the cross. . . . Look! It's Jubal!"

Fitz stood up, raised his rifle to his shoulder.

"Gran'pa, whut . . . ?"

"Cain't save him," Fitz mutterd. "No way to do that, but cain't let him suffer . . . . Cain't do it. God help me, gots to do this."

He aimed carefully. Jubal's scream rent the night again. Fitz's rifle cracked and the scream was cut off. Fitz dropped down again to the cover of the tall grass, pushed his face against the earth, and wept silently. Mark said nothing, but he watched as the cross began to burn itself out.

"Gran'pa," he said after a few moments, "they gettin' the third cross ready. They marched 'round the second one 'til it almost out. They carryin' a cross. Each man carryin' a torch. They chantin' somethin', but loud 'nuff so they didn't hear your rifle."

"Bastahds!' Fitz said fiercely.

"Whut we goin' to do now? They sho' aimin' to hoist poor Dundee up mighty soon."

"We moves in close." Fitz brushed tears out of his eyes. "Close 'nuff so they starts tyin' Dundee to the cross, we begins pickin' 'em off. We gets as many close by the cross as we kin. Mayhap Dundee gets a chance to free hisse'f an' runs. Mayhap we kin get to him an' cut him free. But we ain't lettin them kill Dundee 'thout killin' all the bastahds we kin shoot."

"Mayhap we skeers 'em so they runs."

"Ain't likely, there's so many of 'em, but they sho' goin' to be a lot o' funerals in the next two or three days."

"Mayhap ours included," Mark said grimly.

393

"So be it, Mark. But gots a bettah idea. I moves in close. I picks 'em off an' tries to reach Dundee. You stays heah, in range, an' you picks 'em off too. But when they gets their senses back an' starts lookin' fo' us, you runs to the hosses an' you rides to meet Cap'n Morton an' tells him whar to go. Then you rides to Wyndward. . . ."

"Without you? Like hell I will."

"You does whut I says, Mark. I'm old now. You young an' gots to be sho' Wyndward don't die. Cain't tell whar Jonathan is, he daid o' alive. Up to us now, you 'specially. Do whut I says. Wants no argument. You tries to follow me, I'll use the butt o' my gun on you an' hopes they don' find you fo' you wakes up."

"All right, Gran'pa," Mark said. "Waits fo' you to fire the first shot an' then I starts pickin' 'em off. Goin' to aim fo' the ones with the colored sheets, like the purple one Clarissa sees in Colfax's room."

"Hopes I kin see Apperson," Fitz murmured. "If I gots to die an' I gets him first, I dies happy. Somewhat. Goin' now. Hold your fire 'til I starts shootin'."

Mark said, "Been some time since we left Lynchburg. Reckon Cap'n Morton on his way. Gets directions by the fires easy 'nuff. I don't have to ride away to meet him."

"Prays fo' it. Don't depend on it. You take care o' things now, Mark."

"I takes care," Mark said in a low voice. "Good luck, Gran'pa. I thanks you. . . ." He stopped talking. Fitz was already on his way.

As Fitz neared the spot where the new cross lay waiting for its human sacrifice, he was unable to see what was going on. The light from the second cross was diminishing at a rapid rate. Fitz moved in as close as he dared.

Dundee, tied painfully tight, looked up at the sky and prayed for Jubal, his friend who had died, whose screams had turned his blood cold and robbed him of any possible hope that he might be spared. He knew that Fitz and Mark would be trying to find him, but it seemed impossible they could succeed.

From the moment he had heard Adalia's scream and

heard the muffled threats of the man ready to rape her, he had realized that his usefulness in this wild endeavor he'd planned for so long was coming to an end. He could not have let them harm Adalia, for he sensed they'd likely kill her when they were through. And they'd probably have found him too. So he had broken out of the shed behind the school and begun running across the cleared area. He had planned to get as much of a start as possible and had hoped they'd not shoot at him. Adalia would have had a chance to escape as well. When the other men had come out of the forest though there had been nowhere he could go.

He'd recovered consciousness in the darkness of some barn where he was half covered with straw. His arms and legs were tightly bound and two rifle-armed men sat close by. Neither spoke for the several hours he was held there.

Dundee had had no idea what fate they intended for him, but he knew it would end in death. He prayed it would be a quick one. Then they had dragged in another prisoner and dropped him alongside Dundee. The new man groaned and slowly came out of the unconsciousness caused by several blows to the head.

"Jubal?" Dundee had whispered. "Is it you, Jubal?"

"Goddamn," Jubal said weakly. "They got you too. Dundee . . . where are we?"

"I don't know. I was unconscious too when they brought me. It's an old barn on some farm or plantation. How'd they get you?"

"I heard something big was being planned. I didn't know you were it. I got too close, I think. Or maybe they knew all the time. I think that was it. Someone knew who I was and brought me to the attention of the men who frequented a bar where I found work."

"Was Jonathan there?"

"Yes. I'm sorry to say I think he identified me."

"He's gone all bad. He came back from the war so full of hate it's made him half insane."

"Maybe so, but it does us no good, Dundee. How do we get out of this?"

"You guess," Dundee said tightly.

"I don't have to. And what did we accomplish? Far as I'm concerned, not a thing. This is what we studied so hard for. Developed such hope for. To die in some stinking barn."

"I didn't get far either. There wasn't time."

"Let's hope there are others like us who won't run into this sort of thing. I think it's getting dark."

Dundee squirmed about and managed to raise his shoulders from the straw. "You men! You with the guns. . . . What are they going to do to us?"

"Shut your black mouth or I knocks you out again."

"I was only asking. What harm is there in that?"

"You says one mo' word an' sweahs you goin' to get the barrel o' my rifle right in your black face. You hears me?"

"I hear you," Dundee said.

He grew silent. Jubal seemed to have lapsed back into a partial coma, for he was moaning softly and didn't answer when Dundee whispered to him. Dundee closed his eyes and began to pray. That was all he could do.

They came for Jubal some time later. Dundee didn't know how long it was, though it had grown totally dark. There were four of them. They said nothing, just walked to where Jubal lay, still half conscious and still moaning.

They lifted Jubal, then dragged him across the floor. He cried out in despair as the jolting brought back his senses. Dundee squirmed and tossed and tried to break loose, but the ropes were too tight. He then lay quietly, husbanding his strength in case the slightest opportunity arose to put up some kind of a fight.

Dundee heard the chanting. The guards moved to the door of the barn and opened it to watch. The flickering light of the torches came clearly to Dundee, and when the light grew brighter, he knew a cross had been lit. He heard Jubal scream once. He didn't know what they were doing to him, but the screaming grew more intense. Then Dundee thought he heard the faint crack of a rifle, and the scream was cut off abruptly.

Minutes went by. They came for him then. He was dragged, as Jubal had been, and dropped to the ground beside what seemed to be an enormous cross. Dundee caught the odor of oil saturating the rags tied to the cross. He suddenly knew what had happened and what was about to happen. They had crucified Jubal on a burning cross. Now it was his turn.

The members of the Klan who had been walking in that circle around the cross broke ranks. Dundee caught the smell of whiskey being doled out. There was laughter and shouting and derisive remarks about the way Jubal had died. Someone knocked down the cross on which he had died. They dragged it away. The hole in the ground was going to be filled with another cross—for Dundee.

He lay there, helpless, terrified, trying to convince himself he would not give them the satisfaction of a single scream or plea for mercy. They were going to kill him, and his pleadings would fall on deaf ears.

The guards close by had gone off to join the drinking, for Dundee was helpless. The shouting and yelling grew more intense as the whiskey took hold. He thought they were working themselves up for the next sacrifice.

But one Klansman broke away from the others and walked slowly in Dundee's direction. Dundee prepared himself for being kicked or otherwise abused, a little game they were good at. Or perhaps this man was going to gag him so his cries could not be heard. After all, the burning of two crosses was bound to bring someone, though not in time to save Dundee.

The robed man bent over him. A knife glistened in his hand. Dundee drew a long breath. Then he felt his ropes being severed. The robed man bent closer.

"Whutevah happens," he said, "tells them I could not let my brother die. If they kills me, so be it, but try to get away, Dundee, an' live to tell whut this ghastly organization is 'bout."

"Jonathan!" Dundee said. "Jonathan!"

"Not the Jonathan you used to know. Not 'til this very moment, perhaps. I've gots to go back now. They'll come fo' you in a few minutes. Roll away. Don't get up 'til you clear. Then run like hell."

"I'll stand by you," Dundee said. "We go together or we don't go."

"You a fool! Take your chance. You'll not get another. Oh, damn!"

Dundee remained prone, but moved his head and saw a Klansman in a red robe walking rapidly toward them. He was carrying a rifle.

"Whut's goin' on heah?" he demanded.

"Jes' makin' sho' this bastahd cain't get loose," Jonathan replied.

"Is that so! I'll make sho' . . . this man's untied. . . ."

Jonathan shot him through the chest. Dundee leaped to his feet, but found he could barely move after being tied so long. He did manage to pick up the dead man's rifle. Other Klansmen were running toward them. Jonathan opened fire. Dundee cut down two of them. To the left, others were going down. Someone else had joined the battle.

Dundee felt a bullet hit his shoulder and knock him down. The rifle flew from his hand. He didn't know where Jonathan was. A man in a white robe advanced on Dundee, a knife in his hand. Suddenly he bent over as if stricken by an intense pain and then fell forward. Another dropped, groaning, trying to raise the rifle he held. Someone kicked him in the face, and he stopped struggling.

Someone else picked up Dundee and carried him. Dundee was only half conscious now. The whole night seemed to be exploding all around him. He didn't know that the area was now full of Yankee soldiers. Klansmen were hastily dropping their guns and raising their hands. Someone set Dundee down. He opened his eyes. Jonathan, the mask gone from his face, smiled at him.

"We made it," he said. "My papa an' my son are heah. So are soldiers. It's over fo' now, my good friend."

"Jonathan . . . I can only say . . . thank you. Thank you very much."

"I wish I could o' saved Jubal. I didn' know whut they up to 'til too late. But not too late fo' you. If I nevah do another worthy thing in my life, I'm now satisfied. My papa comin'. I don' know if I can face him."

"You, my friend, can face anything," Dundee said.

Mark, following Fitz, stopped by the spot where the

Klansman in the red robe lay. Mark bent down and used the end of his rifle barrel to lift the loose mask.

"Gran'pa," he called out.

Fitz looked back. Then he retreated a few steps to look down at the face of the dead man.

"Apperson," he said softly. "Goddamn, I been cheated again."

"So long as he daid. They tells me Colfax got away."

"Reckon he be the first to run. You sees your papa over theah?"

"Sees him."

"I see him an' I don't. He sho' no son o' mine." Fitz moved up to where Jonathan sat beside the wounded Dundee. Fitz looked at Dundee.

"You hurt bad?"

"Shoulder. I'm all right. Jonathan risked his life to save. . . ."

"Who this heah Jonathan?"

"Mr. Fitz, don't be like that," Dundee said.

"Shut up, Dundee," Jonathan said. "Let him speak."

"Not to you, you sonabitch," Fitz said coldly. "Nevah again to you. Savin' Dundee a fine thing, mayhap, but from a bastahd like you ain't nuthin'. Once I had a fine son . . . a great son . . . a boy I could trust an' love. Now, far as I'm concerned, he died in the war. He nevah come back. He nevah brought all that hate with him. A wonderful man died on that damn cross. His death sho' on this heah son o' mine's soul. On mine too, 'cause I too damn dumb to know whut was goin' on."

"Papa, let me say somethin' . . . " Jonathan begged.

"Won't heah you. Ain't nobody kin heah the daid speak. Mark, you take care o' Dundee. Gets him to the hospital in Lynchburg, an' you stays with him, a gun at your side, 'til he fixed up 'nuff to come home. I got business with Cap'n Morton."

Fitz began striding off. Jonathan called out.

"Papa!"

Fitz didn't stop, didn't turn his head.

"Good-bye, Papa," Jonathan said. "Good-bye."

Mark helped Dundee to his feet. Jonathan held out a hand to assist, but Mark brushed it away roughly. He got Dundee up, supported him, and walked him slowly to where several carriages were waiting.

Jonathan stood erect, looking out over what was left of the meeting. There were half a dozen men lying still, a dozen others groaning. Some were sitting up. Those not wounded stood in a long line with their hands high. Yankee soldiers guarded them. Other soldiers had lit up the scene with torches.

Slowly, Jonathan pulled the robe over his head, dropped it, impulsively stamped on it, tearing it and driving part of the garment into the ground.

Then he turned and walked away into the darkness.

29

It was morning before the military, under Captain Morton, finished its work. The Klansmen, subdued, some to the point of tears, were identified and allowed to go home. Three, who had been responsible for the kidnapping of Dundee and were identified by him, were locked up. At the hospital, Dundee's shoulder wound was treated, and he was ready to go back to Wyndward whenever Fitz was ready for the journey.

Mark had followed Fitz's suggestion to go to the hotel and rest but had found it impossible. He lay wide awake, his mind churning with the events that had transpired and beset with doubts about his father. He wanted to take Jonathan's side, but couldn't quite bring himself to. And yet he believed Fitz to be unfair in banishing Jonathan. It was something that would have to be worked out.

Early in the morning Mark dressed and went down to get breakfast. He'd not even dozed, still too troubled about events of the night before. He found Fitz and Captain Morton at one of the tables and joined them.

"You sho' don' look any bettah than you did last night," Fitz commented.

"I'm all right," Mark replied quietly.

"Kind o' glad you heah. Cap'n Morton jes' tellin' me somethin' you kin hardly believe. Colfax runs last night. Mighty few knew he was under that robe with the dragon on it. Colfax thinks he got away with it, an' he goin' to make a big speech fo' all the citizens o' this city."

"He sho' ain't," Mark said.

"Now see heah," Fitz said sternly. "You aimin' to kill him, o' bust him up, he ain't yours. He mine. Clarissa killed Bibb, an' he was mine too. Somebody kill Apperson . . . "

"Jonathan killed him. Your son killed him. My papa killed him."

"I said somebody killed Apperson, an' he was mine too. Now all I gots left is Colfax, an' sayin' right now, he mine. You understands that?"

"Whutevah you say, Gran'pa," Mark said.

"Ain't goin' to kill him. That too easy fo' a man like Colfax. Goin' to pull him down. Goin' to make ev'rybody 'round heah know whut he is. We gets that over with, we gets Dundee an' goes home."

"I'll have men posted around the square where Colfax is going to speak," Captain Morton assured them. "People here are very angry over what happened last night, and in this town the Klan is finished. At least for now. It may come back. Sleazy outfits like that often survive and go underground until they find a way to return, but never again with the kind of power Colonel Apperson and Colfax shared."

"Colfax speakin' 'round one o'clock," Fitz said. "Gots plenty o' time 'til then. Goin' to see how Dundee comin' along. Finish your breakfast, Mark, an' we goes to the hospital. Cap'n, you have my thanks fo' whut you an' your men did last night. Didn't think you were goin' to make it."

"The light from the burning crosses led us to the place. I wish we could have reached it earlier. In time to save that poor man they tied to the cross."

"That sho' murder," Fitz said. "But ain't no way we

kin figger who made that happen. Apperson, mayhap, but he daid. Colfax—reckon was him, but we got no proof he was even theah. I kin accuse him when he makes his speech, but to hang him, you needs mo' evidence than we got."

"True enough," Morton agree. "But if you make him pay for that by exposing him, that's good enough for me."

"I brings him down," Fitz promised. "Goin' to hurt that big ego o' his mo'n a bullet."

"An' sho' hurts longer," Mark added. "I ready to go see Dundee."

They found Dundee feeling better. The wound had been treated, there were no bones broken by the bullet, and the wound would heal fast.

"I'm a lucky man," Dundee said.

"Reckon so," Fitz agreed. "Whut you aimin' to do now?"

"I've been thinking about that, sir. I want to keep on with the work Jubal and I started, but . . . well it's too big for me. I realize that now. I want to go back North and organize all the educated blacks I can find. More of us can come down here and do more good than just me, struggling to overcome something that's almost impossible to do. Will you consent to that, Mr. Fitz?"

"Ain't fo' me to say. You the one makin' up your mind."

Dundee nodded. "You're right, of course. Even if I've been free for years now, I still sometimes have a sinking feeling that it never happened. Mr. Fitz, one thing more."

"No!" Fitz said flatly.

"Jonathan saved my life. How can I forget that?"

"Damn near got hisse'f killed doin' it too," Mark added.

"Jonathan betrayed us. He enlists full o' hate, blamin' ev'rybody fo' whut happens to his twins an' to Daisy. Man's got to stand up to things like that, but he go off to fight 'cause he blame the North too. Then he come back. Ain't goin' to say whut happen to him in that Yankee prison wasn't bad. Mayhap happens to me I gets jes' as mad as Jonathan. But when he joined the Klan,

403

when he lied to me, when he gave the Klan information 'bout whut was goin' on, then he stopped bein' my son."

"Mr. Fitz," Dundee said softly, "I agree that he did all those things. I know anger and hate impelled him. But I can recall when I felt the same way. When I wanted to kill every white man—yes, even you—and nobody can say I didn't have cause. You brought me out of that, and yet I can recall that when I was a boy, you hated me. Because I was born to a girl you loved, and I was black while she was almost white. You hated me—as a baby— to the extent that you even told Seawitch and Hong Kong to let me starve to death."

Fitz nodded. "Ain't sayin' that's not so. Ev'ry word's the truth. Made it up to you, Dundee. Best I could. Right now you makin' me jes' as proud o' you as your mama would o' been."

"Jes' whut you sayin', Gran'pa?" Mark asked.

"Takes time to get over sorrow an' hate. Jonathan comin' back some day. Cain't say when, but he comin'. When he gets rid o' his hate, when he stops blamin' ev'rybody fo' whut happened to him."

"Will you welcome him, he comes back?" Mark asked.

"You knows I will. Got some grievin' to do myse'f, but I ain't hatin' ev'rybody fo' it. I had a son an' now I ain't. Had a daughter an' she gone from my life. Got a wife up theah in Washington an' by damn she comin' heah soon as all this dies down. I ain't young no mo', but gots some years left, an' Wyndward goin' to rise again, be the best plantation in Virginia, an' my wife goin' to make me the happiest man in the world. Now let's get ready to mow down this heah Colfax."

Dundee insisted on accompanying them. He had been furnished with a sling and had recovered his strength sufficiently. They made their way to a large park where Sunday band concerts were held and where politicians made speeches from a platform erected for that purpose.

It seemed to Fitz that much of the town had already assembled. They were quiet, not even the children were boisterous. It was more like a funeral assembly, gathered here to listen to what they believed would be a political speech denouncing the Klan.

Colfax, as impressive-looking as ever, wearing an all-white suit, white shoes, and large hat, was driven up in a fancy carriage. While he made his way to the platform, Fitz, Mark, and Dundee moved closer, through paths cleared by Captain Morton's men who were mixed in with the crowd.

Colfax removed his hat, ran fingers through his wavy, thick white hair, and bowed.

"Ladies an' gen'mun," be began. "We are gathered heah to take stock o' things after a night o' blood an' violence brought 'bout by this heah organization know as the Ku Klux Klan. Used to laugh at the name, but sho' ain't laughin' no mo'. Been fightin' 'em evah since they starts up. Makes speeches 'gainst 'em, askin' fo' money to be used in fightin' 'em. But now you thinks mayhap the Klan busted fo'evah. Don't be fooled by that, my friends. It goin' to be stronger than evah, an' we needs mo' folks to fight 'em an' mo' money to give us whutevah we needs to finish the fight. Ain't fo' me to carry on the wuk, not alone. Asks your help 'cause I sayin' now that 'fore long, we gets representation in the Congress in Washington again, an' I now says I goin' to run fo' office. You all knows me an' whut I stands fo'. . . ."

Fitz mounted the three wooden steps to the platform and moved over beside Colfax. "Got somethin' to say," he announced.

"Mistah Turner, suh, you got no right on this heah platform . . . ," Colfax said angrily.

"Got mo' right than you," Fitz said. "Folks, this heah Colfax ain't fit to address you. He run fo' office, I says now I fights him all the way. Mistah Colfax been speech-makin' 'gainst the Klan. Been askin' fo' money to fight the Klan. But Mistah Colfax been usin' that money to finance the Klan, 'cause he the Grand Dragon fo' the whole state. He one o' the biggest Klansmen 'round these parts. Last night he helped burn that poor black who was on'y tryin' to help us all stop this hatred 'tween black an' white. That's whut he died fo', an' that's why Colfax killed him."

Colfax grew crimson with rage and then white with fear as Fitz talked. He did his best to brazen it out, but Fitz had facts and figures and testimony. Yet Colfax tried to defend himself.

"This heah Mistah Turner you-all knows is a nigger lovah. Brings that nigger down heah to make trouble. He lyin' like the bastahd he is. You gots to believe me...."

One tall, sturdy-looking man in his forties elbowed his way through the crowd.

"Mistah Turner ain't lyin'," he shouted. "Knows Colfax is the Grand Dragon heah. Knows it 'cause I served under him 'til I finds out whut the Klan is. Accuses Mistah Colfax o' bein' all whut Mistah Turner say he is. An' gots others heah feel the same way. Whut we ought to do is hang Colfax to one o' them lampposts whar we hangs the six niggers we ain't even sho' were guilty."

Colfax, his face red with rage, faced Fitz. "Goin' to break you, Mistah Turner. Goin' to see you pays fo' this. Goin' to bring you to your knees an' then I kicks you in the face. I makes this promise, an' I goin' to keep it one way o' 'nother."

Fitz turned away in open contempt and walked off the stage. Colfax raised his arms to get the attention of his audience. Someone threw a stone. Colfax staggered under its impact, and a crimson mark appeared on his forehead. Two more stones were thrown and rattled onto the platform. Colfax whirled about, leaped off the back of the platform, and ran for his life.

Fitz, Mark, and Dundee stood to one side as part of the crowd broke free in pursuit.

"You've made an enemy," Dundee said. "For whatever Colfax's hatred may amount to."

"Been used to enemies most o' my life. Colfax goin' to make trouble if he kin. Knows o' all the men who hated me, he sho' the smartest an' at the same time the most miserable. Ain't takin' light whut he said. Sho' goin' to be on guard 'cause we makes a fool o' him today, but tomorrow mayhap folks fo'gets. Colfax a mighty good speaker. He ain't finished, but I ain't either. Let's go home an' put Wyndward in order."

It was a subdued Fitz who returned to Wyndward. Clarissa and Adalia, quickly made aware of what happened, were careful not to bring up the subject of Jonathan. Fitz ordered bourbon, sat on the veranda, and drank alone—by preference, which Mark and Dundee sensed.

He reviewed in his mind every outstanding event of his life, but gave up in contemplation of what was left. He was no longer young. He knew of several men his age long dead, though he didn't dwell on the subject of death.

When he abandoned half his drink and left the veranda to walk down toward the schoolhouse, everyone knew where he was going. He reached the cemetery, stepped over the low gate, and stood facing all of the graves in their neat row. Someone had placed autumn flowers on each one. He suspected Adalia was responsible.

"Well," he said aloud, "it done an' over with. Jonathan is gone from Wyndward 'cause he betrayed it an' me. Think I made a mistake in lettin' him go, but then I believe it was partly his own choice. The man wants to find hisse'f. If you were here, Daisy, this could never have happened, but . . . it did. In the end, he proved himself a man. Now, Benay, I'm married again to a lovely woman of the North. I told you before how she came into my life. She is a woman you'd be proud of as she'd be proud of you. Going to bring Wyndward back from the ravages of the war. I'll make it better than it ever was, and no disrespect to you, Papa and Mama. Wyndward is going to ring with joy and happiness again. Liz will make it so, just as she has brought joy into my heart. Things are too disrupted at the moment to say more. Just wanted you to know what's going on. Papa, forgive me for speaking Northern style. Have to once in a while. I'll be back soon."

He returned to his chair on the veranda and in the late afternoon asked Mark to join him. They sat in silence for a time.

Fitz said, "Tomorrow we begins wuk. This yeah's crop sho' a good one. Some o' the best leaf we evah sends to market. Next yeah we grows half as much mo'. 'Spect you an' Adalia be married in the spring."

"Right after the plantin', Gran'pa."

"Good. Liz be heah by then, an' she sho' goin' to see you has some weddin'. By then mayhap some o' the war hate dies off an' we kin invite the folks who used to come to the soirees heah. We lets Clarissa an' Liz takes care o' that. All we gots to do—you an' me—is bring Wyndward back. Means we hires a hundred mo' folks to wuk heah. We builds two mo' curin' sheds . . . ," he shaded his eyes against the waning sun. "Now whut the hell . . . ?"

They saw the rider coming fast and soon identified him as one of Morton's soldiers. Fitz went down to meet him. The soldier never took the time to dismount.

"A message from Captain Morton, sir. He is being transferred to another post and is leaving tomorrow afternoon. He wishes to see his sister before he leaves, and you as well. He will be at the depot at three, sir. May I tell him you'll be there?"

"Sho' kin. We be theah. Thanks you, suh."

The soldier wheeled his horse and rode off. Fitz sat down again. "Jes' when I thinks ev'rythin' goin' fine, this happens. Why in hell they moves the cap'n? Don't make sense. After whut happen he gots ev'rybody in town respectin' him, an' he been makin' friends. Some . . . not many, but some is a lot these days. Now he goes an' 'nother man comes in, an' who knows whut kind o' officer he be. One man kin sho'ly undo all the good Morton has accomplished."

"That's the military fo' you, Gran'pa. Saw it when I was in the army. You gets orders ain't no reason to 'em, but you does whut you has to. Kin I come tomorrow?"

"Wants ev'rybody to come an' say good-bye," Fitz said. "You tells Adalia to close the school fo' all day."

"Reckon Dundee goin' to stay heah, an' he kin take it over."

Fitz gave him a sharp look. "How you knows 'bout that?"

Mark shrugged. "On'y sayin' whut I thinks Dundee goin' to do."

"He wants to come he sho' welcome. He gots to know the cap'n pretty well too."

"Tells him, Gran'pa. Time fo suppah. Elegant gets mad we ain't theah when she ready."

Fitz enjoyed his supper that night. It seemed to him that Elegant had made a special effort to please him. There were thick slices of ham and a cut of roast beef along with the vegetables she prepared so well. Her biscuits were as good as ever, but when it came time for dessert she remained in the kitchen.

"Elegant," Fitz bellowed. "You gets in heah fast."

She appeared wiping her hands on her apron. "Now whut you wants, Mistah Fitz, suh?"

"Whar is the dessert? You knows how much I likes my sweetnin'."

"Ain't none. You gots 'nuff food in you belly fo' two people. Ain't got time fo' dessert."

"Ain't got time?" Fitz asked. "Whut in hell else you gots to do but cook? An' you knows I likes. . . ."

"Reckon if somethin' ain't burnin'," Elegant said, "it goin' to be."

She bustled out of the dining room. Fitz sighed. "You sets 'em free an' whut do you get? No dessert. Whut's come over that woman?"

"Fitz," Adalia said, "she did prepare a very large supper. I know I couldn't eat dessert even if she served it."

"Well, I could," Fitz said. "Mark, let's go see if we kin find a cheroot o' two. Lessen somebody stole 'em an' says we cain't smoke no mo'."

"You do that," Clarissa said, "me an' Adalia goin' to have some o' that fine port on the sideboard. Me an' Adalia got things to talk 'bout don't concern you menfolk."

"That's right," Adalia said. "There's been little time for woman talk around here."

Fitz bit off the end of a cheroot. "Sometimes I thinks ev'rybody goin' crazy 'round heah. Things gots to settle down. No dessert, gets sent from our own suppah table . . . an' whut in hell you grinnin' at?"

"You sho' gets mad," Mark said. "You gets red in the face an' you gives in. You knows whut that a sign of?"

"Knows, an' you says it an' I sho' goin' to prove I ain't that old. Let's go sit on the veranda with the mosquitoes. Bettah company I gots inside."

In the morning, Fitz and everyone else waited for the carriage to come. It had been cleaned up, and the horses were carefully groomed. Fitz approved.

"Leastwise somebody got 'nuff ambition to see that much gets done. An' sayin' this right heah an' now. This sho' goin' to be the last day we sloths. Wuk to be done heah an' it goin' to be. You hears me? All o' you?"

"Hears you," Clarissa said. "You talkin' mighty big, but we knows whut you means. We goin' to say good-bye to a mighty good friend today, an' ain't no call to bring in anythin' like wuk. That kin wait."

Fitz grumbled, but sat back as Mark took the reins. They reached Lynchburg in plenty of time. The town seemed very quiet, as if it was doing penance for past sins. But Fitz noted that people waved and smiled.

"Likes that," he said. "Mayhap they fo'gets the damn war pretty soon."

Mark pulled up at the railroad station. The platform was empty. Fitz looked around. "Whar the cap'n? Ain't his own men goin' to give him a fine send-off? Ain't like the army to treat an important man like the cap'n."

Adalia said, "Here he comes, Fitz. That carriage. . . ."

"Drivin' hisse'f?" Fitz said. "Wonder how in hell the North won the war the way the soldiers treats their officers."

Before Captain Morton could bring his carriage to a stop behind the one which Fitz and his family were leaving, the train came roaring into the station. Fitz turned around to look for Morton.

"He sho' ain't in no hurry. . . ."

"Gran'pa," Mark said softly, "you knows that lady gettin' off the train? Sho' a fine-lookin' woman. . . ."

Fitz stared. Then he threw his hat in the air and whooped and ran to take Liz in his arms. He covered her face with kisses, began to ask questions, and then stared over her shoulder. Melanie was standing demurely on the platform. Apparently, she'd come with Liz.

"I think," Fitz said softly, "I'm seein' happiness two times. Feels so good inside I's scared."

"I talked to Melanie," Liz said. "She wants to come home. Home, Fitz. That's where I am now. Home again, at last."

Fitz embraced his daughter and then put his arms around both women as he led them to the carriages. He realized now that Captain Morton was merely another conspirator in this plot to surprise him. Adalia joined Fitz, Liz, and Melanie in the first carriage, and their talk was a distinct buzz in the air.

Clarissa, Mark, and Captain Morton walked toward the second carriage. Clarissa touched a handkerchief to the corners of her eyes. Mark glanced at her.

"Reckon it a time fo' cryin' a little, Clarissa. You evah sees a man happy as Fitz?"

"Ain't he bein' happy I cryin' 'bout."

"Then what does bring on those tears?" Captain Morton asked.

" 'Cause theah goes my last chance," she said. "An' if you asks me whut I'm talkin' 'bout, ain't none o' your goddamn business!"

ROMANCE...ADVENTURE...DANGER...

THE BONDMASTER BREED
by Richard Tresillian   (D81-890, $2.50)

Carlton Todd, the Bondmaster, is a happy man. With his marriage to the young, copper-haired Milly Dobbs, he has a new chance to produce a legitimate, white, male heir to his estate. But from his liaisons of the past, others come to stake their claims. A novel of forbidden love in a hurricane of hate by the author of THE BONDMASTER.

BLOOD OF THE BONDMASTER
by Richard Tresillian   (D82-385, $2.25)

Following THE BONDMASTER the saga of Roxborough Plantation—the owners and the slaves who were their servants, lovers—and prime crop! In the struggle for power, there will be pain and passion, incest and intrigue, cruelty and death for these, too, flow from the BLOOD OF THE BONDMASTER.

THE KINGDOM
by Ronald S. Joseph   (D33-074, $2.95)

Out of the rugged brasada, a powerful family carved THE KINGDOM. Joel Trevor was willing to fight Mexicans, carpetbaggers, raiders, even Nature itself to secure his ranch. Then he won the beautiful Spanish Sofia who joined her heart and her lands to his. When control passed to Joel's daughter Anne, she took trouble and tragedy with the same conquering spirit as her father. These were the founders—and their story blazes from the pages of THE KINGDOM, the first book of a giant trilogy.

THE POWER
by Ronald S. Joseph   (D36-161, $3.50)

The children of Anne Trevor and Alex Cameron set out at the turn of the century to conquer the world in their own ways. Follow Dos, the reckless son, as he escalates youthful scrapes into crime. Travel with Maggie from boarding school to brothel to Congress. Meet Trev and the baby daughter to whom all the kingdom, power and glory will belong.

THE GLORY
by Ronald S. Joseph   (D36-175, $3.50)

Meet the inheritors: Allis Cameron, great-granddaughter of the pioneers who carved a kingdom in southern Texas. Go with her to Hollywood where her beauty conquers the screen and captures the heart of her leading man. Cammie: Allis's daughter, who comes of age and finds herself torn between a ruthless politician and a radical young Mexican. They were the Cameron women, heirs to a Texas fortune, rich, defiant, ripe for love.

ROMANCE...ADVENTURE...DANGER...
by Best-selling author, Aola Vandergriff

DAUGHTERS OF THE SOUTHWIND
by Aola Vandergriff (D93-909, $2.95)
The three McCleod sisters were beautiful, virtuous and bound to a dream—the dream of finding a new life in the untamed promise of the West. Their adventures in search of that dream provide the dimensions for this action-packed romantic bestseller.

DAUGHTERS OF THE WILD COUNTRY
by Aola Vandergriff (D93-908, $2.95)
High in the North Country, three beautiful women begin new lives in a world where nature is raw, men are rough...and love, when it comes, shines like a gold nugget. Tamsen, Arab and Em McCleod now find themselves in Russian Alaska, where power, money and human life are the playthings of a displaced, decadent aristocracy in this lusty novel ripe with love, passion, spirit and adventure.

DAUGHTERS OF THE FAR ISLANDS
by Aola Vandergriff (D93-910, $2.95)
Hawaii seems like Paradise to Tamsen and Arab—but it is not. Beneath the beauty, like the hot lava bubbling in the volcano's crater, trouble seethes in Paradise. The daughters are destined to be caught in the turmoil between Americans who want annexation of the islands and native Hawaiians who want to keep their country. And in their own family, danger looms...and threatens to erupt and engulf them all.

DAUGHTERS OF THE OPAL SKIES
by Aola Vandergriff (D93-911, $2.95)
Tamsen Tallant, most beautiful of the McCleod sisters, is alone in the Australian outback. Alone with a ranch to run, two rebellious teenage nieces to care for, and Opal Station's new head stockman to reckon with—a man whose very look holds a challenge. But Tamsen is prepared for danger—for she has seen the face of the Devil and he looks like a man.

DAUGHTERS OF THE MISTY ISLES
by Aola Vandergriff (D93-929, $2.95)
Settled in at Nell's Wotherspoon Manor, the McCleod sisters must carve new futures for their children and their men. Arab has her marriage and her courage put on the line. Tam learns to live without her lover. And even Nell will have to relinquish a dream. But the greatest challenge by far will be to secure the happiness of Luka whose romance threatens to tear the family apart.

If you like romance,
you'll love Valerie Sherwood...

INTRODUCING
THE RAKEHELL DYNASTY

BOOK ONE: THE BOOK OF JONATHAN RAKEHELL
by Michael William Scott   (D95-201, $2.75)

BOOK TWO: CHINA BRIDE
by Michael William Scott   (D95-237, $2.75)

The bold, sweeping, passionate story of a great New England shipping family caught up in the winds of change—and of the one man who would dare to sail his dream ship to the frightening, beautiful land of China. He was Jonathan Rakehell, and his destiny would change the course of history.

THE RAKEHELL DYNASTY—
THE GRAND SAGA OF THE GREAT CLIPPER SHIPS AND OF THE MEN WHO BUILT THEM TO CONQUER THE SEAS AND CHALLENGE THE WORLD!

Jonathan Rakehell—who staked his reputation and his place in the family on the clipper's amazing speed.

Lai-Tse Lu—the beautiful, independent daughter of a Chinese merchant. She could not know that Jonathan's proud clipper ship carried a cargo of love and pain, joy and tragedy for her.

Louise Graves—Jonathan's wife-to-be, who waits at home in New London keeping a secret of her own.

Bradford Walker—Jonathan's scheming brother-in-law, who scoffs at the clipper and plots to replace Jonathan as heir to the Rakehell shipping line.

If you liked Wyndward Glory, you'll want to read...